Chimera

FIVE STAR

Chimera

Lois Carroll

Five Star • Waterville, Maine

This novel is a work of fiction. Names, characters, places and incidents are either the product of the author's imagination, or, if real, used fictitiously.

First Edition
First Printing: June 2006

Published in 2006 in conjunction with Tekno Books.

Set in 11 pt. Plantin by Minnie B. Raven.

Printed in the United States on permanent paper.

Library of Congress Cataloging-in-Publication Data

Carroll, Lois.
Chimera / by Lois Carroll.—1st ed.
p. cm.
ISBN 1-59414-457-5 (hc : alk. paper)
1. New York (State)—Fiction. I. Title.
PS3603.A774585C48 2006
813′.6—dc22 2005030204

To women working long hours
to be everything they can be.

Chimera: a fire-breathing she-monster, an unrealizable dream.

—Merriam-Webster's Collegiate Dictionary

Chapter One

Carolyn Whitney Matison pressed her damp palms against her skirt before she reached up to take the letter from the attorney's age-spotted hand. Tension clutching her stomach, she smiled and thanked him.

"I'll be just down the hall when you're finished." She nodded and he left the room, quietly closing the door.

She looked down at the ivory vellum sheets that felt heavy in her hands, and began to read the familiar but wobbly handwriting of her late great-aunt Louise Whitney.

My dear Carolyn,

I hardly know where to begin. The doctors say I haven't long, so this letter is my last chance. You see, I desperately need your help to right a grievous wrong done to Sara Whitney and Robert Ashford, two lonely souls still searching in vain for peace.

What in the world was this about? Sara and Robert died over seventy years ago. And "providing peace for lonely souls"? That sounded as if they were hanging around waiting for help. The next thing she knew, she would be hearing voices and seeing ghosts. It was laughable, and yet she felt compelled to read on.

You remember that I was quite a bit younger than my cousins, Lora and Sara, the daughters of my father's brother, Lloyd Whitney, and his wife, Alice. On my last visit to Greystone, their summer home on Lost Lake in upstate New York, Sara revealed a very special secret—Robert Ashford was going to ask Lloyd for permission to marry her. She glowed with happiness, but it didn't last long. All their plans to be together went wrong, and she needs you to make things right again. You alone can give Sara the help she so desperately needs.

Needs? Present tense? For the first time, Carolyn began to think that her dear great-aunt's mind had begun to slip into the past instead of staying alert. Not surprising at her advanced age, and yet Louise had always seemed so sharp and knowing.

Hoping to understand, Carolyn read on about Alice's necklace of large, perfectly matched, black emeralds that was still missing, and about Lora Whitney's demise at Greystone.

Greystone was abandoned following Lora's tragic accident there. The newspaper accounts of her death included mention of Alice's missing necklace. Some boldly reported suspecting Robert had stolen it. Suspicion ruined his reputation and he never married. He became Greystone's self-appointed guard, often searching for the necklace to clear his name. Though the rumors about the house are all but gone now, the Ashford name still wears the mantle of suspicion. I had high hopes for Greystone, but could not accomplish what must be done. I'm thankful John's son mows the lawn each week or two. He's a dear—such a dependable boy. Carolyn, the old house is still hiding the secret. I'm sure the necklace is there. You must find it for Sara and for Robert. So I bequeath the house and all my funds to you to transform it into the inn of your dreams you've told me about. But first, you must promise you will personally supervise all of the renovations and search for the necklace. Please, Carolyn. Sara will help you find it. Then she can be with Robert at long last. Promise me you will do this so we all may know peace.

Love,
Your great-aunt Louise

"What do you mean, 'there's a string attached'?" Carolyn asked as she sat in the walnut-paneled office of the Ashford, Ashford and Ashford law firm in Lakeside, New York.

"I'm afraid, Miss Matison, that there is a very long string attached to this inheritance," Thomas, the aged senior partner of the firm, said. "You are to be your great-aunt Louise's sole beneficiary, but only if you agree to certain terms she set down in her will. She described the most important one in the letter you read when you arrived at our law office."

"Yes." Feeling anxious, though intensely curious, Carolyn glanced nervously over at Thomas's son, John, whose friendly face, wire-rimmed glasses, and greying hair gave him an intelligent, no-nonsense appearance that instilled trust. His quiet demeanor reflected honest dependability. John nodded to her, but said nothing, leaving it to his father to explain.

Stooped by the weight of time, Thomas leaned heavily on his cane and shuffled over to sit behind the walnut desk that dwarfed his thin body. "The will states that whether or not you accept the inheritance," he told her with a wave of his bony fingers, "the letter is yours to keep."

Carolyn's eyes widened with astonishment. "Whether or not I accept?" she asked. "How could anyone turn down this inheritance?" She shook her head. "Though I've never been to Greystone, I've listened to Louise's stories about it all my life. I've seen dozens of pictures of the mansion and the people who lived there. Owning it has always been my life-long fantasy—a chimera, I thought, but now a fantastic dream that seems to be coming true."

"You read all the whole letter?"

"Yes," Carolyn responded. "Her handwriting was quite different. I remember beautiful script in the notes I received from Aunt Louise at college. They always seemed to be perfectly timed words of support and encouragement." The corners of her lips rose in a smile while a troubled frown rested on her forehead. "I had hoped the letter would explain why Louise chose to make me her beneficiary instead of my mother, Eleanor, her niece and closest relative."

"She knew you could help her in a way Eleanor never could," Thomas offered easily. John shot him a stern look he pointedly ignored.

"I'm finding it hard to believe she wanted me to have Greystone but never mentioned it to me once. And, I have to add, I find it harder to believe what she expects me to do with it."

"It must come as a shock to you, but I assure you, her will is all in order," John insisted.

"But renovating the whole house and bringing it up to code for an inn will cost a fortune. I know she tried to have some work done decades ago, but I never learned exactly why she failed in her plan to open it as a resort. I always assumed she'd run out of money."

"No, my dear," Thomas assured her with a confident smile.

"Miss Whitney made some very wise investments which have paid off handsomely," John explained. "Even after the estate taxes are taken care of, there will be enough cash to create a working inn—even at today's construction prices. Your income from the rooms and the restaurant will add to it from that point. But then if you find the necklace . . ."

He shrugged and made no attempt to establish how much value that would add to her wealth. And he failed to explain why Louise hadn't succeeded in renovating Greystone.

"John intends to go over the will very carefully with you, but perhaps knowing you have the choice to make is enough for one day," Thomas said kindly.

"I just can't get over it," Carolyn said. "What . . . what happens if I decide it's too much to take on at this point in my career? I'm only twenty-eight. What happens then? Can I postpone renovating it?"

John smiled, a brief break from his otherwise serious demeanor, but at the same time, he was shaking his head. "I told her this might come up, but Louise was adamant."

"You see, when you got engaged last year, Louise was very worried that she'd waited too long already," Thomas put in. "But then you broke it off, so it was all right again," he added, as if that should clear everything up. It didn't.

"But what has my broken engagement . . . ?"

"Nothing," John said with a sweep of his hand, dismissing the idea. "Absolutely nothing. Louise wished that you either accept the house and the responsibilities that go with it, or reject it and them on their own merits, not for any other reasons. We will be permitted to reveal her alternate plan only after you make your decision. Then you will have no further say in the matter. I'm sorry, but there's no provision for postponing your decision past a few days, or for changing your mind after a choice to decline. If you reject the offer, it's out of your hands entirely."

"But what if I never find the necklace? Louise seemed certain I would, but how could I after all these years?"

"Well, she *hoped* you would," John said carefully. "Either way, it won't affect the ownership of Greystone."

"But Mister Ashford, I . . ."

"Please call me John," he offered with a fatherly smile.

"Being partners in a firm called Ashford, Ashford and Ashford, we're happy to establish a first-name basis so we know to whom our clients are speaking," Thomas explained with a chuckle.

Carolyn smiled, too, responding to a jest she was certain he'd used many times before. "What do you think happened to the necklace?" She looked back at John. "Who stole it?"

"Who knows? One of the servants, a stable boy . . . anyone but Robert," John replied with a flip of one hand. "It was a very valuable piece with all perfectly matched black emeralds."

Carolyn nodded. "When I was starting out in the hotel business right after graduate school, I would have taken on a challenge like this in a minute. Now that I've worked in the industry for nearly six years, I know how monumental this job is." She theatrically lifted her gaze to the ceiling. "Oh, Aunt Louise, what have you done?" Carolyn's laughter was tight, reflecting the tension she still felt.

Her face sobered suddenly. "I wish I'd known Louise's intentions while she was alive. When Mom told me she'd passed away in her sleep, I asked the manager of the hotel where I work, to grant me a short leave to go back for the funeral. He refused because she was too distantly related, and it was the busy tourist season. I couldn't get him to understand she was as close as any grandmother could be."

"You saw her every time you visited your parents, and

that was important to her," Thomas offered kindly. This time John smiled his agreement.

"I was so angry and sad. My boss's decision only reinforced my career goal of owning my own inn and being self-employed."

Carolyn thought of her best friend, Tulie—short for Amatulla—Jackson. She was the manager of a smaller independent hotel nearby in Miami, and had commiserated with her. "That's rotten, Carolyn."

"One more thing we'll do differently when we run our own hotel some day," Carolyn had promised.

"You got that right," Tulie had agreed with her ever-ready laugh.

Carolyn and she were close friends though they laughed at the picture of opposites the two of them together presented. Where Carolyn's hair was blond and long, her eyes blue, Tulie's was black and cropped short, her eyes almost as dark. Carolyn was tall, slender and pale complexioned, while her friend was not much over five feet, heavier than she wanted to be, with a smooth, milk-chocolate brown complexion.

John rose from his chair and broke into Carolyn's reverie. "I know it's a big decision you have to make, Carolyn."

She nodded and had to smile at his understatement. "This decision has to be the biggest I've ever had to make, or probably ever will make. How long do I have to decide?"

"Louise stipulated seven days from your getting the offer. But I can't imagine it taking you that much time at all." He crossed to the door. "I asked Rob to escort you on a thorough tour of Greystone before you sign the papers accepting it. He'll take you to dinner, and then install you in the resort cabin we've reserved for your stay."

John's son, Rob, had to be a very patient teenager to be willing to do all that for his dad, Carolyn thought.

"Time for me to go, too," Thomas said as he leaned on the desk for support as he rose. "At my age I put in an hour or so, and then I get to go home," he explained with a grin. "Will you be all right here alone for a few minutes while John finds Rob?"

"I'll be fine," she assured him. "I'm used to being on my own." *And I'm determined to stay alone if I have to in order to avoid another failed relationship like the one I had with Jeff,* she added to herself.

"Rob lives not far from your cabin, so you won't be all alone in the woods. No need to worry, because you'll be quite safe."

Thanks to his assurances about a problem that Carolyn hadn't even thought existed, she now wondered if there really was a reason to be concerned. She was used to worrying about her safety in Miami, but she hadn't given a thought to being anything but safe in this area with its small towns and beautiful natural scenery. What danger could she be in at Greystone?

John paused at the door. "I hope you have more casual clothes with you for going over Greystone tomorrow. It's a mess, and the roads near the lake are dusty gravel. The county gets more paving done around the lakes each year though. Most folks are happy about that." He snorted a laugh. "My son thinks the rough road keeps some nosy tourists and would-be vandals out." He shook his head. "Maybe he's right. Well, I'll go see if I can find him."

"I really hate to bother him. Isn't there a place in town where I can rent a car?" she asked, hoping he would say yes.

"That won't be necessary until you decide to stay. You'll want your own vehicle then, of course. Rob's supposed to be back from an appointment by now, and taking you out there is no problem. He has to go right past the drive to Greystone to get home."

With a look that brooked no further argument, John closed the door after himself. Carolyn shifted in the chair and crossed her legs. She rubbed the back of her neck to chase away a feathery sensation there. She just couldn't understand why Louise had never told her of the bequest in person.

But if she had, what would Carolyn have thought? That the necklace was really still there after decades of looters had hunted for it? Or that Sara could show her where it was hidden when she'd been dead for the better part of a century? Carolyn shook her head and took a deep breath.

She couldn't erase the guilt she felt because she would benefit from Sara's and Robert's loss. They should have married. Greystone should be going to their descendants. But there were none.

Carolyn comprehended their hopelessness and wondered if she would have descendants of her own someday. But she wasn't going to dwell on that now—not when she was finally at the point where she didn't get angry every time she thought of Jeff walking out on their engagement after lying and leading her on just to get the job he wanted at her hotel chain.

Besides, she'd rather think about Greystone. She remembered a photo taken some thirty years ago of Louise smiling happily in front of Greystone's stone façade. She stood by the wide steps under a portico leading up to the tall entrance. That particular photograph was vivid in Carolyn's memory because when she'd viewed it, she had not been merely attracted to the house, she'd felt strongly drawn to it. She'd pestered Louise about seeing Greystone, but Louise had patted her hand and said, "In time, my dear. In time."

The time never came. Carolyn went off to college about the time Louise's health deteriorated too much for her to travel.

"I wish I could take you there. I know you'll love it as much as I do," Louise had told her on her last visit.

Carolyn rose and walked to the window in the law office. "Aunt Louise, we talked about Greystone so often. Why didn't you ever tell me you wanted me to own it?" she wondered aloud, never dreaming that she would get an answer.

"Help me, Carolyn. Find the necklace."

Carolyn spun around, expecting to see Louise in the room behind her. Losing her grip on her purse, it thudded onto the dense carpet. Her rapid breathing thundered in her ears with her heartbeat. She searched the room for the woman who'd just spoken. The voice had sounded so familiar, so real.

Fearful and alert for any movement, she scrutinized the furniture and the corners of the room as she retrieved her purse. Nothing moved except for some dust particles dancing in the sunshine. She was alone in the room. No one could have spoken to her. Yet Carolyn had heard someone. But who?

What was going on? Carolyn had begun to think of her inheritance not as a chimera that was unrealizable, but as a long-held dream that might actually come true. Now, the thought flashed through her mind that it might become the first and more common meaning of the word "chimera." Could her inheritance turn into a grotesque and evil she-monster, a creature that spoke to her when no one was there? Or worse?

"Stop imagining things, Carolyn," she ordered aloud.

"Next you'll think that some alien force out of a horror flick is taking over your body and making you do and say things that you never would otherwise."

Needing to distance herself from her alarming thoughts, Carolyn stiffened her posture and bravely turned her back on the room. She looked out at the main street of the small resort town of Lakeside with its small shops and restaurants, and took in the muted sounds of the traffic, all bathed in the brightness of the sun. It should have felt normal and comforting.

She shivered as the room temperature seemed to drop until she felt chilled to the bone. Despite blaming her experience on her imagination, she was frightened.

With a deep breath, she spun around and strode out of the office. If the attorney's son wasn't here yet to drive her out to Greystone, she would take a taxi rather than wait in that room one minute longer.

The taxi followed a gentle curve through the woods and Greystone materialized before them as suddenly as if Carolyn had conjured up the huge house with the wave of a wand.

"Hey, lady. You sure you want me to leave you way out here all alone?" the driver asked as she climbed from his taxi in front of the huge decaying mansion. "It don't look safe to me."

"Yes, I'll be fine," Carolyn answered with a smile, despite feeling apprehensive. "I'm supposed to meet someone here. I'm certain he'll be along any minute," she added.

"Boy, you wouldn't catch me staying around here a minute longer than I had to." He plunked down her suitcase on the first step and scurried back to the taxi as if he hadn't wanted to be that close to the ominous-looking structure. "Good luck, lady."

Adding a generous tip, she paid him for the ride. With tires spinning on the mud and gravel, the taxi circled the weed-covered driveway and disappeared down the road through the woods.

Carolyn tipped her head up and closed her eyes as she inhaled the sweet, pine-scented air. The April sun warmed her face. A few birds gaily chirped their welcome from the budding maples near the house. The tension from her morning in the attorneys' office slowly drained from her body. Only then did she turn back to the house she'd wanted to see in person for as long as she could remember.

Greystone. Her heartbeat accelerated with excitement just thinking it was to be hers. The foggy-grey structure looked majestic, despite rising from mowed patches of weeds that had replaced its once neatly trimmed lawns. Fingers of ivy clawed at its sides. All the thick wooden shutters were closed. The giant looked asleep.

Far from being frightened by Greystone like the cabbie, Carolyn felt exhilarated—very much as if she were coming home after a long absence. But she'd never been there before, so how could she feel as if she were coming home?

A sudden splash in the water close behind her elicited her startled cry. She whirled around to face Lost Lake a dozen yards away. Blinking in the bright sun, she lifted her hand to shield her eyes from the glare and tried to make out what had caused the splash.

A cedar-strip rowboat with three passengers floated in a zigzag pattern. Sara Whitney's startled shriek when a shower of cold water sprayed across her lap was followed immediately by her sister Lora's laughter that sounded anything but kind.

"Since you insisted on rowing, Lora, you should make a greater effort to be careful," Robert Ashford, the young attorney

handling the other oar, urged. "You'll have your sister seasick as well as soaking wet." He looked so handsome, despite his dark hair having lost the orderliness of its center part.

Determined to row, Lora shared his seat despite both Sara's and Robert's objections. Now she merely looked at Sara, her younger sister by eleven months, and laughed again.

Sara rested her parasol on her shoulder and lifted her wet, long skirt a few inches from her thighs in a futile attempt to shake out the water. On the very next stroke she received yet another shower. "Lora, please. It's quite cold," she pleaded to no avail. She tried to believe the sprays of water were accidents born of the rower's inexperience. She didn't want to think Lora could behave so dreadfully on purpose.

"I'd best take charge of both oars now, Lora," Robert insisted. "If I don't, I believe you'll have us all soaked and down with pneumonia without ever getting us closer to the shore."

"I'm doing the best I can with this heavy oar." Lora leaned her shoulder against his and held out her hands for him to hold and inspect. "Just look at how red my hands are getting," she said with a pout.

"Lora, please move back to your seat so Robert can row," Sara urged.

"Oh, all right," Lora grumbled. The craft rocked as she pushed away the oar, letting it swing free in the oarlock, and returned to her seat facing Robert. Sara wished she'd been riding in that seat, to see and talk with him face-to-face, but Lora had insisted that the seat closer to him was hers. And Lora was practiced at getting her own way. Robert slid to the center of the bench seat and pulled evenly on both oars.

The boat glided smoothly toward Greystone's dock.

And disappeared.

Carolyn couldn't believe her eyes. She squeezed them shut and looked again. A few rings ruffled the surface of the otherwise smooth finish on the lake, as if a fish had broken the surface. She forced a laugh at her own nervous reaction. To think that for a while there, she'd thought she'd seen a rowboat and heard the splash of an oar. She'd even thought the people in it had looked familiar—straight out of the worn, black pages of Louise's album of very old photos taken at Greystone that Carolyn had pored over the previous week. Her mother had sent it to her in Florida when she'd learned Carolyn would be going to see Greystone.

She shook her head. She'd never known her imagination to be as active as it was today. There couldn't have been a boat, and even if there had been, the people in it couldn't have been the people in the album because they were all dead.

And yet it had looked so real.

She folded her arms beneath her breasts and hugged herself against the chill she felt suddenly. Seeing wasn't always believing, she concluded, but just to be certain no boats were on the lake, she walked to a large boulder on the rocky beach. From there, the sun was hidden near the tops of the giant pine trees that stood like sentinels all around the shoreline. The evergreens were reflected on the dark water, their narrowing tips pointing at her like accusing fingers.

Turning on the ball of her foot, she strode back toward the house. The peace she'd felt earlier had disappeared. She vowed to rein in her imagination and get back to thinking about the reason she was here—to see Greystone. To make sure a decision to accept her inheritance would be the right one.

She gazed up at the three-story mansion rising high above the shore like a pale ice sculpture. At an early age Carolyn had heard tales about the grey stones having been carried to this remote rise at great expense. To Lloyd

Whitney, who commissioned the building to please his new bride, Alice, no expense was too great to insure the seasonal residents their cool comfort.

Carolyn's gaze lifted above the main entrance and settled on the handmade circular window. Leaded into its center, the golden sun shone, its rays fanned out into clear glass. Beautifully crafted, the sun appeared to be spinning, defying all the laws of nature. She was glad vandals hadn't succeeded in breaking the resistant clear shields that Louise had put up to protect it. At home she had a sun-teaser miniature of the same design, a gift from Louise years ago. It caught the sun each morning in her kitchen window.

She lifted her gaze to the ornate scrollwork over the windows and doors that featured one curve swooping up before another turned down. The wooden gingerbread trim was the only whimsy in the otherwise staid stone construction.

"A smile and then a frown, another smile and then another frown," Carolyn had said, happily pointing to the trim in one of many photos of Greystone and of the Whitneys Louise had shared with her.

It seemed to Carolyn that the Whitneys, who idled away their summers at Greystone, fell victim to the same description. For each smile there was a frown. For many of their frowns, however, she saw no smiles.

Carolyn glanced at the road, but seeing no car that would announce Rob's arrival and the start of the official tour, she walked up the steps. She tried the entrance door and felt both dismayed and pleased to find it unlocked.

As she stepped into the damp, cold entry, she smiled with delight. The two-story foyer alone was larger than her whole Florida apartment. She clapped her hands and then laughed out loud, only to be startled when the sharp sounds echoed through the dusty, empty rooms.

Leaving the front door wide open to provide light inside the shuttered house, she strolled straight across the marble floor far enough to see a wide staircase rising to the second floor. Beyond the balcony at the top, a wide arch led to a hall over the rest of the house. Plenty of time to look upstairs later when she had a flashlight, she decided.

To her immediate left off the foyer, a double doorway opened into what she guessed must have been the front parlor. As her eyes became accustomed to the dim interior, she took a few steps into the high-ceilinged long room. She imagined that when the exterior shutters were open, the view of the lake would be lovely in any season.

Nearly bursting with excitement, she paused to listen as someone played lively Mozart on a nearby piano. While it was not possible to tell exactly where the sound was coming from, she assumed someone in one of the few homes on the lake must be feeling as delighted at that moment as she.

Carolyn wandered back across the foyer, looking into each room and picturing what life must have been like for her relatives who vacationed there. As she directed her steps toward the entrance from what must have been Lloyd's den, the piano music stopped abruptly.

She barely had time to register her disappointment when, without warning, the front door that she'd left ajar, swung wide open and banged against the inside wall with a resounding crack.

Sunlight flooded the foyer, blinding her. Fear slammed into her and she instantly shielded her eyes with a raised hand. Squinting against the glare, she could discern the silhouette of a tall man standing in the doorway.

Suddenly cognizant of how far from town and how very alone she was, she tasted her own fear.

Chapter Two

"I will not make assumptions about her before I get to know her," Rob Ashford said repeatedly as he steered his pickup toward Greystone.

But damn, the litany wasn't working. How could he not jump to conclusions? He'd seen pictures of Carolyn. Louise Whitney had been sending them regularly since he was a kid. She was beautiful, with a smile that lit up her face and made her big blue eyes sparkle. So what?

She would probably show up to collect her big inheritance and show off to everyone how rich she was. Hell, if she accepted the inheritance from Louise, everyone in town would know she was rich without her broadcasting the news.

Rob wanted to believe he knew her type—the type that flocked to the popular vacation area each summer to play in the crystal-clear glacial lakes, and again in the winter to ski down the slopes of the mountains that surrounded them.

He wanted to believe that, but he couldn't. The evidence wasn't in yet. He sighed. Not that he didn't know plenty about her already. Louise couldn't seem to brag enough about Carolyn's master's degree in hotel administration and about how fast she was moving up in the hotel business world.

"She'll be just what Greystone needs," Louise wrote several years ago.

Now Rob wondered what Carolyn would do with Greystone.

And what was he going to do now that she would own it?

Years ago he'd accepted the fact that he felt compelled to care for Greystone as his grandfather Thomas had done before him and Robert Ashford had done before Thomas. Now it was no trick at all to mow there each week when he mowed around the rental cabins at his fishing camp on the adjacent property.

He could rationalize that Greystone was just a building, but he'd always felt it was more. Much more.

Town folk thought it was haunted, but he felt a sadness about it that he was hard-pressed to describe. When he walked anywhere near it, he felt as if the house were watching him, waiting for him to do something. Damned if he knew what, though.

Rob slowed to pass through one of the many small resort towns that dotted New York from the Finger Lakes area to the St. Lawrence River. He was glad his dad had called on the cell phone to say Carolyn had taken a taxi out to Greystone. At least now he could drive right there without stopping at the office.

As he drove he couldn't help thinking about the trouble his great-uncle, Robert, got into courting Sara Whitney there. His reputation had been destroyed—even though no one ever proved that he took Alice's emerald necklace.

Rob was damned certain he wouldn't make the same stupid mistake of pinning his hopes on an impossible relationship. But then, no rich woman could be happy with the lifestyle he'd worked so hard to create. No, he would never lose his head over any rich woman. It would not be worth the inevitable pain when she got bored with his simple country life and took off. And no woman and no amount of money could make him sell his camp in the woods.

One particular soon-to-be-rich woman interested him

only because she would soon own Greystone. Naturally, Rob was concerned about everything that happened near Lost Lake. Anything that negatively affected the lake could mean his fishing camp would be out of business. Then he would be forced to practice law full-time and be stuck indoors year-round.

Rob pulled onto the rough gravel spur to Lost Lake and glanced around the pickup's cab. Not too littered, but covered with the ever-present layer of gravel road dust. Hell, the least he could do was provide her a clean seat for the ride to her cabin.

He fished for the roll of paper towels he kept under his seat, and using the whole roll like a dusting wand, he cleaned off the other half of the bench seat. One more swipe over the dashboard and the armrest on the passenger side, and he stuffed the soiled roll back where it had been.

Rob ran his hand through his hair. He always let his hair grow longer in the summers when he spent as much time as possible outdoors. Long hair helped protect his neck and ears from getting sunburned so easily.

He turned into the woods on the road between his property and Greystone's and took the fork away from his camp. With nothing else to do outside a deserted and locked house, Carolyn was probably sitting on her suitcase on the porch impatiently tapping her foot.

He slammed on the brakes and skidded to a stop on the gravel next to the entrance steps. Peering through the windshield, Rob couldn't spot her—just a lone suitcase on the step.

The front door was standing open. How had she managed that? He'd left it locked. A sudden uneasy feeling raised the hairs on the back of his neck. Jumping from the truck and running up the steps three at a time, he shoved open the door, disregarding the fact that it slammed against the wall, and paused in the doorway to let his eyes get accustomed to the dim interior.

He located her immediately by her gasp. He could barely make her out in the dim light, but saw her lift her arm as if in self-defense. Guilt tore through him for scaring her.

She stared at him, waiting for him to make a move. The only move that came to his mind was to take her into his arms and tell her he was sorry for startling her. Instead, he smiled.

"You're here," he announced.

And to think he'd spent years studying at the Cornell Law School just so he could make intelligent, accurate assessments of situations. That one had been a winner.

Carolyn exhaled the breath she'd been holding and for no reason that she could identify, felt her fear melt away as quickly as it had come. Struck by the overwhelming sensation she was happy to see this man, she didn't even know who he was. He couldn't be John's kid she was expecting to pick her up.

She inhaled deeply, but couldn't shake a growing feeling of delight. She smiled at his statement of the obvious. "Ah, yes. I'm here. The cabbie had no problem finding the way."

"Good." The man strolled across the foyer toward her. She sidestepped so she could look at him without the light shining into her eyes from behind him.

"I'm sorry I'm late." Long strands of his dark hair had fallen over his forehead and her fingers itched to sweep them back. His square-cut jaw was strong, his lower lip a bit fuller than the upper one. Nothing diminished the intensity of his light blue eyes that seemed to pin her in place.

He was dressed in a dark-grey business suit, somewhat

uncomfortably, she surmised. A carelessly tugged-loose maroon tie hung well below the unbuttoned open neck of his white shirt.

Returning her gaze to his face, she could see that he was examining her, too. Normally confident in her navy, businesslike linen suit with a knee-length skirt that topped matching hose and heels, she felt oddly vulnerable under his probing gaze.

"Are we done with the inspection?" he asked abruptly with a grin.

Carolyn laughed. He was right; they'd both been staring. "I'll finish later," she quipped at once, feeling strangely at ease.

"I look forward to it," he responded.

"Um. You can't be the kid I was supposed to meet here, so who are you?"

"I'm your ride." He stepped closer and extended his right hand to her. She surrendered her hand to his and was surprised to feel it was callused. That only reinforced her conclusion that he couldn't be one of the Ashford attorneys handling the disbursement of Louise's estate. She frowned and let her silence encourage him to continue.

"Robert Ashford, at your service."

"You? You're Robert?" She couldn't resist the feeling that he was drawing her to him. She took a half step back instead and retrieved her hand from his. Only now her fingers felt cold. "Louise often referred to you as a boy. I assumed you'd be a teenager," she admitted with a smile.

Rob laughed. She stared for a moment at his mouth that appeared so kissable. Shaking her head, she crossed her arms and tucked her hands in under them. For some reason, she was fascinated with everything about him and wanted to know more. How could she feel he was someone she'd waited ages to see again? She'd never seen him before in her life. She was 100 percent certain that as handsome as he was, she would remember if she had.

"Sorry about that. I'm . . ." She stopped. "Well, you know who I am. Pleased to meet you . . . kid."

"The pleasure is mine," he responded smoothly. "By the way, people around here call me Rob—rarely kid," he added, a twinkle in his eye. "And while I still mow the lawn, I'm also a partner in Ashford, Ashford and Ashford."

"One surprise on top of another. I didn't know you were an attorney, too. But when I saw the name of the firm, I wondered if every child in the family became an attorney."

She watched a slow, sensuous smile curl his lips. It created a languid warmth within her that startled her. He pushed back the front sides of his jacket and buried his hands in the pockets of his pleated trousers.

"Well, I'm not one when the fish are biting."

"I beg your pardon?"

"I'm a full partner in the firm, but I run a fishing camp next door to Greystone. In fact, Dad arranged for you to stay in a cabin of mine that's close by—until such time as you choose to move into your house. The cabins are rustic, but I hope they're adequate for your needs for the time being."

"I'm sure it will be fine," she said. Their gazes locked for a few moments until a crow cawed loudly outside the entrance, its startling cry echoing in the empty foyer.

Carolyn jumped. Her hand flew to her chest. "I'm easily spooked today, it seems."

He whipped his hand out of his pocket and grasped her upper arm. "What do you mean 'spooked'?" he asked. "Did something else happen here to frighten you today?"

"No. No, of course not," she said to ease the urgency

and concern she'd heard in his voice.

"Good. That's good." He dropped his hand and smiled suddenly. "Well, come on. We have time for a short tour of the house while there's enough sunlight to see by."

"Great. I haven't had time to look much beyond the foyer." She looked up at him, her eyes wide with excitement.

He stood there watching her for a moment before he spoke. "It has a hold on you already, doesn't it?"

How could there be sadness or resignation in his husky voice when she was so happy? "You sound as if Greystone is an living entity and not just an old abandoned building." She extended her arms and turned around in a circle, taking in the foyer in which they stood. "It's all so exciting. Strange though, I can't get over feeling exhilarated, as if I've come home after being away for a long time." Her cheeks felt flushed. Joy bubbled up in nervous laughter until she looked at him and saw only a small wry smile. "What's wrong?"

He shook his head and looked resigned. "Nothing, Carolyn. I guess I should have known all along that you would love it. Otherwise, Louise wouldn't have trusted you with it."

"What's not to love?"

He made a more wholehearted effort at a smile. This one came closer to reaching his eyes. "We should start the tour. When the sun sets behind the hills, it gets dark quickly in the woods."

But instead of leading the way, he put his hand on her arm and stepped closer. She hadn't prepared to ignore his touch and the warmth penetrated her sleeve to swirl through her body. Anyone seeing them might think they were lovers about to kiss.

"Before we walk around, you've got to understand something," he said softly. "It's been a lot of years since anyone has done anything to the inside except in the little apartment Louise had built years ago."

"I know," she assured him with a nod. "I can see that the place is a mess."

He removed his hand. She was startled to discover it wasn't the choice she would have made. She felt chilled. Folding her arms across her waist didn't come close to warming her as his touch had.

"I hate to see you disappointed, that's all. Over the years some jerks really trashed the place," he added angrily.

Without thinking first, she rose to her tiptoes and gave him a chaste kiss on his cheek, as she might have to thank a dear friend for a kindness. "That's very sweet of you to worry about my feelings, Rob," she said, wanting to ease his anger and see a smile sparkle in his eyes again. "Thank you."

His questioning gaze locked on hers.

Instantly embarrassed, she wondered what in the world had made her kiss him on the cheek like some Victorian maiden. She'd never kissed a man she'd just met, and certainly knew better than to react like that in a business situation. She was acting as if she were some other person and not herself. She tried to ignore the sensations that lingered on her lips from the brush against the shadow of his beard.

Best to move away and forget she'd kissed him. He was one of Louise's attorneys, after all. She should maintain an impersonal demeanor with him. Besides, this wasn't the time or place to get involved with a man, even in a casual relationship. She knew next to nothing about Rob, and her experience with Jeff had taught her not to trust a man without knowing everything about him so she would know all that motivated him.

"Where do we begin?" she asked, feeling as giddy as a child set down in front of a Christmas tree surrounded with gifts that were all for her.

He chose the parlor first, and this time she saw a second long room behind the first. "This has to be the dining room. There's plenty of space for a very long table, and wide enough for sideboards and buffets as well." She could almost picture the Whitneys seated around the table.

Rob lightly touched her elbow. She started with surprise. Her hand flew to her chest where her heart beat rapidly. She laughed to cover her startled reaction.

"The old kitchen and the apartment Louise fixed up are that way," he said, pointing toward the back of the house. "You can reach them through there, or this way." He ushered her back through to the end of the foyer and into a large room across the back. "Grandpa says this room was called the morning room. I guess they spent mornings here. Clever, huh?"

Carolyn smiled at his jest.

"The woods weren't as close to the house then as they are now, so it would have been brighter," he explained.

"This must have been lovely, but I'd rather be able to see the lake."

"I agree completely, but the back of the house was very private. A rose garden stretched from the house to the woods."

Today the morning room was dark, despite the bright sunshine outside. The only visible light leaked between the warped slats of weathered wood shutters. She and Rob were too far into the mansion for any light to reach them from the wide-open entrance door behind them.

She watched Rob walk ahead of her to a closed door. When he opened it and switched on a ceiling light in that room, she laughed at being startled this time.

"Voila!" he said with a grin before he turned and disappeared into the lighted room.

Noting his ability to appear and to vanish without warning, she hurried after him, her heels clacking on the dirty marble floor and echoing around her.

In the small apartment, the walls were painted a utilitarian white, and unlike the rest of the mansion, they had little graffiti and damage. The hardwood floor appeared to have been refinished. She walked through, noting a modern kitchen, a smaller room, certainly intended as a bedroom, and a bathroom complete with tub and shower, in addition to the living room where they'd started.

"Treasure hunters haven't bothered this area much. I guess they figured the renovators would have found anything hidden in here. Louise had this built to live in while she renovated the rest of the place, and while she managed the resort, too. But from what Dad says, she was out of her element. All she knew about renovating an old mansion could be written on the head of a pin."

Hearing the insulting, or at best uncaring, comment about her great-aunt, Carolyn's head jerked in his direction. He met her gaze steadily and added quickly, "And I don't mean that unkindly. I'm just trying to make you understand why things happened as they did. She just didn't know anything about the hotel business. All she could do was dream about it."

She studied his face and nodded after finding no malice there. "After Lloyd's death, I guess Greystone went to his brother Arthur—Louise's father. Mom said he'd tried to sell it."

Rob nodded. "He had it cleaned up and painted inside, but they did a sloppy job. Instead of fixing the walls or paying attention to the wood trim, they spread on thick paint to hide damage done by then."

"I guess Arthur couldn't find a buyer and bequeathed it to his daughter, Louise. I think he figured she could eventually sell it."

She raised her arm in an arc. "What was this area before it was an apartment?"

"The music room. The Whitneys entertained their guests here after dinner. The acoustics were said to be quite good, and Sara was something of a pianist. A grand piano was in here, and a smaller version graced the front parlor."

A vital look had come over Rob's face as he spoke of the house and the Whitneys. Carolyn found herself wondering how he knew so much about Greystone.

"Louise told me that Sara favored the one in the parlor, though I don't know if it was the piano or the view that she preferred." She strolled to the door where he stood. "You seem to know a lot about them."

"Enough," he responded with a shrug that snuffed out the brightness in his face as if a shade had suddenly dropped. "The kitchen is this way," he added matter-of-factly, and turned away from her.

Carolyn was sad to see his interested and eager expression disappear.

Rob led her through a door at the other side where the apartment had direct access to the main kitchen as well as to the morning room. The nearby exit to the backyard gave easy access to the outdoors, too. The whole layout had been designed well, making it easy for someone to get wherever they were going quickly.

"It's sad to see everything in such pitiful condition. Oh,

will you look at that? The wood-burning stove and oven combination is huge."

"It had to accommodate the giant pots and pans that must have been used in Greystone's heyday," Rob said.

Several of the iron plates that should have covered the fireboxes were missing. The warming shelf on the top was dented, as if it had been hit with a mighty swing of a heavy instrument. One oven door hung down at an odd angle. The other was missing.

"This was put in when the house was built in the eighteen-nineties. They never updated it, not even to propane," Rob reported.

Carolyn nodded her understanding. She ran her fingers along the long slender grooves in the wide-plank counter that were designed to carry away water from the work surface, in sharp contrast to the crudely carved initials that blemished the surface. "Somebody really did a number on this room, didn't they?" Her voice sounded unsteady, reflecting how the senseless destruction affected her.

"I suppose the people who thought one of the servants took the necklace must have figured she would hide it in here."

A beautiful mansion destroyed by time and vandals. A missing priceless necklace. Unhappy people whose lives had been destroyed by what happened here. Suddenly drowning in her emotions, Carolyn was unable to breathe. The pain and grief of losing her dear great-aunt without saying goodbye or even being able to attend the funeral washed over her again. The unbelievable directive to find the necklace when people had been searching thoroughly for years, and the demanding and frightening challenge of renovating Greystone on top of the joy of seeing the mansion at long last, were too much to cope with all at once.

Tears burned behind her eyes. She floundered against a rising tide of unhappiness. She tried to smile, but couldn't retain her tenuous hold on her composure. Before she could turn her back to Rob to hide them, spontaneous tears overflowed her eyes and slipped down her cheeks.

He immediately opened his arms and tugged her into them to hold her close. His strong hands cradled her against his hard chest as she wept for all those reasons and for no reason at all. Her forehead nestled against his neck where she felt the sure and steady beat of his heart. His comforting embrace provided the safe haven she'd sought without stopping to ask why. Without any explanation from her, he seemed to understand what she was going through. He didn't try to placate her with words, but led her to believe he really cared how she was feeling.

He just held her close, enveloped in his solid warm comfort, as if he'd been doing it for decades.

Slowly, Carolyn regained her composure and resolve, and felt less distraught at the senseless destruction all around her. As she lifted her tear-streaked face to thank him, the front entrance door slammed shut with a loud bang that echoed throughout the empty rooms around them like a shell exploding in the peaceful silence. Carolyn jumped. She felt Rob tense. His grip on her tightened, and she wanted to both run from him and stay in his protective arms.

"It's just the wind," he offered quickly, letting his arms drop from around her as he stepped back. "A breeze off the lake," he added with a one-shoulder shrug.

She thought it strange he'd say so without checking, but she found herself accepting his conclusion. But why? She shook her head to clear it. What was happening to her? Why was seeing Greystone affecting her more than she'd anticipated? The answer to that question would be easier to deal with than all the new and delightful sensations she'd felt when Rob put his arms around her.

He led her back the way they had come through the apartment. In the morning room, Rob pulled a small flashlight from his pocket before switching the last apartment light off. Following the beam of light, they walked on through the foyer where he opened the front door to let in the sunlight again. He picked up a large rock, apparently set by the opening for that purpose, and leaned it against the door to keep it open. She wondered why she hadn't put it in front of the door when she came in.

But wait a minute. Hadn't she done exactly that?

She had no time to remember exactly. He took her elbow and directed her toward the wide stairs. He picked up a wide-beam light that had been stationed on the first step and attempted to turn it on. After a couple of clicks, he opened the top and jiggled the bulb until it lit up.

"Just a little loose, but I put in fresh batteries for you." He handed it to her as she thanked him politely. Then, using his small flashlight, he started up the steps and continued his commentary. "Grandpa had the carpets all removed years ago. They were rotten with dampness and neglect. It smells better in here with them gone, if you can believe it from how musty it still smells."

Carolyn paused barely halfway up the steps. When Rob reached the balcony above her, she heard his footfalls stop. "It was here, wasn't it?" she whispered, suddenly unable to speak any louder. She looked up to see he was still facing away from the stairway.

He inhaled deeply as if preparing for an ordeal, and turned slowly to look down, not at Carolyn, but at the steps beside her. He seemed to know what she meant. "Yes."

Entranced, she returned her gaze to the stairs beside her, remembering the tragic fall that ended in Lora's death there. Carolyn could almost see her . . .

Lora lay there, her ankle-length, bias-cut dress twisted beneath her, her head turned, her hollow gaze fixed on Carolyn.

She recognized Lora from Louise's photos. Or was it remembering those photos that made her see Lora now? Unable to do otherwise, Carolyn stared into Lora's empty, angry eyes. She could hear her last words—as if they were meant for her.

"Sara, you'll never marry Robert now. Never."

Like white nitrogen clouds from dry ice that disappear in moments, the distorted figure evaporated. Carolyn backed away from the cold draft as a startling feeling of doom squeezed the air from her lungs. Her legs trembling, she clutched the railing behind her for strength.

"Carolyn?"

Her head jerked up to meet Rob's questioning gaze. His lips moved, but she couldn't hear his words over the pounding of her own heartbeat. She swallowed hard and dragged air into her lungs. "What?" What did he say? More importantly, what had she just seen?

Not willing to maintain eye contact with Rob, she lowered her head to see that the vision of Lora on the steps had vanished. Relieved, she squeezed her eyes shut and pinched the bridge of her nose for a moment's reality check. She was perfectly willing to blame the vision on her overactive imagination again. And she was tired, too. Yes, that was it. She was tired.

Carolyn scooted sideways to avoid stepping where the vision had been, and hurried up the stairs, hugging the railing the rest of the way to join Rob at the top. He said nothing at first. Neither did she. As they walked on, she pressed a hand on her churning stomach in a futile attempt to calm her nerves.

She felt Rob watching her but couldn't look at him. She didn't want him to see how frightened she felt. She renewed her earlier vow to stop giving her imagination free rein, and walked on past him down the hall, looking briefly into each room. When he resumed his running commentary about the rooms, she welcomed the relief that washed over her.

"How do you know so much about the house?" Carolyn asked when it became obvious he knew more about the house than she did, including who had slept in each room.

"The information was handed down to me in my grandfather's stories. He used to talk to his uncle Robert about the place. I think they went through every inch hunting for the necklace to clear Robert's name. I've spent some time at it, too."

He laughed briefly, but Carolyn could sense his urgent desire to clear Robert's name, too. He wasn't just a distant relative, but a person whose character and activities were well known to him. They shared more than their name.

Chapter Three

As they went on down the hall, Rob never mentioned seeing the specter next to Carolyn on the steps minutes before. But then, she wanted to believe neither of them had seen it.

They continued to examine each room. The furniture had been removed and any built-in cabinets had been trashed as they'd been in the kitchen. The fireplaces were empty of their andirons, and some of the wooden mantels hung at odd angles from having been ripped loose in the search. Fabric wall coverings that must have been beautiful in their day, looked faded and worn. Those fragile remains of a luxurious Victorian decor bubbled away from the wall, the corners drooping and revealing the plaster in several places.

After the master's bedroom and his dressing room, Rob stopped the tour. "The rooms go on to the end of the hall. They're smaller and used for guests mostly. At the end, there's a stairway that leads directly to the kitchen for the servants to use."

"Aaachoo!"

Carolyn's sneeze startled Rob and set him to laughing. "Don't tell me you're allergic to dust. If so, this sure is the wrong place for you."

Unable to speak as she sneezed again, she shook her head, opening her purse for a tissue.

"Time to get you some fresh air to clear your head." He led the way again, despite the fact that her flashlight lit a broader area than his. But then, he seemed to glide through the house as if he needed no light. "Time to get you settled in Cabin One and then see to dinner."

"Cabin One?" she managed.

"Yeah," Rob responded, nodding his head. "It's the first cabin in the row at my camp—the one closest to Greystone."

Carolyn had never been in a north-woods fishing camp and hoped that rustic, as Rob had described it, didn't mean it came with an outdoor privy.

Rob must have seen doubt written on her face. "If you prefer, you're welcome to stay at one of the places in town, but I . . . we thought you'd like to be out here near Greystone. If you choose to accept your inheritance, you'll probably not want to move into the apartment right away—at least not until the rotten plaster is torn out of all the rooms in the rest of the house. Plaster dust can get into places you'd never expect." She scrunched up her nose in distaste.

"You can leave the broad-beam light there on the first step for next time," he suggested at the bottom of the stairs.

Waiting on the porch while he locked the door, she asked, "Do you always keep Greystone locked?"

"Always. I have enough trouble keeping people out when they have to break in. An open door would be an invitation to walk in."

"Well, thanks for leaving it open for me today," she said with a smile.

He slid his keys into his pocket. "I didn't," he said over his shoulder as he crossed to the porch.

This wasn't the first time he'd said something she had trouble believing. "But the door was . . ."

"I must have forgotten. Now, about dinner," he rushed on to say. "I thought we'd eat out here at my place because it would be easier and quicker, but we can go to a restaurant, if you prefer," he said, leaving the choice up to her.

She tamped down her immediate questions about his motivation for such a private dinner. "No, no. I don't want to take the time for a restaurant meal. And I'm sorry to cut into your personal time. I'll be happy to help with dinner."

"The lady cooks, hmmm?"

"Um-hm. The lady cooks, and I take it the man does, too."

Rob nodded. "I guess that's what you'd call it. My cooking ability is born of necessity because I live alone. I couldn't exist on frozen dinners."

Carolyn smiled, absorbing that personal information about him that somehow pleased her even though she shouldn't care one way or another whether he lived alone or not.

"Your chariot awaits, Miss Matison. Shall we go?" He raised his arm with a palm-up gesture toward his truck. His face hid all emotion behind a pleasant smile. Not even his eyes revealed what was going on in his head.

Carolyn plastered an equally fake smile on her own face. "Thank you, Mister Ashford," she replied, attempting a similar *faux* formality.

Rob touched her elbow politely as they descended the steps. She felt a rush of warmth from the contact. Clutching her purse to her midriff to keep the strap from sliding off her shoulder, she tried to concentrate on the feelings of curiosity and frustration she'd felt just before he touched her. At the driveway, she stepped away and walked several feet from him. She wanted to breathe fresh air, not air scented with his sexy mixture of spices and man that she liked so much.

"I was telling your father I should rent a car so I don't

have to impose on you, Rob."

"No reason to do that at this point." He stopped. "Unless it's because you don't want to ride around town in my pickup," he added with a nod of his head toward the red pickup. With no trace of a smile on his face, he added, "Then maybe you should rent one."

She was about to ask that he take her to the rental office when he continued. "But then you can rent the car in town tomorrow—if you're still here."

Startled by his implying that she might not be staying, she couldn't help but want to know why he thought she might leave. Was it just his wishful thinking? "Then I guess that means you'll just have to put up with me out here until tomorrow."

She smiled and crossed to the passenger-side door. Nothing about him fit the conservative-attorney style she'd anticipated. She should have guessed that his mode of transportation wouldn't either.

"You were expecting a Mercedes or a sports car, by chance?" he asked as if reading her mind. "Is that what all the lawyers in Florida drive?" His deep chuckle sent tickles of pleasure down her spine when it clearly had no reason to.

"I'm afraid I can't say," she replied. "I don't know all of them yet," she teased. Amazing. She didn't know how she could have felt comfortable enough with him to do that. Hardly the businesslike demeanor she worked at keeping with men ever since she'd learned the hard way to be wary of one-on-one dealings with them.

Carolyn glanced back at Greystone, almost expecting to see someone behind her. She had the oddest sensation that they were being watched.

Rob lifted her suitcase into the truck bed. While the vehicle was fairly new, the paint was scratched, and the floor of the box bed dented. She noticed the front fenders were pockmarked from the spray of gravel on unpaved roads. Obviously a working truck.

"The inside is clean. You won't get your . . ." He surveyed her derriere and then looked slowly back up to her face. "Your suit dirty."

She didn't attempt to hide her smile, but turned away from his steady gaze that wandered intimately over her body. She splayed her hand across the side of her hip where his gaze had felt like a light, intimate caress. She wished she understood why he affected her so intensely.

The step into the truck cab was a tall one. Carolyn's tight skirt did not permit the ease of movement necessary for her foot to reach the running board. Feeling as agile as a penguin, she did try to step up before he moved to help her. He took her purse and dispatched it to the center of the bench seat. He reached inside her short jacket to settle his strong hands on her rib cage with a familiarity he seemed to take for granted. She grasped his upper arms to ready herself for whatever he might do. "Mind your head."

At his warning Carolyn ducked her head. Her temple grazed his ear. The contact as he lifted her effortlessly onto the seat ignited a hot flame that heated her cheeks. Intent on hiding her visible reaction to touching him, she shielded her face with her hand by pushing imaginary errant hairs back into her French roll. Her fingers brushed her skin, but didn't come close to duplicating the complicated feelings that the contact with him had elicited.

As brief as the contact had been, she couldn't remember a man's touch eliciting such a tingly feeling before. And she didn't tingle only where she touched him. The feathery sensations tantalized her in the most unexpected places.

"Thank you," she muttered politely as she settled into place.

"My pleasure," he had the nerve to say with a sexy smile before he pushed the door closed with a bang.

The surprising effect he was having on her made her feel more unsettled the longer they were together. She wasn't sure whether she ever wanted to wear a narrow skirt again, or if she wanted to wear one each time she drove with him so he would always have to lift her up.

He jogged around to the driver's door and took off his suit jacket. He laid it on the narrow back-bench seat before climbing in.

Another couple of minutes passed as he pulled off his tie, tossed it on top of his jacket, and rolled up the sleeves of his shirt. He finally dug behind the seat cushion to find his seatbelt. "These damn things disappear as soon as I sit down."

His glance in her direction caught Carolyn watching him with rapt attention. "Are you ready yet?" she asked, unable to contain her amusement at the lengthy routine.

"Almost," he answered with a grin.

His grin reminded her of Thomas's smiling face, though his had been pleated with wrinkles. That's who Rob will look like when he's old, she decided, rather than his father.

Rob thrust his hand back behind the seat cushion and came up with her seatbelt latch, too. "Buckle up," he ordered. "I wouldn't want anything to happen to you."

Carolyn didn't want to notice every move he made. She didn't want to, but she couldn't stop. What was it about this guy that made her so aware of everything he did? Aware of every attractive, strong, virile inch of him?

She would definitely rent a car first thing in the morning so she didn't have to ride with him again. Then she wouldn't have to exist in the state of diminished control that she felt when she was with him. She wouldn't have to watch the fabric of his dark trousers stretch taut over his muscular thighs when he raised his foot to the brake. His strong forearms exposed below his rolled-up shirtsleeves wouldn't command her attention as they did when he turned the steering wheel or reached to turn the radio on to play music softly. The spicy scent of his aftershave wouldn't intrigue her and linger in her senses long after the breeze from the open back window vent had swept it away.

But she already knew all those things about him and more, and yet they'd just met.

She glanced over at the heater control and found that it was not turned on. As warm as she felt, that wasn't what she'd expected. She was convinced there wasn't a truck or car in the whole state that was big enough for the two of them to sit in at the same time.

As he pulled the truck around the circle drive in front of Greystone and headed back through the woods toward his camp, Carolyn glanced back through the wide rear window of the cab. "Rob, the shutter next to the front door is open. That must be the first one in the parlor. I thought it was closed. Did you open it?"

"I didn't," he answered and then he pressed his lips into a thin line as if to cut off his own words.

"Shouldn't we go back and close it?"

"Nah. It'll be okay." He didn't take his eyes off the road. "Probably the wind," he offered with a quick glance in her direction after a lengthy silence.

"Yeah, that pesky wind." But Carolyn knew there hadn't been any wind all afternoon, despite his referring to it twice. That was the first thing she'd noticed when they'd stepped outside. The lake was smooth as a mirror. It had been since she'd arrived by taxi. What reason could Rob have for lying to her?

She turned back to watch the road that was little more than two gravel tracks disappearing into a thick stand of trees. Sunlight broke through the leaves and created a fascinating patchwork of shapes and colors. At a fork in the road, he veered sharply onto the other road that headed back toward the lake.

The pickup pitched sideways as Rob left the raised roadbed to drive around a newly fallen tree branch. When Carolyn grabbed the dashboard for stability, he reached out to hold her upper arm until they were level again. His touch had the same effect on her as before and multiplied her excitement and confusion about the whole day.

"Almost there. This fork leads to my place. I generally drive home and walk over to Greystone. I'm glad I didn't today. You wouldn't make it on the dirt path through the woods in those shoes."

"Thanks." Carolyn didn't take her eyes off the view through the high windshield. She didn't want to miss anything.

"Sit right where you are, Rob, and don't move a muscle," Carolyn ordered after enjoying a delicious grilled chicken dinner at his house. "After you did most of the work to prepare the meal, the least I can do is clean it up."

"If you insist," he answered with a devilish grin.

After touring Greystone that afternoon, he'd delivered Carolyn to Cabin One. Any concerns she'd had about it being unsuitable were erased. The one-bedroom cabin with a screened-in porch wasn't fancy, but it felt comfortable. The central room was both kitchen and living room, with a sofa dividing the areas. A large laminate-topped table with four chairs sat in front of the wide window overlooking the lake.

After a quick shower and a change into her favorite jeans, a comfy sweater, and sneakers, she'd donned her jacket and followed the gravel road his truck had taken to the other end of the row of cabins as he'd directed. There the road narrowed and veered uphill into the woods for a hundred yards or so before it turned and opened onto a high clearing that overlooked the lake.

Rob's cedar-sided house with a bark-colored roof seemed to be a part of the woodland. Huge windows ran from floor to ceiling to reveal spectacular lake views. And yet none of the cabins in the fishing camp marred the natural view from any window. She could feel how much the man who owned this house loved the lake and the woods that stood tall around it.

Carolyn felt right at home from the moment she walked in. How wonderfully private and peaceful living here would be, she thought. A far cry from the city living she'd been used to all her life, it felt oddly appealing.

"I can understand why you want to spend your time out here instead of in an office," she asked as she finished loading the dishwasher. "This is a marvelous house."

"The artistry belongs to a friend of mine who built it, Lars Oleson. In fact, he's the one I would recommend to do the delicate wood restoration work at Greystone, if you decide to go ahead with it."

Carolyn felt the smile fly from her face. His comment brought her back to the reality of why she was here, and it wasn't to enjoy his company or his beautiful home. During the past hour she'd enjoyed getting to know Rob so much, she'd forgotten that.

"There's plenty of time tomorrow to consider that." She

rinsed the pot that she'd washed. "You know, having a home like this would make anyone want to play hooky from work."

He laughed in a way that sounded like a snort, as if he didn't believe her. He rose and went through the motions of making coffee. "You can't believe how hard it was to persuade my father that running a fishing camp in the spring, summer and fall was what I wanted to do—a lot more than staying in town and lawyering. My plan didn't go over very well. It doesn't fit his family image."

"Can't he hire someone to replace you?"

Rob shook his head and thought a minute. "He wants to keep the firm in the family. The law work fills my empty hours in the winter when the camp is closed. I go in to the office during the summers if something important comes up and Dad needs me, but otherwise I stay out here for the entire fishing season."

"Something like my inheritance comes up and you're forced to put in hours in the office when you'd rather be out here." And if that was true, he probably resented having her as a client.

"Oh, spending time with you might not be too bad," he said, looking from her eyes to her mouth and back again.

Carolyn pressed her lips together. His gaze had felt like a kiss, and she didn't want it to. "How kind of you to say so," she answered, trying to break the intimate mood. She grabbed the hand towel and dried her hands.

"And if you accept your inheritance, I'll have to work, but it'll be out here at Greystone. I can still manage the camp."

Carolyn nodded.

"How about coffee in front of the fire? It gets cold at night in April. In fact, it's always cooler at the lake than in town any time of the year."

She nodded. "I'll remember that."

He poured two mugs of coffee. "We can just leave those pans to dry in the rack," he suggested.

They settled on the couch facing a fireplace constructed of native stone that stretched all the way to the ceiling. The scene felt tranquil and allowed Carolyn a good opportunity to think back over the day and ask more about Greystone.

"We'll go back over to the house in the morning. You can see the rest of it."

"Good. There's an awful lot to be done, and I'd like to see it all before I agree to accept it."

"Taking on a project that size would scare most people away."

"Maybe if I was smart, that would be enough for me not to accept it," she said with a little laugh.

"Before you see Dad or Grandpa again, I'll take you to talk to Lars, okay? It was his dad's crew that put in the apartment for Louise. But Lars has been through the whole house recently. He'll be able to answer your questions."

What did he mean that Lars had been through the house? Rob was an unofficial caretaker, but other than that, he didn't have anything to do with the house. Was he checking out getting the work done for himself?

"It's getting late and we need to get an early start in the morning." He rose and extended his hand to her. She hesitated only a moment before she slid her hand into his, and he pulled her up to his side.

"I hardly know you, but I'd hate like hell for you to get hurt, Carolyn." He kept his grip on her hand as he studied her face at close range.

All thoughts of Greystone and what he'd meant flew from her mind. She felt his gaze circle her face as surely as if the pads of his fingers had followed that route. Her skin tingled and warmed.

Just when she was convinced that he was going to close the inches that remained between their faces and kiss her, he dropped her hand and walked toward the front door. Disappointment flooded through her. She chided herself for being foolish. This was business, not pleasure. But when her mind revisited the feelings she'd felt when Rob was near, she knew their relationship could be pure pleasure, if they let it.

"I'll walk you back to the cabin," he said, apparently unaffected by their brief closeness. "Here's a battery-operated lantern that you can keep there in case the power goes off. It does that now and again way out here."

Carolyn frowned and took the light. "I hope not too often."

He shook his head. "Sound travels very easily out here. If you have a problem and call me, I'll hear you, even inside my house. I'm not one of those people who have a radio or television on all the time. The outside light at my kitchen door is on all night. Even if the power goes out, a generator kicks on. It keeps the lights on at the cabins, too."

"I'll be fine. I'm used to being on my own," she assured him, trying to duplicate his current impersonal manner.

"On your own, huh? No man waiting for you to come back to him in Florida?"

"No, there's no man waiting for me to come home," Carolyn said, shaking her head. *Not since Jeff,* she added to herself, stirring up memories of anger and hurt resulting from believing in a man who wasn't worthy of her trust on a personal or a professional level. Jeff used her position at the hotel for a recommendation to get a new job while promising her a happy-ever-after life. He'd ditched her the minute he'd gotten the job he'd wanted so badly. She hadn't imagined he'd been lying to her to get it, and felt used and abused.

That was about a year ago. Since then she realized she hadn't loved him as much as she'd thought. He'd wined and dined her royally, and that's what she had liked. It was a far cry from working all the time and eating meals on the go as she'd been used to. Thankfully, she'd learned from the experience. She wouldn't repeat her mistake and trust a man so easily and completely again. Until she met one she could trust without equivocation, she wasn't interested in a close relationship with any man. She looked at Rob. From all she'd heard of lawyers, many didn't fall into that category at all.

She shrugged. "Besides, I'm too busy now trying to develop a career to think about much else. My dream of owning an inn is my top priority. Looks like my inheritance can give me everything I've ever wanted in spades."

"Yes, what more could you possibly want?" he posed, his voice low and clipped.

They started walking down the road toward the cabins. She paused after just a few feet at the sound of footsteps scurrying through the dried leaves on the forest bed nearby. "What's that?"

"Raccoons probably," he answered in a more normal voice, making a sweep of the area with his flashlight without seeing one. "They sleep most of the day and come out to feed at night, but please don't feed them. With rabies around I don't want to encourage them to visit the camp. I have enough trouble with them trying to get into the fish-cleaning shed and the garbage as it is."

Carolyn murmured her agreement to comply with his rules and they started walking again.

"Don't worry if you hear other animal sounds," he suggested after a few moments. "Nothing bigger than a raccoon comes near the cabins. I've never seen a bear on this side of the lake."

"A bear?" she said, halting and grasping his arm to make him look at her.

He laughed. "Don't worry. They don't want to be around you any more than you want to be near them."

"I don't think that's possible." She released his arm and they walked on. Bears. Maybe there was something around Greystone that she should fear after all.

"You'll hear an occasional fish jump and maybe a hoot or two from an owl. For the most part, nights are quiet unless you disturb a bunch of bats."

"Bats?" she asked, her voice raised. She shuddered dramatically.

"Yeah," he said with a laugh. "Don't knock 'em. They help a lot with the mosquito population control."

"Bats are good for something?"

"Very good. Having them around means we have a good ecological balance in the area, and anyway, you won't know they're around."

"I hope I won't."

"Whatever strange sound you might hear, Carolyn, no matter how weird, it's probably some animal. You're not to worry," he urged. "Okay?"

"Fine. I'm too tired to worry about anything tonight after such a long day. I'm going to be asleep in record time."

"Good. You'll find that the fresh country air is a good sleep tonic, even when you're not tired."

At her cabin Carolyn paused on the front porch stoop to thank Rob again for the dinner. He leaned his hand against the doorframe. His shirt stretched across his broad chest. She wondered if she put her ear against his chest if she could hear his heart beating rapidly like her own.

"Tomorrow I can take you to talk to Lars when he breaks for lunch at eleven-thirty, if that's okay."

"Great."

"Then how about coming over to the house for breakfast at about eight? That will give you time to look around Greystone again before we go see Lars. We'll check out the lake, too, and I'll show you a path you can use to walk along it. It's really quite beautiful."

"I'll be there at eight . . . and thanks for . . . for everything."

"Sure."

He glanced at her mouth, but this time she knew he wouldn't kiss her. She also knew that she wanted him to—again, and all her lectures to herself about not wanting it would be futile.

"See you in the morning." She watched from her porch until he disappeared from sight beyond the neighboring cabins into the darkness beyond her porch light. She listened to the waves lapping softly against the rocky shore. The mysterious wind had come up a little. She would open the bedroom window a little and let the gentle sound lull her to sleep. She ducked inside and locked the door, a habit from living in the city.

As it turned out, she'd made an accurate assessment of the time required for her to fall asleep. No time at all.

Chapter Four

The owls and raccoons could have marched up on her porch singing in a chorus and dancing all night for all Carolyn knew. Showered and dressed casually in jeans and a shirt for the morning, she felt ready to face whatever lay ahead.

As it was still before eight o'clock, she directed her steps to the lake. She knew Lost Lake, like most of the deep lakes in the Finger Lakes region, had been created by giant ice-age glaciers that had covered the area.

"The water always feels like ice. Dangerous for anyone who falls in before the summer sun can warm it up a bit," Louise had warned her. "It was always too cold for me to swim in, even by the end of the summer season."

Dipping her hand into the water, Carolyn had to agree. It felt freezing cold, too cold to even want to go wading. Walking a few yards along the shore, she found an enormous boulder and climbed up to view the beauty of the early morning scene.

Two pairs of green-headed ducks caught her eye as they glided across the blue-green water. Their movement left tiny wakes as they swam. The iridescent feathers on the males caught the sunlight burning its way through the morning fog. What fun it would be to see the ducks daily on the lake, she thought, perhaps later in the season with little ducklings following behind. She wondered what Rob thought of the idea of feeding them at his camp.

Suddenly curious about whether or not she could see

Greystone from the lakeside of the boulder, she scooted on her fanny all the way out to the far edge. Not able to see anything through the stand of trees on the point that provided Greystone with natural privacy from the fishing camp, she backed up a little and flipped onto her stomach.

Gambling that the weight of her legs would keep her from sliding into the cold water, she inched her way out again, supporting herself with her hands on the downward curve of the rock. She still couldn't see the house. Creeping out a little farther with her gaze fixed on the woods to catch a glimpse of the grey structure, she moved her hands onto a patch of loose stone, and they slid out from under her. Her startled scream cut through the natural quiet just as two strong hands clamped around her ankles and held fast.

"If you want a cold bath, just don't turn on the hot faucet in the tub," Rob suggested calmly. "It's a lot safer than landing on your head on the rocks at the bottom of the lake."

Carolyn struggled to get her hands back under her and lift her breasts from the rock. Embarrassed, she looked back over her shoulder. "Are you going to help me up or just make jokes?" she snapped.

"When I was a kid, we used to play a game."

"Rob, come on. Pull me up." She wiggled her fanny from side to side trying to scoot back up the rock, but his hold on her ankles kept her where she was.

"As I was saying, the game was hand walking," he continued, as if to annoy her. "I would hold my friend's ankles, and he would walk on his palms."

"Wheelbarrow!" she cried, forgetting her annoyance at the fun of reenacting the childhood game.

"Ready?"

After brushing aside the loose stones on which she'd slid,

she was more than ready to get up. As he lifted her ankles and moved back, she walked on her hands as long as the strength of her arms held out, which was about five hand steps. That's when she collapsed onto the flat top of the boulder in a fit of giggles. Her ankles freed from his grip, she rolled onto her back and sat up, brushing the chips of soil and rock from her palms. "Thanks for catching me. I guess it was a foolish move to go out so far."

He was leaning his hands on the rock, one on either side of her legs. The muscles in his arms bulged out below his short-sleeved knit shirt. He looked a lot more comfortable in his jeans and cotton knit shirt than he had early yesterday in his suit and almost-tied necktie.

"Rob, you look like him, you know."

"Who?"

"Robert. I realized it last night. That's probably why it felt like you were an old friend when we met. Louise showed me enough pictures of Robert to make me feel I knew you."

Rob straightened, brushing off his hands. "Everybody is probably a throwback to some relative," he said, dismissing the resemblance as unimportant. "You hungry?"

"Sure am."

Carolyn slid off the rock unaided and brushed off the seat of her jeans with a few firm swipes. Looking down, she saw her front was covered with dust and tiny stones. She brushed them away and didn't hold much hope for her clothes coming clean.

"Need any help?" he asked with a smirk.

"I'm quite self-sufficient, thank you," she answered, hiding her smile.

"Yes, so you said." He turned smartly to walk toward his house. She ran to catch up. Behind her cabin he paused and gestured for her to lead the way up a narrow path through the woods instead of going to the end of the row of cabins to the road. He followed close behind her. She could feel his gaze covering every inch of her backside.

They entered his house again through the kitchen door, and Rob showed her where to wash her hands in the sink in the mudroom beside the entrance. The dirt she'd collected on the front of her shirt from the boulder refused to disappear even when she rubbed at it. "I'm going to need to get cleaned up before we go to town," she told him, stepping back into the kitchen still brushing at the dirt.

He didn't respond verbally. She looked up to see he was watching her tending a spot over her breast. His gaze was intense, his eyes dark. Looking down again, she realized she'd been pulling the fabric of her shirt tight across both breasts. His gaze felt as if he'd touched her there. Her nipples hardened, visibly pressing outward. She released the shirt, but he'd seen.

"Breakfast is ready," he announced curtly and turned away.

He served the scrambled eggs and bacon from the warming oven while she buttered fresh toast that popped up when she got to the table. In minutes the whole platter full of food in the center of the table had disappeared.

"That was delicious, Rob. Thank you. It must be the fresh air, but I was starved."

They both rose to clear the table. The dishes were in the dishwasher in minutes.

Rob took two broad-beam flashlights from the mudroom shelf and handed one to her after he'd checked the batteries. "This time you can look in every room over there, and then we'll go talk to Lars. After some lunch, Dad can explain more of the will, and you can see Louise's plans for the house."

Carolyn stopped him with a hand on his arm. "Whoa! You have a habit of dropping verbal bombs and then walking on as if they were nothing. See what plans?"

Rob glanced at her hand touching him and then met her gaze. For a moment she saw an expression of reluctance. She retracted her hand immediately as if she'd been burned. He didn't seem to want to be bothered with her questions.

"I thought you knew. Louise had blueprints drawn up to turn it into an elegant retreat where visitors would stay a week or two to get away from the city. But that was a lot of years ago."

"Now people take off for Europe or Florida and California."

"If they've got kids, Disneyland," Rob prompted. He sounded more at ease. Carolyn decided that he couldn't have been annoyed moments earlier, maybe just surprised that she didn't know about drawn plans.

"But it could be a business retreat, too," she suggested. "It's isolated enough for privacy, and with new roads, it's close enough to town for people to enjoy those benefits. Companies could rent the whole facility for conferences. Their families could swim, or sail, or shop, and of course, fish."

"Oh, now you're taking the business away from my fishing camp, huh?"

They laughed together, but it wasn't an easy laugh. She wondered if losing business was a real concern of his. Was he threatened by the plans for an inn next to his camp? To what extent would he go to keep his camp viable so he didn't have to work summers in town? Would he threaten her success? She didn't want to believe that, but thanks to good old two-timing Jeff, she wasn't going to dismiss the idea.

On the return walk to Greystone, Carolyn realized his house was much closer than she'd thought, although she couldn't see one from the other because of the dense woods. The whole distance only took a few minutes to cover. Despite routinely being quite independent, she felt unwillingly comforted knowing Rob would be close.

Before entering Greystone, he opened the shutter on the window on one side of the porch while she followed his instructions to do the same on the other side. The shutter that she'd seen open as they left the day before had been shut, the catch securely in place. "I see you came back to close this open shutter last night. Louise told me you kept an eye on the place and acted as caretaker for her. I know she appreciated it."

He shrugged. "I rigged these two shutters by the door to open from the inside or the outside, but I hid the latch to make them look the same as all the rest that open only from the inside. The thick sturdy boards have turned away a lot of casual vandals who didn't come prepared for heavy-duty breaking and entering. I can't say they turned all the vandals away though."

"Is there still a big problem with vandalism now?"

"Not lately, but I won't sugarcoat it for you, Carolyn," he said as he dug out the door key from his jeans. She was distracted for a few moments because she hadn't thought getting his hand in the pocket of the snug jeans would have been possible. They clung to every curve in his physique as if they'd been painted on. "Vandalism does happen once in a while," he went on, hopefully oblivious to her cheeks warming as she thought about his tight jeans. "I chased out a whole family of squatters several years back who thought they could move in just because it was empty. They had a cooking fire burning in the fireplace in the morning room. I first spotted them by the smoke. They set a squirrel's nest in the chimney on fire, and it's a wonder they didn't burn the place down."

"They must have known about it being empty to expect to use it undisturbed."

He nodded. "Everyone around here knows it's here and empty. They don't all know how close I am to see what's happening. One night last summer some teenagers tried to have a keg party out here. It didn't last long."

Her concern wrinkled her forehead. "That could get dangerous for you if you try clearing them out single-handed."

"Let's just say I have a friendly relationship with the county sheriff. I have a phone at my house, but one's never been put in over here."

They left the front door wide open, and Carolyn made certain the rock was securely up against it before they started their tour. For the next hour they walked through every room. Carolyn found Rob easy to talk to about the mansion's potential as well as its history. His reluctance seemed to have been replaced by a real interest in ideas they bounced back and forth about an inn.

Because the central staircase from the foyer ended on the second floor, Carolyn assumed that was the top floor. She thought the top row of smaller windows that was visible from the outside was in the attic. Today she discovered a full third floor arranged with a long hall down the center and smaller rooms opening on each side accessible via a steep stairway from the kitchen.

"The third floor was used by the Whitneys," Rob explained, "mainly as storage areas and bedrooms for their own household servants and those traveling with their visitors."

"Some of the smaller rooms up here that I don't need for housekeeping or mechanics could be combined into suites. The view from this high is wonderful," she said, opening a shutter on the lakeside.

He stepped close behind her to gaze out the window over her shoulder. "I'll never get tired of looking at that view if I see it every day the rest of my life—and I hope I do," he said softly, his love for the area evident in his voice.

"It's wonderful. So quiet and peaceful. Nothing like the hustle and bustle of the city, that's for sure." She glanced up at him to see his smile disappear so quickly that she figured he didn't like to even think about city living.

The quiet reflective mood evaporated as they headed down the back steps to the kitchen. Carolyn looked around once again, this time with a critical eye, seeing the space in comparison to the minimum required to function efficiently for a restaurant.

Wanting to know roughly how much space would be available, she left Rob checking the security of the back door, and paced off the area all the way through the parlor to the front windows facing the lake. She wasn't concerned with any great accuracy because Louise's blueprints would have the dimensions, and she would see them later that day. She merely wanted an estimate at this point.

"Sara," Robert called. "Sara, you must trust me."

Carolyn heard the male voice calling her by her middle name from the front entrance. "Rob, what are you talking about? And don't call me Sara. I never use my middle name, and I don't like hearing it in this house. It's too weird. I'm Carolyn, not Sara."

"I didn't call you," he said from behind her in the opposite direction from the voice.

Carolyn spun around and widened her stance with a

small step to retain her balance. She felt the blood drain from her face. Rob was leaning on the doorjamb in the old dining room—nowhere near the foyer where the voice had originated. For an instant she thought he might be playing a practical joke on her, but his breathing was calm and even. If he'd called from the foyer and then run through the morning room and the apartment and around through the kitchen to strike his present pose in the doorway, he would be panting or at least breathing hard.

No, Rob hadn't called to her. But who had?

She ran toward the double doors that led to the foyer. No one was there. She felt compelled to call out to be sure. "Hello? Is someone there?"

The front door was still as wide open as they'd left it. She jogged out onto the porch and saw no one. She supposed it was conceivable that someone had come in, called to Sara and then run out again. But who would do such a thing? And why? Was someone deliberately trying to frighten her away?

The wind was more in evidence in the waves she could see breaking on the shore below the house. The branches of the giant pines swayed in an uneven rhythm. She wanted to believe the vocal sounds had been the wind.

But could a wind over Lost Lake call out to Sara? Or was it someone else calling to Carolyn, as someone had in the attorney's office? She pulled her jacket closed against the chill that settled around her. Who was trying to frighten her, and why?

Rob strolled from the parlor into the foyer, acting as if nothing had happened. "Ready to get cleaned up to see Lars?"

Still in the front doorway, Carolyn looked back over her shoulder to study his face for any signs of deception and was alarmed by what she saw. Rob's pale gold shirt and jeans caught the sunlight pouring through the yellow portion of the stained-glass window above the entrance. The bright rays transformed his appearance into a preternatural golden phantom. The leaded braces between the panes of thick tinted glass created shadows like dark streaks, emulating folds in an ethereal robe. Her gaze darted to his face to see the shadows that fell there were from the "frown" side of the stained-glass sun. His mouth and brows appeared to be curved downward. He looked fierce, angry, and threatening.

She stumbled backwards as her gasp echoed around them in the empty two-story foyer.

"Carolyn? What is it?"

Stepping toward her, he moved out of the colored light, and the frightening image projected on him disappeared. She saw real concern on his face. Her breath left her in a gush, and she quickly turned away, tamping down the fear she'd felt. She still wanted to believe that all she might have to worry about was a wandering bear or two. "It's nothing. I know. Must have been the wind again."

She couldn't look back at him. She didn't want to see if the concern she'd seen on his face and heard in his voice was real or not. Right now she needed it to be; therefore, without looking, she could believe it was. "Rob, I think we should go now. I want time to wash away the dust and change."

"Me too, but I want to check around the outside, if you don't mind. It'll only take a minute or two."

She smiled and nodded. "I'll wait in here for you."

"Be right back," he called over his shoulder as he jogged out the front door past her and took the steps down to the drive two at a time.

Carolyn stared after him until he disappeared around the house. She looked toward the lake and for some reason, the light stones in the driveway reflected the sun so brightly that she blinked against the light. She lifted her arm to shade her eyes and looked again.

A black Model T Ford was pulling into the drive toward Greystone.

"I did it, Sara! I did it!" Robert Ashford called as he parked his father's touring car in front of Greystone.

Unable to contain her excitement, Sara Whitney ran down Greystone's wide porch steps to greet her beau. "Wonderful! I was so worried when you didn't arrive when you said you would," she admitted anxiously as she toyed with a ribbon at her waist.

Robert laughed and pushed back the dark hair that stubbornly crossed his forehead as he unfolded from the driver's seat. "Nothing could keep me from your side, sweetling."

Sara's heart sped up. Smiling down at her, he took her hand and led her the few yards from the driveway to the shore of Lost Lake. They ducked beneath the branches of the huge weeping willow that granted them a little privacy.

"You needn't fear, Sara. I couldn't wait to see the gold of your hair, the blue of your eyes, and to feel the softness of your lips." He raised her hands to hold them against his chest and gently kissed her lips.

Sara felt warmth flood her cheeks. "Robert, I love you so that I can't bear to think that summer is almost ended and my family must return to Manhattan. I wish we lived close to Lakeside so I could be near you all year-round."

"But you will soon," he predicted eagerly. "That's what I came to tell you. I did it! I've reached an agreement with the owner of the property next door—about buying it to build our home there in the woods for after we're wed."

Sara twirled around with joy. Facing him again, she stood on her toes and bravely kissed his cheek. "You couldn't have picked a more perfect place for us. I'll love living here at the lake all year long."

"I would live with you anywhere," Robert vowed. "But my father and uncle would skin me like a fresh-shot rabbit if I left their law practice," he added with a grin.

Sara laughed. "Oh, guess what. Mama allowed me to try on her black emerald necklace last night. She said I must wear it when I wed someday. I longed to tell her we planned to wed next summer."

Robert stepped back and poked at the rocky sand with the toe of his shoe. "Are the emeralds quite beautiful?" he asked, not meeting her gaze.

"Oh, yes," she answered, nodding excitedly. "And Mama says wearing the necklace will bring me good luck."

"It will be years before I can afford to buy you even the smallest jewels," Robert confessed, turning back to her. "You're so beautiful. You deserve much more than I can give you, Sara."

"Dearest Robert, you are all I need to be happy, not jewels." She lifted his hand and kissed the back. "Only you."

"Then if you're sure you want to marry me, I'll ask your father for your hand right now. Is he at home?"

"Yes, yes," she whispered breathlessly.

Unable to imagine being happier than she felt at that moment, she felt like dancing. But she didn't dare even hold his hand any longer when she saw her father coming out from the house.

"I thought I heard your auto," Lloyd Whitney called from the circle drive.

"Yes, sir. Hello, sir," Robert replied awkwardly as Sara and he walked toward Lloyd.

Sara's older sister, Lora, her dark hair drawn into a tight bun that accentuated her sharp features, appeared at the front door. She lifted her hand to shield her solemn face from the sun as she took her customary place at her father's elbow.

Robert politely greeted Lora, then turned his attention back to Lloyd. "May I speak to you, sir?" He glanced at Lora who was listening to his every word. "In private, sir?"

"Why, whatever do you have to talk about with a small-town attorney, Papa?" Lora asked with an incredulous laugh.

"Lora, please," Sara whispered urgently, wishing her sister would stay out of this, but knowing she was wishing for a miracle.

"Now, now, Sara," Lora purred before turning to Lloyd and wrapping her hands around his elbow. "I was just going to say to Papa that we should invite dear Robert to stay for dinner."

Sara held her breath, waiting for Lloyd's answer.

"Robert is welcome to stay, my pet," he said finally, patting Lora's hand and granting her every wish, as usual. When Lora turned back to Sara, Lora's smile disappeared at once.

Sara wished she'd been the one to ask if Robert could stay. The way Lora always butted in, one might mistake Robert for her suitor, instead of Sara's.

"Thank you, sir," Robert responded. He tugged at his high stiff shirt collar with a hooked finger.

"You girls run along and change for dinner. Robert can keep me company in the library until then." Lloyd redirected his steps toward the house.

Robert smiled at Sara and ran to catch up with Lloyd at the door. Sara followed, walking quickly to stay ahead of Lora to avoid another confrontation.

Sara barely had time to change when she heard raised voices downstairs. She hurried down the hall, her legs weak with trepidation. She leaned on the railing as she slipped silently down the steps past the huge family portraits that hung from the picture rail high above her. The library door opened.

"You misunderstand my intentions, sir," Robert was saying. "I'm asking for Sara's hand, not Lora's. It's Sara I love."

His voice sounded higher than Sara was used to hearing. She ran to clasp the hand Robert extended the moment he saw her. Her heart pounded and her hands felt cold against his warm ones. When she saw the furious look on Lora's face as she stood beside her father, Sara feared she might faint. "Please, Papa, please."

"Sara, for a pretty young girl like you, there's no need to rush into marriage. Why, your older sister is not even spoken for as yet. And it wouldn't do to have you engaged before Lora. No, there's plenty of time. I see no reason to decide anything now."

"But Papa . . ." Sara's shoulders slumped under the weight of her sadness. Tears stung her eyes. She clung to Robert's hand like a lifeline.

"You must understand these things. My boy, for now I think you shouldn't stay to dinner."

Lloyd dismissed them all with an upward wave of his hands as he walked to the front door. "I'll still have time to check on Champ's leg. Tell your mother I'll be in the stables," he called over his shoulder, exiting as if he hadn't just broken Sara's heart.

"Please, Lora. Can't you talk to him?" Sara pleaded. "Make him understand. Papa always does what you want."

"Talk to him?" Lora smiled smugly. "Oh, yes. You can count on it. I'll make sure he knows exactly what he must do, no matter what happens." Her head high, Lora strutted up the stairs.

"Robert, what will we do?" Trembling, Sara clung to Robert's lapels as his hands circled her waist. Tears spilled from her eyes.

"Sara, I'll talk to your father again. We'll find our happiness. It just won't be quite as soon as we'd hoped." Robert gently kissed each damp cheek. "Please, don't cry. You must trust me. I promise you that our love will bind us together for all eternity. Someday we'll be as one, and then nothing will part us. Nothing."

Sara loved Robert with all her heart, but in the light of what had just happened, she couldn't bring herself to trust his prediction. But she nodded bravely and tucked her hands in his bent elbow as they trudged outside.

"I hate to tell you this now, Sara, but I must go to Albany for a week or so to meet with a client for the firm. Please don't worry while I'm gone. I hate to see you so unhappy."

She tried to smile, but her lower lip trembled.

"We'll be together one day, my love. Trust me."

Sensing someone watching, Sara glanced up past Robert's shoulder to see Lora staring down from her bedroom window on the second floor. She didn't get a chance to tell Robert. With his palm beneath her chin, he turned her face back to his and kissed her lips, pressing and nipping sweetly for more than a few moments. Heat coursed to her cheeks and she forgot that Lora was watching.

Robert chuckled. "There. Now you're not so pale."

Sara smiled shyly as they said their goodbyes. She watched Robert leave, her arms wrapped around her waist in the only hug she'd get until she saw him again.

"No!" Carolyn closed her eyes and turned away from the retreating figure. "This has got to stop. I didn't see that." She pressed her eyes with her palms to erase the nebulous images.

Opening her eyes moments later, she looked around the foyer. She couldn't have seen Sara and the others. They were all dead. Greystone wasn't fresh and clean as she'd just envisioned it. What was going on? She didn't remember her imagination ever being this vivid. Why did it have to start now?

"All set," Rob announced from the front door. Startled, Carolyn cried out and spun around to face him. "Hey, I'm sorry. I didn't mean to make you jump like that."

She smiled. "It's nothing," she assured him. And that's what she wanted to believe.

After removing the rock to free the door, Rob locked up. As they returned to the cabins, he led her into the woods beyond the driveway on a new path near the shoreline.

"This is the path I was telling you about. It keeps going all the way around the lake. It's a beautiful walk even if you don't have the time or stamina to make it all the way around."

Arriving at her cabin, he asked, "Ten minutes enough time to change?"

She nodded and turned up the steps to her cabin door.

"Carolyn?"

"Yes?" she answered without turning back.

"It could have been anything. You were concentrating on counting off your steps to measure the room. I was watching you. I couldn't hear anything, but I believe you heard something, for whatever that's worth."

She whirled around. "You believe I heard someone call out to Sara?"

Slipping his hands into his back pockets, Rob shrugged and dropped his gaze to his toe that was tapping a stone on the path. She stepped over to face him and grasped his upper arms, forcing him to look at her. "Do you, Robert Ashford, believe I heard someone call out my middle name when no one was there?"

As if he saw that escape from her and from the subject

was futile, his gaze fixed on hers. "Yes, damn it, I do."

What would he say if she asked about the other things she'd seen and heard today—and the boat just after she arrived? For now, she'd settle for explaining the voices. "And? Don't stop there, Rob. You believe me because . . . because . . . ?"

Carolyn waited for him to speak, but instead, he looked up and away from her with a sigh. Shaking him with her tight grip brought his gaze down to lock on hers. She wasn't about to let him get away with avoiding the issue this time. She was going to learn what was going on.

"Why, Rob? Why do you believe I heard someone speak to Sara? Are you just saying it because you think that's what I want to hear? Keep the client happy?"

His eyebrow rose as he inhaled deeply through his nostrils. "Because I've heard someone calling to Robert," he whispered so quietly that she could barely hear him from just inches away. He continued to stare into her eyes until she released the breath she'd been holding and dropped her forehead to rest on his chest. His arms found their way around her waist to pull her close. She pressed her ear against his hard chest and heard his steady but rapid heartbeat.

"Then I'm not going nuts, thinking I hear voices?" she asked softly. *And thinking I see people who aren't here?* she wanted to add but couldn't.

"Voices? Plural?"

"Yeah."

Without stepping away, she briefly explained hearing her aunt's voice in the law office after reading her letter.

His chuckle rumbled in his chest. "Well, I've never heard them there, but if you're going nuts, we both are."

Tears of relief stung her eyes. His fingers slowly

threaded back into her long hair that she'd worn loose over her shoulders and tipped her head up. She couldn't move. She knew what was coming—not just his kiss; more than that. She somehow anticipated the flood of sensations she would feel. Without questioning why, she knew they would feel wonderful.

His lips touched hers, lifted, and with a sigh, settled once more to give and to take as they pressed against hers. She didn't turn away. All her expectations had been correct. Her body tingled with a new awareness. His kiss warmed spots she hadn't realized had turned cold over the years. Reminding herself of Jeff and why she had chilled toward men, she knew she shouldn't enjoy the kiss so much. But she did.

When he eventually lifted his lips, he smiled. His breath embraced her face in warm puffs. "Before we get ah . . . sidetracked any further, you wash off the dust, and we'll go see Lars. He's expecting us. When we get back, we'll have plenty of time to talk . . . about everything."

He punctuated his promise with another quick kiss, this one on the tip of her nose that brought a smile to her lips. Without another word he was gone, whistling as he jogged home.

While she washed up and changed into clean slacks and blouse, Carolyn wondered about Rob. She'd never known a man who thought that kissing was getting sidetracked. She smiled at the thought, but she agreed that this particular sidetrack wasn't a desirable one for her to stay on. But hadn't she heard you could trust a man who could whistle on key? She hoped so, because Rob was a good whistler. His secret must be his gorgeous lips.

She frowned suddenly. Or was the old saying that you could not trust good whistlers because they made such good liars?

Chapter Five

The conversation in Rob's pickup on the way to Lars's job site was about anything except who or what had spoken to Carolyn.

"Is creating an inn what you really want to do with your life?" Rob asked. "No plans for marriage? A family? You're a very attractive woman. I'd hate to believe you're a misogamist."

"No, of course I'm not," she responded with a brief chuckle. "But marriage isn't something I'm looking for now. I want to make something of myself first before I even think of committing to someone in some arrangement as lifestyle-altering as marriage."

"You've already worked your way up to assistant manager of a large hotel. What was next?"

"You mean before I got the call from your dad?"

"Yeah, before that."

"That's easy. Another move up. I want to build a career. A damn good career that I've been dreaming about since I was a kid. I dream of owning a hotel or an inn someday that would be a roaring success."

"Like at Greystone."

"Exactly. The opportunity came a lot sooner than I ever thought it would, but developing Greystone into a luxury resort is just the challenge I want, to prove myself. So in that sense, creating an inn is all I want right now." She looked out the car window through eyes clouded by dreams playing in fast-forward through her mind. "The challenge is more exciting than anything I've ever felt. Aunt Louise took the possibility of everything I've dreamed of, and gift-wrapped it with the money to accomplish it. What more could I ever hope for?"

Rob's silence was all the answer she received and at once she turned away, embarrassed at revealing so much of herself. "Besides," she said in an exaggerated manner to break the uncomfortable stillness. "I don't imagine there will be much opportunity to meet many unattached men way out here in the woods. Spending every day at Greystone will mean I won't be seeing men other than workmen sporting lower-back cleavage above their low-slung jeans and leather tool belts."

Rob laughed. "On the other hand, you'll probably get lots of men interested in you for your money."

"Hmmm. I hadn't thought about that," she admitted. "But I'll have to remember it."

Rob gave her no more time to consider it. He turned into the driveway of a startling Victorian house. "Here we are. The town is trying to get the owners of these old relics to fix them up in an effort to attract the drive-by tourists."

Carolyn climbed out of the truck and looked up at the gaudy ornate woodwork on the house. Every gable, every window and every door was surrounded with fancy wood scrollwork. Three, no, four different colors of paint, a different one on each kind of decoration, gave the house the appearance of a poorly done paint-by-number drawing. "I almost expect to see a fence I saw in North Dakota that looks like the rows of paper dolls you can cut from folded paper with every one the same shape. But at this house, each one would be a different color."

"Please, Carolyn, don't suggest it. The owners might go for it." He feigned a shudder at the thought.

"You mean they're adding to this? It's not the original trim?"

"Some was, but the guy's added more. Lots more. Lars hates being a party to it, but in a town this size he has to take what jobs he can find."

"It gives the phrase 'painted lady' a whole new meaning," she said, stifling a giggle. "I'm not sure this one's a lady."

As if on cue as they neared the house, the door opened and two men in sawdusty work clothes came out carrying lunch boxes. The first was a tall and very slender man with straight, greying blond hair that had been cut short and then allowed to grow out with little attention to the direction it took. His skin showed evidence of the sun except for his forehead, which was lighter because he obviously wore a hat while he worked outdoors.

That could also explain the tornado-style hairdo, Carolyn realized. Hat hair. Her conclusion was proved correct when he whipped out a folded baseball cap from his back pocket and pulled it onto his head the moment he was out the door.

The second man didn't have to worry about what his hat did to his hair because there was very little of it, she noted before he plopped on his cap.

"Perfect timing," the slender man said with a huge grin and an extended hand for a hearty handshake with Rob.

"Lars, how are you doing?" Rob asked, shaking his hand vigorously. "I'd like you to meet Carolyn Matison. As I told you, Miss Matison wants to talk to you about the possibilities for Greystone."

"Yah. Sure. Nice to meet you," he said with a melodic Scandinavian accent. His warm callused hand enclosed

Carolyn's for a much more gentle shaking that it had given Rob's.

Lars turned to the big man beside him. "And this here is Tiny. He can frame a square corner better than anyone I know."

"Ma'am." The big man nodded, touching the bill of his cap with his index finger, but made no move to shake her hand. He stood over six feet, as did Lars, but Tiny had forty pounds more on his frame and probably ten years more of living under his wide, leather tool belt.

"You've got to watch out for Tiny. He'll talk your ear off," Lars added with a good-natured jab of his elbows to Tiny's ribs.

The incongruity of the statement made everyone laugh. Lars slapped his coworker on the back, saluting his good humor, and suggested they walk over and sit on the end of the porch. "You'll forgive us if we eat while we talk, but we only have half an hour until we have to get back to work."

"Please. Go right ahead," Carolyn told them.

While Lars and Tiny arranged the contents of their boxed lunches and poured their drinks into their thermos lids, Rob announced, "I showed Lars what your aunt had in mind for the house as a summer lakeside inn."

"The plans were drawn up a long time ago," Carolyn pointed out. "And I haven't seen them yet, but what about the possibilities of turning it into an inn now? I would need guestrooms on the second and third floors. I pictured using the present dining room and the parlor for the restaurant. The back of the foyer would be the reception area near the foot of the main stairs. I'd need an elevator on the other side of the door that leads into the morning room. That room would be a ballroom or at least a large meeting area with room dividers to make the space more versatile. And I think the walnut-paneled den in the front could make a handsome lounge with a bar along the inside wall and seats by the windows overlooking the lake." Carolyn looked up from the mental image she'd been describing to see all three men staring at her.

"She gonna do it, Rob?"

"You'll have to ask her," Rob answered, shaking his head.

Lars turned back to Carolyn. "You gonna live in that spooky place while you fix it up?"

She really wished people would stop calling the place spooky. "That's what my aunt intended."

Lars's eyes widened. "You got guts, and the answer to all your questions is 'yes.' All that can be done."

She could feel his respect for her go up a notch, but she couldn't quite understand what living out there at Greystone had to do with anything.

By the time Carolyn stood up to leave at the end of Lars's and Tiny's lunch break, she knew they could work well together. A detailed examination of the house would be required to make an accurate estimate of the cost and time factors for the work, but today she'd found out that the transformation of Greystone to an upscale lakeside inn and restaurant was feasible. She felt her excitement and determination build within her like pressure inside a volcano.

"After sitting and watching them eat in front of us, I'm starved. What about you?" Rob asked as they drove away from the garish house.

"Sure, and then I want to go over the will and see my aunt's plans for the house. I want to visualize what she wanted to do."

"First, we eat."

Arriving at the restaurant well after the lunch hour, they

were shown to a table at the windows that overlooked another of the many smaller lakes in the region. Carolyn thought the view from her seat created a perfect picture of spring. The deciduous trees were leafing out and the gardens below the windows boasted yellow daffodils and red tulips in full bloom.

As they ate, they talked over numerous possibilities for Greystone. The flush of warmth she felt in her cheeks reflected how excited she was about the possibilities. But by the end of the meal, she noticed she was doing all the talking and Rob was silent.

"You're taking very good care of me, Rob," she said as the waitress removed their plates. "This is a lovely place to eat, and the crab salad was delicious." An impulse to touch him struck her, and she reached over the narrow table to pat his hand. "Thank you."

He captured her fingers and rubbed the back of her knuckles with his thumb. Exciting ripples of pleasure slid up her arm. "I've got strict orders to treat you like visiting royalty, which is where you'll rank in a town the size of Lakeside." He looked at her a moment before he released her hand and leaned back. He abruptly signaled the waitress for the bill and busied himself getting out his charge card.

Carolyn lowered her gaze and set her napkin on the table. A chill settled over her. How could she have forgotten? Rob was her escort to a business appointment with Lars and to lunch because it was part of his job. She should be thankful that he hadn't disguised the reason. As one of the partners in the law firm, he'd been assigned the care and feeding of the heiress. She was sure the firm was being paid well for their efforts from the estate funds. She would do well to remember he was a paid escort—certainly not a lunch date.

She didn't like the idea that she'd felt any intimate pleasure from the touch of a man who was paid to spend time with her. She shuddered. *Find his motivation,* she reminded herself. *But when you do, don't let it hurt so much!* she added firmly.

By the time they left the restaurant, Carolyn had accepted that his kindnesses, and yes, the wonderful kisses they'd shared, were just to keep his client happy. Well, she liked the kindnesses, but the kisses were going to stop. While they had felt exciting and genuine, she couldn't imagine what had made her allow them to happen so quickly. Theirs was a business relationship after all.

She would reinstate the impersonal distance she normally kept between herself and all the men with whom she worked. She should have wised up sooner, but when she looked at Rob and remembered his kisses, it was hard to remember to be wary.

As they drove back to Lakeside, Rob was more talkative than he had been in the restaurant. "Louise lived in Lakeside about six months while she had the plans drawn up to renovate Greystone. She had some sketches of both the interior and exterior rendered from the floor plans."

"I wonder why she never showed them to me, or even told me about them."

Rob shrugged. "Well, you'll see them all in a few minutes."

Back in the law office, Carolyn watched Rob lay out the drawings Louise had commissioned. They covered the walnut conference table. The elevations showed the house with a wide covered entryway so guests could get out of their cars under the protection of an extended roof similar to the original one in Louise's photos. Sketches of the guestrooms reflected an attempt to keep the Victorian look from the period in which Greystone was built. The floor plan, however, included no elevator or any plans for third-floor guestrooms.

"I'd need the third story accessible for guestrooms," Carolyn told Rob who had circled the table, looking at the drawings with her. "The whole project wouldn't be financially feasible at today's costs without utilizing all the income-producing possibilities."

With a familiarity that lovers share, he leaned over her to look more closely at the drawing. A fragrant blend of the outdoors and spice tickled her nose. His hard chest pressed against her shoulder. Puffs of his breath ruffled her hair. Suddenly, her arms felt heavy with a desire to hold him. She wanted the contact to continue long after he straightened.

"I think Louise pictured the third floor being used for the staff housing. She pictured this resort just for the summers, remember."

Carolyn looked again at the plan and tried to ignore the longing curling within her. "Of course. But I think this area could support a year-round inn today. There's so much to do in any season." Her gaze had slipped beyond seeing Rob standing next to her, to visualizing the mansion in the winter. She smiled and a sigh escaped her lips. "It would be beautiful in the snow."

Rob's words were so quiet she almost missed them in her concentration. "Do you know your face positively lights up when you talk about Greystone?"

She laughed lightly. "I'm excited about all the possibilities out there."

Rob nodded and continued to examine the drawings. Carolyn looked down as well, but she was looking back at the times Rob had told her about Greystone. His face had lit up too, she remembered. Was that an indicator of a more than average interest in the mansion? He'd certainly made a point to find out a great deal about the structure and the people who'd lived there. He knew a great deal about Louise's plans for it even though he would have been a teenager at the time, not an age to be interested in an old lady's pipe dream, as an average teenager might have perceived it.

The light knock on the partially opened door broke her reverie and announced John's arrival. The rest of the afternoon and early evening was spent talking about Louise's will and the extent of the available funds for the renovation. After learning how all the money was invested, Carolyn knew she had to seek advice from a financial planner on whether to use the money or leave it invested and borrow against it. So many details to tend to.

By the time they were ready to stop for a late dinner, they had covered everything. Carolyn's head was spinning from the sheer size of the project. But barring any unforeseen catastrophe or structural failure, she knew there were sufficient funds to get an inn up and running.

"It's been a long day," John concluded. "Rob, do you have reservations for dinner or are you taking Carolyn out to your house?"

Carolyn didn't give Rob a chance to respond. "Neither, but thank you," she said without a glance in Rob's direction. "Rob gets the night off. I have so much to think about that I'd like to eat alone so I can study these drawings more. May I take them all to the cabin for the night?"

John assured her it would be fine and started to leave. Carolyn stopped him by asking, "John, there's one more thing I'd like to know." He turned back toward her. "What happens if I don't find the necklace?" she asked, remaining tense anticipating his answer.

He smiled wryly and contemplated his answer before he spoke. "Well, you'll be a lot less rich because you won't have the funds it would bring if you sold it, or the borrowing power you could have using it as collateral."

"And if it isn't found, we'll never prove Robert had nothing to do with its disappearance," Rob said softly from behind her.

She glanced back at him, but he was gathering the papers and didn't look up. "Clearing Robert's name is important to you," Carolyn said. His father remained silent.

"Let's just say that if we could do that, all the Ashfords could get on with their lives without that hanging over our heads," Rob conjectured. Carolyn heard John sigh.

Rob put the last of the rolled-up blueprints in the cardboard box and pulled it to the edge of the table. "Carolyn, are you sure you wouldn't like to grill the steaks I planned for dinner? That should give you some energy so—"

"I appreciate the invitation, Rob," she interrupted. "But if you don't mind, I'd like to stop at a grocery store to get a few things so I can eat something light at the cabin while I study all these."

She glanced back at John. "I do have a favor to ask, though. I'd like to use this office for a few minutes to call my parents and a friend in Florida before we leave. I haven't called them since I got here, and there's no phone at the cabin. They're expecting to hear from me, but I don't have my cell phone here. I don't want them to worry any longer."

"Fine. No rush. Just come on out when you're finished."

Rob picked up the box of drawings. Carolyn couldn't tell if he was relieved or upset in her change of plans for them. In fact, she couldn't read anything in his face. She smiled, thinking that he must be a good lawyer in the courtroom. No one could tell what he was contemplating. He followed his father out of the room. The box on one hip, he turned back to close the door and said, "I'll wait for you in the reception area."

Carolyn nodded. "Thanks." Inhaling deeply to give her body an infusion of fresh air, she crossed the beige carpeting to the phone on the credenza. Setting a chair from the table closer to the phone, she sat down as she punched in her parents' number.

Her mother answered after the first ring. "I'm so glad you called. We were beginning to worry, but we figured John or Thomas would have called if there were anything wrong. We know you must be busy."

"You talk about John and Thomas as if you know the Ashfords, Mom."

"Well, no, we've never met, but Louise told us enough about them so we feel we've known them for years. John has a son, too, but I can't remember his name offhand."

"It's Rob."

"That's it. He sure did Louise a lot of favors. He must be a nice young man."

"Yes, he's nice," Carolyn responded as a smile bloomed on her face. "Nice" didn't begin to describe him. He was handsome, strong, polite, definitely sexy, and he might be a liar who was not to be trusted, but she didn't think her mother needed to hear all that. She kept her thoughts to herself.

"Mom? Can you get Dad on the extension? I want to tell you both about what's happening up here."

With both Eleanor and Don on the phone, Carolyn told them all about the will, the letter from Louise, and the choice she had to make.

"It must take your breath away, honey."

"You're right about that, but Mom? Why didn't Louise leave it to you, her niece?"

"That's simple, dear. Two reasons. One: I wouldn't know what to do with it. And two: you do and you've always loved it even though you'd never seen it," Eleanor told her. "Louise knew that."

"You've got a bigger decision to make than most people face in their whole lifetime," Don offered. "We're behind you which ever way you want to go."

"Thanks, Dad. I haven't told them my decision yet, but they must know it would be impossible to turn down. By the way, I'm staying at one of the fishing camp cabins that Rob owns right next door to Greystone. No phone in the cabin, but Rob has one up at his house a few minutes' walk away, if you need to reach me."

"You be careful, sweetheart," her mother urged.

"I will, Mom. And thanks for the words of encouragement, Dad."

"Carolyn, I mean it about your being careful," Eleanor insisted. "There were accidents when Louise was up—"

"Eleanor, you'll scare her with the way you're going on," Don warned, cutting her off. "Louise was an old lady and prone to tell tales. She probably blew everything that happened decades ago all out of proportion."

Carolyn didn't understand exactly what they meant, but she wanted to put her mom's mind at ease. "Really, I'm fine, Mom. If anything happened, Rob said he could even hear me inside his house if I yelled real loud. I guess sound carries well out there. Please, don't worry."

"Well, call us again soon, dear," Eleanor urged. "We'd love to hear what's going on."

"And we want you to know we think it's wonderful that

Louise had such confidence in our daughter. We're very proud of you," Don told her.

"Thanks, Dad."

Carolyn assured them she'd call again soon. Before she finally said goodbye, Eleanor urged her once more to be careful. She was used to her parents' loving admonitions, but not so often in one call. She shook her head as she punched in the second number and waited for Tulie to answer.

"You're not going to believe this. You'd better sit down," Carolyn said as soon as she'd greeted her friend. She told her all about her inheritance.

"You go, girlfriend. It's finally happening for you. Wow! I am so happy for you."

"It looks like our dream is going to come true a lot sooner than I expected. I just wish I felt better about the lawyer they have me working through. He's the youngest in a three-generation firm."

"Is he nice and good-looking, or one of those fast-talking jerks who make their own TV commercials with nonstop talking?"

Carolyn laughed. "You would ask that. I'd have to say that he's very good-looking."

"Then you shouldn't have a problem working with him, girl. Just enjoy!"

"I wish it was that simple. Everything's weird. I feel like I've known him for years, and yet I don't . . . I don't trust him, I guess. I've caught him saying things that I don't think were true more than once. On top of that, some very strange things have been happening to me."

Tulie listened as she described the door slamming and hearing voices. She didn't bother telling her about the boat or the people she'd imagined seeing in the house. That was too much. She didn't want Tulie to think she'd gone off the deep end.

"Sounds like it could have all been the wind," Tulie suggested easily.

"Yeah, that's what Rob said," Carolyn muttered in response. "Well, anyway, I just wanted you to know what was going on. So don't sign any long-term contracts now because if this all works out, I want you to come up here and work with me to pull this off."

"Girl, are you sure? I mean we talked about working together and all, but . . ."

"Yes, I'm sure, Amatulla Jackson," she scolded. "Mind you, I haven't officially made my mind up, but frankly, I don't see how I can pass it up. Tell you what. I'll call again when I get a phone of my own. Then we'll keep in touch regularly so I can let you know what's happening and when the place will be ready."

"I won't be able to sleep a wink till you call again, girlfriend. I'm so excited I feel like jumping up and down."

Carolyn laughed. "Thanks, Tulie, I needed that. I'll call as soon as I have definitive news." Feeling a lot more relaxed, she ended the call and went to find her ride to the grocery store and then back to the cabin. Rob helped her carry in her grocery bags and made it in one trip from the car. He didn't stay, saying he had frozen food in the bags he had bought for himself. They said good night and Carolyn went straight to change into something comfortable. Grabbing a bottle of soda water she'd just purchased, she went straight to the table by the window and started going over the drawings one more time.

As she ate her sandwich for dinner later that evening, her mother's words of caution came back to haunt her. Carolyn wished she'd asked her what she'd meant about accidents, but then her father had as much as said they were nothing.

Once Louise's papers were stacked back in the box, Carolyn stretched her arms high over her head. Her eyes felt sand-filled from studying the tiny figures that noted the sizes of the rooms. Her shoulders and back were stiff and aching from sitting hunched over the drawings. Wanting to take a walk to unwind and get the kinks out of her muscles, Carolyn grabbed her jacket and an apple, and stepped outside. Seeing how dark it was, she retraced her steps to get the powerful flashlight she'd bought with her groceries. It had a strong, narrow beam, and it was smaller and easier to carry than the six-volt lantern Rob had given her to use. With the fresh batteries the light traveled a long way.

Leaving the kitchen and front porch lights on, she headed down toward the water and took the path close to the lake. She walked away from the fishing camp in the direction of Greystone. She'd never realized how dark it became at night outside the city where no light reflected back on the clouds. It was pitch black when the cloud covered the moon.

The amount of animal life scurrying around her in the night surprised her, too. She'd heard their movements in the woods from the time since she'd left the porch of her cabin, but she was determined to think of the sounds as merely unfamiliar and not frightening.

Carolyn rounded a gradual curve in the path, hoping that the mansion was close ahead. In the dark she really couldn't tell how far she'd come. Waves splashed on the rocky shore a few feet away. She raised the zipper higher on her jacket against the wind that was kicking up. Blowing through the trees, it sounded eerie—almost like a woman crying.

Time to rein in your wild imagination again, Carolyn warned herself.

Having no television or radio, she hadn't heard a weather forecast, but the air smelled like rain was on its way. She felt she would be all right as long as there were breaks in the cloud cover. Rain wasn't likely immediately.

A banging sound coming from Greystone up ahead made her quicken her steps. One of the shutters must be open and slapping the house in the wind. Carolyn smiled. This time she really could put the blame on the wind.

The path came out of the woods about fifty yards to the side of the mansion. Using her flashlight to illuminate the façade, she saw an open shutter, the same one that had been open when she and Rob pulled away yesterday. It pounded against the house in an uneven rhythm. She checked the others with her flashlight, aiming the bright beam across all the stories of the house. She was relieved to see them all closed. The latch on the one doing all the banging must be coming loose.

The moon appeared through the trees, but she saw its light only briefly before another dark cloud rapidly covered it. However, the few moments of moonlight made her more cognizant of how very dark out it was after it disappeared.

Leaving the woods, she picked her way across the yard and up the steps to the porch to fasten the shutter. She didn't want the storm to blow the shutter into the glass window and break it. Once fastened, the latch seemed to hold just fine. She couldn't understand why it kept coming open.

Looking up at Greystone from this angle, the flashlight cast a shadow that delineated an inset panel and square holes in the front wall above the front door. That had to be where the roof had been attached. In the photo of Louise, it extended over the steps and part of the driveway. Guests could get out of their cars and enter the house without getting wet in the rain. She'd been so interested in the round stained-glass window above the entrance, she never paid any attention to the depression before. She crossed back to the steps and sat on the top one for a few minutes with her knees pulled up to her chest. She imagined the grand horse-drawn carriages circling the drive and stopping under the old entrance roof.

The moon peeked out again long enough to light a path across the lake that disappeared into the black horizon. She was fascinated by how the moonlight frosted the tips of the waves with white for several seconds in the midst of the black night.

Carolyn was so enchanted with the exciting and beautiful scene that she didn't notice a new rasping sound beginning directly above her.

Chapter Six

Rob was an angry man. He was slamming pots and pans around his kitchen cleaning up after a dinner he'd had no appetite to eat once he'd cooked it.

He felt disgusted with himself because he couldn't get Carolyn out of his mind. Despite not wanting to get involved with her, he kept imagining excuses to spend more time together. The memory of the fullness of her breasts pressed against his chest would not leave him. He could still feel the softness of her cheeks. Her yielding lips . . .

Rob stood up so suddenly that his chair fell back. Hell, he'd erase his memories of her with a brisk walk. He grabbed a flashlight, but as he opened the door, he knew his feet would take him down to Cabin One to see how she was doing.

He stood on his porch outside his kitchen door long enough to put on his jacket. The television weather broadcast had predicted a thunderstorm. He'd better hurry to get down there and back before it hit. At least he didn't have to worry about her in the storm. She would be in the warm cabin—safe. He was confident she'd have enough sense to stay indoors with the wind kicking up. He'd have to remember to give her a radio so she could at least get the news and weather forecasts.

The cabin's kitchen and porch lights were visible from the path as he approached. He knocked lightly so as not to startle her and called out her name. After two tries without getting a response, he opened the unlocked front door and called out again. No answer. A quick survey of the whole cabin sent him outside on the run. She was gone.

Only one place she would go. Greystone. He cut through the shortcut in the trees that he hadn't shown her yet. The path went straight across instead of following the curve of the point. Cursing himself for leaving her alone, he broke into a run.

"Robert!"

Had someone just called his name? Rob halted momentarily to listen, but heard only his own panting and the wind in the trees. Leaping over branches the wind tossed onto the path, he raced on, his sense of urgency renewed.

Carolyn rose from her seat on the step when she heard the rapid footsteps coming in her direction through the woods. No raccoon could be making that much noise. She saw the bobbing beam of light and worried who would be out there at night. Thieves? Vandals? Her heart sped up and she swallowed hard.

All her muscles tensed, and ready to run, she glanced around for an escape route. But she didn't know what lay in the opposite direction from the camp. She clicked on her flashlight and aimed it at the approaching light.

"Rob, is that you?" she called out hopefully. Her voice wasn't as loud as she wanted, but he'd said sound really carried out here, hadn't he? She cleared her throat and called again, more strongly this time. "Rob?"

The figure reached the clearing. The light swung across to find her on the steps. Then, just as quickly, the beam rose onto the upper stories of the house high above her.

"Carolyn, run! Get off the steps!" he shouted.

She reacted instantly. Already frightened and nervous enough to jump out of her skin, she leapt down the few remaining steps and promptly tripped in her haste. She tumbled and rolled on the weedy gravel.

Before her body came to rest, she heard a crash behind her and the sound of splintering wood. She lifted herself up to her hands and knees to see that one of the heavy shutters from an upper floor window had fallen and smashed to pieces where she'd been sitting. Like a theatrical spotlight, the flashlight she'd dropped in her flight illuminated the scattered shards of wood on the steps.

Reaching her side, Rob dropped to his knees and hauled her into his arms, dropping his flashlight into the weeds beside them. "Are you okay?" he asked breathlessly, his lips buried in her hair.

He held her so tightly she could hardly breathe, much less answer, but she didn't care. She was clinging to him just as hard. In his arms she found warmth and security—a safe haven from the terrors in the night. Reassured she was unhurt, he was suddenly kissing her. And she was responding with the same frantic need. They pressed against each other, unable to get close enough. Their mouths opened and their tongues twirled together. They thrust and parried with no regard to the danger of the match they had begun.

Though their lips eventually separated, they clung together, still holding on for dear life. His hands circled her back; his cheek pressed against her ear. "My God, Carolyn, you could have been killed if that had landed on . . ."

"No, I'm okay, Rob. But if you hadn't come down the path and called out to me at that moment . . ." She laughed a nervous, scared little laugh as she strengthened her resolve and moved back from his arms to sit on her heels. She couldn't break the connection and held onto his hands. "Thank you for being there."

The moon shone brightly through a narrow break in the

cloud cover. Trying to smile, she squeezed his hands and dropped her grip on them, feeling suddenly awkward. What had she done? She didn't belong in his arms drawing comfort . . . yes, and pleasure, from him. She shouldn't want to be there, and she certainly ought to be able to resist the strong attraction she felt. She wasn't acting like herself, hadn't been since she arrived at Lakeside.

Rising, she inhaled deeply and rubbed her hands against her thighs, not just to clean her palms of the dirt from her fall, but to erase the memory of the feel of his hands she'd just released.

"What were you coming over here for tonight, Rob?" she asked as she brushed dirt from her clothes. She'd have to put a visit to a Laundromat on her list at the rate she was going getting her clothes dirty.

Rob reached to pick up his flashlight from beside her and rose. "I came to see if there was anything you needed at the cabin and found you'd gone. I figured this is where you'd be." He leaned over to brush off his own knees.

Carolyn started back to the steps for her flashlight, but Rob stopped her with his hand on her arm. "Wait." He inspected every window with his beam of light. Finally, with his nod of approval, she ran and grabbed the light. Spurred on by a crash of thunder, she cried out and she raced back to his side.

Clouds had completely filled the sky, denying the moonlight access to Lost Lake. "I've never been in such total darkness," she admitted.

With both of their flashlights trained on the ground ahead of them, he took her hand and started toward the camp, tugging her along at his side. "We could use a drink. Come on before we get soaked."

"Thank you for the kind invitation," she said sarcastically, not liking his sudden proprietary manner.

"I'm not taking 'no' for an answer this time, if that's what you had planned," he spat out. "We have to talk."

Carolyn could only wonder what had suddenly made him so angry. She didn't understand. One minute Rob was friendly, the next, he sounded ready to punch her lights out. "Wait just a little minute here," she demanded, pulling back on her hand but keeping up the fast pace on the path through the woods back to the cabin. "Why are you angry with me? I didn't loosen the shutter or sit under it on purpose just waiting for it to fall, you know."

He stopped so abruptly that she bumped into his shoulder. He steadied her and then dropped his hands to his sides. "I know. I'm sorry. I'm not angry with you, Carolyn. What I am, though, is frightened for your safety and angry at how close you were to being seriously hurt. I've been trying to avoid it, but it's time we had a long talk. I don't care if you have that drink or not, but you must listen to what I have to say," he concluded in a less-demanding tone of voice. "Please."

"Say about what?"

"About some strange things that have happened at Greystone."

Without giving her any opportunity to question him further, he grabbed her hand again and towed her behind him at the same rapid pace, heading up a new path to his house. She'd have to check the woods out for more shortcuts.

Lightning lit the sky above the forest canopy. Thunder boomed closer this time. If there were any animal sounds in the woods, they were masked by the wind howling in the branches. Despite walking away from them, Carolyn could hear the waves pounding on the shore below.

A loud crack spurred them into a run. A large branch of

a white pine broke loose and crashed to the ground behind them with a heavy thud. Rain began falling in large drops. The beams from their flashlights bounced rhythmically ahead of them as they ran. The air was heavy with the odors of damp leaves and molds as the wind kicked up the forest bed.

Carolyn was thankful Rob held her hand firmly all the way until they were at the back entrance to his house. At the pace they'd been going, seeing the narrow path would have been impossible for her. She knew that without him she could easily have gotten lost in the woods.

"We made it," she said, "without getting too soaked."

He hung their jackets on the rack in the mudroom to dry and made hot chocolate laced with crème de cacao while Carolyn washed her hands dirtied in her fall.

"Good thing we arrived when we did," she said, joining him in the kitchen. "It's pouring out there now."

"You seem to have good luck with your timing tonight. Let's hope it stays with you," he said without looking at her.

She frowned as they sat in front of a crackling fire. Carolyn sipped her drink and pretended to concentrate on the flames. All the while she was acutely aware Rob was watching her. He set his mug down and surprised her completely by reaching over and picking a couple dried leaves from her hair that must have stuck there when she fell.

"You're sure you're all right?" he asked, sounding concerned. "You didn't get hurt tumbling on the ground?"

"I scraped my palms and maybe my knees." She held her free hand out palm up to show him the reddened areas. "That's all. I may be a little achy in the morning, but I'm fine."

"Turn your head that way," he told her, pointing toward her opposite side.

"More leaves?"

"No," he said softly. He reached over and pulled loose the fabric-covered elastic that had bound her hair at the back of her neck. He lifted a handful of long waves forward to rest over her shoulder. When was she going to learn not to trust him to do what she expected?

"Your hair's beautiful. You should wear it down more often." His voice sounded deep and breathy.

Carolyn felt herself being drawn to him, but tried to deny the attraction. She looked away at the fire and recrossed her legs in a desperate attempt to mentally place him at a distance that was more comfortable. "Thanks, but it gets in my way too much. Frankly, I'm not comfortable at work with it over my shoulders. It emphasizes the fact I'm a woman, and when I'm conducting business, that should be the last thing on anyone's mind."

Rob played idly with the strands, winding and unwinding them on his fingers. "Always the businesswoman, huh?"

She laughed. "When you're in the hotel business, there's never a time when you close the store and go home."

"I can relate to that."

"Yeah. Owning a fishing camp, I guess you can." She forced herself to relax again. "Anything else you'd like to talk about before you get around to telling me what you really have to say about Greystone, Rob?"

Chuckling, he reached behind him for his mug and settled in more comfortably, facing her with one leg bent under him. He took a deep breath and let it out slowly like a long sigh.

"It's okay, Rob. I can take it. I'm a big girl."

He laughed briefly, looking at her incredulously as if she hadn't guessed that he knew that fact only too well.

Carolyn chose to ignore his pointed gaze that covered

her from head to toe. She went right on questioning him. "Look. If there's a problem with Greystone, I'd sure rather hear it now than after I sign the papers. What it is? Are my dreams about to be smashed like the shutter that crashed on the steps?"

"I'd have to say, Carolyn, that's up to you. But before you decide to sign anything, I want . . . I need to tell you about some . . . some events that have happened at the house." He leaned his temple against his palm, his arm resting on the back of the couch. "Grandpa should really be the one to tell you about the first big one. He was there and I wasn't."

"The first big one?"

"The first incident I know about that involved someone in your family and mine. Before that there was the painter who broke his leg falling from a ladder over the stairs—the same place Lora fell, as a matter of fact."

"But that could have happened to anyone. Maybe they weren't careful people. They didn't have the sturdy metal ladders we have today," Carolyn pointed out, trying to provide a rational explanation.

Rob nodded. "I suppose," he said, but he didn't sound convinced. "Whatever the reason, his drop from a ladder at the top of the stairs was a long way to fall."

Carolyn shuddered but wanted to hear the rest. "So what was the first one involving our families?"

"It happened the last day Louise was here the summer she'd spent planning the resort. By the way, did you know that Louise sent pictures of you every year?"

"You're kidding. Why would she do that?"

"I'm not sure, but Grandpa has shown me so many over the years that I felt like I knew you before I ever laid eyes on you. It was almost as if you were a cousin, or at least someone close who my family would keep track of growing up only a few years after me."

"Louise never had a family. Maybe sending my picture was the next best thing for her. But tell me, what happened that final day she was here?"

"Well, Grandpa told me about it. I can't get Dad to talk about anything dealing with the happenings at the house. It's only fair to tell you that Dad says Grandpa's ideas about what happened at Greystone are baloney. With that in mind, I'll tell you."

He put his mug down and with another deep breath he began. "Grandpa brought Louise out to Greystone for one last look before he drove her to the train station in Syracuse to go back home. She and Grandpa walked through the house once more, threw pebbles into the lake, and sat on the big rock by the shore. In other words they did all the fun little things one does to etch memories of a favorite place on the brain before you have to leave it—even if you expect to return."

Carolyn nodded.

"The time to catch the train came. Louise got a camera out of her purse and asked Grandpa to take one last picture of her in front of the house."

"That must be the picture I remember seeing, the one under the portico that isn't there anymore. I keep forgetting to ask you what happened to it."

"That's what I'm coming to. It was noon and the bright sun shone on light-grey stone walls. Louise stood on the steps under the portico, but Grandpa thought it was too shady for a good picture with the glaring stone on each side. Too much contrast. So he asked her to stand in front of the roofed area, where the sunlight could catch her. She complied with his wishes and . . ." Rob shrugged.

"Well? You can't stop there."

"Well," he said, pausing again to take a gulp from his mug. Carolyn shifted, feeling he was toying with her by being overly dramatic. "Grandpa says that asking her to move out there saved her life. He took the picture, and when she'd taken a step or two toward him to retrieve her camera, the whole extended roof over the entrance collapsed and crashed down behind her just like the shutter did tonight."

"No! She never told me. Was she hurt?"

"She got dusty from the flying debris, but there were no injuries. The ancient timbers that spanned the area just couldn't hold it any longer, Grandpa thought."

"What did she do?"

"She wanted to change her reservations and see to cleaning it up, but Grandpa talked her into leaving as scheduled and promised that he would take care of it. She trusted him because he'd been caring for the house for years. Actually, Robert had been checking on it and cleaning up the place ever since the Whitneys moved out, and Grandpa kept it up after he died."

"Your family has been caring for it all that time?"

Rob nodded. "There was no one else to do it. After the 'twenty-nine stock market crash, very little was done for a long time. Grandpa thought it might have been sold. When Arthur Whitney inherited it from Lloyd, he paid other people to do a little work, but he never came to see about anything in person. Though he tried, it didn't sell, not even after they slapped on the thick paint to spruce the inside up. Arthur eventually, and I think reluctantly, contacted Grandpa about hiring the law firm to officially supervise the caretaking, handling the taxes, and that sort of thing. He didn't seem to want to own it, but he didn't want it sold for taxes either."

Carolyn shook her head. "After all the Ashfords did for them, how could they still believe Robert stole the necklace?"

Rob shrugged. "A lot of people still think he's guilty. Anyway, after Louise inherited it years later, she came up for visits and made attempts at getting work done, but she continued to let our firm handle the details. Attorneys often managed properties back then. That's how she became friends with Grandpa—and Grandma, too, before she died. Louise never believed Robert was a thief."

"Even though the firm supervised caring for the house, you couldn't have known when the roof would collapse."

"Carolyn, that's the whole point. Louise had been so serious about fixing Greystone up as a resort that she'd had it inspected that summer. The engineer said the roof structure was fine."

"But if it was fine, why . . . ?"

"Exactly. Why indeed? Grandpa took Louise to the train that day and went right back out there with a builder friend of his. He wanted a second opinion. They found the ends of the crossbeams that supported the extension had been snapped clean off. They could have been sawed off except they couldn't find the evidence of a saw—no marks or sawdust. The cuts were clean like a knife cut. They never did determine what broke the supports and sent the whole thing crashing down."

He stretched his arm along the back of the couch and went back to playing with her curls. "Dad kept saying it could have been storm-weakened. Heavy snows or ice could have pulled it away from the house and just the right wind that day could have sent it down. Who knows?"

Carolyn winced when she heard him blaming it on the

wind. "There certainly seems to be an active and often dangerous wind in this area." Suddenly, she snapped her fingers. "Wait a minute. I wonder if my parents knew that. When I called them this afternoon from the office, they told me several times to be careful. I think the last time they sounded that concerned was when I tried in-line roller skates."

"If you've tried skating on those things, Lars was right. You have got guts." Their laughter helped relieve the tension a bit.

"Rob, your family is largely responsible for keeping the structure in good shape by watching for problems over the years."

"We had to," he said, sounding resigned to his duty. "People were counting on us."

"Now that I'm here, is shedding that responsibility bittersweet?"

He shrugged in his one-shoulder manner that was becoming so familiar to her. "There's a certain family pride involved here. I want to see Robert's reputation cleared. I think we all do, so we want the necklace found. I believe the emeralds are still in the house, or else we would have heard about the discovery or the sudden appearance on the market of the emeralds. One is big enough to make all the newspapers in the country if it showed up."

She turned and looked into the fire to consider what he'd said. "I've never seen a black emerald unless it was on a hotel customer and I didn't recognize it."

"And now you could be the owner of a long string of perfect ones set in a yellow-gold chain."

She ran her fingers through her hair and pushed it back. "Why do you suppose someone would want to hurt Louise, or me? It can't be to get the property, because if she'd died then, my mother, as her nearest kin, would have inherited, wouldn't she?"

"Probably. I don't know about any will earlier than her present one."

"If I died, it would depend on the options of her will, but my folks are my only kin. I'm an only child and not married. No one else could gain by removing me from the picture. I know my parents aren't behind this. I wonder who is."

Rob stared into the fire. "I wish I had an answer for you."

"The culprit is someone who suddenly makes the roof collapse, opens shutters and crashes one on the steps, slams doors, and calls out to unsuspecting people."

"If you count all that, it's someone who has been strong and active for over half a century."

"Pretty powerful being. Listing everything that's happened makes it sound like someone is really trying to scare people away or worse." She wrapped her arms around her waist. She hadn't mentioned seeing the hologram-like figures in the house or the rowboat. Rob would never believe her, and she was embarrassed to admit she thought she saw them. "And hey, after tonight, they're succeeding in scaring me."

She leaned closer to the fire for more warmth. Rob raised his hands in a helpless gesture, but he said nothing further.

"I'm willing to admit my limitations and fears of managing this size renovation job," she said into the silence as she stared at the dancing flames. "But now we're discussing an added danger element that has nothing to do with the building project. The danger is real and seems very potent. What is it that they say about fools rushing in?"

She glanced up to see he was smiling. Suddenly, an idea struck her. She turned her whole body on the seat to face him. "Wait a minute. Maybe it has to do with what happens if I decline to accept the house."

"I don't think anyone believes you will decline," he told her with a wry smile.

"I don't suppose many people could."

"But if the accidents at Greystone escalate, accepting it could be dangerous to you and maybe even to others who will be working there."

"Rob, that could sound like your conclusion or a threat. Either way, I don't like feeling frightened."

"It's no threat, and I hope it's the wrong conclusion." He gathered her into his arms and tucked her head under his chin. "It's okay to feel frightened sometimes because it makes you cautious. And in this situation, perhaps you need to be for safety's sake."

"I think you may be right." Carolyn relaxed against him.

"Starting with the disappearing emerald necklace and Lora's death, to say the house was accident-prone would be an understatement." His fingers slowly stroked her upper arm.

"There's been more of them?"

He nodded. "Lesser incidents involving people working there. And I'm sure there are more stories than I know to tell, too."

"I wish I could figure what's behind all this."

"I would guess twenty-five things."

She sat up to meet his gaze. "What? Why so many? What do you mean?"

He smiled. With his index finger, he drew a curve around the front of the base of her neck. She held her breath as the pleasurable warmth of his touch skittered over her skin and tightened her nipples until they stood up taut, longing to be held.

"Twenty-four perfect dark emeralds the size of your thumbnail." He picked up her hand and looked at her nails. "Yes," he said with a grin. "I had to look to be sure you didn't have those long dagger types. The twenty-fifth emerald in the center was the size of the end of my thumb from the knuckle to the tip."

"Hmmm. I can't imagine wearing something like that. I don't go anywhere it would be appropriate."

"It would take a dress and an occasion to pull it off, the likes of which modern Lakeside has never known." He snorted a laugh but quickly looked serious again. "I understand it was a truly unique piece for its overall simplicity. It must have looked beautiful on Alice, and I'm certain it would have looked as lovely on Sara."

"And Lora?"

Rob looked back at the fire. "You must have seen photos of her. She was, I'd say, ordinary-looking at best, but next to Sara, she must have looked very plain. Maybe that's what made her so manipulative. From the stories I heard, she had her father wrapped around her little finger and seemed to be able to have her way most of the time. She was always getting her parents to side with her against Sara. And if she didn't get her way, she became angry very easily."

"Not an easy person to live with. Maybe I should be glad that I'm an only child," Carolyn suggested with a laugh. "No sibling to compete with."

"Yeah. Me too."

Carolyn shook her head. "I just can't imagine being able to find the necklace after all this time. How could it still be there?"

Rob shrugged. "I don't know. Thieves have pounded

holes in the walls, pulled up floorboards, hunted in fireplaces, and even dug holes on the grounds looking for it. But we'd know if anyone had found it. The stones are just too big and too perfect to be sold without anyone hearing about the sale."

"Well, if I stumble across it, I certainly won't mix it up with any run-of-the-mill, green emerald necklaces that were left lying around."

"Right." His laughter sounded good even if it was brief.

They settled into a comfortable silence, watching the fire. Unwise as it was, Carolyn felt pleasure nestled beside him and couldn't bring herself to move away. She tried to concentrate on Greystone and not on the hint of his aftershave that tantalized her senses, or the appealing strength of his arm, which held her against his side.

"I have to ask one more thing, Rob."

"Hmm. What is it?"

She turned and looked up at him. She wanted to read his face when he answered. "Has anyone else heard voices calling them? Or . . . or maybe seen anything strange happening over there?"

"It was just . . ." Looking down into her face, he apparently couldn't go on with what he'd been going to say.

"What?" she prodded.

"Well, yes, if you believe rumors that have been around for decades. People who sneaked into the house told everyone who would listen that they saw ghosts. Kids used to try to get in all the time as a challenge to their bravery."

He turned to look at the fire. "Tonight, I heard someone call to me. At least I think she was calling me. That's why I ran over there. And, as I told you, I've heard it before. The voice always sounds like a woman, and she's calling for

Robert. That's all she says. She just calls out the name Robert."

"What about the others in your family?"

He took a deep breath, showing her how difficult talking about this was. "From what Grandpa's said, he's heard voices or something. I don't know. Dad says that's one area where Grandpa no longer has a good grip on reality."

Carolyn could understand that. She'd blamed the sounds and visions on her own overactive imagination, not anything real that she'd seen. "What about lately?"

"Frankly, I think Grandpa doesn't want to talk about it nowadays because Dad will think he's gone off the deep end and put him in a nursing home or something. Grandpa enjoys his independent living and doesn't want the arrangement changed."

"But that doesn't explain who is behind what's happening. The original Sara and Robert lived nearly a century ago. Nobody who was an adult then would be alive to carry out any vendetta, or whatever you want to call this, against the families today. They'd all be dead by now. And who could be still so upset about what happened way back then that they would want to even the score today?"

"I don't know what it is, Carolyn. For years I've wished I knew what was happening over there. I almost hate to see you get involved and put yourself in danger after what happened tonight. That shutter came too close. But listen. I stay out here most weekdays now. If you decide to accept your inheritance, I'm hereby promising you, I will do my best to watch out for you to see that nothing happens to you."

Despite the warmth of his arm around her and the fire just a few feet from them, Carolyn felt strangely chilled by his pronouncement. She should have felt comforted by his promise of protection, but there was no realistic way she could trust it. Only the person or persons creating the accidents could stop them, so how could he make such a promise? How could he prevent things from happening? "Thanks," she murmured anyway.

The wind advancing the thunderstorm howled outside. The wood crackled in the flames dancing in the air drafts in the chimney. Rob squeezed her briefly. "You can count on it. I'm going to be all over you the whole time you choose to be here."

"All over me?" Carolyn said with a laugh as she felt the heat of desire rise at his choice of words.

His chuckle was deep and sensuous. "Ah, how about, 'I'll be staying close by in order to keep you safe'? Is that better?" Heat rose in her cheeks. His laughter was infectious. "Oh, Carolyn, I've never met a businesswoman who blushes as delightfully as you do."

"Please! Don't remind me. It's a curse that a lot of blondes have to put up with, just like sunburning easily."

He caressed her cheek with his palm, tipping her face up to his. "Are you for real?"

"No, maybe I'm a ghost." She laughed harder. What she'd proposed was ludicrous.

"Prettiest ghost I've seen in a long time."

Before she could ask if he'd seen many others, Rob captured her jaw in his warm hand and lowered his mouth to cover hers. His lips dipped, rose, and moved to nibble gently on hers. She promptly forgot to ask.

She raised her arms around his neck and twisted to press her breasts against his hard chest to soothe the vague ache she felt building there. He moved his hand from her cheek, threading it through her hair to the back of her head to hold it while his other arm held her firmly against him. He ran his tongue along the edge of her lower lip and when she opened her mouth with a quick gasp for air, he took advantage. His tongue dove in to dance with hers. Her little moan stirred him on to deepen the kiss.

When he eventually lifted his head, she couldn't deny the regret she felt. There was no question about it. They both had wanted the kiss and more.

He placed a brief kiss at each corner of her mouth and then raised his jaw to rest against her hair. "Your hair smells like a bouquet of flowers."

For a minute or two, they clung to each other and waited for their breathing to return to normal.

"Carolyn, it's time I walked you to your cabin before we do anything else we both would most certainly enjoy, but might regret later."

"Yeah, you're right, but the way my knees feel, you may have to carry me to the cabin." She extricated herself from his arms and pushed her hair back from her face as she stood up. In the kitchen she pulled on her coat. "Hey, the rain has stopped."

Grabbing her flashlight, she walked out ahead of him onto the porch. A sky full of clouds still hid the moon completely, but persistent strong winds bent the trees and sent Carolyn's hair flying. Thunder rolled not far away. "The temperature sure has dropped while we were inside."

"We'd better hurry," Rob suggested as he closed the door behind them. "It's supposed to rain off and on all night and it feels like it might turn on any minute."

Pulling her jacket closed across her chest, she quickened her pace to match his. At the door to her cabin he paused. Carolyn turned back to him and studied his face in the porch light. "Rob, really. What if I don't find the necklace? Does anyone truly still think Robert took it?"

He turned slightly to face the wind that parted his hair down the middle and made him squint. His lips were pressed shut, narrowing their fullness. Carolyn's breath caught. He looked exactly like Louise's photo of Robert. Exactly. His gaze came back to meet hers. The wind flipped his hair back to his normal side part. Carolyn blinked to clear her vision as unbidden tears welled up in her eyes. This time she wanted to blame them on the stinging wind, too.

"It apparently matters to someone. You'd better hope you're the one to find it," he said quietly before he bade her a good night.

Rob waited until Carolyn was inside the cabin and her door lock had clicked before he jogged back to his house. He had promised his father he would let Carolyn make up her own mind about the choices she had to consider under Louise's will. But Rob knew she couldn't turn Greystone down. No one in his right mind could. Not even him, even with everything happening over there.

He worried that she didn't know what she was getting into. He'd tried to explain part of the problem, but maybe he should say more about all that was really going on.

But even if she hired a bodyguard or two, they couldn't do anything against the forces she would be up against, forces Carolyn knew nothing about. If she accepted her inheritance, she would be in the worst danger of her life.

By the time he'd climbed into bed, Rob still hadn't figured out what he could do to keep Carolyn safe—not when someone wanted so badly for her to stay away from Greystone—someone who would even try to kill her to keep Greystone as it was, with the necklace still hidden.

And from what had happened already since Carolyn arrived on the scene, he knew that particular someone was getting more desperate and might do anything.

Chapter Seven

Carolyn woke to hear a soft whirring sound, followed by a plop of something like a small stone dropping into the lake. She heard nothing for a few seconds before a series of light clicks began. Then the sequence started over again.

Curious to identify the sounds, she crawled across the bed to the window near the foot and looked through the opening in the striped cotton curtains. Seeing nothing, she pulled on her thigh-length silk robe over her short silk nightgown that she used when she traveled because they took so little space in her suitcase, and wandered out through the living room.

Nothing accounted for the sounds until she looked out toward the flat rock where Rob was sitting with his back to her. She eased the squeaky screen door open far enough to slip through and stand barefoot on the cold porch for a minute or two to watch what he was doing. She smiled to discover the sounds were from his spinning reel when he cast his jig out into the water, waited, retrieved it, and cast it again.

As if programmed to happen when she entered the quiet scene as the audience, the lure disappeared under water in a swirl of waves, rings, and a splash. Rob flicked the rod upwards and reeled in the line.

Jumping down from the rock, he reached down to lift a beautiful trout from the water by the gills. The rainbow of colors on its back sparkled in the sunlight. Busy taking the hook from the fish's mouth, he spoke without ever having looked in her direction. "How about some fresh fried fish for breakfast?"

"That sounds yummy. I'd love it," she answered with a smile.

No more had to be said. Her smile broadened when she noticed the box on the picnic table on the porch. There was flour, a couple of cooked potatoes, a bowl with an egg in it and a carton of grapefruit juice standing next to a thermos. The man had been confident he was going to catch a fish.

Carolyn took the box with her and put it on the kitchen counter before grabbing her clothes and heading for a hot shower. By the time she was dressed, she could smell the fish and potatoes sizzling in the frying pan. She dispensed with the idea of putting on makeup, and chose only to cover her skin with a moisturizing sun lotion she normally wore under her foundation to protect her face from the Florida sun.

Not wanting to take the time to bother with her long, wet hair before breakfast, she wrapped a towel turban-style around her head and went to the kitchen. "I could get used to having my breakfast made for me every morning."

Rob pulled the dish towel from the refrigerator handle, folded it over his arm, and turned back to her looking every bit like a butler. "Breakfast is served, ma'am," he intoned in grand, stuffy butlerese.

"It smells heavenly."

He helped her with her chair as a good butler would. But stepping out of the role, he leaned down and inhaled deeply with his ear just below hers. "So do you."

Carolyn felt goose flesh rise across her shoulders and skitter down her spine. She looked up and found herself wishing he would lean down farther and kiss her, but he straightened and moved to his place at the table. She felt strangely sad over his decision and immediately chided herself. She shouldn't want or expect his kisses, no matter how much she'd come to enjoy them.

The delicious break to her night-long fast passed talking about the fishing and the lake in general. Rob's love for the area was clear. Not wanting to alter the light mood, Carolyn refrained from asking even one question about Greystone.

She learned the lake was good for fishing and that few people lived around its shoreline, most of them just visiting seasonally. New Yorkers called their summer cottages camps, and the few people who owned them on this lake owned significant acreage with them. Hence there were fewer of them. The general consensus was to leave it that way, as far as he knew. That meant fewer boats, less pollution and a lot more privacy.

After the two of them made quick work of hand washing the dishes, Rob walked to the front window, his fingers in the back pockets of his jeans. He heaved a big sigh and Carolyn guessed from that and his stiff stance that the relaxed atmosphere in the cabin they had enjoyed throughout their meal was about to tense up.

"I talked to Dad last night, Carolyn," he said as he turned back to her. "I told him about the shutter, and he agrees with me that we should get an engineer out here to study the structural integrity right away, before you spend any more time over there. We have to determine what's safe before someone gets hurt."

"That's a good idea. I concur completely."

"Dad hoped you'd say that because he's going to contact a friend of his who owns a very reputable inspection firm in Albany. The engineer has been talking about coming up here to fish and Dad thinks he can talk him into taking a look at it this weekend. But we don't want to take the choice of inspector out of your hands though, if you know a better one."

She shook her head. "No, he sounds fine."

"Frankly, from the sounds of it, Dad's friend is looking for an excuse to take the weekend off for some fishing. He'll be squeezing the look at the mansion in between bouts with the trout." The smile faded from his face. "I don't know anyone else who would come out that quickly."

"And the sooner we know how safe Greystone is, the better. Your dad's friend sounds perfect, especially if he can come tomorrow," she agreed, not really understanding why Rob seemed to be working hard to convince her. She could easily check the engineer's credentials, and Rob was right. Getting one out could take weeks otherwise. She couldn't imagine that a lot of engineers would be interested in this kind of trade for fishing time.

Rob nodded. "Good."

Carolyn thought she detected relief on his part, but what could he be relieved at? That she'd agreed to his choice of engineers? She didn't doubt that John would pick an excellent one. But Rob's manner, suggesting he'd put something over on her, made her nervous. *Don't trust a man until you learn his motivation,* her old mantra insisted. She had to remain wary.

And, she suddenly realized, she wouldn't be able to go back to Greystone without taking chances, not until she got the green light from the engineer. That meant that if someone else trying to find the necklace had dropped the shutter to keep her away, whoever it was had succeeded. Now he or she would have several more days free and clear of other people interfering.

But why would someone be searching now after all these years? Had her arrival driven someone to make one last desperate attempt at finding it? So many questions and so few answers.

"Which brings up another matter," Rob added, looking back at her. He appeared ill at ease under her scrutiny. He moved his gaze away from Carolyn to study the calendar on the wall.

"What is it?" she asked, walking past the table to stand beside him so she could read his face. He'd shaved this morning. Her fingers itched to run her hand over his cheek to test its softness. She shoved them into her pockets. "Is something else wrong?"

"The cabins," he said hesitantly. "From now through fall they're filled most of the time with fishermen or vacationing families."

"This cabin," she said, holding her hands out palms up. "You need it for your guests?"

He shook his head and smiled sheepishly. "No. I've kept it open for your use as long as you want it. Although, I had thought briefly about saying 'yes.' "

Her forehead wrinkled into a frown. "Why?"

"I had it all worked out. I'd have to kick you out of here, and the only place for you to go was up to my house."

He reached up and loosened the towel turban from her head. Her nearly dry hair fell across her shoulders in a mass of tangled waves. He threaded his fingers through it for a few moments and then nestled a hand on each side to hold her head still while he kissed her tenderly.

Keep your mind on the conversation, not the wonderful feeling from his kiss, she ordered herself. "What changed your mind?" she whispered, watching him through half-open eyes as he kissed the corners of her mouth. But that was near to impossible as he continued to cradle her head. Though they didn't touch anywhere else, every nerve in her body was tingling and longing for his hands to soothe them with his touch.

"I decided . . ." He kissed her lower lip and nipped it between his lips. ". . . that when you come to my house to stay with me . . ." He kissed her upper lip. ". . . you would come because you wanted to . . ." He slid the tip of his tongue all the way around the edge of her lips making them tickle. ". . . and not because I'd tricked you." He kissed her gently. "That's why," he concluded, dropping his hands and smiling. He stepped away from her to gather his kitchen things and put them back into the box he'd brought.

Carolyn found herself swaying slightly at the loss of support. He could turn her knees to pliable putty faster than she'd believed possible. What was it about him that could make her forget to be wary? Her gaze went from the box he was filling to the box of Louise's plans that sat on the couch beyond them. She sighed. Why couldn't she have met Rob at another time and place when they didn't have Greystone looming large between them?

A car crunched the gravel in the driveway approaching the row of cabins. "I gotta go," Rob announced. "That'll be Sandy. She cleans the cabins and makes up the beds for the guests. I still have to take the shutters off the windows on the last three cabins this morning so she can clean them for the people who arrive this weekend. If you need anything, just find me by following my grunting sounds, or ask Sandy. She'll know where I am."

She followed him to the door. "Until the engineer gets here, I'll spend my time going through Louise's plans. And thanks for breakfast. It was delicious."

"My pleasure." He leaned down for a firm but quick kiss. "Come on out and I'll introduce you to Sandy."

Carolyn caught the porch door and stepped out behind

him. Sandy stood by her car, removing cleaning equipment from the trunk. She appeared to be in her thirties with dark hair, a friendly smile, and a ready handshake. Her bright chatter about hoping Carolyn was enjoying her visit to Rob's camp made Carolyn smile.

"If there's anything she needs, I told Miss Matison to ask you if I'm not around," Rob told Sandy. "I'll see you both later."

Sandy leaned over to see the remains of the breakfast provisions in the box he held. "You fixing breakfast, boss? Why didn't you tell me? I could have come out earlier."

Rob lifted an eyebrow. "Be right back to pull those shutters," he promised.

"Don't rush back on my account," Sandy called after him as she turned to her car to get a divided carrier that held her cleaning supplies. "The man's a slave driver," Sandy called in good humor loud enough for Rob to hear as he jogged into the woods toward his house. She set the cleaning supplies down on the steps of the cabin next door to Carolyn's and turned back to her. "It is nice meeting you, Miss Matison."

"Please call me Carolyn."

"Thanks. And I'm glad you're here. You've put a spring in his step already."

"I beg your pardon?"

"Rob. I've never seen him smile so much this early in the day before the season picks up. He's too worried about how the fishing will be and how many cabins he'll rent."

"Oh, but I don't want you to misunderstand. I'm not Rob's . . . ah . . . personal guest. I'm here on business about Greystone with his law firm."

The errant thought that he might be happy and smiling because Greystone would be empty all weekend until it was inspected popped into her head. She frowned. Where had that idea come from?

"Whatever you say," Sandy said agreeably enough, but she wasn't smiling any longer. "But don't talk to me about that place," she warned with a jerk of her thumb toward Greystone. "I don't go near haunted houses. That one gives me the creeps." She shuddered dramatically. "Well, I gotta get to work."

"Nice meeting you." Shaking her head, Carolyn returned to her cabin. One look in the mirror at her mussed hair told her why Sandy might have imagined another reason for Rob's mood. She'd forgotten he'd pulled off the towel turban and she'd left it that way to go outside. Now as she brushed it and contained it in a cloth binding at her neck, she thought about Sandy saying Greystone gave her the creeps.

She must have been joking about the rumors Rob mentioned. Dismissing the woman's comment, Carolyn strode into the kitchen and put on a pot of coffee. She found making coffee a greater challenge than she'd expected because she'd never perked it in a nonelectric pot on a propane stove before. She had to add more water when the first attempt boiled over, but when she got the height of the flame adjusted right, it worked fine.

After filling her mug, she set the pot on the worn spot in the center of the stovetop. From having seen steam rise from there after wiping up the boiled-over coffee, she surmised it covered a pilot light that could keep the remaining coffee warm.

By afternoon she wished she'd known to take out the grounds as soon as it was done perking. Each cup of coffee tasted stronger and stronger as the day progressed.

The hours flew by and she worked through most of the

afternoon before taking much of a break. Heading along the lake path again, she stopped in front of Greystone. She climbed up on one of the larger rocks at the water's edge and sat looking, not at the lake this time, but at the mansion.

The smashed shutter was gone. Rob must have swept up the pieces since Sandy had refused to go near the place. All the remaining shutters were closed, even the one on the front parlor window next to where Sara's piano had stood.

Louise's notes had mentioned the baby grand piano being there. They confirmed that Sara played well and often. Carolyn liked the idea of having a piano placed in the same spot again for soft live music for the dining room guests.

She lay back on the flat-topped rock and smelled the sweet and clean air. The sun warmed her through her dark jacket and jeans. It felt good to just relax for a few minutes and lie in its rays.

Wouldn't it be perfect to have a big tree by the shore—perhaps a weeping willow? In her imagination, suddenly she could almost see one growing there beside a dock.

Her mother's piercing scream sent Sara racing into the house. She found Lora already at Alice's side in her bedroom.

"It's gone!" Alice said in a voice that trembled as much as her hands. "I came up to dress for dinner and I can't find my emerald necklace."

"It must be here somewhere, Mama," Sara assured her. "You wore it last night, so you must have misplaced the box."

"No, I tell you it's stolen."

"You know the servants would never take it. They've all been with us forever," Sara insisted.

"Yes, I suppose," Alice agreed, looking no less worried.

"And we can't consider for a moment that Robert might have

taken it when he was here earlier," Lora volunteered, too willingly in Sara's way of thinking. "Though I did wonder why he then visited a second time only to be sent away by Papa."

"A second time?" Sara asked, wide-eyed with surprise.

"Yes. I saw him running into the woods from the rose garden just after lunch. Hadn't he been here with you?"

Bewildered, Sara shook her head. Robert hadn't arrived until past four. Had she missed him earlier?

"But Robert certainly wouldn't have taken the necklace," Sara hastened to say. "He's an honorable man. We all know that. So don't worry, Mama. We'll find the emeralds if we have to search every room in the whole house. I'll go find Papa at once. With his help we'll find it."

Lora's words stopped her at the door. "Mama, did you know that Robert is trying to buy the land adjacent to Greystone?"

Sara whirled around. "How did you know that?"

"One does wonder where the man just starting out in life is getting all that money."

Sara swallowed past the sudden dryness in her throat. She opened her mouth to defend the man she loved, but didn't get the chance.

"I hate to be the one to say anything," Lora continued, sounding as if she meant anything but that. "But the purchase of property by a young man in his station just doesn't seem possible. And now, with the necklace missing after his being here without talking to anyone . . . Yes, one does wonder."

"No, don't say that." Lightheaded, Sara clutched the door. "We don't even know the necklace was stolen. Mama could have misplaced it."

"Of course, we won't know for certain unless the emeralds don't turn up," Lora concluded. "Then we'll know that he . . . that someone stole them."

"No!" Sara could take no more. Tears flooded her eyes as she

ran blindly to find her father in the stable. "Papa, you must come quickly. Mama's emeralds are missing."

"Missing? Damnation! Has she no sense of what they're worth?"

"You must help us find the necklace so we can assure Mama that no one took it," she urged as they crossed the garden.

Another scream from the house sent them both running. Bursting into the foyer, they discovered Lora had fallen down the foyer stairs. She lay halfway down at an unnatural angle, her face turned toward them. Blood ran from an open gash where her head must have hit the edge of the step.

Alice appeared on the balcony just then and rushed down the stairs to her side. She lifted Lora's limp hand and called her name.

Lora didn't move. Lloyd called her name as he knelt at her side. Still no response.

Sara tenderly brushed aside the strands of hair that had fallen across Lora's forehead. She withdrew her handkerchief from her sleeve and pressed it against the open wound. "Papa, look. She's blinking her eyes."

"Send for the doctor!" Lloyd shouted to Betty, one of the servants who'd come into the foyer to see who had screamed. "Tell him to come at once!"

"Lost my balance . . ." Lora's voice was hardly audible.

Lloyd took her hand and stroked it. "Lora. My dear Lora."

Sobs shook Alice's body. Her bloodless fingers gripped her husband's arm. "She'll be all right. Tell me she'll be all right!" she screeched.

"Robert . . . necklace . . . leaving town," Lora rasped haltingly.

"What does she mean?" Lloyd demanded of Sara. "Did that boy take the emeralds? Has he left town with them?"

"Robert left for Albany today, but he couldn't have taken

. . ." Sara stammered. One glance at the angry look on her father's face left her speechless. Unable to breathe, she tugged at the tight high collar on her dress.

"Young lady, I forbid you to see Robert again until the necklace is found! And if Lora doesn't . . ." He broke off and leaned down to comfort Lora.

Feeling as if her father had struck her, Sara gasped, dropping the bloody handkerchief.

"Sara can't marry . . . thief," Lora managed to say. She gasped a tiny breath. "Never . . ." The air escaped from her lungs and her head fell to the side. She stared vacantly into the foyer.

"Lora," Alice whimpered through her tears.

Sara looked at her father, who shook his head. He reached down to close Lora's eyelids and rose slowly. He lifted away the ladder-back chair that had fallen beside Lora and threw it into the corner of the balcony beyond the top of the stairs where it splintered into pieces.

Returning to Alice's side, he helped his weeping wife to rise, gathered her close in his arm, and slowly guided her up the stairs to her room. His quiet reassurances had no effect on her hysterical weeping.

Tears fell from Sara's eyes as her gaze returned to her sister's lifeless face. Lora seemed to believe to her dying breath that Robert had taken the necklace. "No, Lora. No!" she sobbed. "Robert didn't take it. The emeralds have just been misplaced, I tell you." She desperately wanted Lora to be wrong about Robert.

Lora was wrong. Wasn't she? Robert wouldn't do that to get money for the property next door, would he?

Carolyn was not aware of falling asleep with the sun warming her until she awoke cold and stiff. It was dusk and the temperature on the rock had dropped considerably. She remembered bits of a strange dream she'd had about the missing emerald necklace. Or had she witnessed it and then fallen asleep?

Sitting up, she peered up at Greystone. She rubbed her eyes and looked again because she could have sworn the parlor shutter was closing as she watched.

"Okay, this is getting ridiculous," she mumbled as she jumped down from the rock and jogged toward the house. She tugged on the shutter. Locked. She looked at all the others. No movement. Heading for the front door, she tried to open it and found it locked, too.

"I need a reality check," she muttered as she leapt down the steps two at a time and jogged toward the warmth of her cabin.

But as she started down the path, she heard feminine laughter coming from Greystone and wanted to assume it was echoing from the camp ahead. Sandy must have heard a good joke. No other woman was near enough. Carolyn didn't want to look back at the shutter, but a thought crossed her mind that made her wonder where Rob was at that moment.

Leaving the woods near her cabin, Carolyn could see Rob standing at a cabin down the row talking with two men who were unloading fishing equipment from the back of their enclosed pickup. A glance farther down revealed two other parked cars with boat trailers. Lights shone in the adjacent cabins. Apparently she was no longer the only guest at the fishing camp.

The men laughed at something and the group broke up. Rob walked her way after giving the men a parting salute. Strangely relieved to find him here and not near Greystone, she waited for him on the stoop and called out a hello when he got closer.

"Hey, I still have the steaks you turned down last night. How about having them with me tonight? If it'll make you feel better, I'll even let you do all the cooking while I shower and clean up."

"Some invitation, but you caught me at a weak moment. I'm starved. Let me just get my flashlight to use coming back later."

Rob had stepped inside the door behind her. He took a key off a hook by the door and handed it to her. "You'll want to use this in the front door from now on. You don't want to find out what people will do when a beautiful temptation is attracting them."

She frowned and an uneasy chill skittered down her spine. She knew Rob was referring to her not being alone in the camp anymore. But what about the temptation in Greystone? She wondered what people would do faced with the temptation of having a beautiful emerald necklace hidden somewhere to find. To what lengths would someone go to find it?

"Thanks." She took the key and locked her cabin door. With the key safely tucked in her jeans pocket, she did her best to look less concerned than she felt as she strolled with Rob to his house.

The engineer friend of John's arrived very early Saturday. Carolyn awoke to the now-familiar crunch of tires on gravel as his car pulled past her cabin, the first in the row, down the way to his. The man must have gotten up at three to arrive so early.

In her nightgown, she peeked out to discover she was apparently the last one in the camp to wake up. She'd never thought of herself as lazy, but getting up before the sun each morning was a bit much for someone who wasn't into fishing.

Boats were out on the lake, and the newest arrival joined them as quickly as he could get his equipment in his boat and the craft launched from the concrete ramp next to Rob's main dock.

The blue sky and bright sunlight looked so inviting that Carolyn resisted the temptation to return to bed and headed for the shower instead. Her breakfast of cold cereal tasted like a poor substitute for fresh trout, but she consoled herself with the thought that it was quicker and that she had a lot fewer dishes and pans to clean up afterwards.

She pulled on her jacket as she went out onto the porch. The envelope on the table caught her eye at once. A note and key were inside.

Gone fishing.

Didn't know how long your food supply would last. Here's the key to my kitchen door. Help yourself. The truck keys are on the counter if you need to go to town. It drives just like a big car.

Rob

P.S. You do drive a stick shift, don't you? You're welcome to use the phone, too.

Carolyn didn't need the truck, but the phone was another matter. She gathered a few of the papers from the box of Louise's plans along with her notebook in which she'd taken copious notes the day before, and jogged to Rob's house. She made herself at home with her papers spread across his kitchen table.

The fresh pot of coffee she'd made was nearly gone and her ears ached from talking so long on the phone by the time she heard Rob approaching the kitchen door.

"Bless you. Fresh coffee."

Rob dropped two trout into one of the double sinks and washed his hands in the other. Taking off his jacket and sweater, he tossed them on the washer in the mudroom.

"And good morning to you, too." She rose and lifted her arms high to stretch.

Turning back to her, he wrapped his arms around her so she had no choice but to lower her arms around his neck. He kissed her hard. His unshaven face felt bristly to her tender skin. "Ouch. You didn't shave before you went in search of the elusive trout." She scratched a fingernail across his jaw.

"Sorry, but discounting the whisker burn, this is the way I prefer to say good morning." He kissed her again briefly and released her just as suddenly as he had pulled her against him. "Have as productive a morning as I did?" He poured the last mug of coffee for himself.

He seemed so casual about their kisses. And what kisses they were. They felt like he'd been kissing her for ages instead of days. Each one worked like the gas burners on the stove. They heated her up instantly. She'd never had a man affect her in this way before, but his whole attitude was so casual, she wondered if the kisses meant anything at all to him. Maybe he said good morning with a kiss to other women he knew, too. "Yeah, I got a lot done."

"I see you're back at the plans for Greystone. The hiatus that you seemed to be enjoying last night must be over."

She nodded. "Yeah, I've been getting cost estimates for renovating and furnishing Greystone. You know, beds and dressers for the guestrooms, tables and chairs for the dining room, the bar, and the equipment, too, like the furnace, air conditioner, elevator, and machines and appliances for the kitchen and laundry."

"You have been busy. How did you manage to do all

that on a weekend morning? Wholesalers generally aren't open on Saturday, are they?"

She shrugged. "I woke up friends of mine and asked them. The guy who does the buying for the chain where I work gave me most of the figures. They're not on the dollar, but they're within the ballpark and good enough for this stage in my thinking."

"Your friend didn't mind being bothered about all that stuff early in the morning on a day off?"

"No, but it was hard not letting him know what I was doing the research for. He was curious, but I didn't want to say it was for myself. I told him I was helping a friend who was thinking of opening a bed and breakfast. It got a little sticky when he wondered about the quantities. He must think it'll be the biggest bed and breakfast in the state." Carolyn chuckled at her own joke, but stopped when she realized Rob was not laughing with her. She gathered the notes from her calls and stuck them in the notebook. "I'll get this stuff off your table."

"The guy must be a good friend to blow that much time on the phone with you." He opened his mouth as if to say more, but didn't. He studied her with the strangest look on his face.

"Yes. I suppose."

He turned away and put his empty mug in the sink. "By the way, were you at Greystone this morning?"

"No. I saw your note after breakfast and came right up here to use the phone. Why?"

"No reason. I just wondered." He started toward the living room.

She stepped quickly to his side and gripped his arm. "Rob, why don't you tell me what you really mean?"

He looked at her and then admitted, "All right. I could

see Greystone from the lake. The front shutter was open again and . . . and I thought I saw someone inside."

"Maybe it was my guardian angel just checking the place out for me," Carolyn suggested with a strained laugh.

"From what's been happening, it's more likely your guardian devil—or somebody's at any rate."

What could she say to that? She didn't want to think about the possibilities.

Rob saved her from having to say anything by continuing. "It was probably the mist rising from the cold water when the sun hit it. It does that sometimes."

Carolyn nodded, having seen the phenomenon herself. "The shutter was closed yesterday. I sat on the rock by the lake late in the afternoon and saw it close . . . I mean I saw that it was closed." She put her coffee mug down in the sink beside his. Why hadn't she wanted him to know she thought she saw it closing? He'd confided a similar incident to her. In the time they'd spent together, he'd been helpful and cooperative.

What an understatement—he'd saved her life! And yet now, thinking about it, she realized she really wasn't sure she trusted him. There was still too much about his role in the whole situation that she didn't know.

"I'll check the latch again when we take the engineer over there after lunch."

"Good." Then they would know for sure. No more talk of spirits, good or evil. No more explaining or guessing at reasons for distrust. She gathered up her remaining papers into organized stacks.

"By the way," Rob went on. "I knew you'd want to talk to the engineer before the inspection, so I invited him to lunch. Actually I told him he could come only if he brought the trout he caught. That way you and I could eat these," he admitted with a grin.

"Way to go," she responded, happy to lighten her own mood.

Rob rubbed his bristly chin. "I'm going to get cleaned up. That should give you time to clear room for me to show you the expert way to fix fresh trout. I'll even think about allowing you to use my secret recipe in your restaurant next door." He raised his eyebrows up and down in a Groucho Marx manner.

"Go. Get out of here," she ordered with a smile she couldn't repress.

Her restaurant next door. How natural that sounded. How perfect. She would bet his special trout recipe was mouth-watering, like the one Rob used to fix breakfast at the cabin. As she concentrated on clearing her things from the table to set it for lunch for three, her stomach reminded her that the bowl of cold cereal she ate had been hours ago.

Chapter Eight

The whole weekend disappeared rapidly going over Greystone with the engineer, Mac Arnold. When he wasn't fishing, that is. The fishing boats went out on the lake early each morning and again in the evening.

During the daylight hours, from late morning to late afternoon, Carolyn and Rob followed Mac in and out and all around the huge house. He studied and tested every floor and wall in minute detail with special equipment that employed sound waves to detect wet or dry rot in the ancient, thick, rough-hewn wood.

Fascinated, Carolyn watched the television-like screen that projected the tests on the thick supports. He pounded, poked and pried his way through each room. He'd been on the roof, and before he was done, Mac had also dug several test holes beside the foundation.

By Sunday night after dark when the fishing was over, he gave Carolyn and Rob his preliminary oral report over their last fish-fry dinner together at Rob's house.

"I'll have my secretary type up my notes into a written report for you, but for now I can say renovating the house is certainly workable."

Carolyn felt the tension flow from her body to be replaced by an immense surge of excitement.

"It's a damned well-built building, considering how old it is," Mac went on to say. "It would cost a fortune to put up one like that today. The biggest safety hazards right now are the chimneys on the back and the end of the house.

They should come down before any work starts on the old place."

Rob and Carolyn shared a look, but they didn't say anything as he continued his report. The details chased around after each other in Carolyn's aching head as the three of them walked together down to the shore. Mac said good night and disappeared inside his cabin. Rob walked Carolyn to her door, but she knew sleep was a long way off.

"I'll say good night, but I'm going for a walk. I'll never get to sleep right away with all I have to think about."

"I'll go with you."

"Rob, don't be silly. It's late and you were up before the sun this morning to go fishing. Go home and go to bed." She gently pushed on his chest to send him on his way, but he reached to hold her shoulders and didn't move.

"There's no way I'm leaving you to go wandering off in the woods. If I did, I'd never get to sleep either, no matter how tired I am."

She could see the concern in his eyes. It was real concern, wasn't it? And not a desire to keep tabs on her for some undetermined reason? Resigned to the fact that he wasn't leaving, she nodded.

Rob slipped his arm around her shoulders and held her close so they could walk side by side on the narrow lake path to Greystone. She didn't want to acknowledge how wonderful it felt being close to him. She held the flashlight with both hands and concentrated on lighting their way.

They were nearly to the clearing when an owl fluttered its wings and hooted. Carolyn was so startled that she cried out, startling Rob. The two of them laughed at their own shows of nervousness.

"Sorry to bother you, Mr. Owl," Rob called up to wherever it hid in the treetops above them. "I'll try to keep her quiet from now on."

His conversation with the bird was just what she needed to laugh and it broke much of the tension she felt. But a loud bang from the house made them both look in that direction. The smiles disappeared from their faces.

"Rob, what was that?" Carolyn held the flashlight with one hand and clutched at his jacket with the other. "It sounded like someone's in there."

"We opened all the shutters to give Mac light. We even opened a few upper windows to let in some fresh air because we were spending so much time inside. Maybe one of the windows slammed shut, or a bird could have flown in."

She looked up at him and shook her head. "You can't convince me that sound was a bird."

He took the flashlight and moved the beam from window to window. "Do you see anything moving?"

As his light rose to the third floor, her gaze drifted to the first floor, to the window with the shutter that seemed to have a mind of its own. She gasped as she saw someone standing just inside the window!

"Rob!" Carolyn's voice sounded as if she was choking. She swallowed and tried again. When he started to turn to her, she grabbed his arm to hold the light where it was. "Rob, leave your light aimed up there, but look at the parlor window."

He looked at the window. "Yeah." He looked back at her. "What about it?"

"Don't you see anyone there?"

"Just a dark window."

"Oh." Carolyn squinted to be certain she wasn't seeing things, but now she couldn't see anything there either.

"Hey, you're shivering." He put the flashlight under his

upper arm and turned her to face him. Like an adult would care for a child, he zipped her jacket up under her chin. "There, that should be warmer."

"I was so sure I saw someone there."

He wrapped both arms around her shoulders this time, and hugged her. Her head, still facing the house, rested against his chest. "That better?"

"Much."

"I think so, too."

She closed her eyes to erase the image of a woman in a light-colored dress she'd seen in the window. But no, there couldn't have been anyone there. And in a dress? If someone had broken in to look for the emeralds, they certainly wouldn't wear a white dress.

As Rob's warmth penetrated her jacket, Carolyn felt more at ease and much safer than before. She was amazed at how comfortable she felt in his arms, but didn't know why, when they'd just met a few days ago.

"Rob?"

"Hmmm?"

"Why do I feel like I've known you forever?"

"If I knew the answer to that, I'd know why I feel the same about you."

"We're not just reacting to the fact that your given name is Robert and one of mine is Sara, are we? We're not some weird continuation or reincarnation of past lives. I don't like that idea. I don't believe in that stuff, and I wouldn't like that to be the reason."

"We're both smarter than that."

She didn't have a chance to respond. Another loud bang from the house, like a door slamming on one of the far sides, echoed in the darkness. Rob aimed the light back at the house.

"Rob, tell me someone slammed a door at the fishing camp," Carolyn insisted, her nervousness evident in her voice.

"Can't do that. And you're right. That's no bird. Maybe you did see someone at that window." He switched off the light. "Stay here and leave this off!" he ordered as he shoved it into her hands.

She grabbed for his sleeve. "No, wait. What are you doing?"

"I'll be right back," he whispered as he pulled out a small flashlight from his pocket and turned it on. "I'm going to check the backyard and find out what the hell is going on. You watch the front. If someone comes around this way, you sing out. If there are teenagers out here again, I want to find them and make damned sure they don't come back."

"Rob, no. You could get hurt," she called after him in a stage whisper as he hurried toward the house.

He must have heard her, but he didn't stop. He'd covered the end of his light with his fingers and allowed only a sliver of illumination to show him the way over the uneven ground as he disappeared around the side of the house on a run.

Carolyn didn't like the idea of standing in front all alone. Or being at the edge of the woods in the pitch dark. Or the idea of Rob going to check out the noise alone.

And she sure didn't like feeling frightened again.

Her eyes accustomed to the moonlight again, she looked around and listened for any movement. Had someone broken into Greystone the back way? She didn't want to wait there to find out. She turned on her light, covering most of the lens as Rob had done, and started after him.

His light had been out of sight behind the house only a

short time when she distinctly heard a woman's voice calling out to him. She paused to listen, trying to place where the sound came from. At first the voice resembled an aspirate echo from far away, but the words were not repeated the same as in an echo.

"Robert, no. No!" the voice shouted. "Robert!"

If only it could be Sandy back at this hour for some reason. But Carolyn knew it wasn't. She quickened her steps along the side of the house.

Then a woman's scream pierced the night. Carolyn heard a sound like a couple of large stones sliding together down a rocky hill. Fear gripped her like needles piercing her temples. She uncovered the lens of the flashlight and increased her speed to a jog.

"Rob!" she cried out. "Rob, where are you?"

More and more rocks tumbled down, each one hitting the ground with a heavy thump until they all roared together, crashing into each other like a landslide. Carolyn's fear threatened to paralyze her. She didn't waste any energy calling his name again; she just ran.

A root twisting out of the ground caught her unawares and threw her to the ground with a grunt. Though the fall knocked the air from her lungs, she was up in seconds, found the light that had flown from her hand, and ran again.

Flying dust and debris rose in a giant cloud-like puff that reflected the illumination from her flashlight as the pounding of the rocks stopped. She ran toward it.

"Rob? Rob!" Carolyn cried out. She swept the whole backyard area with her light, looking for him. "Rob!" she screamed, choking in the dust, but she heard no response.

Running footsteps behind her in the woods, announced the arrival of two of the fishermen and Mac. They were in their nightclothes with their jackets thrown on. "What's going on?" Mac called.

"Help me," she pleaded. "Quick. Rob came back here when we heard a noise, and I can't find him."

She coughed as she moved through the dusty fog that soon thinned enough to reveal a pile of rocks and rubble below where there had been a wide chimney built against the back of the kitchen. She raced along the rock pile.

"Rob? Rob! Where are you?" she shouted. "Answer me!" she demanded, her panic rising to choke her. Tears blinded her as she set the flashlight on the ground and began to pick up the rocks and throw them behind her.

The men fanned out around the pile, all calling Rob's name and tossing the rocks behind them. The one who had gone around to the far side saw him first. "Over here," he called. Carolyn grabbed her light and ran with the others around the end of the rock pile to his side.

Rob lay on his stomach in the weeds just beyond the rocks. Blood ran across his forehead from a gash in his hair.

"Rob?" the man called as he knelt to feel for a pulse in his neck. His shoulders slumped as he relaxed from the tension of not knowing. "He's just unconscious, not . . ."

Carolyn cleared her eyes of her tears with the back of her sleeve and fell to her knees. "Rob?" She lifted Rob's hair aside to see an open wound. Blood seeped steadily. She rummaged through her pockets for her packet of tissues and pressed several against the gash to stem the flow.

"Should we carry him back to camp?" one of the men asked.

"Don't move him," Mac ordered as he squatted on the opposite side of Rob's limp body. He carefully felt his arms and legs. "There are no obvious breaks, but because he's unconscious, it would be better to get an ambulance instead of moving him. There might be something wrong that I can't feel, like a broken neck."

Carolyn gasped.

"I'll run up to call the paramedics," one of the men volunteered. "I've got a cell phone in my cabin."

Before he could move away, Rob groaned.

"Wait. He's wakin' up," Mac called to stop the man.

Rob blinked several times and finally managed to keep his eyes open.

"Rob, talk to us. Are you okay? Can you move?" Carolyn asked, impatient to know he was okay, unable to bear thinking otherwise. She lifted the tissues, but could see the cut was still bleeding.

Rob struggled to roll over onto his back with the ready advice of all those around him as to how to do it. He tried to sit up, but Mac stopped him with a hand on his shoulder.

"Just lie there a few minutes to be sure you're okay. How do you feel?"

"All your damned flashlights on my face would be giving me a headache," Rob answered, "if I didn't have a doozie of one already." The lights were all moved away from his face with quick apologies and a few chuckles.

Rob lifted his hand to the head wound and then held his fingers in front of his face. "What the hell happened?"

"We were hoping you could tell us that," Carolyn said, pushing the hair up from his temple so she could press the folded tissues on his wound again. "Hold still. This should slow the bleeding."

Mac rose. His gaze followed the beam of his light over the back of the house before he told Rob what everyone else had already seen. "The chimney fell, and from the looks of it, you caught a piece of it on the side of the head." Mac shook his head and looked down at the injured man still lying on the ground. "That's one less chimney that will have to be taken down, but you might have picked a safer way to accomplish it, Rob. You could have been killed."

With help and more advice from everyone, Rob sat up. Carolyn removed the tissues and saw that her hands were shaking. Tears stung her eyes as she looked at Rob and realized how devastated she would have felt if anything had been seriously wrong with him. She took a deep breath to steady herself. Folding a clean side of the tissues out, she pressed the stack against his head.

"I didn't know what was happening, but if you hadn't called to me, Carolyn, and given me that shove, I would have been standing right under the avalanche. You were lucky you didn't get hurt. Damn, my head hurts." He drew her hand down and saw that the tissues were bloody again.

"Let's get him to my cabin," Carolyn said to the men before Rob could say more. "It's a lot closer than his house, and we can get a better look at his head and stop the bleeding."

She didn't like the way Mac was looking at her after Rob's talking about her being back there when the chimney fell. He'd arrived in time to see her run up to the rocks, looking for Rob. He knew she hadn't pushed Rob away.

"Good idea," Mac agreed.

Carolyn let Mac take charge as the men helped Rob to Cabin One. He insisted on walking, but with his arms over their shoulders, two of the fishermen practically carried him. Carolyn ran ahead to unlock the door. The fishermen set Rob down on the couch and took seats in a circle facing him on chairs they'd pulled from around the table.

"If you men can get his jacket off, I'll get a cloth to wash the blood away so we can see how badly his head is cut," Carolyn said as she walked directly to the bathroom.

"I hope it's not as bad as it feels," Rob muttered.

With all three of the men working to help Rob, the simple task took as long as it took Carolyn to get a wet cloth and her first aid case. She was glad for a few extra moments when one look in the mirror revealed a dirty, tear-streaked face. She frowned. She'd been trained to be capable and efficient in emergency situations—without any of the emotional involvement she'd felt tonight. How had she come to care so much about Rob in just days?

She splashed some water on her face and rushed to dry it before grabbing the first aid items and returning to tend to Rob's wound. Sliding a towel under his head, he leaned against the back of the couch. "That's better. The management would be upset if you got blood on the couch," she joked to relieve the tension.

Rob gingerly rubbed his shoulder. "I think some rocks must have bounced off my shoulder. It's killing me."

Carolyn couldn't stop her quick intake of breath when she heard his remark about something killing him. Could he be right? Was someone trying to kill people at Greystone? The falling shutter was a near miss, and now the rocks?

Mac gave her a quick look and then opened Rob's shirt. He leaned forward so Mac could see the back of his shoulder. "It's red all right. It'll be black and blue by morning. It's not broken?"

Rob rotated his arm to test the shoulder. "Seems to work, so it must be just bruised."

" 'Just,' the man says. The good news, Rob, is that your pupils aren't dilated, and they react evenly to the light. Your head should be good once you get rid of the ache—as good as it ever was, that is," Mac joked.

"Thanks for your help, Mac," Rob said with a chuckle. "Ow! It hurts to laugh."

"Lean back so I can see your head," Carolyn said.

Rob looked at the men standing around him. "I'll be fine now. I just need to rest here for a while before I go up to the house."

"I can stay and drive you up when you're ready to go," Mac volunteered, concern evident on his face.

"Mac, you're such a nice guy," one of the other fishermen offered with a laugh. "Nice, but dense! If you had the choice between me nursing your head or a beautiful woman like Carolyn holding your head on her lap and doing her best to make you feel better, which choice would you make?"

They all laughed, including Carolyn, but the expression she saw on Mac's face told her he wanted to stay for more than to watch Rob. She didn't want to answer any of the questions he would ask once the other men were gone.

"I can take care of the first aid," she promised. "My hotel school training has taught me what to do, but I can't promise to hold his head on my lap, fellas," she added with a grin. The knowing looks they gave each other before they said good night amused her. After all, they were the ones standing in her cabin in their pajamas.

"Hey, will you guys just leave and give me a break here?" Rob pleaded. The men all wished him well and exited the cabin. "Thanks," Rob called as they left.

Carolyn had sorted out the first aid materials by the time she and Rob were left alone.

Mac was the last to go. "Please, Carolyn. Don't go near Greystone again until those chimneys are taken down. You might not be so lucky next time. Promise?"

Carolyn nodded to put him at ease. "Sure. I'll talk to John tomorrow morning and see how quickly it can be done. We certainly don't want anyone else to get hurt out here. And thanks for coming to help tonight, Mac."

He nodded and looked back at Rob. Carolyn held her breath, hoping he didn't ask about Rob thanking her for being where he knew she hadn't been.

"Yeah. Well, take it easy, Rob."

After shutting the door after Mac, Carolyn turned her attention to cleaning the dust and dirt from Rob's wound. It wasn't easy getting the blood out of his hair, but better to do it now, she thought, than after it had dried any more.

"Ouch! What is that, rubbing alcohol?" he asked when she patted the wound with disinfectant.

She couldn't help but laugh. "When I complained, my mother always told me that if the medicine didn't hurt, it wasn't working."

"I suppose she told you medicine had to taste bad to be effective, too."

"Doesn't it?" she asked innocently as she dabbed on the antiseptic cream. "Oh-oh."

"What? What's the oh-oh?" he asked with a worried sense of urgency.

"I can't put a bandage on it without taping it to your hair." She studied his head in mock sincerity. "Hmm. I suppose I could shave your head on that side."

"Hey!" he cried, ducking his head away from her in mock horror and then regretting it when the pain from the quick movement hit. He pressed his fingers against his temples.

"It could look very modern. If I shaved the capital letters R-O-B on the side, I could plan it so the gash would be in the 'O'. Then I could stick the ends of the bandage in the shorn middle of the R and the B."

Her comments elicited a smile and a raised eyebrow this time.

"Then again, maybe if you just slept on a towel, it would be all right uncovered. It doesn't look so bad now. I don't think you need stitches. The dirt that mixed in the smeared blood made it look worse than it actually was. How does it feel?"

"All right, considering, but I still have a headache." He leaned back on the towel she placed on the back of the couch and sat with his eyes shut.

While he rested for a few minutes, she put away the first aid items and washed her hands. In the kitchen area, she put on water to boil. "Now that the others are gone, tell me what really happened back there while I make some tea for us," she said over her shoulder.

"What do you mean, 'what really happened'?" he asked as he stretched out lengthwise on the couch, putting the towel under his head again.

"Rob, all that business about me pushing you away and saving you was rubbish," she said, turning to face him. "I can't see the need to puff me up into a hero for a bunch of your camp's customers."

He looked at her with a questioning frown and straightened to a sitting position with his feet on the floor. She returned from the stove to sit next to him.

"What is it?" she asked, feeling concerned for his well-being. "Are you seeing double?"

"No, Carolyn. It's you." He took her hand and held it in his, resting on his thigh. "You saved my life, and I'm wondering why you won't let me say thank you."

"Rob, that's the whole point. I didn't. I wasn't anywhere near you. By the time I got to the back of the house, the chimney already had fallen. All I could see was a choking cloud of dust. We didn't find you until the dust settled and we'd circled the whole pile of stones looking for you."

Rob turned away and raised his free hand to massage his forehead as he leaned against the back of the couch.

"Tell me again what happened," she prompted. "Maybe we can make some sense out of it."

"I went around the back and examined the whole yard with my light. I saw no cars or bikes, or any evidence of anyone being there. I walked over to check the kitchen door, but it was locked. I saw no one, but I remember hearing something above me, so I looked up. I never got the flashlight raised to investigate the noise before you yelled."

"What did I say?"

"I don't know," he said impatiently. "You yelled 'Robert, no!' or something like that. That's when I heard the rocks start to fall. You shoved me so hard that I took several running steps just trying to keep my balance, but I couldn't manage to stay standing. I fell forward. The next thing I knew, everyone had lights shining in my face, and my head felt like it would explode. Still does."

"I'll get that tea," she responded as she crossed to the kitchen area. She digested what he'd said while she served two steaming mugs of lemon-flavored herbal tea.

She wished the answer to the puzzle would appear like magic in the black of the night. The porch light lit the area in front of the cabin, but the light didn't extend far into the trees that rimmed the other side of the drive toward Greystone. Instead of inviting and beautiful, the woods looked dangerous and foreboding.

Try as she might to gather the facts, Rob seemed annoyed that she'd quizzed him again about the events. Was he trying to hide something? There were too many strange things going on. Was the ugly mythical monster side of her chimera rearing its evil head? She hated thinking of a monster each time she thought of Greystone. She wanted the

Greystone Inn to remain her fantastic hope-filled dream, not something frightening.

Rob placed his hand on her arm. She jumped and then gently settled back against him. "I'm sorry I was testy. That isn't what happened, is it?"

She shook her head and glanced at him before looking back into the darkness outside. "No, Rob. I was nowhere near you when the chimney fell. Someone else saved you from more serious injury. Someone . . . when no one else was there."

She crossed her arms against her midriff. She felt cold despite the warmth of his body against her. "Someone must be trying to scare me—to scare me away. At moments, like right now, I feel they're succeeding, and I don't like it."

"No one's trying to do that," he said, a little too easily for her to believe. "I probably just don't remember what happened because of the hit on the head. My story about a voice and someone pushing me must be a dream I had while I was unconscious."

"Don't, Rob. Don't say something that isn't true to make me feel better. Please. No lies between us. I need to be able to believe you."

One part of her wanted to believe him while another screamed that she shouldn't get caught again in the trap of believing in a man who could gain immensely by using her.

"You can believe me," he assured her, taking her hands in his. "Now. You didn't call out to me?"

She shook her head. "No, and I couldn't have pushed you away from the danger either. The rocks would have hit me if I'd been standing behind you. And besides, I wouldn't call you 'Robert.' I'd yell, 'Rob, look out,' or something like that."

"Robert?"

"Yes, you said the woman called out to 'Robert.' That's the word I heard her call, too."

Rob gripped her arm and met her gaze. "You heard her, too?"

Carolyn nodded.

Rob looked at her a few more moments and then released her arm and leaned back on the couch. He released a heavy sigh.

"What is it? What's going on, Rob? You've got to tell me," she urged. "Don't make this any more damn mysterious. What do you know?"

He gathered her in his arms and held her head against his good shoulder. She sat stiffly in his arms and pressed her hand against his chest, not to feel the warm firmness there, but to be ready to push back from him. She needed to remain objective, and that wasn't what she felt in his arms.

"Carolyn, I find myself not wanting to tell you, yet wanting you to believe and trust me because I wouldn't lie to you. But I guess I have to tell you. You should know everything anyway before you decide about Greystone."

Straightening, she pulled out of his arms and asked, "Tell me what?" She shifted her weight onto a folded leg, so she could look directly at him, and so she wouldn't be tempted to let him circle her with his arms again. His hand stayed on her near shoulder, his elbow resting on the back of the couch. He hadn't broken the tenuous contact between them.

"You're not the only one who's heard voices calling to them. She . . . whoever it is . . . always calls me 'Robert.' When she does and I look for someone, there's no one there. Not ever. Sound familiar?"

Carolyn laughed a hollow-sounding laugh. "Oh, come

on, Rob. The next thing you'll be telling me is that you've seen a ghost over there, too. Listen. Just because the figure I saw in the window looked like a woman, doesn't mean . . ." She stopped when she realized from the look on his face that she hadn't told him about seeing the figures. "It could have been moonlight reflecting on the dark window," she said with a shrug.

She stood, breaking their contact, and paced the floor. "Wait a minute. Look at it from the point of view of the person trying to scare me away. Hearing voices should be enough. I wouldn't need to see the ghosts. Someone could use a little tape recorder. You said sound carries really well near the lake."

"A tape recorder. That's all it would take. Oh, damn, that's good," he said as if only now seeing it that way.

She stared at him, suddenly really seeing him for the first time, and took a deep breath. "Now that I think about it, a recorder would have worked every time. But who would know where I would be and when I would be there?"

Her eyes opened wide and she turned away. "Oh, no," she said as a revelation of what had been happening played over in her mind. "It can't be."

"What is it, Carolyn?"

She couldn't face him. "Someone *was* there each time besides me," she said in a breathy soft voice. "Even in the law office when I heard Louise." She drew a jagged breath. "The voice tonight and the one in the office could have been the same. Any female voice would have worked, considering the state I was in after reading the letter about the inheritance."

Carolyn hugged herself. She felt very cold. Slowly she turned to look at him. "Rob, you could have been watching from the street where you would see me near the law office window where I heard Louise's voice. Then at Greystone when the voice called out to a 'Sara,' you were with me then. And the rest of the stuff that happened at Greystone. The flashlights, the vision at the window, the shutter falling—you were always there. You're very handy next door at your camp. You could have rigged it all."

Tears burned in her eyes, but she couldn't stop. "Wow, what a production," she said, the strength of her voice increasing with her anger. "I've got to hand it to you. You must show me the hologram equipment some time. That's slick. With all the time you've had since Louise died, you had everything ready before I arrived from Florida. You know exactly where I will be, and you could control when I will be there." She raised her hands palms up and then slapped them against her sides. "Now I know why you were late picking me up the first day. You had to give me time alone to see the scene on the lake."

Rob frowned and opened his mouth to speak, but she gave him no opportunity to answer. "You rig a shutter to open and close. You make a few things fall, but you get me out of the way first and make me think you saved my life. I was truly grateful. I fell right into your arms. But you were after a lot more than a few kisses, weren't you?"

She ran her hands through her hair and pulled fistfuls beside her temples. "Why didn't I see it sooner? And tonight, the chimney. That must have been tough, even if Mac did say they were ready to fall. Real blood, too, or was that an accident when you didn't get away fast enough after pulling down the chimney?" She shook her head. "I've always heard that lawyers have to be good actors. Well, buddy, you deserve an Oscar."

She ignored the fact that he wasn't saying a word in response. "But what's supposed to happen next, Rob? Maybe

I'm terrified out of my wits. And then I run back to Florida. Is that next? Sure. You can't kill me because then someone else would just be in line to inherit, and you'd have to start all over. But the big question remains: if I leave now, what happens to Greystone?"

She raised her fisted hands to her forehead. Bitter tears of disappointment were spilling from her eyes, blinding her, and she was glad. She didn't want to see him sitting there—silent.

"You've taken such good care to be with me—not because you wanted to, or even because you had to for the law firm—but to control me and use me. I'm certain you even knew what your expert kisses would do. You said Louise told you all about me. So the good-looking, disarming fisherman-*cum*-lawyer makes me melt in his arms with his fantastic kisses." She groaned. "How could I be so naive as to fall for it? To think I thought I really cared for you!"

Rob looked surprised and then slumped forward, his elbows resting on his knees. Silent, he didn't look up to meet her gaze. With all her heart, she wanted him to deny her accusations, but he didn't. Was it because he couldn't or wouldn't?

"Who else could so cleverly plan it all? It's got to be you. Damn! You get Greystone if I turn it down, don't you? If Sara doesn't get it, Robert will. Aunt Louise was enough of a romantic to do something that crazy with her will. Then you would own the whole end of the lake, wouldn't you? An Ashford would end up with all the money and the property. With or without the necklace, that would be the ultimate revenge against the Whitneys for accusing Robert of theft and ruining his life. Wouldn't it?"

Her final accusations paled Rob's face. He rose and held her gaze for a moment before jerking the front door open and disappearing into the darkness beyond the scope of the porch light. The screen door bounced in his wake.

Carolyn's head dropped into her hands as she gave in to heart-wrenching sobs. Betrayal hurt. He'd promised to stick by her, to protect her, and he'd been the one threatening her all along.

Men were just one broken promise after another as far as she was concerned. She couldn't trust any of them. With the evidence fitting so perfectly, she never thought for a moment that she might be wrong and that she'd chased away an innocent, injured man from the comfort of her care. All she could do long into the night was to ask herself, why did it have to be Rob?

She didn't know which hurt more: knowing she could not trust him, or knowing she was falling in love with him despite it all.

Chapter Nine

Carolyn surprised John, who found her waiting in his front office when he arrived the next morning. Invited into his private office, she didn't waste any time before getting to the heart of her visit. "I need to talk to you about what's happening to Greystone. Can you spare me some time now?"

"Of course."

First, she explained what had happened the night before when the chimney fell. John was visibly shaken by the news of his son being hurt. She patiently waited while he called Rob's house to find out for himself that his son was all right.

"Yes, she's sitting right here." He lowered the phone from his mouth and asked Carolyn how she got to town. She told him.

"Says she hitched a ride in with two of the men staying at the camp," he said into the receiver. "Apparently they came in to town to get a breakfast they didn't have to fix for themselves."

He listened a moment longer and hung up.

Carolyn couldn't wait for John to volunteer the news, but she was angry with herself for asking, "Is Rob okay? His head doesn't still hurt?"

"He seemed fine, but I'm glad you told me about the accident. His mother and I worry about him out there all alone." He stopped and appeared to regret having said that much. "Enough about Rob. What did you want to ask about?"

"Greystone. The chimney falling shows just how dangerous it is." She told him about Mac's inspection and summarized his findings. "Something must be done right away before someone else gets hurt."

"Have you made your decision, regarding the inheritance?"

"Yes, but just to be certain, I have two questions first." He nodded for her to continue. "What's to happen to Greystone if I don't accept it because of the demands of the will or for any other reason?"

"I'm sorry. My father and I were made privy to that information, but as I noted when we went through the will, it's a stipulation that you're not to be told prior to your decision."

"But after . . . Oh, no. What you just said—you and your father . . . Both you and Thomas know what is to happen if I don't accept it?"

He nodded.

"And Rob? Was he told all that the will says?"

"No."

Carolyn found it hard to breathe. Didn't John trust his son either? "Why not? Why not tell Rob?"

"I'm afraid only Louise could have told you that. It was her decision, not ours. She said Rob was not to know the alternative plan before your decision was made."

"There's no way he could find out? I mean, he works here. Wouldn't he have access to her files? Couldn't he find it in a computer or somewhere . . . if he went looking for it, I mean?"

"I can't imagine why you'd even consider that Rob might do such a thing, but no, Carolyn, Rob does not and could not know." He leaned back in his chair. "I think I know why Louise made a point of making certain he wouldn't know. She felt that he might influence your decision. I know you're . . . in a situation out there where you two must spend a good deal of time together. Since you're staying at his camp, it was easiest for him to be the one to show you around. The contact has been unavoidable. I think Louise's decision was the right one."

Carolyn hardly heard the end of what he was saying. Rob did not know what would happen to Greystone if she turned it down. It might go to anyone: her mother, a charity, anything besides to Rob—or it could go to him. But he didn't know which. He'd be a fool to count on the latter, and he might be a lot of things, but he was no fool.

Last night! Damn. How wrong could she be? She wished she could take back everything she'd said to Rob. She'd jumped to conclusions from circumstantial evidence. Anyone would agree that the circumstantial evidence appeared to be pointing directly to him. It had all seemed so logical, so clear. In fact, now that she looked at it from a new angle, it was as if someone was trying to stack the evidence against him on purpose.

Of course! How could she let that someone sucker her in? Rob couldn't be the one trying to scare her away in order to get Greystone all for himself. But someone was.

Carolyn felt more determined than ever—whoever it was, wouldn't succeed. *You won't ever scare me away,* she vowed silently. *Never.*

"And the other question?" John asked, bringing Carolyn out of her reverie.

"Yes. The necklace. How could Louise think I could locate it after all these years of other people trying to find it?"

John smiled and shook his head. "The will only states that you must look for it—not find it. But as to why you should be able to locate it?" He took off his wire rims and pulled out his silk pocket square to wipe them. "You don't know how hard it is for me to say this. It goes against everything I believe in."

He put his glasses back on and tucked the square back into his breast pocket. "You see, Louise assured me that Sara would lead you to where it was hidden."

When Carolyn exited the law office an hour later, the air smelled fresh and clean. The day felt like one of those rare spring days when all of nature seemed to pop out with tender green growth all at once. She couldn't wait to get back out to the lake to begin a fresh start herself—with Rob. If he would let her.

She directed her steps toward the local car dealer down the street a few blocks who, according to John, rented cars. She'd only gone a few steps when the door of the dusty red pickup parked at the curb opened. "It took you long enough," Rob called calmly.

Carolyn's heart sped up. She swallowed the hard lump that suddenly blocked her throat. She stepped over to the door. "I had a lot to say and do. It took a while."

He nodded but said nothing. He looked at the steering wheel and scraped at something there with his thumbnail.

Carolyn looked down the street in the direction she'd been heading and then back up into the truck at Rob. "I'll certainly understand if you say no after the awful things I said to you last night, but would you mind giving me a lift? I need to go somewhere, and I have some things I'd like to say to you on the way." She paused. "If you'll let me."

"More of what you said last night?"

She bit her lower lip and looked down the street. He wasn't making this easy, and she didn't blame him one little bit. "It's about what I said last night," she answered softly, her gaze locking on his. "But it's going to be a sincere apology, not more of the same."

By way of invitation, he waved his hand toward the empty seat beside him. Having slacks on, she climbed in easily and sat facing him after pulling the door shut behind herself.

She caught his hand as he lifted it to turn the key. Looking into his questioning eyes, she brought his hand to rest on her thigh where she held it with both of hers.

"Will you forgive me, Rob? I'm so sorry I said what I did last night. I had no excuse for flying off the handle with accusations before I had proof other than the circumstantial evidence that appeared to make it a logical conclusion. I wasn't thinking clearly because I was frightened by all that had been happening. And I was terrified that you might have been really hurt, Rob."

"You had a funny way of letting me know it."

"I had a lousy way of letting you know it. And I have no excuse."

She looked down at his hand. He hadn't pulled it away. It lay limply in hers. "Frankly, your close call bothered me more than I expected. I know I can't take back my mistakes in life and do them over, but if I could, I would take back everything I said when I accused you last night of causing my problems at Greystone. I hadn't even thought about it all that much, yet everything suddenly seemed so clear." She chuckled. "It was as if some stranger took possession of my mind and made me accuse you without giving you the benefit of a doubt or checking the evidence first." Her face sobered. "I know it's hard to believe, but it just wasn't me saying those things."

"What changed your mind about me being the bad guy?"

She eased the tight grip she had on his hand and leaned

back into the seat. "Well, for starters John said that you didn't know what would happen to the house if I declined the inheritance. I know it won't help after what I said, but I've always wanted to think that you couldn't be the one who is trying to scare me away."

"Thanks for that much."

"At the same time, I couldn't figure out any other logical explanation for what's been happening." She shook her head. "But I didn't work very hard at it. Someone did a wonderful job of making you look guilty so I'd come to those conclusions. And I was too frightened to see anything differently. I still am scared, Rob, but I'm also so very sorry for what I said. Please forgive me."

He watched her for a few moments and suddenly smiled broadly. The smile brightened her day and eased the constriction that had made her breathing difficult.

"When I'm working on a criminal case, I often have to discount the obvious in order to find the facts. As to what you said last night—I'd be the first to admit the evidence was stacked against me. You were right there." He shrugged. "I'd collected all the evidence against me before you did. And as for being concerned for me? Thanks. You can't be concerned if you don't care."

He leaned over suddenly and kissed her. Her hopes rose.

"Does the kiss mean we can still be friends even though I acted like an idiot? Does it mean you forgive me, Rob?"

"Yup! But don't ever let it happen again," he threatened playfully. He reached to fasten his seatbelt and told her to do the same. "Where to, ma'am?"

"To the car rental agency."

His head jerked in her direction. "You mean . . ."

"I mean to rent a van. I'm going to have a lot to carry around. Turning a . . . a haunted house into an upscale lakeside inn ain't easy, ya know, buddy."

"Yes, ma'am," he said with a snappy salute.

Their laughter filled the cab as they headed for the car dealership.

The next weeks were unbelievably busy for Carolyn. She quit her job in Florida, and not wanting to spare the time to return, she asked Tulie to pack and ship her things from her apartment. She was happy to help. What Carolyn couldn't use in the cabin, she stacked in a rented storage unit near town until the apartment in the mansion was clean and safe for her to move into.

Tulie was so excited that she was ready to quit her job with two weeks' notice and come up to help. "I'll just pack myself into one of these boxes and ship myself on up."

Carolyn persuaded her to bide her time and not cut off her source of income until they knew how long the renovations at Greystone would take.

Mac's recommendations about the mansion were taken to heart, and the first thing Carolyn did was to have the stone chimneys and heavy shutters taken down. The house appeared a lot brighter inside with the sunlight streaming through the tall, uncovered windows.

Once the building was safe to walk in and around, Carolyn arranged for her folks to visit for the weekend. She wanted them to see Greystone and the plans she was developing with an architect.

Finally, after the contracts were awarded, the actual renovation work began. Roadbeds and parking areas were graded and topped with coarse gravel. Later, when the truck traffic ceased, they would be blacktopped. The huge earth-moving machines shook the house on their passes along the driveway. The diesel engines and the grating roar of gravel sliding off the steel truck beds was enough to drive Carolyn out of the house and the birds out of the trees.

Her ensuing headache motivated her to grab her car keys for a break in town where she could find quiet. She was patiently waiting for a dump truck that blocked the road to move before she could pull her rental van out. The foreman, who was also waiting for the truck, loped over to her car. "Had enough of the noise and dust?" he shouted.

She nodded. "I don't know how you stand it all day long," she called out.

He held up a finger to halt her words and reached up to remove an earplug that he had been wearing. "What'd you say?"

"I was wondering how you stand it, but you've answered my question," she said with an easy laugh.

"I'm surprised you lasted as long as you did since we were working so close to the house. Man, I don't know how the lady you got working on the second floor can stand it. But maybe I shouldn't mention it, 'cause I don't want to get her in trouble."

"What do you mean?"

"Well, whatever you gave her to do ain't getting done. She's been at the window watching us all morning. It's like she's never seen road-building equipment before. Really weird."

The truck beeped its loud horn, letting them know he was now waiting for Carolyn to move her van. The foreman stepped back. "Have a good one," he shouted, as he put his earplug back in place.

Her heart pounding, Carolyn pulled onto the graded surface and drove slowly to the tree line. Just before Greystone would disappear from view, she stopped and looked back. Was that a woman standing in the second-floor window? A woman in a light-colored dress? The same woman she thought she saw the night of Rob's accident?

A quick count of windows from the corner told her it was Sara's bedroom. She even looked like Sara.

Carolyn's hands were shaking so badly she changed direction. She would work at the cabin instead of going all the way to town. Maybe she'd read a novel to take her mind off Greystone altogether. She needed to relax. Then she would be her old realistic self again. The self that didn't imagine seeing and hearing people who weren't there.

She never finished chapter one before the phone company showed up to install a phone in her cabin. The line would be moved to her own apartment in the house when it was habitable. She called Tulie to give her the new number. She almost mentioned the lady in white but decided not to. If she ever told her, it would have to be in person.

Rob arrived next with papers to sign, and Carolyn didn't have time to think about telling him. There was too much to do.

Throughout the initial work stage, Rob acted as the liaison for the law firm. He supervised the accountant who'd been hired to keep track of the bids, the bills, and the payments. The final decisions were left to Carolyn, who relied heavily on architects and engineers to advise her.

The roof was replaced and the outside walls repaired first. Additional stairways and exits to the outside were added to meet code. The old chimney openings were closed in. Dumpsters as long as the bed of an eighteen-wheeler were parked beneath the windows. Long chutes of plywood were attached to various windows to carry debris directly to the Dumpsters. Finally, the integrity of the structure insured, the time had come to begin on the inside.

Carolyn saw Rob every day, although she often went for

several days without really talking to him. Other days they seemed to find a reason to be alone together talking for hours. Those were the days Carolyn liked best.

She came to expect to find him somewhere in Greystone, checking on something or just watching. No matter where she was, Rob seemed to be behind her when she turned around—just out of reach. Her fingers itched to touch him, to hold him again, but those occasions were rare. He was up before dawn for the fishermen and fell asleep earlier than she did each evening. Their relationship felt like trust, and she wanted to trust him. Yet as hard as she tried, something always held her back.

In the weeks since she'd accepted her inheritance, a few strange events and voices had occurred at the house, but she couldn't discuss them with Rob. He dismissed the incidents as being merely accidents. When a section of a ceiling fell on workmen, Rob insisted they had hit the ceiling with the ladders, making the loose plaster fall.

Missing tools reappeared in a different room; sheets of plywood sailed off the stack as the crane lifted them; workers quit because they didn't like working in a haunted house where they heard mysterious voices. The logical explanation was their overactive imaginations fed by local rumors, but they wouldn't believe that. She hired other workers.

In time she could even discount the truck driver seeing a woman watching him. Most of the windowpanes were the originals and not at all smooth. They could easily reflect sunlight in an uneven way, resembling a figure standing there. Simple. She'd already seen it happen herself in the moonlight when she thought she saw a woman in a white dress on the first floor.

Ready for a break late one afternoon, she decided to invite Rob to her cabin for a special dinner. She wanted to put thoughts of Greystone aside and just enjoy an evening alone with him. After making sure the workers were all gone and Greystone was locked up, she jogged to her cabin to clean up.

Before heading for the shower, she phoned Rob to ask him to join her. When there was no answer, not even from his answering machine, she wrote a note that said she had a lamb shish kabob and a Greek salad with his name on it. She jogged the short distance to his house and tucked the folded note in the screen door that led to his kitchen. Rob would see it when he came home, but even if he were distracted, the note would fall onto the floor when he opened the door. Either way he couldn't miss her invitation.

Yet by the time she'd showered, dressed, and prepared the salad for dinner, she still hadn't heard from him. She called again after the meal was assembled, but she still got no answer.

Disappointed, she didn't even bother to light the charcoal barbecue. She wrapped up the skewered meat and put it in the refrigerator for the following night. Sitting on the screened porch feeling more lonely than usual, she ate the salad. Pouring a glass of the wine from the bottle she'd opened earlier so it could breathe, she silently toasted her absent dinner companion. Taking the glass with her, she took advantage of the daylight left and walked the lake path to Greystone.

Perched on the large rock, she sipped the wine until movement in Greystone's parlor caught her attention. She blinked hard and looked again. Yes, a woman was seated in the front room, just inside of the end window where the shutter had opened the first day she saw Greystone. Dressed in a pale dress, her equally pale hair was done up with long curls that trailed softly over her shoulder.

A piano. Though Carolyn could see only her, she knew the figure was sitting at a piano. She could even hear the lovely sonata she was playing.

Barely realizing what she was doing, Carolyn noiselessly slid from the rock and crept toward the house. At the bottom of the entrance stairs, she stopped and stood transfixed, staring at the window.

The figure rose and turned to the window, as if knowingly meeting Carolyn's gaze. This was the closest view Carolyn had ever had. There could be no mistake. She knew who it was. Sara.

A gentle smile graced the figure's face. Her hands rose to touch the bow on her dress just below her breasts in a shy manner. She said nothing, but her smile—that said it all.

Sara was saying, "Thank you."

Responding with a smile of her own, Carolyn watched as the figure turned and disappeared without ever moving away from the window.

"Wait! Don't go," Carolyn cried out. Running up the steps and looking at the same window from the inside, Carolyn saw what she knew all along she would see. Nothing. No one was in the room. She knew if she searched every room in the whole house, she would find no one. But something about this vision of a woman looking out the window was very different. Or was it only her reaction to it?

Why don't I feel afraid? In fact, she felt more than an absence of fear—she felt happy. She'd just seen a vision that defied all rational thinking, and she'd smiled at it . . . at Sara.

Could this shy and smiling apparition be the same one who sent the shutter and the chimney crashing down? Carolyn didn't think so, but she couldn't say why. The only fact she knew for certain was that the figure wasn't the sun reflected on old wavy panes of glass, or a new pane for that matter. The sun hadn't been shining directly on the window at all.

Carolyn was still on the porch at the window digesting it all when Rob called from the end of the driveway. "Hey, I wondered where you were."

She immediately closed her eyes to block it, but a nagging inner voice asked, "Isn't he always nearby whenever something strange happens?" Where had that thought come from? Carolyn didn't want to think that way, and purposely shoved the unwanted thought out of her mind. She turned toward him as he strode across the porch to her side.

The moment their eyes met, he opened his arms to her. She fled to the comfort he offered her. She clung to him, her arms around his waist, hanging on to his shirt so he couldn't disappear as silently and suddenly as he'd appeared.

"Something's going on, isn't it?"

"Not anymore."

"What was it? Did you see something at the window again?"

She raised her head to look at the house. "Right there, in the sitting room. I thought I saw . . . I saw a woman with light hair and a white dress with a bow."

"You saw her?" He held her tighter after she nodded.

"She said . . . Well, no, she gave me the impression that she wanted to say 'thank you.' I could tell just from the look on her face, her smile."

"She's gone now." He wasn't asking. He was telling her—assuring her that the vision was gone. He lifted her face with a hand under her chin.

"Yes," she breathed before his lips covered hers.

Heat coursed through her veins as she opened her mouth to his. Their tongues danced a timeless dance. She pressed her aching breasts against his chest. How long had she longed to be held this way? Forever.

When the need to breathe more deeply forced their lips to separate, Rob blazed a trail of kisses to below her ear. He sucked on her earlobe. She rolled her head back and to the side, insisting on the same treat for the other ear.

"Can I walk you home, Carolyn?"

She blinked her eyes open and saw that his were dark with desire. "Yes," she whispered. He kissed the corners of her mouth and slowly loosened his arms from around her. The breeze from the lake felt cool against her heated skin as they walked down the steps.

Steering her with his arm around her shoulders, they took the lake path so she could retrieve her glass as they passed the rock.

"I've got some more of this wine," she said. "Would you like a glass?"

"Sure."

"Allow me," he offered as he kissed her softly in her cabin minutes later. She curled up on a folded leg on the couch while he got them each a fresh glass of Chardonnay. He sat beside her as they each sipped their wine. He turned the stem of his goblet between his thumb and index finger, staring at the swirling wine.

"I'm surprised it took so long," he said softly after the oddly comfortable silence between them.

"Rob, are we thinking about the same thing here?" Her voice trembled. She'd just seen a ghost she recognized and had been kissed so thoroughly that she felt it to her toes. Now she couldn't tell which he was talking about.

"The lady in white in the house," he said as if her existence was no more astonishing than a grocery list.

Carolyn grasped his arm. His gaze met hers.

"Have you seen her before, Rob? I . . . I mean, we've talked about hearing voices, about some things happening, but we've never talked about actually seeing anyone. You only said you heard a voice and felt the push."

He nodded and went back to watching the wine swirl around in his glass. "I think I've seen her several times. I've just never told anyone." He looked up and their gazes locked. "And if you tell my clients that I see dead people who can evaporate into thin air, or voices when there's no one around, I'm out of business altogether. Nobody would trust the loony lawyer," he added with an effort to laugh.

"If you're loony, so am I."

"Because you've seen her before?"

"Yes, and I've seen others too." She bit her lower lip. "The whole family, in fact, but I was afraid to admit it to myself, much less tell anyone else."

Nothing was as it seemed to be. And nothing between them was simple anymore.

Rob set their glasses on the table at the end of the couch and took her into his arms. "Hey, don't look so worried. This inheritance is your chance to get everything you've ever wanted. You told me that your life-long dream was coming true. Trust me. You shouldn't look so glum."

She had to smile. She wanted to believe him, and when she was this close to him, she wanted more than that.

Rob was different from the other men she'd known. Wasn't he there for her wherever she turned to him? And he'd never pushed to move their relationship to a more intimate level.

Then what was it that still made her question him? Was it still the circumstantial evidence pointing to him as being involved in a scheme against her that kept her from trusting him? She'd tamped down her doubts time and again, but they never seemed to disappear.

"Hold me tight, Rob." She laid her head on his shoulder and slid her arms around his waist. She wanted to forget about the house for a while.

He tightened his arms around her and caressed her back, moving his hand in circles. "There. Is that better?"

"Hmm."

"You can ask me to do this anytime," he added with a chuckle.

She smiled up at him. "Just think, if you'd come to dinner, I never would have gone to Greystone, and all this wouldn't be necessary—to make me feel better, I mean."

"I've got news for you. 'All this,' as you put it, is something I've wanted to do for months." He kissed her. "And I would have come for dinner if I'd known you wanted me here."

She sat up straighter, her arms remaining at his waist. Her gaze captured his. "Haven't you been to your house at all this evening?"

"Sure. We hadn't made plans for tonight so I ate a lonely bowl of soup and a sandwich and then fixed a fishing reel I broke. Then I went for a walk and found you."

"You entered your house through the kitchen door?"

"I always do. Kind of a country custom, I guess you'd say. I never use the formal front door."

"But I left you a note, Rob, inviting you to dinner. I tucked it in your back door. You had to see it."

"Sounds like I should have, but it wasn't there. I'm sorry I didn't see it. What did I miss eating for dinner?" he teased, his eyes wide to make him look eager and hungry.

She playfully slapped his chest. "Fried polliwog tongues."

He laughed, apparently dismissing the lost message. "Yuck. I hate those. Remind me to ask what you're serving before I accept any future dinner invitations."

"You haven't complained about all the others I've fixed for you."

"I wouldn't dare. You might not invite me again." He kissed her briefly on the lips. "But they were all too good to complain about," he added. His watch beeped the hour. "Damn. I didn't realize how late it was. We both have to be up and at 'em early, so I'd best go." He lowered his head to kiss her more deeply.

Knowing it would be the last one, Carolyn lost herself in his kiss. She drew comfort and found pleasure at the same time as his lips caressed hers. Rob seemed as reluctant to separate as she was, but he had the fortitude to do it. If it had been up to her . . .

She said good night and watched until he walked beyond the lighted path. She thought of all the kisses they'd shared during the summer. Some of them had made her sizzle more than the hot weather had. He'd shown her so many ways that he cared for her and that he wanted more. And yet he always stopped before they became intimate. And even with her body aching to make love with him, she'd let him walk home alone. She chuckled. Theirs was an almost Victorian-type relationship.

She frowned. After all this time . . . There had been no reason not to, and yet . . .

Carolyn had a difficult time getting to sleep. She thought about Rob and what she wanted their relationship to be. Finally relaxing into sleep with a smile on her face, she'd decided that the best way to tell him what she'd decided was to show him.

When the sunlight woke her the next morning too early

for the first trucks due at Greystone, she heard only the birds serenading the rising sun.

Or was that the only sound? Lying still, she could make out the familiar "whir . . . plop" and knew at once where Rob was. At least she hoped it was Rob and not one of the other fishermen in the camp.

Showering quickly, she pulled on her jeans and loose shirt and ran to the lake. When she found him, she climbed up on the boulder and sat next to him, her feet dangling over the water.

"I've heard fishermen would rather fish than sleep."

"Good morning." His arm reached around her waist to pull her close as he lowered his lips to hers.

Last night hadn't been her imagination. His kiss brought back all the warm sensations that pooled in her belly. She tasted peppermint and coffee.

"Good morning to you, too," she said moments later as she nipped at his lower lip and then met his tongue with hers for another taste of his morning coffee. She managed to make him forget about fishing so completely as their kiss deepened that he nearly dropped the fishing rod.

"I'd rather do this than fish any day," he volunteered once the rod was secured under his thigh so he could put both arms around her and kiss her again. "Do you really have to go to work today?"

She laughed. "Hmm. I wish I didn't, but how would I explain my absence to the men waiting for me?"

He growled and pulled her head closer and kissed her again. When he raised his head, she smiled. "If that's the way you feel about other men waiting for me, I'll have to mention them more often."

"Or I could throw you into my truck and steal you away from them all."

"And what would I tell them when I got back," she asked with a giggle.

"I didn't intend that you would ever come back," Rob managed before his lips covered hers again.

"You two gonna do that all day, or are you gonna open Greystone so us working stiffs can get in?"

Chapter Ten

"Lars, you're early," an embarrassed Carolyn chided as she scooted out of Rob's arms and off the boulder. She felt a different warmth than she had moments before, this one rising into her cheeks.

"Not by much. You two are just taking your own sweet time, that's all. Mornin', Rob."

"The morning was shaping up just fine until you showed up," Rob complained over his shoulder with a chuckle. He picked up his fishing rod and cast the bait into the water.

Carolyn understood why he didn't want to turn around. She wasn't happy to have Lars see her flushed face. She ran toward her cabin. "Give me time to get my shoes and the keys, Lars. I'll be right there."

"And give Lars a key to the house, will you?" Rob called after her.

"Good idea," she agreed.

Before she got into the cabin she heard Lars teasing Rob. "Hey, I heard real fishermen don't kiss girls. Isn't that right?"

When she returned a minute or two later, Lars had gone on to Greystone. Rob was leaning against the rock, waiting for her.

"Carolyn, wait." She stopped a few feet away and looked at him expectantly. "I want you to promise me something."

He sounded so serious that she worried Lars might have mentioned something that had gone wrong. He stepped closer to her.

"Promise you'll be careful working inside. While you're in Greystone, don't take any chances." He cradled her cheek with his palm. "I don't want anything to happen to you."

She exhaled her relief. "I'll be careful. I promise."

"Good. I care a great deal about you, and I want you safe over there."

She stood on her toes and kissed him tenderly.

"Hmmm. Isn't this where we were before we were interrupted? Maybe we could pick up where we left off and . . ."

A horn beeping at Greystone separated them. Carolyn reluctantly ran off with a wave.

"Can I have a rain check?" he called after her. Their laughter floated away on the breeze.

The screeches of nails being pulled from wood echoed in the empty rooms as the wood moldings were removed for stripping. The intricately cut designs had been slopped with so much paint, the delicate scrollwork had been nearly hidden. Room by room one crew worked on that time-consuming job while another crew took out the old plaster.

Considering that Carolyn had run to work this morning with nothing for breakfast more nutritious than coffee-flavored kisses from Rob, she was delighted when he arrived in his motorboat with sandwiches and cold drinks to share with her for lunch. He motored slowly down the lake so they could enjoy the relaxing ride while they ate.

"With the warm sun and the fresh air, I could fall asleep right here. The gentle waves' lapping at the side of the boat makes it like rocking in a cradle."

"Be my guest," he said as he cut the motor near the middle of the lake.

"Okay, I will," she said with a grin. She adjusted her seat

to the flat position and stretched out. “This is the nicest lunch I’ve had in a long time, Rob. Thanks.”

He plucked a grape from the last bunch in the bag and kneeled down beside her. “Want more dessert?”

He held the grape above her mouth and slid it lightly around her lips, but lifted it quickly when she tried to bite it.

“That tickles,” she said, laughing.

He leaned over her. “Does this help?”

His lips rubbed against hers, stroking back and forth with only light pressure. His hand rested on her midriff, his fingers massaging little circles.

“Hmm. That helps a lot.”

She plucked off his hat and dropped it on his seat so she could thread her fingers through his hair.

“Very thoughtful of you to want to help,” she said as she slipped her arms around his shoulders and pulled him to her. She needed to press her breasts against him.

His arms slid around her as they kissed. One hand found its way under her loose shirt. Circling around to her breast, he slid aside the lace confinement and kneaded it gently. She moaned with pleasure as his thumb swept back and forth across the nipple until it stood firm. She twisted her shoulders to deliver the other breast for his touch.

His lips left hers to trail downward where he teased the tips of her breasts through her shirt with his tongue. She arched her back, insisting that he do more to relieve the delicious ache she felt building within her. He pushed aside the fabric and drew the rosy tip of a breast in his mouth and sucked until she gasped. He dragged his tongue over her sensitive skin to tease the other.

She whispered his name as he lifted his hip onto the narrow seat beside hers. He pressed his pulsing manhood against her thigh. Kissing her, his tongue thrust with the same ancient rhythm that rocked his hips against her.

They fit so perfectly together, but she couldn't get close enough. She slid her hands under his shirt and yanked it off over his head. Pulling him down, she pressed her breasts against his bare chest. This was what she wanted to feel. Hot skin touching hot skin. Not the sun's heat, but the intimate heat their bodies created being together.

The roar of another motorboat engine startled Carolyn. She froze. Kids' laughter and shouts echoed across the lake.

Rob uttered a short, succinct phrase and slid off the seat. He reached for his shirt. Kneeling, he tugged it on and looked for the other boat. "Don't worry. They're not even close."

Carolyn pulled her clothes into place and buttoned up. The boat they'd heard was turning in a big circle near the far shore, towing a skier behind it.

"The Emmetts' grandkids are here," Rob explained.

Carolyn lifted her seat back into the sitting position while Rob slid into his own place behind the wheel. He quickly started the motor and steered back toward his camp.

The noise of the motor made talking impossible. If they shouted, people on shore could probably have heard their voices more easily than they could hear each other.

Carolyn sat back in the cushioned seat and tried to enjoy the ride. The wind whipped her hair around. At least she didn't have to worry about what it looked like when they got to shore. Anyone seeing her would blame the tangles on the boat ride.

But were her cheeks pink from rubbing his? Her lips rosy and swollen from their kisses? Would anyone be able to tell how aroused she'd felt?

She glanced at Rob, but he kept his gaze on the lake ahead of them. As he neared the shore, he slowed the boat. The motor quieted down enough to let them talk without shouting. He reached over and squeezed her hand.

"Don't worry." He glanced at her then. "I thought you'd like to go back to your cabin first, before you go back to work. Am I right?"

She nodded. "Thanks."

They sat in silence for the remainder of the ride to the fishing camp. Two of Rob's camp guests were fishing from lawn chairs they'd set up near the tie-off cleats and caught the rope he tossed. There was no opportunity for her to say anything more to Rob. She just said hi to the fishermen and jogged to her cabin.

How could she have let herself get so carried away out in a boat? Yet she couldn't deny how she'd felt out there. She didn't want to. Not anymore.

After the workers all left for home that afternoon, Carolyn went back through the whole house to check on how much they had accomplished. As usually happened, she was diverted to various cleanup duties that she accomplished as she checked each window. And as she also did each day, she looked to see if any new hiding places that could contain the necklace had been uncovered.

With no permanent wiring or fixtures in place yet, the lights were all portable ones on simple stands made from heavy iron pipes and some clamp-on work lights. She made certain they were all turned off. When the sun dipped behind the hill beyond the lake, it suddenly appeared much darker inside, even though it was not yet officially sunset time.

From the third floor she made her way down the new

back stairway and crossed the second floor to the main stairs to the foyer, a route that passed every room in the house. Nearing the Whitneys' bedrooms, she heard piano music. The workmen often had radios playing while they worked, and she wondered if one had been left on. Or it could have been someone living nearby. Only this music sounded way too close.

Following the sounds toward the balcony, she stopped in front of an open door when a breeze of fresh air swirled around her. Not scented with the dust and rotten plaster she'd been inhaling all day, the air smelled of lilies of the valley. But how? Those flowers bloomed in the spring. How could she be smelling them now?

Counting the rooms from the end, she realized the breeze was coming from Sara's room. With hesitant steps, she crept to the door. The workmen hadn't progressed this far and the windows were shut. However, the air was definitely sweet and fresh.

The mantel and the wood trim on the walls cast odd, long shadows in the harsh illumination of the single work light that stood beyond the fireplace.

Carolyn wiped her damp palms on the sides of her jeans. She took a deep breath and held up her hand to shield her eyes from the glare as she moved toward the light stand.

The breeze became so strong that it ruffled the curls that had worked their way loose from the bandana she wore to protect her hair from plaster dust. Wondering if it was coming from the fireplace flue, she stepped over to check. On the stone flooring in front of the fireplace, she was startled when a slab of slate moved beneath her foot. She jumped back and knelt down to assess any damage.

The mortar around the slab was cracked as if it had been loose for some time. Picking out the loose chunks, she planned to lift the foot-square piece to see if loose bits had worked their way under the slab, causing it to wobble. She got a finger hold on the corner and lifted it to a vertical position.

Balancing the slab on end, she gasped. In a narrow space between the rough-cut boards that supported the slate lay a thin package. It appeared to be wrapped in floral paper, but when she touched the top, she could feel that it was fabric and not paper.

She exhaled and dragged in a deep breath, trying to contain her excitement. Louise had believed that Sara would lead her to the necklace. Carolyn bit her lower lip. Is that what she'd found? Some clue to the mystery?

She flattened her hand against her heart as if she could manually slow the rapid beat. She laid the stone slab in the fireplace for safekeeping and sat back on her heels. She had to laugh at how tense she felt.

She took another deep breath to calm herself, but then frowned. She couldn't imagine why the necklace would be all wrapped up in fabric and hidden in Sara's fireplace. That would mean someone in the house had taken it and hidden it. But why in Sara's room? Sara didn't take the necklace. Carolyn was certain of that. It had to be someone else who thought that Sara's room was the safest place to hide it—or it was someone who wanted to frame Sara.

Carolyn pressed at her temples with her fingers. She had misjudged circumstantial evidence and accused Rob of sabotaging her efforts. Now she was doing it again, trying to draw conclusions from little or no evidence.

She rubbed her damp palms on her thighs and took another steadying breath. Treating it gently, she lifted the package from its hiding place. The unevenness in the shape of the contents told her that whatever it was, it wasn't in a box. She shook it gently to be certain, but heard nothing.

Carolyn slid her hips sideways to sit on the floor and extended her legs out together so she could lay the package on her lap. The floral fabric had been tied with a silk ribbon in a bow. Unable to contain her curiosity a moment longer, she tugged at the end of the ribbon and loosened the wrapping. The fabric slid down and revealed a thin, hand-bound book, not a box containing the necklace.

Carolyn raised her face and nervously laughed out loud as disappointment clobbered her. Her gaze jerked back to the book when she realized it could be just as valuable. It might describe where the necklace would be found.

Her heartbeat sped up as she gingerly lifted the book. The cover seemed to be leather, now stiff and dry with age. She opened the front far enough to see the precise old-fashioned handwriting on the first page.

" 'The Very Private Diary of Sara Whitney,' " she read aloud. "Oh, Sara!"

Carolyn couldn't believe her good luck. If Louise had thought Sara would show her where the emeralds were, then surely this book would describe how she would accomplish the seemingly impossible task of finding them.

She held the book tightly between her breasts. Unable to resist another moment, she tilted her face to the ceiling and whooped a loud "Yahoo!" that echoed throughout the house.

Having no clean place to study it there at Greystone, she decided to take the diary to her cabin. She held her treasure against her midriff and hurried through the remainder of her routine for closing up the house. She walked rapidly along the path through the woods, and almost dropped her keys as she fumbled to open her cabin door one-handed.

Once inside, she set the book on a clean towel she spread

over the table and closed all the drapes against the outside world. Respecting the ancient find, she ran to scrub her dirty hands. After stopping only to turn on the lights, Carolyn returned directly to the table.

The pages were bound between the leather covers with another thin ribbon threaded through holes near the left side. Since the leather was no longer pliable, the front piece would not bend back when opened. Picking at the bowed knots, Carolyn untied the strands of silk, but left them in the holes. Once loose, the stiff cover lifted off the first page. She slowly flipped it over onto the towel like she would the cover of a three-ringed notebook.

She read the title again and swallowed against the excitement that bubbled up inside her. Turning the title page over to lie upon the cover, she began reading the faded script.

Dear Diary,

I have created you to keep me company and share my secrets because I can share them with no one else, save dearest Robert. I shall tell you of my prince who has captured my heart and promised to love me forever.

The confidences granted the diary described Sara's boundless love for Robert. As proper as their relationship had to be in that decade, Carolyn could tell that Sara was quite ecstatic as their summer season together progressed.

She wrote of boat rides on the lake in the family's cedar-strip rowboat with Robert at the oars. Carolyn could picture her riding with her parasol high over her head to deny the sun the opportunity to leave its rosy glow on her cheeks.

Diary, you must never tell that I noticed how strong he is, how broad his shoulders. He kissed me today under the willow tree. I was so filled with happiness and love I thought I would faint.

Carolyn smiled and wondered what it would be like to be so in love, so trusting of a man that she could let herself go and feel that way.

This must have been Sara's last summer at Greystone. She wrote excitedly that Robert was going to ask Lloyd for permission to marry her. Sara never doubted that it would be granted.

She described in detail what her wedding dress would be like, and how beautiful she would feel with her mother's magnificent emerald necklace on for that special day, bringing her good luck.

Near the end, Carolyn read of Lora's death.

Papa is so upset there is no talking to him. He blames the tall chair for tripping Lora as she crossed the balcony to descend the stairs. He's banished them all to a room upstairs. Mama has taken to her bed. Greystone is silent as a tomb except for her weeping. There is nothing I can do to comfort her. Mama and Papa quite ignore me now that their precious Lora is gone. But when I think that I shall never see Lora again, I cannot stem my own tears. I can give no thought to our disagreements. I can only feel loss and grief without her. We must return to the city tomorrow, and I shall not see Robert again this summer, for he is still in Albany. I long to discover where the necklace is hidden to prove Lora was wrong to call him a thief. Oh, Diary, he must be innocent. How can there be any doubt in my heart? And yet I wonder . . . Was my beloved in Greystone when the necklace disappeared?

Sara's final entry was just six sentences.

The services for Lora are in the city on the morrow. Mama's necklace has not been found. Papa still forbids me to see Robert, and he refused him entrance when he rushed back to Lakeside to see me. Papa would not even accept Robert's expression of sympathy. My heart is broken, but I cannot stop loving him. I'm so confused, I don't know whom to believe or trust.

The passage brought tears to Carolyn's eyes. Until recently she hadn't known very much about Sara except that they shared a name. Quite unprepared for her own empathetic reaction, Carolyn found that the pain she felt for Sara was real enough to be her own.

A sob choked Carolyn. She rose to go splash water on her face. Drying her cheeks, she looked into the mirror at her reddened eyes. "Oh, Sara," she said as if it were Sara in the mirror listening. "I know what it's like to want to trust a man and not be able to because of a nagging doubt. Your doubt leaves you bewildered, and you don't know whom to believe. You . . . No, this is about me now. I need to believe in him, Sara. I need to believe in Rob. I must be able to trust him. I could never let him know I love him until I'm certain I can trust him with my heart."

The knock at the door elicited a startled cry. Patting her face once more, but knowing she couldn't hide her red eyes, she answered the door.

Rob stood on the porch. "What's wrong?" he asked, pulling her into his arms without hesitation.

Sobs overwhelmed her again and kept Carolyn from doing anything but holding him tight. When her trembling had ceased and he'd kissed away her tears, she showed him the diary. Curling up on the couch near him, she waited while he read every word.

"It's so sad," she told him. "Sara must have died without ever seeing Robert again. We know they never learned what had happened to the necklace."

Her breath caught and Rob moved to her side and held her close. "You can't change that, Carolyn. You can't go back and make Sara happy."

"I know, I know. But I think that now I need to find the necklace so that I can know what happened to it."

"Then we would both know," he said in a whisper as he kissed her tenderly. "It would mean a lot to me to prove that Robert didn't take it."

She pulled his head down and met his kiss eagerly. "Hold me, Rob. Hold me tight," she pleaded moments later.

"I want to hold you. More than anything. I want to hold you all night, if you'll let me, darling."

She wrapped her arms around his neck and gave him her answer. "Yes. You must. Don't leave me tonight."

Their lips met and melded. Their tongues curled around each other and dove to taste the hungry desire exploding within them both.

Carolyn had enough of fear and sadness for now. She longed only for caring and loving. She wanted Rob.

The movement of his shoulder muscles under her palms as his warm hands caressed the curves of her back and hips enticed her. When his hands found the heavy softness of her breasts, she moaned. His thumbs circled and teased the hardening tips. Her shirt came off over her head and her bra quickly followed it. His eager mouth traveled the path his hands had taken.

Her trembling fingers worked the buttons on his shirt

until they were all open. She circled the firm planes of his chest with the pads of her fingers and reached up to push the shirt off his shoulders. Her captive for a moment, restrained in the buttoned cuffs, she kissed him hungrily before he yanked the shirt from his wrists to free his arms to hold her. The buttons bounced on the vinyl-covered floor.

When the tide of their lovemaking was poised to carry them out to sea on a wave from which there could be no escape, he lifted his head an inch or two. His hands that had brought new luscious excitement to her body stilled.

"Carolyn, I'm flesh and blood, not a ghost."

"I know," she whispered with a smile. "You feel too warm in my arms to be a ghost. Too warm and definitely too hard." She rocked side to side, rubbing her breasts against his chest.

"And hot. Hot is how I feel right now." His breath tickled her ear. "What I mean is . . . I'm a warm-blooded creature who's getting much warmer every minute near you. I've wanted you since the moment I saw you. I can't take much more of this and still be able to pull back."

He kissed her smile. "I wasn't sure what you wanted our relationship to be, and I've been struggling against my desire for you for weeks to give you all the time you needed. You've had so much on your mind, but you have another decision to make here and now. It's up to you, but you've got to tell me now if you want me to stop. Because if you don't, I will make you mine."

Floating in a whirlwind of emotions, Carolyn was amazed he was still in control. She gazed into his eyes darkened with desire and knew there was only one decision she could make. "Rob?"

"Hmm?" he asked, his gaze never having left hers.

"Make love with me."

Those were the last words spoken until after they were propelled together to a place that not even their imaginations could improve. Clinging to each other, they experienced anew the thrills of loving that were older than Lost Lake.

Much later, satiated and happy but barely awake, they lay nestled in each other's arms in Carolyn's bed.

"This bed is too small," Rob grumbled when he knocked his toes on the footboard.

"You should complain to the management," she said sleepily.

With a chuckle, he pulled the light cover over them against the chill of a cool summer night in the woods by a lake.

"Carolyn?"

"What is it this time?" she asked, trying to sound annoyed when she felt completely content.

"I think we've stumbled onto something else I like better than fishing."

Their laughter echoed over the water with the delicate strains of a sweet Brahms lullaby played softly on the piano.

Carolyn didn't question the origin of the music as she fell asleep, feeling safe in Rob's arms.

Chapter Eleven

Carolyn continued her rounds at Greystone, but made no more discoveries under loose slabs of slate. It hadn't been for lack of trying. After the workmen left each day, she devoted more and more time to her never-ending search for the necklace.

Her search was not without some success. She discovered another secret compartment in Lloyd's bedroom, but it was empty. If the necklace had been put there for safekeeping and Alice had forgotten putting it there, it was long gone. But finding such a hidden niche was enough reinforcement of her search methods to keep her looking for longer and longer periods.

When her hunger drove her to quit one night, she headed down the second-floor hall. Coming out onto the balcony over the entrance foyer, she stopped to pick up some finishing nails someone had dropped on the hardwood floor. She didn't want them to further mar the surface.

She smiled when she heard the piano music floating up the stairs. At once, she felt comforted by the soft strains. She listened a moment and then moved quickly to the head of the wide staircase to see if it gave her clear sight lines into the front room. Would she actually see Sara playing tonight? She leaned over the railing for a better view, but she could see nothing. Moving to the head of the stairs, she leaned over to look again.

Unexpectedly the melody stopped. A misplayed chord was struck loudly as if all ten fingers of the player had been slapped against the keys at once.

As Carolyn straightened to run down the stairs to investigate, something behind her caught her eye. She instinctively ducked at the waist to avoid whatever it was coming at her, but she couldn't dodge it. A powerful force rammed into her shoulder. She cried out as she lost her balance and fell. To break her fall, she lunged for the banister, but her hand swung by it—empty. The stairs came up rapidly. She tried to tuck and roll. Pain enveloped her.

When her forward momentum stopped, she had plummeted half way down. And she wasn't alone. On the bare steps above her, she recognized an image she'd seen there before.

Lora.

Lora was laughing. Her ugly, evil-sounding laugh echoed in the high-ceilinged foyer.

Carolyn realized the specter was laughing at her! To see such power from beyond the grave enjoy hurting someone was more frightening than having been hurt.

How could Carolyn protect herself against such power? Until she figured that out, her only avenue was escape from Greystone. Trying to sit up, she yelped as the movement sent searing pain through her back. She could feel where each of the steps had left a broad and painful imprint. Closing her eyes, she swallowed the tears that had come with the pain.

Keeping her eyes closed blinded her to the danger so near her, but she could convince herself that she'd just tripped and fallen. Lora didn't exist. Not today.

Strangely, after a few moments, Carolyn felt no more pain. Though her head throbbed, the rest of her body felt only chilled. When she tried to move her hand to press on her aching temple, she couldn't make her arm move.

As the panic that she'd been holding at bay rose within her, she opened her eyes, but she couldn't see anything! Instead of Lora, or the stairs, or the foyer, all she saw were dark shapes swirling around her. She no longer heard Lora's laughter. She only heard the pounding of her own heart. Waves of nausea rose within her. She swallowed past her fear to repress it. At least she could swallow. And she could do more. She had to.

She had to get help. She tried to call out, but no sound came from her throat. She couldn't tell if her eyes were open or shut. The faces of everyone she knew swarmed in the darkness around her along with the faces of Lora, Sara, Robert, and dear Aunt Louise.

Somebody help me, she wanted to scream. But an inner voice answered her only with questions. Who could help her? Whom could she trust? Every time she reached out to one of the familiar faces, it would disappear and elude her reach.

Of all the faces, she saw none she could trust. Not even Rob. They all abandoned her. She was completely alone.

Greystone felt cold despite the summer heat, she thought—her last thought before all the faces she saw swirled into total blackness.

"Carolyn! Carolyn! Darling, are you all right? Can you move?"

Carolyn heard Rob's voice calling her name and groaned. At first he sounded very far away. "Help me," she rasped through lips that would barely move.

Valiantly struggling to blink her eyes open, she saw him kneeling right beside her. His wide-beam lantern provided the only light in the cavernous space. The area behind him looked black as velvet.

"Where are we?" she managed to ask. She closed her eyes and grimaced with her effort to move her head.

"Greystone. It's just past dark. We just got in from fishing, and I didn't see a light on in the cabin. Since I'd promised you fish for dinner, I came to find you. Can you move?"

"I don't know. Everything hurts. What happened?"

"I was hoping you would tell me. But right now, will you be okay for a few minutes while I run to call an ambulance to get you to the hospital?"

"No. Wait. Let me try to sit up and see how I am." After the few minutes required to test her limbs, she concluded that nothing was broken, just very painful. "I think I'm going to have black and blue marks where I didn't even think I could get them," she tried to jest, feeling extremely relieved that Rob had found her.

Once she showed evidence she could move, Rob helped her to sit up and lean on him. "Just rest a minute before you try to get up. Do you remember what happened?"

The warmth of his firm chest as she leaned against him felt so good. She laid her hand on his arm. The hairs tickled the pads of her fingers. She smiled, knowing she could feel something other than fear and pain. Tears stung her eyes as relief nearly overwhelmed her. "I was just closing up and checking everything like I always do when I heard the piano music again. I was standing up there by the banister."

She moved her hand to point and was relieved that she could move it without pain. She didn't hold any hope of being able to do the same with the other arm. That shoulder ached.

"I was pushed from behind. I guess I managed to roll down sideways. I probably would have broken my neck in the fall like . . ."

"Pushed?"

Carolyn turned her head to meet his gaze. She nodded. "Definitely pushed."

"Damn it, no! This can't be happening."

"I think I'm getting scared again, Rob. Thinking that some shy lady was playing a piano and watching the workers or that a friendly ghost directed me to a diary? Fine. I mean, I enjoy the funny ghost cartoons like everyone else. But falling chimneys and being pushed down the stairs are quite different matters."

"You got that right."

"Do you think she got mad because the men took their big toy trucks she used to watch and went home? Maybe I could leave her a note with the construction company address. She could go there and watch all she wants and leave me alone."

Rob cut through her nervous ramblings. "You haven't lost your sense of humor. You must be okay. Come on, let's get you back to your cabin."

He helped her up, stopping only long enough for her to lock the door on the way out. At her cabin Carolyn groaned with the effort needed to climb the two steps.

Once inside, Rob enfolded her stiff body in his arms. "I'm so glad I came looking for you."

"Me too. Did a lady in the white dress tell you I needed you?" she asked with a laugh, but one look at his face and she wasn't laughing. "It's not funny anymore, is it?"

Rob ran his hand through his hair and said nothing.

"I'm glad I had Sara to thank for slamming her hands down on the piano keys to startle me into noticing that something was coming up behind me." Carolyn hated to leave Rob's arms, but she had to. "I'm going to soak in a warm tub."

"Good idea," he told her. "You go soak until your muscles feel better, and I'll get dinner started."

In the tub Carolyn thought about Sara, the helpful ghost. She pictured her as the one who seemed to be there when they needed her the most.

But what was the force doing the damage and trying to hurt people? She remembered that Lora had appeared after she fell. Had she pushed her? How could that be?

The force against her shoulder blade had felt strong as flesh and blood. And no weakling had made the chimney crumble, or pulled down slabs of plaster. What spirit wielded that much power?

Carolyn's hand went to her mouth. Was there a third spirit involved here? She'd heard a man's voice call to Sara. Could another spirit, perhaps the spirit of Robert, be stronger than she guessed the sisters to be? He sure had a right to be angry enough to be causing the problems. But why would he be angry with her? She was trying to find the necklace to clear his name.

Carolyn, get a grip, she told herself. *You're talking about ghosts as if they were able to act in the live world.*

But if not a ghost, what was it then? Was there a live person involved here? Carolyn didn't want to suspect Rob. Could there be someone else?

Definitely not Thomas. He was too old to carry out any of the "accidents." And John wouldn't do it. He appeared to be the model of an honest and dignified lawyer. Besides, he wasn't at Greystone enough to set anything up. Who else was around here?

When she made mental lists, they always came down to the same people. The one heading the lists was Rob. He . . . No, she wasn't going to go there with her thinking. Not tonight.

Damn, trying to make sense of it all only made it appear

more muddled, and while the bath's hot water made her sore body feel better, it did nothing to clarify what had happened. Thinking about it constantly didn't bring her any closer to the answers. Taking her mind off it for the night seemed to be the best thing to do. At least her head didn't hurt anymore, she realized as she rose from the tepid water to dry off.

Wrapped in her terry robe, Carolyn dried her hair and finally appeared back in the kitchen. "How close are you to dinner time? Time for me to get dressed?"

"Given a choice of eating or you not dressed, I'd be a fool to prefer a meal," Rob answered as he folded his arms around her. His kiss was warm and inviting. "Tell you what. You put on enough to be decent, and I'm taking you up to my house. My bed's king size, plenty of room to give you a massage to soothe your aching muscles."

She RSVPed his inviting kiss with one of her own. After she managed to throw on clean slacks and a knit shirt, they left.

Rob broiled two trout, which they ate with a delicious fresh vegetable salad and raspberry vinaigrette dressing.

"This is great with you doing most of the work," Carolyn told him lightly. "Could you wait on me every night?"

His eyes darkened a moment and then he smiled, but the smile didn't reach his eyes. She frowned and wondered what she'd said that had upset him. She rose to help with the dishes, but when she leaned over to clear the table, she winced.

"What's wrong?" Rob was at her side at once, his expression filled with concern.

"My shoulder." She unbuttoned her shirt and slipped it off her shoulder to see what the problem was.

"You've got a purple bruise that's growing darker by the

minute on the back outside of your upper arm," he reported, his brow knit with concern. "To bed with you! I'd carry you, but I'd probably hurt your bruises more than if you walked."

"I'm not sick, Rob. You don't have to put me to bed," she teased. His chuckle rumbled in his chest as he hugged her.

"That's not why I'm putting you to bed." He kissed her ever so tenderly. "I'm the doctor and you're the patient. I'm going to locate all your bruises and kiss each one away."

She quivered with anticipation. "Well, in that case, I think you should begin with the one that I have right here on my lower lip," she suggested as she let the shirt drop to the floor and slipped her arms around his neck.

Doctor Rob took care of kissing that one and all the others they found together. And as Carolyn was falling asleep in his arms an hour or two later, she heard a soft piano sonata.

Rob had been right. Sound did carry a long, long way.

Though stiff and aching from the fall, Carolyn rolled out of Rob's bed the next morning to get back on the job on time. He insisted she not leave his house until they'd both had a good breakfast. Since Lars had a key to Greystone now, appearing later was no problem for her.

To top that, dressed in his work clothes, Rob announced that he was going to keep her company today.

Carolyn watched his nonchalant act with one raised eyebrow and her hands resting on her hips. "I'll be okay, Rob. You don't have to come to keep an eye on me. Besides, there's no way that you're going to protect me from everything."

He stepped close, but didn't touch her. "I'd just feel better being there. I can't stand to see you hurt, Carolyn. It hurts me." He slid the back of his bent fingers over her cheek. She turned her head and kissed his knuckles.

The look in his eyes told her he wouldn't settle for less than at least a compromise. They finally agreed Rob would show up at Greystone more often, but at randomly selected times instead of the same time each day.

"That way there won't be any pattern to when you're there," she explained.

"No one would try anything funny if they suspected I might show up any minute, huh? Yeah, that might just work."

Carolyn didn't want to have a part-time bodyguard, especially not Rob. But every place she hurt reminded her of the stairs she'd bounced down the previous night.

However, if they were dealing with the supernatural, what could Rob do except make her feel better by being around? If it were someone else and not ghosts causing all the accidents, having him around Greystone wouldn't be all bad either, she decided.

"Carolyn, Dad would like to see the progress at Greystone in person," John Ashford told Carolyn the following week. "From what Rob has told us, it sounds like it's coming along nicely."

Happy to oblige them, she arranged to meet the senior members of the Ashford law firm at the mansion on Saturday afternoon. She felt excited and anxious to show them around.

She worried though. She couldn't imagine Thomas attempting any stairs, and the elevator was not yet functional. She brought some lawn chairs borrowed from Rob's cabins into the house to allow her guests a clean surface on which to sit if they wished. Thomas could wait seated while the others went upstairs.

As it turned out, Thomas managed a short tour of part of the main floor and then seated himself in what had been the front parlor. Carolyn began to describe how that room plus the former dining room together would create the inn's dining area.

"Carolyn, while you explain that to Dad, I'd like to walk around upstairs with Rob," John said. "That okay?"

"Sure, but while you're both up there, could you do me a favor? I opened some windows on the second floor to bring in fresh air that wasn't white with plaster dust for you. Could you shut them when you're done? It's supposed to rain tonight, and we don't want water damage."

"Sure thing. Take good care of her, Grandpa," Rob kidded with a smile.

"Go right ahead and don't worry about us. Carolyn and I will chat and listen to the music," Thomas said easily.

Rob glanced quickly at Carolyn and then back at Thomas. Her tiny shrug told him she hadn't heard anything. Yet. Rob jogged across the foyer to catch up with his father, and Carolyn began describing the restaurant dining area plans to Thomas.

After hearing all about it, Thomas wanted to see the other end of the dining space where it would lead to the kitchen. The two of them were just turning to go back to their seats when the soft piano music began.

"Doesn't she play beautifully? Uncle Robert used to talk about how she would play for him." A little smile brightened his face. "I guess she still does."

Carolyn was speechless. Thomas could hear the music that she'd been attributing to Sara. And he was talking about Sara as if she were a friend in the room with them.

They'd stepped through into the archway when she was aware that Thomas was getting more unsteady on his feet. She reached to take his elbow to aid in supporting him as he shuffled across the room toward the chairs. Just then a woman in white came into view near the front window.

Sara. She was playing her piano, but a moment later she rose. She looked from them to the foyer and back to them in an agitated manner. Carolyn had little time to wonder what was wrong when the back of Sara's hand flew to her mouth and her eyes widened. Was she surprised? Or frightened?

Before Carolyn could decide, Sara seemed to go out of focus and disappeared like steam rising into cooler air.

"Oh, dear," Thomas said. "Trouble's a-brewing."

The next moment there was a shout and a heavy thump coming from upstairs.

"Come on, Mr. Ashford," Carolyn urged, not wanting to leave Thomas standing on his own. "We'll get you to a chair, and then I'll run upstairs to see what the ruckus is all about." She tried to maintain a calm demeanor to reassure him, but actually she was afraid to leave him. His arms and legs were trembling. She couldn't tell if he was extremely tired or if he was trembling apprehensively. "Will you be all right if I leave you for a few minutes?"

"Yes, dear. You needn't look so worried. I'm just tired. Sara will return soon to keep me company until you get back. I'll be just fine."

He looked less pale now that he was seated, and Carolyn felt better about leaving him. She ran out of the room and up the stairs. "Rob?" she called. "Rob, where are you?"

"In here, Carolyn," John called from the master bedroom. She found Rob on the floor holding his ankle, and

John helping him take off his sock. His shoe lay a short distance away.

"What happened?" She ran to his side and knelt next to him with her hand resting on his shoulder blade.

"He nearly fell out the window, that's what happened," John offered tersely.

"What? Rob, are you all right?"

"It wasn't that bad, Dad. Don't scare Carolyn."

"Then you tell me," she ordered deliberately. "Tell me what happened." The look she gave him added, "And it had better be the truth and the whole truth."

"The window with the refuse chute leading to the trash bin was open."

"I didn't open that one. It wouldn't bring in any fresh air."

"Well, it was wide open and I couldn't get it to close. I climbed up on the sill to get better leverage and I . . ." He glanced at his father and then back at Carolyn. "I came close to losing my balance. I grabbed at the frame to keep from falling out, and I fell in onto the floor instead. I landed wrong and ended up twisting my ankle. Hurts like hell actually."

His expression told her that he had more to say later—when his father wasn't with them. John had pulled his sock off, and they all could see Rob's ankle was swelling and turning blue and red already.

"Is it broken?" she asked.

With gritted teeth, Rob wiggled his toes and rotated his ankle. "No, I'm sure it'll be okay. Just a sprain."

"Good. But we've got to get you home and get ice on that," Carolyn responded.

They helped him up and Rob hopped on one foot with an arm around each of their shoulders. It was a slow process, but they eventually made it to the foyer.

Thomas had risen to meet them at the door. He didn't seem to require an explanation of what had happened upstairs. With more energy than Carolyn had seen him display before, he went out the front entrance ahead of them to open the car door so Rob could climb in.

Carolyn took a minute to close up the house before John drove them right up to Rob's kitchen door. She and John practically carried him in to his couch.

"I'll get some ice to keep down the swelling," Carolyn volunteered immediately.

"There are freezer bags in the drawer beside the sink that zip shut. They won't leak when the ice melts."

She reappeared moments later with a bag of ice to see that John had pulled the footstool over and put it under Rob's leg. She watched as John looked more closely at the swelling ankle.

"It doesn't look good. You're sure nothing's broken? I can still drive you to the hospital for an X-ray," John offered.

"No, Dad, I'm fine. It hurts, but I can move all the toes. See?" He wiggled them all again and then tried to turn the ankle. "Ouch!"

John looked worried, but Rob assured him the ice was all he needed.

"Well, if you don't need my help, then I should get Dad home. This has been a lot of excitement for him. You're sure you'll be all right, Rob?"

"Don't worry. Carolyn will take good care of me, won't you—ow!" He yelled at the moment she placed the ice pack on his ankle. "That's damned cold."

"Yeah, it's the way they make the ice these days," she answered with a grin.

"Some nurse you are. You've got no sympathy for the patient."

"Well, I can see you two will be fine," John concluded with a strained chuckle. "Don't let him give you any trouble, Carolyn."

"I'll go out with you to say good night to Thomas," she responded.

Exhausted by his excursion to Greystone, Thomas had fallen asleep in the back seat. He awoke when John climbed in the front. "How's Rob?" Thomas asked immediately, his voice filled with concern. He turned to Carolyn who stood outside the open car window. "Can you tell what's wrong with his foot?"

"He'll be fine. He's certain it's just a sprain. Don't you worry. I'll take good care of him."

Thomas smiled. "I know you will, dear. I've known that all along."

They all said good night, and John drove off. Before the car disappeared into the woods, Carolyn sent a little wave to Thomas and he returned it. He always made her smile. Before today she knew he was a sweet old man, but now she knew something else. She knew that he was one of them—three of them. They all could see the figures and hear the music. She didn't know what that meant, however.

Suddenly she grew more wary. She prayed that it didn't mean Thomas would suffer an "accident" like those happening to her and Rob at Greystone.

Still occupied with her thoughts, she directed her steps toward the house. She and Rob were going to have a long talk.

Chapter Twelve

Detouring to grab a hand towel from the bathroom, Carolyn returned to see Rob sneaking the ice bag back onto his foot.

"I saw that," she said with a grin. "It won't help if you take it off, silly."

"Hell, it's cold!" he complained. "It hurts more than the sprained ankle."

"I've brought this to put under the bag to make it more comfortable." She draped the towel over his foot.

"Thanks. You're all heart," he responded.

"It'll come in handy, too, in case the bag springs a leak." She steadied the ice pack over the bruised area and then sat next to him. She took his hand and idly stroked it. She looked up and their gazes locked. "Okay. You first. What really happened up there?"

He sighed and gave her hand a squeeze. "It was just about the way I said it. All except for the fact I didn't lose my balance. I was pushed. Something—or someone—wanted me out that window, but the only people in the room were Dad and me. With the refuse chute attached to the window frame, I would have tumbled into the bin of plaster chunks and pieces of lumber. What if I'd hit a nail or fallen head first, or been stabbed by a broken . . ."

"Stop!" Carolyn groaned and laid her cheek against the back of his hand. "I can't bear to think about that."

"I grabbed the frame like I said and pushed backwards so I fell inwards. I came down on my foot the wrong way and sprained my ankle."

"Did John see what happened?"

"I think he believes I just lost my balance. Hell, I didn't see anything . . . It all happened so fast, I only felt it. Then Dad tried to help me up, and I discovered my ankle hurt. I don't think Dad saw anything. He never has."

"No, not him."

"What do you mean, 'not him'?"

"Your grandfather might have, if he'd been there. He saw Sara in the parlor today. In fact, we both saw Sara, and we both heard her play briefly at the piano. She got very agitated and disappeared at about the time we heard you fall. After that he told me to go see what was happening to you because Sara would return to keep him company."

"God, I didn't think he'd mention her to you. I thought I was the only one he talked to about seeing Sara."

Carolyn shrugged. "He seemed to take for granted that I saw her, too."

"But if Sara was playing for you, I wonder who or what tried to push me out the window? And why?"

"Sara wouldn't do something like that," Carolyn insisted. "She always seems to be shy and friendly, or at the very worst, agitated. I'd never describe her as threatening."

"Okay, but where does that leave us?"

"If Sara's the good ghost haunting this house, then who or what's the bad force?" Carolyn thought about it a minute before she lifted her head and looked into his eyes. "I've been thinking about that a lot." She wondered if she should voice her conjectures. "Um, you don't suppose Ro . . ."

"No, I don't think I want to hear what you are about to say," he warned, holding his hand up, palm out. "And we shouldn't even talk about Sara as if she was really there this afternoon and these appearances were facts. There could be other explanations."

"But you said . . ."

"This whole thing is getting out of control," Rob insisted. "All I ever said was that I thought I heard voices."

"Well, who else are we going to suspect? Your father? Lars? Maybe Tiny? What if his grandmother was a maid who stole the necklace, and now he's covering up her crime?"

Rob laughed, but whatever they were getting into was frightening her more, and she didn't like the feeling. "No, don't answer any of those," she said suddenly. "We are just two people . . . no, three if you count your grandpa. We're three people with very vivid imaginations. Someone was probably playing the radio loud and the sound carried in through the open windows."

"And Grandpa is very old and might see people who have been dead for years all the time because his mind isn't what it used to be. That's all."

"A very logical explanation," she said, nodding and wishing she could accept it. "Just manifestations of our imaginations!" She slapped her thighs to punctuate her conclusions. "Right!"

"Yes," he agreed and reached to lay his hand over hers.

They were both silent a moment. They stared at their hands and laced their fingers together.

"Carolyn?"

"No."

"Me neither. I don't believe a word of our conclusions."

"Rob?"

"Hmm?"

"Should I be frightened for my life?"

"I certainly hope not."

"I hate not knowing what is going on. Your grandfather identified Sara by name. Today was the closest I've been to her, and I felt no fear. I wonder why I'm not scared—of her, at least. There's got to be something else going on, too. I'm not so sure we shouldn't be afraid of . . . of that, whatever the other person or force is."

"It's easy to be afraid of what you don't know."

She nodded. "But if we did know . . . If Sara is a benevolent spirit, the choice for the role of malevolent spirit isn't too hard to narrow down. It was very strong like a man and . . ."

Rob cut her off suddenly by kissing her soundly. "I'm hungry, Carolyn."

"Hungry?" She pulled her hand from his and looked at him incredulously. "But I was just saying . . ."

"Yeah, hungry for you and for dinner."

Carolyn rolled her eyes. "Rob, not talking about it won't make it go away."

"What'll it be? The kitchen or the bedroom?"

That got a laugh out of her and broke the tension. "Okay. Okay. I love it when you talk sexy." She playfully punched his arm and resigned herself to postponing their discussion of the paranormal. When Rob was feeling better, she would ask him why he wouldn't talk about it.

As the evening passed, Carolyn rounded up supper for the two of them while Rob sat with his foot up.

"I think you should stay here until morning, Carolyn. I might need help getting up during the night." He sounded so innocent, but he couldn't fool her for a minute. She already knew he was an excellent actor.

"You've never had a problem getting up before," she said sweetly, but fully intending the double meaning.

Rob laughed, failing completely in his attempt to keep a

straight face. But he did eventually manage to convince her to stay.

They made no further mention of the ethereal figures in Greystone, but that didn't mean Carolyn had stopped thinking about them. Had Rob cut off her discussion of them because he didn't want to face the fact that the strong spirit doing the harm could be Robert's?

She wondered about the land on which his fishing camp was built. Was that the land Robert was trying to buy for his and Sara's home? How had Rob come to own it? He'd never volunteered that information to her, and she hadn't asked.

And why do I keep coming up with reasons to be suspicious of Rob? I must stop that, she told herself as sleep finally came.

The next morning Rob's foot appeared even more colorful and so swollen that they had no hope of getting a sock over it.

"It looks like it must really hurt," Carolyn said.

"Only when I put my weight on it, or try to bend the ankle, or move my toes up or down, or . . ."

"Okay, I get the point. Time for a vacation for you. Honestly, what some people will do to get out of working."

Her teasing did nothing to make Rob look contrite. In fact, he looked as if he was enjoying being waited on. He seemed to like the wash down Carolyn gave him in the shower the best. They nearly ran out of hot water by the time they were done.

John wisely waited until late morning to call. Rob described his ankle, and his dad finally convinced him to drive to the hospital and have it X-rayed after all. Carolyn volunteered to take him.

"Just as I had expected. No breaks, just a bad sprain,"

the radiologist told them after the X-rays were developed.

"At least we know for sure," Carolyn noted.

The doctor prescribed crutches and a mild pain reliever. "Stay off your foot for at least a week or longer until the pain and swelling subside," he told Rob.

"Not being able to walk is a good excuse for taking the rest of the day off," Rob announced on the way home.

"It's a weekend, Rob. We don't have to work."

"Oh. Here I'd thought up great ways of passing the day with you, and they were going to be all the more special because it would be like sneaking a day off."

"Tell me about them. I'll bet we can think of ways to make them very special—and not hurt your ankle either."

As it turned out, Carolyn was right. The weekend that had begun so badly ended wonderfully. However, Rob's return to work on crutches Monday morning began the reign of terror of King Rob the First.

While Carolyn opened up the windows and answered questions the crews had, Rob made his way into the former parlor and established himself in a chaise brought over from his cabins.

With his ankle comfortably elevated, he wanted to try to be useful. By noon, however, the restorers, using the room for working on stripping the wooden molding, requested that he be moved. They'd wasted too much time getting things for him to do.

Monarch Rob did not take being deposed very well.

"Rob, come sit in the foyer where you can watch me chip the thick paint from the wood molding around the hall windows on the balcony. Or if you don't have work from your office, you could look through the fabric sample books and tell me which ones you like," Carolyn teased. He groaned. "Are you sure you wouldn't rather be out fishing? You could sit on the dock or in your boat with your foot up."

"Hmph!" was her only answer as he maneuvered across the foyer on his crutches. She slid the chaise to the foot of the stairs.

"What are you going to chip paint for?" Rob asked as he got his ankle comfortable. "Haven't you got enough to do? Hire more workers if you need them. You don't have to do that stuff."

"I know. I just feel I want to do this. It could be fun, you know."

"Where will you be working?"

"Up there," she said, pointing at the picture molding near the ceiling all around the balcony and over the stairs where the giant portraits of the family once hung suspended on wires. "The rail doesn't have to be removed. The plaster behind it was in good shape and the length of wood isn't so intricate as to warrant special stripping. However, there was so much paint glopped in there years ago that some picture hooks are even permanently imbedded—there where those loose wires dangle down along the wall," she pointed out.

"Isn't there something lower down that you could do? How about the baseboard?"

"Why, Rob, I do believe you're worried about me. That's sweet. Anyway, it should go quickly. Lars gave me this neat scraper with a wooden handle that's sharp on the inside of the hook end and at the point. See? Slick, huh?"

"Looks sharp."

"Yeah. It has to be."

She climbed up the ladder that Lars had set up for her at the end of the balcony. "See? The curve of the hook hugs the top of the molding, scrapes it clean, and empties the trough above it. Presto! It's ready for painting."

"I'll admit you make it look simple," Rob called. "But

really, you don't have to do the scraping. Why do you want to work chipping paint yourself? It's dangerous."

"I don't understand either. Every time I try to go back to the cabin to finish the decorating plans, something pulls me over here again." She shrugged. "But hey. It could be fun."

Rob grumbled something Carolyn couldn't hear as she worked in earnest to clean the rail. Before long, she'd finished past the windows, and she had to move the ladder around the corner to the wall leading to the stairway. When she was half way to the top step, Lars and his crew were breaking for lunch and walked down behind her.

"When you get that far," Lars said, pointing to the rail over the top step, "I'll show you how to change the length of one of the ladder legs so you can set them up on the stairs. That way the ladder will be level like on the flat floor."

"I'm not sure I like the sound of that." She chewed on her lower lip and looked up at the rail. It looked higher now for some reason.

"I hope you're not afraid of heights," one of the other men taunted with a laugh. "By the time you get to the bottom of the steps, you'll be over two stories up by today's standards."

"I'm so glad you mentioned that," Carolyn retorted with a faked smile. She didn't add that it felt even higher from the top of the ladder looking down.

"You can't be serious, Carolyn," Royal Rob said from his chaise/throne at the foot of the stairs. "Let one of the men do the part over the steps. They're used to hanging from ladders like monkeys. You only have to supervise the work, not do it."

Carolyn had been willing to let someone else work over the steps, but now she felt annoyed that Rob was telling her what to do, and telling her in front of the other men. Her annoyance grew to anger, and she decided she wanted to make him understand so he wouldn't do it again.

Instead of immediately responding to Rob, she urged Lars to go ahead with his lunch for now. "But I want you to show me how to fix the ladder legs when I finish over to the first step."

Carolyn could feel the visual daggers that Rob was sending Lars as he passed his chaise.

Lars nodded. "She's one hard-workin' lady," he told Rob as he descended the steps. "She got as much done as one of my men would have, and she still had time to check how much was getting done in the rest of the house."

Carolyn could see Rob's puzzled frown. They both knew she'd worked where he'd been watching her all morning, but they said nothing as Lars continued.

"The guys respect her all the more for workin' alongside 'em. I was worried, but it seems to be workin' out with the boss-lady on the crew," he teased, ducking as if she might throw something. Laughing all the way, he jogged out of the house to eat with his men by the lake.

"And to think I thanked the man," Carolyn called after him. She carefully hung the hook over the end of one of the lower rungs on the ladder where she hoped no one would disturb it. It was too sharp to carry in her pocket, and she didn't have a leather tool belt to store it in.

She handed Rob his crutches from where they leaned against the wall behind the chaise. Her attention was drawn up to the hall beyond the balcony on the second floor. She thought she saw someone slipping back into the hall. But who could have been up there? All the workmen had knocked off for lunch. Getting the shivers wasn't the same as being frightened, she hoped.

"Thank God for lunch break," Rob said, standing up and placing the crutches under his armpits. "I'm tired of sitting all morning."

"Rob, has everyone left for lunch?"

"Yeah, I think so. Why?"

"Oh, nothing. Need any help getting to the car?"

Rob shook his head and maneuvered his way without help. She decided not to mention the figure upstairs. One of the workmen probably went back up for his forgotten lunch.

She waited for Rob to slam his door before she started the van and pulled out of the driveway. He yawned and leaned his head against the back of the seat.

"Why don't you take a nap after lunch?"

"As much as I like the idea, I can't." He looked across the seat at her. "Unless you'll join me," he said softly, his face hopeful.

Carolyn smiled. "You know I can't."

"Hon, the will didn't say you have to be there every minute. You can take an hour off."

Carolyn was hurt by the sudden exasperation in his voice. By contrast, hers was very soft. "Why don't you say what you really mean, Rob?"

"What are you talking about?"

"You don't want me on that ladder over the steps, but you'll agree that it would be safe for one of the men on the crew."

After a hesitation he admitted she was right. "Can you blame me for not wanting to see you get hurt?"

"No, of course not. But Rob, you can't protect me every minute of the day and night like you've been trying to do. I have to do my own thing. I am not weak, sheltered Sara who wouldn't dream of doing anything without Lloyd's or

Robert's permission. I'm not like that. No one is going to dictate to me what I can or cannot do."

Rob sighed, which was as much as admitting he understood that she was right.

"I'd like to see this through in my own way. And not because it's in the will. Not even because a great-aunt I loved very much would want me to. And certainly not because I harbor any hopes of finding an emerald necklace which is probably long gone, broken up into a dozen different pieces of jewelry decades ago." She saw the disappointed look cross his face instantly. The necklace being gone could mean Robert stole it. That made her breath catch.

She pulled the van in behind his house and helped him into the kitchen. By the time their lunch was consumed, Rob was still trying to talk her out of doing any actual work at Greystone.

"Listen, Rob. Please try to understand. I can't let you or any pale specters or imagined evil forces of some sort scare me away from what I'm capable of doing. I can't let them succeed, whoever they are."

She kissed him gently and immediately placed her fingers on his lips to silence his retort. "You have a good nap and keep off your ankle. I'll come back on the coffee break and get you and bring you back over there. Don't worry. You'll be there when I work out over the steps."

Without waiting for him to disagree, she walked out of his house and jogged back to the inn, leaving the van by Rob's kitchen door in case he woke and wanted to come over. It was an automatic transmission, and she was guessing he could drive it with one foot.

The crews were already at work when she arrived at Greystone. Before she climbed up the ladder and went back to work herself, she took the time to check on the progress of the two upper floors. She was just coming back down when she heard a yelp of pain and then a stream of swear words so foul that she wasn't familiar with all of them.

When she reached the balcony over the foyer, she saw one of the Sheetrock workers sitting on the top step. Lars was checking out his shoulder.

"What happened?" Carolyn called as she jogged up to his side.

"You should know what happened since it's your fault," the injured man grumbled. She looked up at Lars who held out her paint-chipping hook in his hand.

Carolyn took the hook and examined it. "I left this on the rung of the ladder. How did you get it?"

"He took it out of my shoulder, that's how. You left it up there, and it fell on me."

The man grabbed the hook from her and threw it into the corner of the hall at the head of the stairs. It skidded through the paint chips that she'd scattered that morning and came to rest near the wall.

"That's what comes of women doing men's work," he continued. "Following me around wherever I go. It's almost like you're in two places at once. No more. I've had enough of this place."

"He's right," Carolyn agreed at once. "Get someone to take him in to a doctor. And Lars? He won't have to come back." Lars nodded his understanding.

Nothing she said now would get through to him anyway. And the less said of a woman upstairs the better.

Lars directed one of his men to drive the injured worker to town. One by one the other men who'd gathered to see what had happened went back to their work.

When no one remained within earshot, Carolyn sat down on the top step. "Okay, Sara. I can use a little help here," she whispered. "There can't be any more people hurt. Tell me what I can do to stop the accidents before someone is seriously injured. There have been too many problems already."

She leaned back against the banister and closed her eyes for a minute. *Damn, if anyone hears me talking to Sara, they'll think I'm ready for the funny farm. But I've got to put a stop to the accidents.*

With the noise in the parlor where electric sanders buzzed, no one could possibly hear her, she decided. "Sara, is it Robert?" she asked out loud. "Is he trying to chase us away so people will never know for sure he took the necklace?"

Carolyn could feel a strong breeze coming through the house and swirling up the stairs around her. Remembering the breeze she'd felt when she'd discovered the diary, she looked around. No sign of anyone. No hint of lilies of the valley. This time the cool breeze really was coming off the lake.

Summer weather would soon be gone, but it would be easier to work in the cooler fall, Carolyn concluded, trying to remain upbeat. That didn't stop her from feeling sorry for Sara, especially if Robert actually had been the thief and the strong spirit causing the present-day problems. And for Rob, if that proved to be true.

Carolyn shivered and hugged herself, rubbing her upper arms with her hands. Poor Sara. How terrible it was, she thought, to be in love with someone, to build a mutual intimate trust, and then have something destroy your trust.

Carolyn watched Rob hobble across the foyer and come to the bottom of the steps. He looked like a man with something on his mind.

"Dad called. The workman will be fine. What was this all about? He said your scraper hook stabbed him. He almost had Dad convinced you stabbed him!"

"That would be laughable if it wasn't serious. The worker said it fell on him from up there," she said, pointing at the top as she came down the ladder.

"I know you left it on the third rung from the floor when we went to lunch. I saw you."

"Thanks. I needed that. But I also need to stop thinking about it. I've gone over it so many times in my mind. I'm positive I left it there, too. And none of the workmen would have moved it."

"You're right. No one touches anyone else's tools without permission. The men are extremely careful about that since the condition of the tools is so important to being employable."

"I need a break." Carolyn smiled broadly and climbed down. "Or did you come to watch me work some more?"

Rob smiled and ran a hand up and down her upper arm. "You look tired. Why not take the afternoon off?"

"Well, a nap sounds good, but it won't get the work done."

He stepped closer. "My bed is pretty comfortable," he said softly so they couldn't be overheard.

"You got that right," she responded with a smile. "Did you get a nap?"

"No. With the storm coming up, I drove down to the dock to make sure all the fishing boats were tied securely. I went back to put ice on my foot for a while, and then Dad called about the accident. I thought I'd come down here and see how you were doing."

"With all you've just done, no wonder you're leaning heavily on those crutches. Let me guess. You had to put weight on the sprained foot while tending to the boats, right?"

"You had me followed?"

She laughed. "Tell you what, Rob. You sit down there on your throne and put your ankle up while I finish what I can reach to the first step. Then I'll quit for the day and drive you home. And this time I'll make sure the hook is safely put away."

"Deal."

Carolyn returned to the ladder while Rob hopped to the chaise. He settled himself and raised his sore ankle to rest over his other one. "What are you looking for?"

"The hook," she said. "I put it on the third rung again and now I can't find it. But unless someone sneaked by me while we were talking, it's got to be here."

"Carolyn?"

His tone of voice made her look over at him. He was pointing up toward the ladder. Her gaze followed in that direction. High over her head, the hook was hanging on the molding near where she'd stopped working.

Suddenly her palms felt sweaty, and she needed to wipe them on the sides of her jeans. The guys working in the sitting room beyond the foyer laughed at something at that moment. Instead of the laughter releasing her tension, it only heightened it.

"Ah, thanks," she called, but she didn't dare look at Rob. "I must not have brought it down with me after all."

She moved the ladder over a few inches under where the hook hung and pressed down on it to be sure the rubber-tipped legs were stable and at a safe angle. She rubbed her palms dry on her jeans once more and began her ascent.

Chapter Thirteen

Once at the top, Carolyn wrapped one leg around the vertical bar of the ladder and hooked her toe under a rung to secure herself so she could have both hands free to work.

"Remember, Sara, no more people get hurt . . . including me," she whispered under her breath.

"What did you say, Carolyn? I couldn't hear you."

Carolyn called out that it was nothing, but she didn't look down. She couldn't look down at him sitting in the foyer from this dizzying height. And right now he didn't need to find out she was talking to a dead person, asking her for protection from someone else, but she wasn't certain from whom.

No, there was no way she was going to let him know how terrified she felt at the top of this ladder, hanging on for dear life. She didn't even want to think about how it would feel on a ladder with uneven legs over the stairs.

And while she didn't consider herself a coward, she'd decided she wasn't about to find out. She would be more than happy to let someone else do that work. Then she would have made her point, had her fun, and be able to stay on the ground from then on. She could go back to finishing the room decor plans. She wanted those designs done before her friend, Tulie, arrived and could begin work gathering bids. She was never quite sure what had made her so interested in helping chip paint, but for some strange reason, it seemed very important that she do so.

She stabbed in the hook behind the picture rail and wiggled it from side to side. "Oh, come on. Get out of there," she urged, having trouble freeing the hook. It was stuck in a section where the picture wire clip was buried in paint that completely filled the trough above the molding. She wiggled the handle from side to side with a grunt.

"What's the matter?" Rob asked.

"I can't get this wire thing to move." She laughed nervously. "It almost feels like someone is holding it there while I'm trying to pry it out."

"You're working in your own shadow. Your head is blocking the light from behind you. And you're not getting any help from sunlight through those windows either because it's getting dark out from the storm that's moving our way."

She could hear the storm was about on them. She glanced out the windows on the end of the balcony. The afternoon appeared as dark as evening. The only light in the building now was from the bare-bulb work lights. The light they cast was harshly bright in sharp contrast to the long dark shadows they created.

"I think you're right. I just can't see well enough."

Carolyn couldn't help but notice the rumbling thunder was getting closer with each clap. She wasn't overly fond of thunderstorms, and she liked working in a storm while high on a ladder even less.

"Carolyn, are there any more of the spotlights down there that you can spare for upstairs?" Tiny asked from the other end of the balcony. Startled by the deep voice behind her, she grabbed the ladder with both hands. "It's getting so dark we can't work."

"Just wishing I had more light myself," she managed weakly as she tried to calm down her frayed nerves.

Tiny leaned over the railing and called to the men in the sitting room. "Hey, down there. You guys got any lights to spare?"

They did. By the time they handed them up the stairs, and Tiny set the light closer so Carolyn could see better, the storm sounded like it was in the front yard.

Carolyn's knuckles were white as she gripped the sides of the ladder. When the blood in one leg threatened to stop circulating, she switched feet and wrapped the other leg around the ladder.

Back to work, she ordered herself. *Ignore the storm. The faster you finish the little bit left to the steps, the faster you can quit and drive Rob home.*

A flash of lightning lit the trees outside the windows and was followed immediately by a booming crack of thunder. Taking a deep breath and gathering her nerve, she leaned forward against the rungs and released her grip on the ladder sides. She pulled on the smooth wooden handle of the hook, twisted it to the side and then upward.

With a grunt, a half-inch chip of paint finally flew out over her head and the wire that had been hanging there fell to the floor. At that same moment there was a lightning flash, a crack of thunder, and then total darkness.

Carolyn cried out. The hook flew out of her hands, and she instinctively grabbed the sides of the ladder. She squeezed her eyes shut and pressed her forehead against a rung. The hook bounced down the steps below.

"Carolyn?" Rob called. "You okay?"

"I . . . I'm still up here, Rob," she answered after swallowing hard to recover her voice. "I haven't convinced my legs to move yet." She tried to laugh to hide how nervous she was.

"Please come on down, Carolyn," Rob called.

"Exactly my intentions," she answered. "Watch out for the hook. I dropped it."

"I'm going to get the lantern from the van," Rob called.

As the workmen migrated to the first floor from all over the house, they talked and laughed about how far they had jumped at the last flash and boom. Carolyn guessed they had all been as startled as she was. Good thing she hadn't jumped. The leap to the floor was a big one!

Before she could lift a foot to climb down, something hit hard against the side of her ladder. Carolyn screamed again and hugged the ladder, praying it would remain upright.

"God, is that you up there, Carolyn?" Lars yelled as he grabbed the ladder to steady it. "I was feeling my way along the wall, trying to make my way to the stairs, and hit the ladder. I've got it now. Come on down."

"I'm trying to get my shaking legs to move. I hate being on ladders in a storm."

"I'm awful sorry I bumped it, boss. I couldn't see a thing," Lars explained.

"Carolyn!" Rob shouted. "Where the hell are you? I heard you scream. Are you all right?" Soaked from the rain, Rob appeared in the foyer, his wide-beam lantern searching the foyer for her.

"Rob, I'm okay. Just give me a minute to get down. My legs don't seem to be moving when I tell them to."

He shone the beam up on Carolyn who raised her arm to shield her eyes from its brightness before he lowered it again to the steps below her.

"Come on, Carolyn," Lars called. "Don't worry."

"Thanks, Lars."

Slowly Carolyn lowered herself to the floor. She hadn't even noticed Lars's hand on her hip to steady her for the last couple steps until she glanced at Rob. He was watching Lars's hand warily.

"Thanks. Has anyone discovered why the lights went out?"

"The lines must be down at the road, or maybe lightning hit a transformer," Lars conjectured. The remaining workers who'd been upstairs came down the stairs past them.

"When I was out front to get the light, I didn't see any lights on at the cabins either," Rob offered. "The yard light normally comes on automatically at night or in storms like this one. It didn't this time. I'll have to go check the gas generator."

"Well, if the whole area is without power, there's no sense in anyone staying around," Carolyn announced loud enough for everyone to hear. The men cheered the chance to leave for home early.

A couple of them rounded up some flashlights from their cars and went back through the house with Carolyn to be sure everything was closed and locked up. When the last of the crews were out, Carolyn locked the door and ran ahead of Rob in the rain that had begun, to open the van door for him.

Once in the car herself, she was soaked to the skin. "This isn't going to do the upholstery any good."

"Home, James," Rob ordered.

"Oh, I'm a chauffeur now, am I?"

"Get me home and I show you what else you are." He raised and lowered his eyebrows rapidly as he puckered his lips trying to look funny.

She laughed. "Ooooh, Elvis doing a Groucho impersonation and talking sexy." She leaned over and boldly kissed him. "Hmmm. Your lips are cool. I'd better get you home and warmed up in bed. Don't want you catching a cold."

"Best idea I've heard all day," he said, relaxing back in his seat.

Carolyn started the engine and flipped on the headlights. It took only a few minutes to drive to Rob's house, and not many more to get inside and take all their wet clothes off. After that, in no time at all, they were very warm.

When they eventually made it back into the kitchen to eat, the power was back on, enabling them to enjoy a hot supper. They washed their wet clothes, and set them to tumble dry. Wrapped in his terry robe, Rob built a fire to ward off the chill of the storm. Similarly attired, Carolyn snuggled up next to him to enjoy a cup of tea.

"I can't believe the summer is almost gone," she said, staring into the flames.

"You've been working so hard, Carolyn, I'm surprised to hear you knew it was summer at all." He kissed her temple. "You work too hard, you know, but it's all coming along smoothly."

"Smoothly?" She looked at him incredulously with one eyebrow raised.

"Well, except for a few accidents. But you're doing a great job. I mean it," he claimed.

There was a big lump in her throat, and she couldn't even say thank you. But she could kiss him and she did. She also helped him onto his crutches and down the hall to his bed.

It was nearly eleven that night when she woke again in his arms. Rob was sound asleep so she tried to slide off the bed without waking him, but it didn't work.

"Hmm. Don't go."

She leaned back down and kissed him while she pulled on his robe. "I hate to, but I should go to the cabin. I have to shower and wash my hair and get different clothes for tomorrow. It wouldn't do for me to show up in the same ones. And I'm so tired, I'll just stay down there tonight, but you can save my place," she said, patting the bed beside him.

"Every night." He pulled her down next to him, and his kiss was so inviting that Carolyn was tempted not to leave at all.

"I wish I'd met you before Louise died."

"What a strange thing to say, Rob. Am I too busy to get to know now?"

He shook his head sadly. "No. Well, yes, but that's not why. I would have been an ordinary guy meeting a wonderful woman. That's all."

He kissed her lightly and moved to get out of bed. Carolyn pressed her hand on his shoulder to keep him there. "You stay put," she told him before he could swing his feet out of bed and put any pressure on his aching ankle. "I'll get my clothes from the dryer, throw them on, and lock the door on my way out. Your crutches are here by the bed when you need them. If you need help, just phone me."

She kissed him good night again. He closed his eyes, and she could tell it wouldn't take him long to get right back to sleep.

As she went to get her clothes, she thought about his wishing they'd met before Louise died. Strange wish.

It was her inheritance, after all, that had brought her here. Carolyn had a good job and wouldn't have left Miami, and Rob was well established here. The inn was what they had in common. It had brought them together. She didn't consider at that moment that her inheritance might be the very thing that would keep them apart.

Her jeans were still damp, but a few minutes more in the

dryer would fix them right up. She turned it back on and wandered into Rob's den to dress where the carpeted floor would be warmer on her feet than the tiled kitchen.

She sat down in his desk chair to pull on her socks, and noticed a large blueprint spread out on the glass-covered surface. Looking more closely, she could see the shoreline of Lost Lake, the point between the camp and Greystone, the row of cabins and Rob's house. It was a detailed plan of the entire fishing camp with one major addition: a large lodge with more than a dozen rooms. The elevation drawings showed it straight uphill of the dock behind the cabins. And the date in the corner was way back early in June.

Fear constricted Carolyn's throat, making her choke and gasp for her breath. She clutched the edge of the desk and tried to regulate her breathing. Rob had never mentioned plans for expansion. This kind of building project would take a lot of money to carry out.

A legal-sized pad of paper stuck out from its partially hidden position under the edge of the drawing. She pulled it out and gasped at what she saw. She bit down on a knuckle of her index finger to keep from crying out. Tears stung her eyes.

There on the pad was a large ring of dozens of dollar signs. Interspersed among them were several large and small question marks. She deduced he was trying to figure out how to come up with the money to pay for the lodge. And then she saw the drawing of his solution to the problem. In the center of the rings of dollar signs was a sketch of Alice Whitney's emerald necklace. She counted the twenty-five emeralds, each one cracking her broken heart in a new place. No, she wanted to believe. He wouldn't do that, would he?

Her tears were bouncing off the paper and she rose

abruptly. She had to get out, to get away from the evidence of his deception. She felt weak with disappointment and bit her lip to keep from sobbing. Jerking on her jacket, she turned out the light and went back to retrieve her jeans from the dryer. She didn't want to look again, but she had seen it all drawn out.

All the while, she was trying to deny the conclusion she kept coming back to: Rob was hunting for the necklace to fund the building of a lodge. The accidents had continued because he was still trying to scare her away, or at least slow down the work, to give him more time to search. When those attempts didn't work, he'd taken the only avenue left—making her fall in love with him. Once they were intimate, he had an easy excuse for being at her side to search for the necklace any time of the day or night. He could take her away from the house for romantic interludes, anything to delay her hunt.

And then tonight. Carolyn folded her arms across her stomach and bent over at her waist. She pressed her lips together to keep from vocalizing her anguish. He must have had a moment of weakness tonight when he wished out loud that they had met each other earlier. Could he really care for her and momentarily have some regrets about what he was doing? Well, if so, he deserved all the pain he was feeling.

Damn. How could he do this to me? I love him! Her tears flowed anew, and she had to hurry and leave. Dressed, she looked around for anything she might have left. She wouldn't be coming back to get it.

The camp yard lights illuminated the path as she made her way down toward her cabin. The rain had stopped, but the dripping tree branches and the dropping temperature left her wet and chilled. It was only after she'd arrived at her cabin that she realized she'd left her van at Rob's kitchen door. She'd blindly run right by it.

Her frustration level rising as high as her pain and anger, she was fiddling with the key in the cabin door when her gaze was drawn in the direction of Greystone. Was it the wet leaves reflecting the cabin lights, or the smoky humidity suspended expectantly in the air? She thought she could see light coming through the trees. She wiped away her tears with her jacket sleeve and looked again.

The lights. Of course. The storm had cut the power. When the workmen went home, it didn't occur to anybody to switch all the lights off when they shut the windows.

Carolyn stepped into her cabin far enough to grab a flashlight and diverted her steps toward the path through the trees to Greystone. The distant rumble of thunder accompanied her running footfalls. She let herself in the front door and quickly closed it against the damp cold.

The thick stone walls had kept in the heat of the early day despite the outside temperature dropping with the storm. She welcomed the comfort the warmth provided. She tucked the flashlight under her arm and rubbed her hands together, blowing on them to warm them as she went up the stairs.

Starting on the top floor and working her way down in her usual pattern, she turned off the lights. The workmen had left lights on in most rooms, but it wasn't long before she stepped out of the hall onto the balcony over the foyer. A work light stood at the end near where she had been chipping away the paint from the picture molding.

Near the light that stood between her and the ladder, she felt a warm breeze in her face that drew her gaze upward to the ceiling near where she'd been working.

Carolyn froze when she saw the glitter of the golden

chain, so conspicuous against the greying walls. She drew in a ragged breath. Without taking her eyes off the dangling object high above her, she inched her way to the base of the ladder. She could almost make out the links in the chain from where she stood.

Did she dare think what she wanted to think? Her chest felt constricted, each breath painful. Setting down the flashlight, she held the ladder with both hands and slowly climbed up until her face was just inches below the level of the molding.

Her attention snapped to the scraper hook stuck in the thick layer of dry paint beside the chain. She knew she'd dropped it that afternoon when the thunder frightened her and the power went out. She hadn't thought to look for it after everyone had left Greystone. She didn't know where the hook had ended up, but it certainly wasn't way up there when she left. It couldn't be there now, but it was.

Next to the hook, the length of gold chain lay draped over the rounded top of the molding. An ornate clasp hung from the end of the sturdy links. Could this really be it? The clasp on the end of the antique necklace everyone had been searching for?

Trying to swallow her excitement past the large lump in her throat, Carolyn removed her hands from the ladder one at a time and wiped the sweat from her palms on the seat of her jeans. Focused on the chain, she forgot where she was standing and didn't bother to wrap her leg around the ladder for stability.

Pressing her body forward against the rungs, she slowly wrapped her fingers around the hook's worn handle. With her other thumb and forefinger, she grasped the gold chain and tugged up a little. It wouldn't move. The end disappeared into the dusty layer of paint beyond the curve of the wood.

Gingerly, Carolyn poked the hook well beneath the buried end of the chain and pried it upward. Another small chunk of paint loosened. She moved the hook deeper while lifting the chain up out of the way and pried again. A chunk of paint fell out over the golden links and echoed as it bounced down the steps in the tomb-like silence beneath her.

That sound coming from so far below suddenly made her painfully aware of how high she was. The legs of the ladder stood only inches from the edge of the top stair. She swallowed again and tried to repress her mental comparisons of a fall from the ladder and her recent fall when she'd been pushed off the top step. She didn't want to think about how much worse a fall from the ladder would be.

She turned her attention back to painstakingly prying out another inch of the chain. Her breathing was shallow and her heartbeat thundered in her ears as loud as the thunder beginning again outside. She continued her task without looking away from the chain.

The scraping hook was poised to press in again when she heard the piano. It was soft at first, just what Carolyn needed so that she wouldn't feel quite so frightened in the empty dark house.

"Sara? Is that you?" Carolyn's voice cracked with the tension she was feeling. She tried to let the sweet melody flow around her and soothe her jangled nerves. It had to be Sara, and that made her feel safe. Pleasant sounds of music wouldn't accompany danger.

"Louise said you'd show me where it was. And I'm sorry I didn't believe her before now, but I'd almost given up hope."

Her whisper had been barely louder than the scraping sounds the hook made as she went back to work more swiftly, but no less carefully. The next loosened piece wouldn't fall out. It cracked and rose but turned on its side. She gingerly poked at the cracks with the hook point and forced a flake away from the treasure.

The dark black-green of the first emerald uncovered was a stark contrast to the greyed-white paint that stuck to the side of the stone and its setting. Quite unable to stop until the entire necklace was in sight, Carolyn ignored everything else around her. She was determined to loosen the paint from the wall and from the molding without a scratch or any damage to the precious jewels or the gold settings.

The metal ladder dug into her thighs. Her feet ached from the pressure of the rung in her arches. Perspiration ran down her back and even between her breasts.

There was no way Carolyn could tell how much time had passed, but at last she came to gold chain again beyond the last emerald, and finally, reaching over the stairs as far as she could, to the other half of the large decorated clasp. The whole chain was freed. Much of it was still encased in chunks of dried paint, but it had to be Alice Whitney's emerald necklace.

Hanging the scraping hook back on the molding where she'd stopped, she extracted the entire necklace from its hidden bed and slid it into the safety of the pocket in her shirt. She'd buttoned the flap to keep it secure when she realized that the music had stopped.

She looked toward the parlor, and seeing the distance down to the foyer floor, a wave of dizziness nearly overwhelmed her. She closed her eyes and hugged the ladder.

"Sara?" she called weakly after her stomach had settled a bit. "You know, don't you? You led me here. I've found the necklace and that will clear Robert's name. Everyone will know he couldn't have taken it now." *And hopefully I've broken the cycle of accidents that had been happening at Greystone,* Carolyn added to herself.

Rob should be happy that she'd cleared Robert's name, but at the same time, he wouldn't gain any of the proceeds from the necklace to fund his new lodge. *No, I won't think of that now. I should be happy.*

"Sara, you should be happy, too. You should be playing happy music." But instead, Sara was silent. The music had stopped. "Why have you stopped playing?"

There had been no missed chord, but Carolyn felt something was terribly wrong. She fought the fear and panic that gripped her. She grasped the ladder sides and shifted her weight to one foot so she could step down one rung. She stopped there when she heard a door open behind her. Drawing on all the courage she could find, she slowly turned her head and watched the scene that unfolded on the balcony as if Carolyn and her ladder weren't there at all.

Lora ran on tiptoes in a stealthy fashion from her room to the head of the stairs. There she pulled one of the tall ladder-back chairs by the window to a spot against the wall, just above the top step. Standing on the chair, she reached up, but could not extend her arm above the portrait of her father hanging there.

She moved the chair even closer to the step and this time she turned it around and leaned it against the wall with the back facing out. Tucking her skirt up, she gingerly tested the chair's stability as she climbed onto the back edge of the seat. Leaning her hands against the wall for balance, she stepped up the rungs on the back as if they had truly been on a ladder and not just a chair design feature.

Her body flat against the wall to keep from falling, she slowly extracted Alice's necklace from her pocket. After two tries, she managed to flip it onto the picture rail behind the portrait. It slid into the picture-hook groove above the rail and disappeared from sight. She released her breath and rested her forehead against the wall between her outstretched hands. "That will show them all. When they can't find the emeralds, I'll make sure they believe Robert took them." An ugly sneer spread across her face. "I'll see to it that Papa never allows Sara to marry him. Never!"

She slapped the wall with her palm to punctuate her evil vow, and suddenly the legs of the chair slid away from the wall. One leg caught on the carpet that ran down the stairs while the other slid over the edge of the top step. The chair twisted and Lora lurched out over the steps, her arms thrashing as if she were swimming. Her panicked scream echoed in the empty foyer. Landing head first from her midair dive, she rolled down two more steps before she lay totally still.

The tall chair clattered down with her and came to rest against the wall.

Carolyn screamed and turned away from the horrid scene she had witnessed. She buried her face in the sleeve of her shirt. Tears burned her eyes, and she had to open her mouth again to accommodate her rapid breathing. She wouldn't look down again. She couldn't.

"How could Lora do that?" Carolyn mumbled. She, not Robert, had stolen the necklace. And Lora died hiding it from the others in her family. Covered with carelessly laid layers of paint, it had remained hidden there until tonight.

Little by little, Carolyn became aware of heavy rain that pounded on the tall windows at the end of the hall. The storm made it impossible to notice much else than the sudden flashes of lightning and the almost immediate cracks of thunder.

She sniffled and wiped her eyes on her sleeve so she

could see. Down. She had to get down. Lora had died in a fall from a lower height.

What if someone or something pushed Carolyn's ladder now?

Chapter Fourteen

Grasping the ladder sides in both hands, Carolyn forced her trembling knees to bend outward to continue her descent. Her feet felt numb, and it was difficult to ascertain when one was securely resting on the next rung to shift her weight to it.

More lightning cracked, the thunder booming in the emptiness around her. She flinched and squeezed her eyes shut with each loud report, opening them again only after the blue-white flash had filled the hall and disappeared.

Afraid it would make her dizzy or that she might see Lora again, she didn't look down, not even when a sudden cold breeze swirled up the stairs past her. Not like the fresh breeze Sara had brought, this was damp and stale, and it chilled her to the bone instantly.

"Sara, help me!" she pleaded in a whisper.

She moved down another rung and managed to keep her gaze focused straight ahead at the wall until a shuffling sound and movement below her in the foyer forced her to look down the wide stairs.

A dark vision rose up the stairs toward her. She couldn't breathe. Her nerves taut, she couldn't even move. She blinked, trying to make out what was there.

"I've come for you," the foreboding figure announced harshly.

Rising between her and the foyer work light, the threatening figure appeared otherworldly. He was surrounded by a halo of flashing sparkles that glistened from his dark clothes. Slicked down, his dark hair was parted in the middle and covered much of his face. He looked like . . . It was Robert, rising from his grave to get her.

"Robert, no!" Carolyn screamed. Her guess had been right. He was the evil force that had pushed her down the stairs. He looked furious. Was it because she'd found the necklace and not Rob?

The vision raised both hands and pulled heavily on the railing as he climbed up the steps unsteadily toward her. His voice was hoarse and evil sounding. "You're coming with me—now!"

Torn from the terrifying male figure, Carolyn's gaze flew to the center of the stairs. There she saw Lora still lying at an awkward angle, staring up at her through vacant eyes. She was much paler than the male image and looked more like a mirage. With a sudden swirl of red vapor, she seemed to move through the air toward Carolyn, too. Lora raised her arm and pointed her finger up at her accusingly, her face filled with such hatred as Carolyn had never seen. She had to escape.

She dragged air into her lungs. The necklace weighed heavily against her breast, but she forced her feet to move to the next lower rung. She had to get away before the darker figure got up the stairs. There. Another step downward.

"Never marry Robert," Lora cried out, her voice echoing as in a deep tunnel. "Never."

Carolyn felt a deathly chill as the threats and shouts of both figures swirled around her in a frigid mist. Lora reached up to wrench Carolyn from the ladder. She raised her arm in self-defense, but her other hand cramped and her grip on the ladder slipped.

"No!" Carolyn tried to shout as she grabbed for a hold

on the ladder. Her strangled scream floated out into the stormy night.

The icy hands of the glittery male apparition clawed at her thighs with supernatural strength. She tried to kick free, but his arms enclosed both her legs and held them still. She struggled to hang on, to somehow escape his grip. *"No!"*

But where could she go? She couldn't go up the ladder again. She couldn't jump free of the cold, grasping fingers that circled her thighs in a deathlike grip, pulling her down. *"No!"* She saw no escape. No escape.

Finding the necklace was supposed to solve all the mystery—to make everyone happy. But finding it had brought Carolyn face to face with the greatest danger. Finding it changed everything. She saw that now. She could trust no one now. No one.

Unable to escape the evil forces tearing at her, a blackness she welcomed as deliverance overwhelmed her consciousness. Her body slumped and she fell from the ladder into the cold wet arms of the unknown.

After Carolyn left the circle of his arms in his big warm bed, Rob tossed and turned, unable to do more than doze without her close. He rolled over and punched the pillow.

"When am I going to learn?" he grumbled in the dark room. How could he miss her so much when it wouldn't be long until she would have everything she ever wanted? And it wouldn't include him.

Then she would blink her beautiful eyes and take a close look at him, a small-town lawyer with no ambition to make lots of money, a man totally happy living in the woods near Lost Lake, a guy who loved to fish more than just about anything—until he'd met her.

And then? When she saw who he was, it was easy to predict what she would do—anything she wanted to do. And he couldn't picture her selecting Lakeside as the place to do it.

When you had the best in the world—money, jewels, talent, beauty, and prestige—there wasn't much more you could want. Certainly nothing as ordinary as a man named Rob Ashford.

Rob's ankle pulsed with pain from turning repeatedly with his restless movements. Finally reluctant to roll over again and subject his swollen joint to another bump, he lay still and listened to the sounds of the night.

The rain had begun again. He'd been vaguely aware of the volume of the thunderous storm increasing. He was comforted, knowing that Carolyn had left before the rain started. These late-summer storms could be nasty.

She would have finished her shower by now, probably be drying her long luxurious hair. Rob visualized the pale strands softly flowing over her naked shoulders, and he needed to shift slightly.

He eyed the phone on the nightstand beside his bed, and without any further hesitation, he pressed the number for her phone in the cabin. She wouldn't be asleep already. He would just say good night and wish her sweet dreams. Maybe he'd say how much he missed her in his arms. He wondered if her eyes would turn the deep blue of molten glass with desire as they had earlier.

The harsh ringing in his ear was nearly drowned out by the repeated crashes of thunder. Lightning lit the expanse beyond his window as the phone rang for the tenth time. He shouldn't be on the phone in such a storm.

And Carolyn couldn't be sleeping through the rings and the storm. Therefore, she wasn't there! he concluded, slamming the phone back into its cradle.

"Robert," a woman's voice cried through the night. *"Robert, help!"*

"Oh, God, no!" Panic tensed his muscles into action and he lurched into a sitting position. The voice sounded so clear that Rob looked around the room to see where the woman who had spoken was standing. He saw nothing. He wasn't surprised, though. He knew no one was there. He also knew the voice was calling to him because Carolyn needed him.

"I'm coming." He threw the sheet off his naked body and slid to the edge of the bed. Clenching his teeth at the inevitable sharp pain when he put any weight on his sprained ankle, Rob managed to dress in the first jeans and shirt he could find. He forced a sock on his swollen foot after the other foot was shod.

Hobbling into the kitchen on his crutches, he tugged on a shiny, rain-repellant jacket. He went straight to the van that Carolyn had left for him, throwing in the crutches before he climbed in behind the wheel.

He drove to her cabin, the gravel spraying from under his tires. Without taking the time to get out the crutches, he hopped up on the porch. He turned the knob and hoped it was not a bad sign that the door was unlocked. The short trail of muddy footprints he saw when he opened the inside door filled him with dread. The prints led across the vinyl flooring to the table and then back to the door. She couldn't have!

"Carolyn? Carolyn! Are you here?" he called out, hoping he was wrong in thinking she'd gone out again.

As fast as he could manage, Rob hopped to look in the bedroom and then the bath. No one. The footprints must mean she'd come in for something and then went out again.

Where was she? Why did she leave? Was she okay? Questions filled his head without eliciting any answers he liked.

He looked down the row of dark cabins. He had few guests during the week this time of year, after school had started. Most could only spare the weekends for fishing or hiking in the woods.

Rob hopped back to the van and pulled himself up behind the wheel. He had to massage the cramping muscles in his good leg. He'd done a lot of hopping on that leg and the muscles were objecting.

"Robert!" the voice called again, no less urgently.

"Yes, yes, I know," he muttered through his clenched teeth. "I'm coming!" he shouted.

Finger-combing his long wet hair straight back off his face with both hands so he could see, he started the car and drove toward Greystone. He thought for a second about walking the path she must have taken, but crutches on the soil softened by rain would be nearly impossible to manage.

He would check out the house first. If she wasn't there, then he'd walk back toward the cabin on the path.

The thunderstorm was right over the lake now. Jagged streaks of brilliant lightning seemed to come out of the sky and spear the churning black water. The booming claps of thunder at the same moment vibrated the van as Rob stopped at the steps of Greystone. Rain came down as heavily as he'd ever seen it.

"Oh, Carolyn, why didn't you stay in the cabin?" he shouted.

The light from Greystone's foyer fell onto the porch from the windows on each side of the closed entrance door. The light shining through the round sun window above the door mocked the storm as it raged. A paler glow was evident through the windows of the sitting room beyond, but from the van he saw no one through any of them.

Not having the patience to bother with his crutches, Rob got out and leaned on the van for support as he hopped to the steps. There he wheelbarrowed to the porch on his hands and one foot. On the porch he stopped only long enough to turn the knob and discover that the front door was unlocked. "Thank God," he mumbled, knowing he hadn't thought to bring the key.

"Robert. Help me."

"I'm coming, damn it!" He raised both hands to push his rain-soaked hair back from his face again as he hobbled into the foyer. With a growl of piercing pain as he landed on his sprained foot, he lurched to catch the door and fought the cold wind to shut it again.

Leaning against it momentarily to catch his breath and gather his strength, he couldn't believe it when he heard himself calling out. "Where, Sara? Where is she?"

Rob had always tried to deny her existence. Now he was calling to her for help. But if Carolyn was in trouble, he'd take whatever help he could get to come to her aid. He had to find her.

The work light at the back of the foyer was on, and he could see light coming down the grand staircase from a second light near where Carolyn had been working that afternoon.

Dear God, no! She wouldn't go up the ladder at night alone, would she? What if she'd fallen? Didn't she understand that nothing that she could gain here, not even finding the necklace, was worth her getting hurt?

Fortified with the few moments' rest, Rob pushed off from the door, hopping toward the stairs. He grabbed the newel post at the bottom of the balustered railing for support and looked up. He gasped and his fingers tightened around the railing.

Carolyn stood near the top of the ladder, her face hidden from him by her bent elbow. He didn't think she was even aware he was there.

Afraid of frightening her and making her fall, he spoke softly. "Sweetheart?" She didn't turn to see him, but inched her way down the ladder one rung. Maybe the storm was too noisy for her to hear him. "Carolyn?"

Rob couldn't wait for her response. He started up the stairs as best as he could. He leaned heavily on the railing with both hands for support and jumped up each step on his uninjured foot. After he'd progressed a step or two, her choked scream made him look up to her.

"Honey, I've come for you." He bit back the lecture he was about to deliver about working alone at night. Relieved that whatever startled her hadn't made her fall, he hobbled up another step.

When he looked up again, Carolyn wasn't even looking at him. Damn. Was she trying to ignore him after the scare she'd given him? She was saying something, but he couldn't make it out with the noise of the thunder echoing in the empty foyer and the rain on the windows beyond her.

"No arguments now. Please. You're coming with me."

This time she must have heard him, but she reacted with another scream. Looking behind him, she appeared terrified. He wondered what had happened to scare her.

At last he'd pulled himself up to the top step and reached for the ladder. Carolyn was low enough for him to wrap his arms around her thighs to keep her from falling. He could feel the muscles tense in her legs.

"Never!"

The voice had come from the steps behind him, but before he could turn to see who it was, he felt Carolyn's leg muscles jerk several times and then go limp and buckle under her. Although unable to brace himself with his injured foot, he accepted her weight into his arms as she fell. With a lunge aiming them away from the steps, he fell with her safe in his arms. He was able to take the brunt of the impact on the back of his hip as they landed on the balcony.

"Honey, are you all right? Carolyn?" He turned her face so he could see it. She'd fainted into his arms and showed no signs of waking.

Rob pushed himself to a sitting position and lifted her gently on to his lap with her head resting just under his chin. Holding her there with one arm, he was able to scoot backward by pushing with his other hand and his good foot.

Reaching the corner, he leaned back and cradled her in both arms. For the next few seconds as he tried to catch his breath, he was thankful she wasn't aware of what was happening around them.

Cold mist rolled up the steps. A bolt of lightning literally sliced through a tree beyond the windows like a giant axe. He could hear the decades-old tree split with a loud crack. The falling branches clawed at everything in their reach, including the power lines. All the lights went out. The tree crashed to the ground as another deep rumble of the thunder shook the house.

With every light bulb darkened again by the loss of power, Rob could see nothing except when the lightning flashed. He opened his jacket and wrapped it around Carolyn's limp body in his arms.

"Thanks, Sara, for getting me here in time," he called out without feeling a bit foolish.

His voice was raspy in a hoarse throat repeatedly dampened by rain. Rob tried to ignore something in her breast pocket jabbing him in the chest. He didn't want to disturb her to remove it.

Her breathing was more even now. He kissed her temple and felt her muscles tense as she began to stir. Her head tossed one way and then the other. "Never . . . Not Rob," she mumbled. "No!" She sat up with a start and struggled frantically to free herself from his arms.

"Honey, it's okay," he called out to her. "I'm here. You're safe with me now." He held on tight until her writhing ceased.

"Who's there?" she asked in a small scared voice. "I can't see anything."

"It's me," he responded, expecting her to know his voice. "Don't worry. The power is out again, but I'll keep you safe."

"Am I safe with you?" she asked, and then relaxed against his chest.

He continued a stream of quiet assurances and in moments she was asleep. "Yes, Carolyn. You sleep. There's nothing else you can do now that I've got you right where I want you." He kissed her hair, leaned his head back, and shut his eyes. He felt so completely exhausted, so absolutely wrung out mentally and physically.

"Right where you want me," she mumbled.

She was safe in his arms. That was all that was important to him. Despite his vow not to get emotionally entangled with this rich girl, Rob knew in that moment, he had. He'd fallen in love with her even though it was just a matter of time until she lost interest in him and they parted company.

Exhausted, he couldn't fight sleep any longer. Neither his throbbing ankle nor the occasional thunder now some distance away disturbed the two as they slept.

John Ashford hated thunderstorms. He could hear the indistinct rumble of the distant thunder. The storm was probably over Lost Lake and would hit the town soon. Rain off and on until morning, the television had said, but the worst wouldn't last long. Or so he hoped.

John wished he hadn't stayed up for the late news and weather. Maybe if he'd gone to bed early, he could have gotten some decent sleep before his father called. And John knew he would.

He chided himself for not being very charitable toward Thomas. *Hell, if I live that long I hope Rob is more kind to me.* But he knew all the while that Rob would be. He'd always been very good to his grandpa. There was a bond between the two of them that John envied. He'd seen it for years. They had their favorite things to do together. Their favorite places to go, like Lost Lake. Like Greystone.

Thomas had encouraged Rob to develop the fishing camp. He'd sold him the land instead of giving it to him. Thomas had inherited it from Robert who had gone ahead with the purchase even after Lora's death. Robert had never given up hope that he and Sara would live there together—until Sara died the following year and his dreams had been shattered.

John was well aware that Rob loved living out there. He was happier running his camp than he was practicing law, that's for sure. And John couldn't complain, because whenever he needed Rob's help, he was there for him.

Rubbing his hands over his face, John rolled over on his side. He'd never known much to interest him outside of being an attorney. His law work at the office or in his den at home filled as many hours of the day and night, as many days of the week as he wanted it to, even in this town.

The lightning flashed and he could make out Ruth's face momentarily in the blue-white light. She stirred at the sound of thunder, and he stroked her with a comforting hand across her stomach. He'd been able to plant only one seed that grew there. Rob. They couldn't ask for a brighter or nicer son. They were very proud of him, but Rob was his own person.

John guessed Rob had gotten his degree and passed the bar to fulfill a sense of responsibility to his family. He was doing his part to help with the firm, but did little to increase its size or scope.

Rob didn't have aspirations of getting rich. In fact, he sometimes appeared to feel uncomfortable around rich people—even those among their clients.

"Rich people wouldn't be so bad if they didn't have all that money," Rob used to joke. Happy being a small-town lawyer, working enough to keep himself financially comfortable, he did what he liked best. He ran his fishing camp at the lake.

The ringing phone cut off John's reverie. He knew who would be calling, but he asked anyway. "Yes? Is that you, Dad?"

"I'm worried. The storm's a bad one. No good can come of it."

"It's okay, Dad. It'll pass over by morning."

"Rob's at Greystone, too."

John sighed. All his father seemed to care about during storms lately was what was going on at Greystone. "No, Dad. Rob's home in bed. He's not doing much for a week or two with his sprained ankle. Remember? I understand that you're worried about him, and if you want to see him, I'll drive him over to your place in the morning."

"It's no good, Rob not being able to walk."

"No, it's not, but it's just a sprain. He'll be back on his feet in no time. Dad, is Mrs. Panchek with you? Does she know you're phoning?"

"Yes, she's hovering right here. You'd think she'd rather be asleep than watch me talking on the phone," he added, his annoyance clearly evident in his voice.

"Put her on the phone, Dad."

John spoke before Thomas's housekeeper/caregiver could get in a word. "It's all right, Mrs. Panchek. I'm going to take care of it. Like I promised, I'll be there as quickly as I can after I get dressed."

"What's going on, John?" Ruth asked, rising to lean on one elbow. "Is it your father? Why can't he ever call during the day?"

John lowered the phone from his mouth and explained to Ruth what was going on. By this time, thinking he was no longer listening, Mrs. Panchek was shouting, "What I do? What I do?"

Calm under fire as a practiced attorney had to be, John rose to the occasion. "Mrs. Panchek, you are not to worry. I'm getting out of bed right now. I'll be over there in twenty minutes to take charge of my father, so you needn't worry any longer. If you could just keep an eye on him until I get there. And for heaven's sake, don't let him go out the front door. Hide his shoes or something," he told her, his voice rising uncharacteristically. He hung up the phone and got dressed quickly.

"Would you like me to go with you, dear?"

"No, Ruth, it's nonsense for us both to be up all night. You go back to sleep. Heaven knows how long it will take to calm him down this time."

When John left, Ruth appeared to have already fallen back to sleep. It took only ten minutes more until he stood at his father's side and demanded to know what was going on.

"You wouldn't understand."

"Probably not, but try me anyway."

"You're a good lawyer, John, but all you know about is what you see and put your hands on. Only cold hard facts for you."

"That's what they teach in law school, Dad. Get to the point."

"Can't. I need Rob." His lower lip jutted out in stubborn defiance.

John sighed. "Dad, can't it wait until the morning? The sun isn't even up yet. The boy's probably at home in bed sound asleep at this hour." John didn't want to go into the details about the fact that he suspected if Rob was in bed, he wasn't there alone. This wasn't the kind of news you presented to a man this old about his beloved only grandchild. He'd probably make him marry her in the morning.

"He ain't."

"What? Sorry, I was a mile off. What do you mean?"

"He's right, Mr. Ashford," the housekeeper offered. "Your father made me call Rob on the telephone."

John had forgotten that Mrs. Panchek was still in the room. "Dad, you mean you called Rob at this hour?"

"She found his number and pushed the buttons for me, but he didn't answer. His answering machine didn't come on either."

"Maybe he's busy . . . ah, or sleeping so soundly he didn't hear the phone." *Or down at Cabin One,* he added to himself.

"You call him."

"Will you go back to bed then, if I call Rob and he's okay?" John waited a moment for his father to weigh the pros and cons of his deal. Reluctantly, he finally nodded.

John walked to the phone and dialed Rob's house. He waited twenty rings. Then he pressed the buttons with the number for Cabin One. "I'm trying again to be sure I have the right number," he said to cover the second call. Again he waited twenty rings.

Thomas only became more agitated. "We gotta go out there. You can't feel it, but I can. Somebody out there needs help. They need help at Greystone."

Mrs. Panchek saw her charge getting upset, and she tried to calm him. "John take care of problem. You got no need to worry."

"She's right, Dad. You need to stop worrying so much. You go back to bed, and I'll go out to the lake and check on things. It's almost sunrise." He shrugged, raised his hands and slapped them down at his sides. "Hell, maybe Rob went fishing."

"In a storm? The boy's not daft."

"I'm telling you, Dad, if he's okay, and I've gone out there for nothing, you'll hear from my attorney," John retorted in a louder voice.

"I'm your attorney!" Thomas shouted.

John rubbed his face with his hands to give himself a moment to calm down. "Sorry he's been a bother, Mrs. Panchek. You be sure to go right to bed, Dad, so she can get to bed, too."

"You promise me, John. Tell Rob she needs help. He'll understand."

John scowled at him, but said nothing as he let himself out of the house and drove out to the lake. When was his father going to forget this nonsense about knowing what happened at Greystone?

The nearing dawn lightened the sky. The last of the storm had passed, and the rain-drenched leaves glistened in his headlights.

John ran his hand across the back of his neck and moved

his head around from side to side to try to work out some of the tension.

How could Thomas seem so sharp of mind at his age and still talk about people from seventy years ago as if they were here today? If the man wasn't his own father, he might consider him certifiable.

John slammed the car door and strode to Rob's kitchen door. "Rob?"

The door coming open in his hand worried John. It wasn't like Rob to leave the house open, but his truck was in the garage, so Rob must be home, John thought, feeling a bit more optimistic. He switched the kitchen light on, but nothing happened. Not knowing where to look for a flash-light, he ran back for the one in his car. Then he walked through the whole house to no avail.

John drove down to Cabin One next. It was also un-locked and no one was there either. Another few seconds and he was out the door and driving toward Greystone. He was worried now on two counts. First, he was worried that they might be really hurt or in trouble as Thomas had told him; or second, he worried they might be enjoying the night together at the inn or anywhere else, and not in need of help. And he sure would be making a fool of himself bursting in if that was the case.

John couldn't get all the way to Greystone in the car. A tree had fallen across the road. He started to walk around it when he heard rather than saw the crackling sparks. The power line was down and twisted in the branches—the break that had left Rob's house and the cabins in the dark. He backed away and ran to the car. Using his cell phone, he called the town police and informed them about the downed lines.

Realizing a deadly danger now, John picked his way carefully. He skirted wide around the tree, sloshing through mud that soon covered his shoes. Water conducted electricity, but he hoped not very far. Not knowing made him more nervous and worried. Once he was beyond the fallen tree and line, he climbed back on the road and broke into a jog.

In front of the inn, parked practically on the first step, he discovered Carolyn's van. It was faint, but he could see the dome light was on, running on what power the battery had left. He jerked open the driver's door that had been left ajar and found the van empty. He slammed the door and ran up the steps to try the door to the inn. Unlocked. Not a good sign.

The predawn light allowed him to see around the foyer. No one. Nothing but a lone work light stand and an empty chaise. He wanted to call out, but he couldn't. Concern for his son and Carolyn had frozen his vocal chords.

He looked in the open door to the former parlor and found nothing unusual. The den on the opposite side was enclosed in plastic for refinishing the walnut-paneled walls. No one there.

As he approached the stairs, John scanned the balcony, shining his flashlight from one end to the other to brighten the dark shadows.

A sound from outside made him look back out the front door.

Chapter Fifteen

John saw nothing outside, just mist rising from the driveway and steps in the sunlight. He turned back to his search of the house. He had the rest of the first floor and then upstairs to check. He turned toward the morning room when a moan made him raise his light back up the stairs.

The sight he'd missed in the far corner froze him in place. Rob lay slumped against the wall with Carolyn cradled in his arms. Their clothes looked damp and rumpled, and Rob's sprained foot in a wet, muddy sock lay extended out in front of him.

Guilt tore through John. Thomas had said something was wrong. He'd said someone needed help. But because John hadn't believed, he hadn't come . . . until now.

"Rob! Rob! Carolyn!" He sprang into action and raced up the steps. Only when Rob drowsily lifted his head, did John's heart start to beat again. "Oh, thank God you're alive."

"I feel stiff enough to wonder," Carolyn said as John grasped her shoulders to help her slide her weight from Rob's thighs to the floor, where she managed to sit unaided. She blinked her eyes and looked back at Rob who was rubbing his thighs. She smiled a weak apology at him.

"That's the last storm I want to get caught in if it means sleeping on a hard floor," Rob announced.

"But staying here was the smart thing to do with all that lightning," John told him. "You might have been under one of the trees that fell if you'd tried to get home. There's a big one blocking the road and it brought the power lines down with it."

Carolyn rotated her head. "My head hurts." Rob gave her a brief massage on her shoulder muscles. She closed her eyes and moaned with pleasure.

Suddenly, the memory of what had happened the night before broke through her sleepy haze. She gasped and felt the blood leave her face. "Last night." Slowly she rose to her knees and dared to look over the edge of the balcony down the stairs. "Down there, on the steps." She swallowed past the fear that had lodged in her throat. "She's gone. They're both gone."

"Who's gone?" John asked, looking down the empty stairway.

"Nobody, Dad," Rob responded. "It was just the storm. Come on," he said, as he scooted on his fanny to the steps, his sprained ankle lifted off the floor. "Whatever happened is over. Carolyn, you must be as tired as I am. You'll feel better after we've gotten some real sleep. Later, when you're rested, there will be plenty of time to talk about what happened."

Carolyn pulled on John's proffered hand to stand up. The necklace in her pocket bounced against her breast. How could she not have thought of it until now? Her back to the men, she pressed her hand over her pocket and felt the uneven and cold stones through the fabric. She checked to be sure the pocket was securely buttoned. She tamped down her returning excitement and tried to steady her breathing that had sped up as she thought about the previous night. Finding the necklace had been so important and . . .

And what? Why wasn't she shouting the news?

Because she wanted to keep it to herself, she realized.

She'd learned last night when she saw Rob's resort plans that she could no longer trust him. Then she saw the specters come up the stairs after her and she'd been frightened. Terrified.

She'd been thinking that the specter of Robert could be the danger to her, but now so was Rob. He was a clever and bright attorney. What better way to commit a crime than to have all the evidence be only circumstantial and then point it at yourself? Without hard evidence, he'd be in the clear because it would look too obvious to have him be guilty.

"Can you give me a hand?" John asked.

She took a deep breath and reached down to help lift Rob onto his good foot. His arm around John's shoulders, Rob held on to the railing with his other hand and hopped down the steps.

"How did you happen to come out at this hour?" Carolyn asked warily.

"Your grandfather sent me, Rob."

Rob nodded, and at the bottom of the stairs, he moved his hand from the railing to Carolyn's shoulder. "Tell Grandpa we're fine. He'll be worrying until he hears from you. You'll tell him right away?"

"I told him I'd call, but I'll go right back to town once you're settled and see him. I called from my car to report your lines down, so they shouldn't take long to repair that. You probably should cancel work for the day though. No telling when there will be power again." He looked to Carolyn for approval.

Carolyn nodded and thanked John when he volunteered to make the necessary phone calls. "I have a copy at the office of the schedule of who was due to come in. I'll get right on it to catch them before they leave home."

Despite Rob needing to lean heavily on his father for

support instead of using his crutches that sank in the path, it wasn't long before Rob and Carolyn were in her cabin and John had left for town without questioning leaving them both there.

As Carolyn turned up the heater in the bathroom, she shivered even though she still had her jacket on. "You take the first shower," Rob called as he took off his damp clothes and hopped his way to the bed. Standing in the doorway, she opened her mouth to speak, but couldn't. She couldn't say, "Rob, I found the necklace. Robert was innocent. He wasn't a thief."

She rationalized that she didn't want to tell anyone until she knew if the necklace was the real thing or someone's idea of a joke. One of their regular dinner meetings was scheduled at John's house tonight, and she felt it was important to have established its authenticity and possible worth at a reputable jewelry store first. In fact, she couldn't bring herself to even mention it until she knew for sure. Not even to Rob. Or especially to Rob.

And if it was the real thing? Then what?

Carolyn had done what Louise wanted. What Sara wanted. What Robert wanted. What Rob wanted. She'd found the necklace and cleared Robert's name. But was that what Rob really wanted? If he'd been the one to find the necklace, would he have told her? She'd never know, but her heart wanted to think that he would have shouted, "Here it is," and handed it to her, the rightful owner.

But then how would he pay for the secret new lodge?

A few more months of work and the inn would be completely renovated and ready for business. What then? The will said she would be free to do what she wanted. She didn't have to stay here and run it. She could even sell it. Once the initial excitement of running it was gone, would there be any reason to stay?

Rob had never intimated that he wanted her to stay. He seemed to enjoy their time together, but would he care if she left? Really care?

Was she keeping the necklace a secret because she worried that was the only reason Rob hung around? Would he walk away now as Jeff had? But after deceiving her, did she want him to stay?

Lost in her own thoughts, Carolyn wasn't certain how much time had passed as she showered. She peeked into the bedroom to see Rob was sound asleep. The muted roar of a distant chain saw probably meant the power company crew was already at the scene of the line break. It shouldn't take them long to clear the road.

Tucking the necklace into a terry washing cloth, she silently retrieved her purse from the dresser and slipped the bundle inside. She set it on the kitchen table for the time being.

She crept across the bedroom to retrieve a suit dress from the closet. Rob stirred but didn't wake. She didn't want him to ask about last night—to ask about what she'd been doing. She couldn't tell him. The drawings left her feeling sad that their intimate relationship was over. Their trust was lost. The link that had joined them since the day they met had broken, and she didn't have a ghost of an idea how to fix it.

Carrying her purse and heels, she slipped into her sneakers for the walk to the van, still parked at Greystone. She paused again at the bedroom door. Rob was sleeping with his arm stretched out across her side of the bed. His face looked so serene, so guileless.

So trustworthy?

Tears threatened as she turned away and stepped outside, holding the door to close it silently behind her. She pulled down on the screen door to keep it from squeaking as it opened, and jogged along the shortest path to Greystone.

Thwarted by the van's low battery, Carolyn had to seek help from the men who were clearing the fallen trees. Clutching her purse containing the treasure between her breasts, she hurried up the road to find them. The foreman was more than happy to drive her back in his pickup and jump-start her van. She got the distinct feeling that was not all he'd be willing to jump-start, given the chance.

Driving back up the road behind his truck, she waved her thanks to the other men who hoisted the trunk of the tree to the side of the road so she could pass. Having passed the impressive display of masculine strength, she smiled, but not at the men, at herself.

Her timing was perfect. She parked in front of the Lakeside jewelry store half an hour before it opened, just as the owner was arriving.

"Who was her appointment with?" John's wife, Ruth, asked the three Ashford men sitting in her living room. "Could she still be there this late?"

Rob knew Ruth had dinner ready and was worried it would be ruined if they had to wait much longer for Carolyn to show up.

"Rob, did she say where she was going?"

"No, Mom, not to me." Rob looked at his father.

John shook his head. "I don't know where she was either. But she'll be here, Ruth," John assured his wife. "Don't worry about dinner. It'll be fine."

They hadn't told her much since he'd arrived. She frowned. He didn't know what to say. No one had seen

Carolyn all day. The tension and expectant feelings in the room were palpable. What should have been a regular dinner meeting that they had every two weeks to discuss the progress at Greystone, had turned into something more. The silence hung heavy enough for them to feel it pressing on them.

Two cars pulling up drew Rob's gaze out the window.

"Here she is now," Ruth reported. "Oh, and there's another car pulling up right behind her van. John, you didn't say there would be two more for dinner."

"I didn't expect there would be. Just wait and see who they are before you get into a tizzy," John answered, his annoyance uncharacteristically evident.

"Besides, Mom, knowing you, there's enough food for an army," Rob said with a smile, trying to ease her worrying.

With a smile at her son, Ruth went to the door and opened it in anticipation of Carolyn's arrival on the porch. "Hello, dear. Come right in."

"Thank you, Ruth. Forgive me for bringing two unexpected guests, but they won't be here long."

Ruth politely showed them all into the living room.

While Rob stayed seated in the easy chair with his obviously swollen foot propped up on the stool, John rose to his feet. Thomas stayed seated as his age allowed him to do without excuse.

"Mr. Simons tells me he is acquainted with all of you," Carolyn began awkwardly as the men exchanged handshakes, "but this is Hal McNair. He is a private, armed guard that Mr. Simons employs at certain times when he needs his special services. Mr. Simons is, as you know, a jeweler."

Rob sat up straighter in his seat and damned the

sprained ankle that kept him there. He watched Carolyn command everyone's rapt attention. She smiled toward the men who had entered with her and then looked back at John. Her smile disappeared immediately, and Rob could see she was very nervous. He suspected her hands were at her waist with her fingers locked to hide their trembling. She didn't get a chance to speak before Thomas did.

"You've done it," he announced quietly without taking his eyes off Carolyn. "Rob, she's done it."

"What has she done?" Ruth asked, but no one answered.

Carolyn looked at Thomas and finally at Rob. The bottom of his world was about to fall away, and he couldn't meet her gaze. He closed his eyes and leaned back into the easy chair. Opening his mouth, he dragged in a deep breath. Had she found it last night and never said a word to him? She must have. He felt devastated when he realized why she'd left that morning without a word. She'd left him asleep and sneaked out as silently as a thief.

Out of the cabin and out of his life, he was certain.

He gripped the arms of his chair as he tried to turn his deep sense of loss into anger. Anger aimed at himself might relieve the constricting pain he felt in the vicinity of his heart.

If Thomas was right, she had everything she'd ever wanted now. She didn't need him for anything. There was no longer any reason for her to stay at his camp or even in puny little Lakeside.

Rob opened his eyes and looked at her. She'd been watching him for the seconds during which his heart broke, but quickly turned her gaze away to Thomas.

"Yes, Mr. Ashford, I've done it. Mr. Simons confirms it. I've found the missing necklace."

As everyone in the room watched, she unbuttoned the

waist-length, high-collared jacket that she wore over a creamy off-white, scoop-neck dress, and took it off. There, a few inches below her slender neck, lay the black emerald necklace. The twenty-four matching rectangular-cut emeralds and the larger center one sparkled from their gold settings that hung from an ornate gold chain.

"Oh, dear!" Ruth gasped, her hand going to cover her mouth as she stared at the necklace.

"Very dear indeed," John intoned.

Everyone was still staring at the gems as Carolyn went on softly in a breathy voice. "Mr. Simons has spent the day cleaning up the necklace and securing the stones well enough for me to wear it long enough to show you all this evening. There are still bits of paint caught in the gold settings. He will remove the stones, clean the gold chain, and then reset the emeralds on new, stronger settings for security. You can understand the presence of Hal. Nonetheless, I've already contacted the insurance carriers to establish a policy on it."

John cleared his throat. "I'll tell the accountant to watch for it," he offered.

She nodded. "Thank you. The necklace will be kept in the store safe until his work is done, and then it goes to the bank vault until such time as the disposition is decided."

"But it's yours, Carolyn," Thomas explained. "Louise left you the house and all its contents."

"That's easy to say, but the concept is still difficult for me to comprehend."

Carolyn stepped in front of Simons. She turned her back to him and lowered her head. He undid the simple clasp of the necklace. Rob wished the man would get his hands away from her, but he had no right to think that way.

McNair held out a black velvet box he'd brought for that

purpose, and Simons fastened the jeweled chain down to the satin bed with the padded wires set in a circle. Closing the box, Simons put it in his breast pocket and wished the others good night. McNair nodded and, with Carolyn's thanks, the two men left.

She turned to face in his general direction, but Rob noticed she was avoiding looking at him as she spoke. She toyed with her jacket in her hands. "You'll all have to forgive me if this all appeared a little on the dramatic side. You must understand that I had reason to be very cautious."

John murmured his understanding.

"I feel numb. My life has been taken out of my own hands completely since I entered your law offices in April. I believe the magnitude of what has been happening to me is just now truly sinking in. May I sit down?"

That simple request, pointing out the social shortcomings of the situation, produced an immediate reaction from John and Ruth. She thanked them for their offer of a chair.

"Here, Carolyn. Come sit by Grandpa."

Rob jerked his head toward his grandfather. Thomas was smiling broadly. He'd just invited her to sit close by, and he'd offered her the honorary relationship as his granddaughter. The irony didn't escape Rob.

Carolyn smiled and sat at his side on a chair John pulled over from a desk. She surrendered her near hand to Thomas who grasped it in both of his. They talked as if they were alone in the room while Rob and his parents listened.

"I knew you'd do it," Thomas told her, his face looking younger with his bright smile.

"Thank you for your confidence, but I didn't do more than pick it out of some thick paint." She took a deep breath. "I found it during the night when I went back to turn out the lights in the house. It was hidden above the picture molding. I have no rational explanation to offer for how I know, but I believe Lora stole it and climbed up there to hide it behind a portrait. She took it to make Robert look guilty so she could thwart her sister's plan to marry him."

"So it was right by the stairs all the time, huh," Thomas asked, interrupting for clarification.

"Right above the top step." She told them about seeing the chain and chipping out the rest. "Sara's description in her diary of Lora's death mentioned a ladder-back chair that fell with Lora. Instead of tripping on it as her father suspected, I believe she must have been climbing on it to hide the necklace."

"So much hate," Thomas said as he patted her hand.

Carolyn nodded. "She must have been mad with jealousy. Now so many strange things are happening, and people have been hurt. I hear piano music where there isn't any. I was propelled down the stairs, and Rob was almost pushed out a window."

Tears appeared in her eyes, and though she hadn't glanced in his direction, Rob could see she was fighting for control over her emotions.

"Pushed? You never told me that, Rob," John interjected.

Rob only shook his head and waved the notion aside with his hand. Their attention went back to Carolyn.

"And then finding the necklace . . . That means Robert is clear of suspicion." She took a deep breath. "If that were only the end of it."

This time when she turned, everyone in the room could see her tears trailing down her cheeks. She picked up her jacket and purse from her lap and rose. "Please, forgive me. I'm sorry, but I just can't stay for a meeting or dinner." Her voice was barely audible.

Pausing in the archway to the foyer, she looked directly at John. "Please tell me now. I've done all that Louise asked, and I must know. If I hadn't accepted the inheritance, what would have happened to Greystone?"

John looked at Rob and back at Carolyn. "You must understand that Louise believed that there were too many hearts broken in that house. Too much unhappiness. And I guess she could afford to be a romantic."

"Was Rob to get it?" she prompted.

"Rob? Why no," he said with a frown. "If Greystone could not be fixed up right, the necklace found, and Robert Ashford vindicated . . ." Everyone stared intently as he paused dramatically. "Then the house was to be destroyed."

Carolyn cried out, "Oh, no! Destroyed?"

John nodded. "Leveled to the last stone and planted over with wild flowers. Louise hoped that the 'unhappy spirits,' as she called them, who were still looking for their happiness there, would be free of the sadness that was connected with Greystone. The land was to be turned into a wildlife refuge and much of the money she'd saved used to maintain it in perpetuity." John slumped into a chair looking more tired than Rob had ever seen him.

"Um. The will stipulated that I am to supervise the work closely," Carolyn said slowly. "Then I would be there to find the necklace or to claim it if someone else found it. But now that it has been found?"

"That was not stipulated." John didn't look up from his folded hands when he spoke. "Everything is all yours, Carolyn. No more strings are attached."

Carolyn nodded and took a few moments to refold her jacket over her arm and tuck her purse back under her elbow. "Ah . . . I need some time away from Greystone. I intend to carry out all my obligations to my aunt to complete the inn, but right now I need to get away and think for a little while. You're certain this whole deal isn't going to come crashing down around me, if I take some time off?"

John looked up at her and shook his head. "No, and with all the stress you've been under, taking some time off is probably a very good idea. We'll keep an eye on things for you."

"Thank you," she mumbled. "Oh, and as soon after I return as she can, the friend of mine from Florida will be here, the one who is moving up here to be my assistant manager at the inn."

"You can afford to hire all the help you need," Rob offered and then, from the hurt look on her face, wished he hadn't.

She looked in her purse. "Greystone and now the necklace—I have gained what other people will think is a great deal. I can't help but wonder why I don't feel happier. Maybe getting away will give me time to deal with the shock of it all." She pulled her keys and picked out the one to her van.

Rob stopped breathing. His hand clutched the arms of his chair so tightly his fingers were white. Finally, tipping her head up again, she looked directly at him. He held her gaze for only a few moments. Then she looked away.

"I'll be back on the job in a couple of weeks. Goodbye," she whispered.

Rob's stomach clenched as she stepped out the door. She was leaving.

"Not worth it, if she leaves for good," Thomas murmured weakly as she closed the door behind herself.

Rob stared at the floor where she'd stood. He'd known something was wrong from the moment he woke alone in the cabin. But he hadn't wanted to believe she would leave. He wanted his expectations to be wrong. Just as he'd tried to ignore the strength of the forces at work in Greystone.

And look where it had gotten him.

Carolyn was gone. She'd said two weeks, but Rob was struck with the increasing belief that Carolyn would leave Greystone for good. She'd found the necklace. That could buy her anyone she wanted to hire to see the renovations through, and she could leave. Go back to Florida. Hell, she could go to Europe and flit from one resort to another, one country to another, living on what the necklace alone would bring on the open market.

She was free to go, but until now, he hadn't let himself think she would. But what was there to keep her here? Certainly not a guy who owned the fishing camp next door to her high-class resort.

Damn. What happened to his vow not to get emotionally involved? This was exactly what he knew would happen.

If she came back to supervise the work, his visits on the inn's business as her attorney would be his last opportunities to see her. To touch her. To smell her fresh fragrance that always brought a smile to his face. To soothe his aching heart.

But the visits would never satisfy the intimate desire he would always have for her. The need he felt just to be near her.

The thought of her leaving hit him with a gut-wrenching pain the likes of which he'd never felt before. Like a nightmare he couldn't wake up and escape from, he knew the pain would stay with him because there was no way he could keep her near.

She had everything she wanted to make her life-long dream come true, and it didn't include him. The inn hadn't been a chimera after all. He'd just witnessed it becoming a reality.

In comparison, he had nothing—just as Robert had ended up with nothing.

And Rob felt as lonely and desolate as Robert must have felt.

Chapter Sixteen

In less than an hour Carolyn had returned to the cabin, packed a suitcase, and driven out of town. A sense of urgency directed her to hurry, but she couldn't think why. Something had pointed her to the necklace, and perhaps something pointed her toward her parents' home now. She didn't know what to believe any more.

Exhausted, she arrived at their home just after midnight. Eleanor and Don were happy to see her, even if she had awakened them. Carolyn made up her bed in the room where she grew up, insisting her mom and dad go right back to sleep. She barely made it into her nightgown and couldn't even summon the energy to eat something for her missed dinner before she found the great escape in sleep.

After the urgency she'd felt at the start of her trip, it felt odd that the first four days of her two-week break went by having done little else than telling Tulie and her parents about finding the necklace, and eating and sleeping. She laughed when she remembered how important it had felt for her to come.

At meals they spoke of the progress at the inn, and she mentioned Rob only in passing. Her parents listened attentively, but she was thankful they didn't ask any questions about him beyond what she'd told them.

During the daytime Carolyn wandered out into the yard a couple of times to help her mom with the hedge trimming that needed to be done each fall. Her dad wanted to take her golfing, but she declined.

After he left without her, Eleanor expressed her concern. "Honey, you can't just keep moping around like this. It just isn't like you. You've told us everything is going well at the inn. Are there other problems that are unsolvable?"

"Oh, Mom, I've been thrown into a fantasy land. It's getting hard to tell the real from the imaginary—what I really want from what I thought I wanted. I thought creating the Greystone Inn offered me everything I've ever wanted. It's all Tulie and I ever dreamed about wanting to do. I've been given more wealth than I ever dreamed I would possess, and yet I don't feel like it should be mine. That must prove I'm crazy." She tried to laugh, but tears welled in her eyes.

Eleanor opened her arms and gave her daughter a hug. "You sound just like Louise. She never felt satisfied with her lot. She tried to fix up the inn and couldn't do it. I was never sure why she failed. It wasn't money, I don't think. I don't know. She just couldn't seem to make a go of it. Maybe she just wasn't meant to do it. Though judging by the boxes of stuff she accumulated, she sure worked on it long and hard."

"Boxes? What boxes?"

"The ones stacked at the end of the attic. I keep meaning to go through them. Your father wanted me to throw them out, but I couldn't. Something made me keep them. They've been up there for years since Louise moved into the nursing home. Say, maybe you'd like to go through them?"

"Would I!" Carolyn smiled for the first time in days. She couldn't believe her good fortune. She gave her mom a quick hug and then ran up the stairs two at a time. She was thankful the attic was an okay working temperature now that the cooler days of September had arrived. She pulled out all the dusty boxes from under the eaves and looked through each one.

For the next six days she spent all her waking hours except for meals in the attic. She even tried to take sandwiches up with her one noon, but Eleanor put her foot down. "I will not have you eating up there in that dust. It's bad enough you have to breathe it the rest of the day."

So Carolyn would gulp the sandwich and wash it down with a glass of iced tea. With a quick "Thanks, Mom," and a kiss on her cheek, she would run back up the stairs.

At the end of the six days, she'd repacked several boxes and received her parents' blessing upon her plan to take them back with her to Lakeside. Her father had smiled broadly at the idea of getting the boxes out of his attic.

On the eleventh day of her two weeks off, Carolyn plunked herself down in front of the card catalogue in the public library. Pleased with the historical costume section, she checked out several books on clothing worn in the 1890s. Eliciting Eleanor's help, the two of them spent day number twelve poring over the drawings.

"Can you do it for me, Mom? Can I hire you and your sewing friends in the church group to come up with the period costumes to use as uniforms at the inn? Do you think it's possible?"

Eleanor's "I don't know why not" was just what Carolyn wanted to hear. She clasped her hands together over her head. "Yes!"

"This is so exciting," Eleanor said, a smile filling her face, too. "I haven't felt this good in ages."

Carolyn put her hand over her heart and leaned back in her chair. "I wish Aunt Louise was here to see her dream coming true."

"If you keep her in your heart, she'll be there with you."

"Thanks, Mom." She sat up and leaned toward Eleanor with a worried frown. "Now, the important part. Can I convince you to take all these books back to the library when you're done with them so I'm not socked with an overdue fine?" The two women laughed.

Carolyn was happy she'd asked her mom to make the costumes. It would be fun working together on a project again. Eleanor made a series of phone calls and found several friends who agreed to help, too. They all decided, however, that the pay should go to the church, not to the women.

The next evening the sewing group gathered in Eleanor's living room for dessert. Carolyn outlined the project and its time parameters. Once they understood that most of the actual construction couldn't even begin until the staff was hired to know the sizes, they still agreed to do it. She thanked them all for their support and knew she could count on them.

"I'm so glad I came home," Carolyn told her mother as they went up the stairs to bed that night. "Those boxes were a treasure of information. Aunt Louise used to send me letters at college just when I needed them. Reading all these notes that she kept about Greystone when the Whitneys lived there was just what I needed now. And the portrait and photos I'm taking back—they're going to make it all almost perfect."

"Almost?"

"As close to perfect as I can make it. The rest . . . well, it depends on other people . . . other things . . ."

On day fourteen Carolyn left with her van loaded with boxes that smelled of musty attic. She made a lengthy stop in Syracuse on her way back. She talked with an oil painting restorer and watched while he and two assistants looked over the things she'd brought. They put her in touch with a portrait painter—her next stop. When all the possibilities matched her requests, contracts were agreed to, and Carolyn left for Lost Lake.

She raced a cart through a Lakeside grocery store just before it closed and pulled in next to Cabin One about an hour after dark. Her groceries stashed away, she grabbed her jacket and keys, and jogged toward the mansion.

She was amazed to see how much had been accomplished in two weeks. The walls were all plastered and the wood trims back in place. The central heating and air-conditioning systems had appeared. The elevator was in, though a big "Danger, Do Not Use" sign hung on a rope across where the doors should be. The walls were up for the lobby restrooms and the plumbing in.

Stainless steel counters and sinks shone beneath bright new fluorescent lights in the kitchen. Throughout Greystone, the pipes had been installed in the ceilings for the sprinkler system, and all the guestroom bathrooms had been roughed in.

Stepping back into what had been the front parlor, she wondered momentarily why she heard no music, saw no figure at a piano. Sara should be happy now. Yet on Carolyn's whole tour she'd seen and heard nothing unusual. Nothing but her own footfalls on the wood floors. Shaking her head, she turned off the lights and came full circle back to the foyer.

She was about to cross to the entrance when she heard not music but a woman crying. Drawn to the sound, she saw Sara sitting on the top stair. A very unhappy Sara. Carolyn couldn't move closer, but she couldn't run away either. The shape stirred as if to disappear.

"Wait. Please. I . . . I want to thank you for your help,

Sara. You led me to the necklace, didn't you? Well, I know you did. But I don't understand what's happening now. To you or to me. Why are you so unhappy? Wasn't finding it enough?"

The figure lowered her head into her hands and sobbed.

"What's wrong? I found the necklace. I'm doing all I can to finish the inn. I promise you, Sara. I don't know what else you want me to do."

"Robert."

The whisper of his name swirled around her as she watched Sara lift her arms in supplication. Her eyes were wide with an innocent sadness that brought tears to Carolyn's own eyes.

"Robert."

Carolyn swiped at the falling tears with the back of her hand. "I can't bring Robert to you. I cleared his name, but that's it. I can't do any more than to finish the inn."

Before Carolyn could say more, the figure was caught up in a pale whirlwind that rose and vanished.

Switching off the last light and locking up, Carolyn headed back over the path to Cabin One. Even after a hot shower aimed at relaxing her, it was a long time before she fell asleep.

The wind rustling the colorful autumn leaves outside sounded too much like weeping.

Carolyn couldn't hear him because her cabin windows were all closed against the cool fall night temperatures, but she saw him sitting by the lake as soon as she was up and dressed. She slipped on her jacket and stepped out onto the screened-in porch.

The early-morning fog was slowly rising from the lake. The rays of the sun breaking through the highest branches painted strips of lighter blue on the dark water.

The high-pitched whine of a few electric trolling motors signaled that fisherpersons were already out in their annual fall pursuit of the elusive trout.

A squirrel scurried across the driveway and disappeared up a tree with a new-found tidbit from the picnic table nearby. The scene appeared so beautiful. So peaceful.

Her gaze was drawn back to the man on the flat rock. His arms and broad shoulders, covered with warm, blue-plaid flannel, extended beyond the down-filled vest he wore over jeans. She remembered the strength of those arms around her, holding her, comforting her. Loving her.

His long legs, crossed casually at the ankles, stretched out toward the lake. She could almost feel them intimately entwined with hers as they lay together.

A tremor shook Carolyn's body, not from the cold but from fear. About to face Rob, she was more afraid at that moment than she'd been facing the specters in Greystone. She knew by the expression on his face when he saw the necklace the night she'd left, she'd hurt him badly by not trusting him enough to tell him. But what about her pain when she found the drawings and realized he was searching for the necklace to use it for himself?

What would their relationship be now that she knew the intimate moments she'd shared with Rob had been proven false? She might be better off thinking of them as two adults with normal sexual appetites who happened to be thrown together. That was better than thinking he'd made love to her to be close to her in order to find the necklace himself to bankroll the new lodge.

While in her heart she hated to think that being her attorney was all that connected them now, how could she even trust him in that capacity?

The familiar whir-plop drew her out into the crisp morning air. The porch door squeaked as always. The air smelled so clean and fresh that she stopped to inhale deeply.

Starting her slow walk to the big rock, she watched him cast out his bait, let it sink a half minute or so and reel it in, only to start the routine again. He didn't turn even though he had to have heard her approach. The first word would have to be hers.

"Catch enough for breakfast for two?"

"Don't tell me the rich girl is panhandling for grub?"

Carolyn staggered back a step. She felt as if she'd been slapped. It hadn't sounded at all like a joke. She watched him slowly retrieve the unsuccessful cast and climb off the rock.

"You can walk on your foot now." She immediately felt stupid for having said it. After all, it had been two weeks.

"Just bothers me when I run." He walked to the water's edge and pulled in a stringer of two rainbow trout. "Do you want to come up to the house?"

"Or we could eat here. I stopped at the store last night."

"Suit yourself."

"Here then, I guess. You can bring me up to speed on Greystone." It would be too painful to return to his house where they had shared so many happy meals.

The two people who had been lovers walked up to the cabin acting every bit like casual acquaintances. They worked together getting the meal fixed, but never came close to helping each other, or touching each other. Instead they each picked a job and did it all alone. When they ate, Carolyn thought the fresh fish must be delicious, but she couldn't tell. She could barely swallow it past the dry lump in her throat.

"You'll want to talk to Dad today. You're at a point where the contractor that specializes in code requirement monitoring should be here full-time now."

"That would be good. I'll be glad to have him do more of the day-to-day supervising and checking. I want to get the apartment over there habitable so I can move in this week. You can have your cabin back for fishermen for the fall season."

"Sure. Thanks."

They each carried their own dishes to the sink. Two short stacks of dishes looked up at her in a wide-eyed stare. They hadn't even stacked them together.

"I guess I should get to work. I'll call your father this morning." Carolyn turned to face him, but couldn't hold his intense gaze. "Thanks for breakfast. Delicious."

"Yeah. No problem."

Against her better judgment, she wanted so desperately for him to say he'd missed her, to hold her, to . . . But he obviously wasn't going to. He didn't say anything, and it was just as well. He stood there looking, well, more tired than she remembered ever seeing him. Maybe his ankle still disturbed his sleep.

"I'll do these later," she announced with a wave of her hand toward the sink. "I really should run. I can't wait to see the progress in the inn. I only took time for a quick tour last night."

"You arrived early enough to go to Greystone?"

She nodded and watched him slowly blink his eyes and sigh. He didn't move to leave, but he didn't say anything either. He must be waiting for her to make the first move again.

Tell me not to go, she silently pleaded. *Take me in your arms and hold me here. Tell me it was all a big mistake. Explain why I should trust you again and ignore the plans I found.*

She pulled her jacket from the rack and glanced at his fishing rod leaning in the corner of the porch. "Take your time. Just snap the lock on the door when you leave. I have the key."

He nodded, but still not a word.

"I . . . I'll see you later then."

He leaned down to pick up a spoon left on the table and turned his back to her as he put it in the sink.

Feeling like a fool, she ran from the cabin down the path to the inn. The exertion of running didn't explain the tears in her eyes when she arrived at Greystone, but no one asked. The greetings from the workers followed immediately by their questions and complaints took her attention away from her personal problems.

And that was good. She couldn't dwell on what she'd lost. She had a wonderful dream inn to complete. And since that's all she had, it would have to be enough.

When she got back to her cabin to grab some lunch, she discovered Rob had done all the dishes and cleared everything away from their breakfast for two. It looked as if they had never been together at all.

Maybe that's what he wished. He'd left her—emotionally. And by winter—physically as well. He'd be going back to his law practice full-time and move on to another client.

Why? Why had she let herself fall in love with a man she couldn't trust?

In a few days' time, the manager's apartment in the inn was cleaned up and furnished. Carolyn learned that Rob had set a crew on it as soon as she'd left, trying to have it done before she returned. It appeared to be his engraved invitation to get out of his cabin and out of his life.

The new van she'd ordered with the name "Greystone Inn" painted on the side had arrived while she was gone. It easily transported all her belongings in one trip from the cabin to the inn. On her next visit to town, she retrieved the rest of the boxes from storage where they'd been since Tulie shipped them from Florida.

The day after she moved out of the fishing camp, Bill Swenson, the new supervising contractor, moved into Cabin One. Tall, blond, and of Scandinavian descent like Lars, Bill, or Super, as the workers called him, was friendly and easygoing. He had a fantastic ability to remember details of all sorts and had a memory for lists that didn't quit. In other words, Carolyn concluded, paired with his construction supervision know-how and years of experience, his uncanny memory made him perfect for the job.

Carolyn conferred with Bill daily, but from the time he'd signed on, she left the construction and the meeting of codes to him as she turned her attention to the decorating and marketing plans for the inn.

Rob showed up at Greystone with checks for her to sign and sometimes just to look around. He was always cordial, but when his business as liaison attorney tending to Carolyn's interests was done, he left. His demeanor was so impersonal on his visits, she'd given up hope that he derived any pleasure from seeing her. Sometimes he appeared to do little more than watch her, but other times John came in his stead.

Carolyn hurried to complete what she could outdoors before winter set in. She had much of the landscape planting done as soon as the roads and parking areas were blacktopped. The trees and shrubs would get a head start on spring-planted ones.

She'd decided to restore a long-handled pump over the

old well in the area set aside as the flower garden. Guests might get a kick out of pumping water the old-fashioned way.

For indoor decor ideas she turned to the treasures from her folks' attic. She'd found Louise's copious notes of what she remembered about every room she saw as a child. Carolyn didn't set out to duplicate what she read, but rather to use it as a basis on which she made her own design decisions. The decor for each guestroom would be different. She wasn't going to institutionalize the inn with the same vinyl wallpaper throughout. The modern plumbing and lighting fixtures she'd selected were reminiscent of the Victorian era when Greystone was built, but definitely contemporary in function and convenience.

When she had her decorating plan firmly in mind, she and Tulie would price it out and then hire a decorator who could get the job done within the tight time constraints that Carolyn was determined to keep.

As to marketing the inn, it wasn't difficult. Some news of what happened there made the national wire service and broadcasts over which Carolyn had no control. Someone leaked the story about her finding the emerald necklace. The item appeared in newspapers and on some evening national network news programs across the country. Reporters called and came out to interview her. Rob insisted on being at her side to advise her. She suffered the pain of her heart breaking when he was near, but remained businesslike.

"The inn will be completed soon," she announced. "We'll be ready for bookings some time in midwinter if all goes well."

The reporters eagerly listened to the story of brokenhearted Sara and Robert. "What about you two? You're the modern Sara and Robert. Any romance between you two?" they asked nosily.

Carolyn looked up at Rob, leaving him to answer the man because her voice had suddenly failed her.

"The Sara and Robert who were romantically linked lived a long time ago," he said without hesitation. "Carolyn and I have a business relationship. That's all. As we told you, I'm her attorney, and Carolyn is the owner of the Greystone Inn and a priceless emerald necklace. Hey, what more could she want?" he asked them, grinning and getting a laugh. The reporters weren't willing to give up so easily, but Rob managed to cut them off and whisk Carolyn away.

Old newspaper stories of Lora's death were dug up and rewritten. Those written by more imaginative reporters even suggested that Sara's ghost might still be in the inn waiting for Robert to return. The public loved it.

But none of them knew it was all true.

"You should feel fortunate getting the free publicity," Tulie told her after seeing the story in a Miami paper.

"I couldn't have gotten such extensive coverage even if I'd tried to create a nationwide ad campaign."

"And you can't complain about the cost," Tulie added.

No one will ever know how much this has cost me, Carolyn added to herself.

As Halloween neared, publicity of the Greystone as a haunted house picked up.

"Damn. I never guessed that necklace was hidden right under our noses," Tiny told Carolyn one morning. "I heard about the house on the news again last night."

Carolyn smiled. "Great publicity, isn't it?"

"You might not think so if you saw the cars that have been turned back from entering the road here all day," Lars announced, coming in just then, much later than expected.

"I wondered when you were going to get back," Tiny teased.

"Hell, I've been fighting the traffic—all the nuts wanting to get a peek at this place."

"We'll need to have a gate or checkpoint at the entrance to the driveway," Carolyn told him. "If people have no business here, we'd better keep them out. It's not safe to have them wandering around the work area."

"Got that right," offered Lars. "Wait until Rob discovers that he'll have to show his ID to drive to his own house." Laughing all the way about how Rob would react, Lars and Tiny went into the bar to finish the final coat of varnish on the bar they had built to match the walnut paneling on the walls.

At John's suggestion, a metal gate was put up across the road on her side of the fork next to the road to Rob's camp. It left his road open, but it connected with a fence that led into the woods far enough to prevent vehicles from going around it to Greystone.

The name, Greystone Inn, was set into a wrought-iron pattern of pine trees with a circle at each end capturing the spinning sun from the stained-glass window over the entrance. Enhancing the entrance when swung open or shut, the tall gate added to the grand Victorian decor. However, it was locked each night, and manned by someone to check people who wanted to enter during the day.

The gate kept the curious away, and from the time Carolyn moved to the manager's apartment, Rob seemed to stay away, too. She rarely spent any time with him when other people weren't present. Once in a while their eyes would meet and hold, but someone would call their attention to something, and the moment would end.

Rob couldn't have made himself more clear. He was no

longer interested in her in a personal way. Deep inside herself, she was trying to piece together the pieces of her shattered heart. Not even the fact she was rich could entice him to stay. Of course, she couldn't accept money as the reason for his interest, any more than she could accept that it had been the necklace that kept him close up to the day she found it.

When her former fiancé in Florida finally got his promotion, thanks to her, he'd moved out without a word. She never had to see him and be reminded that she meant nothing to him anymore. But seeing Rob at least weekly made her love for him a painful lesson that she would never forget.

"Carolyn Sara Matison, what's the matter with you, girl?" a strong female voice called from the foyer.

Chapter Seventeen

"Tulie!" Carolyn cried in surprise. She ran to hug her best friend, who stood at the front entrance of Greystone.

"You trying to keep me out o' this place? I had a heck of a time convincing the owly wooly character at the road that I really knew you, much less that I was supposed to be here."

"Sorry about that, but you can't imagine the number of gawkers that have driven up here lately to see the haunted house that gave up its jewels."

"Well, the guy wasn't prepared to fight a little brown bear and couldn't keep me out."

Carolyn laughed. "When I got no answer at your apartment last week, you had me worried. You'd never told me exactly when you could come."

"I had another week on that lease and decided to visit my folks for a few days before I packed the car and moved north."

"I'm glad. How are they doing?"

"They're fine. They're just afraid I'll freeze to death way up here."

"Oh, it's so good to see you." Carolyn blinked rapidly as their reunion triggered tears that welled in her eyes.

The friends hugged once more, but Tulie stepped back and examined Carolyn's tearful face. "Well, you don't look none too good. What's this place been doing to you, honey?"

"It's not the place," Carolyn announced with a wry

smile. "Come on. Let me show you around. You'll love it as much as I do."

"I'd love to see it, but that doesn't mean you're gonna get away with not telling me what is bothering you, girl."

Carolyn smiled. "You got that in one, but I'll tell you about it later." She sniffled and grinned. "Gosh, I'm glad you're here. And have we got work to do. Would you believe letters are arriving requesting room reservations? It's been all the publicity about the necklace."

"Fantastic! So what are you doing about the letters?"

"I sent them all the informational brochure and wrote that I would notify them as soon as the opening date had been determined."

The women were interrupted by the driver of a truckload of bath fixtures that had arrived. Carolyn signed for them and called to some men to help make room and unload them.

"This is like Grand Central Station," Tulie said, dodging a dolly of boxes.

"Yeah, feels like Christmas every day with all the truckloads of boxes," Carolyn said. *Only Christmas should be a much happier time than fall at Greystone has been,* she added to herself.

The women took the elevator to the third floor to start their tour from the top.

"I'm impressed," Tulie admitted as they walked through the rooms. "Greystone is really starting to look like an inn."

"Finally," Carolyn amended. "It's been a long haul, and there's so much left to do to get this place opened."

"Hon, just tell me what you want me to do, and I'll get started."

"Thanks for coming, girlfriend," Carolyn whispered, her voice hoarse with emotion. "You can always make me laugh, and I need that." She blinked away the tears that stung her eyes. "Not to mention needing your help for all the work I have to do." Standing on the balcony over the foyer, she and Amatulla laughed and hugged again, even more excitedly, rocking from side to side.

"I'm here and ready to start to work," Tulie told her.

"Carolyn?" Rob called up from the foyer.

Carolyn stiffened. The smile flew from her face, to be immediately replaced by a faked one. She reinforced the barrier around her heart to keep the hurt from spilling out. "Rob. Hi. We'll be right down."

"Uh-oh," Tulie said beneath her breath after watching the changes in Carolyn. "From the looks of you, girl, I think this is just the man I want to meet."

At the bottom of the steps, Carolyn introduced her to Rob. "Besides being my new assistant manager, she's my best friend," she added.

"I hope a friend of Carolyn's is a friend of mine," Rob said smoothly as they shook hands. He smiled broadly, but Carolyn noted his smile didn't make his eyes sparkle as they used to. Was he on guard because Tulie had arrived to help her?

"All the northern men this friendly and good-looking?" Tulie teased. "I'm going to like it up here despite the cold winters."

Rob laughed. "And I think I'll like having you here," he responded. "How soon can you start to work? Carolyn can sure use the help. She works too hard."

Carolyn glanced at Rob. He'd sounded concerned about her, but he wasn't even looking at her.

"I am here to stay!" Tulie announced with a laugh and a wiggle of her ample hips.

"Welcome to the Greystone Inn," Rob said. "Say, why

don't I take you both to dinner? It's getting close to that time, and we can tell you all about what's happening."

"Sounds great," Tulie agreed before Carolyn could get a word in. "After airplane food for lunch, I'm starved."

"Ah, I'm not dressed to go out," Carolyn finally managed, looking at the other two dressed in business suits in sharp contrast to her jeans and sweatshirt.

"Will forty minutes be long enough to get ready? I'll show Tulie the camp and then take her up to my house. We can have a drink while we wait for you to join us."

Tulie slipped her hand in Rob's bent elbow. "Honey, you're just what I've been looking for—a man who wants to take me home with him."

They both laughed, but then looked back expectantly at Carolyn. "Ah, sure. Forty minutes. It won't take me any time at all."

"Why don't you give me a call when you're ready? We'll come pick you up," Rob announced as he put his hand over Tulie's dark one and ushered her through the reception area.

Tulie looked back over her shoulder. Her broad smile lit up her face as she winked at Carolyn. "No need to rush on my account, girl. I can see I am in good hands." She laughed as they disappeared out the door arm in arm.

Carolyn showered and dressed with uncustomary speed. Standing at the telephone ready to call Rob, she caught sight of herself in the mirror. Her image startled her. She looked very much like a jealous woman. All the guns in her arsenal of clothes and makeup had been pulled out to make herself look as great as possible, and for what? A dinner with her best friend and her . . .

Pesky tears stung her eyes. "Don't go messing your makeup," she ordered herself aloud.

With a sniff, she dabbed the corners of her eyes with a tissue and looked for her purse.

I have no right to feel jealous, she thought. *I have no claim on Rob. I can't feel jealous in a relationship that doesn't exist.*

But as she went to meet them, she wished the evening had ended already.

On Halloween day the Greystone Inn name appeared in upstate newspapers again with a story about the "ghosts" that haunted it. Some workmen were quoted as saying they had seen or heard a ghost. That only spurred the reporters on to weave more imaginative tales.

Carolyn noticed that Rob hung around as the men and women working in the inn left for their homes that evening. She found him in the foyer when she came down to lock up the front after checking all the rooms.

"Has Tulie left yet?" she asked.

"What? Ah, yeah," he answered distractedly.

"Rob? Is there something else you wanted?"

He studied her a moment and dropped his gaze to a packing staple on the floor, which he leaned over to pick up. He tossed it up and caught it before he spoke. "Yeah. I . . . I wondered if you wanted to join me for dinner."

Carolyn's heart beat hard enough to affect her vision. Her hands gripped the railing on the balcony where she stood looking down at him. She couldn't let her desire to be near him cloud her view of his motivation.

She breathed deeply and started to walk across to the stairs. She slid her hand along the smooth walnut railing, welcoming its solid support as she descended to the foyer.

"Why, was there something else we needed to discuss?"

"Discuss? No," he said with a shrug. "I just thought you wouldn't want to eat alone." He wrapped a fist around the staple and slid his hands into his pants pockets and followed her.

"I see." She spun around and faced him squarely. "Let me be sure I understand this. Since I got back from my parents' house nearly two months ago, you've made sure you've never been in a room with me alone for more than a few minutes. Other than business lunches or dinners, you've left me to eat every meal here by myself, but suddenly you think I wouldn't want to eat alone?"

"Damn it, Carolyn. I worry about you."

She straightened her spine. "How very unnecessary," she said coolly. "I am fully capable of taking care of myself."

"I know that. I'm worried there might be trouble tonight. Damn it. It's Halloween." He stepped closer and raised his hands. To touch her? To plead with her? He dropped them when she spoke.

"Haven't I told you? I'm planning a party tonight, but I didn't think you'd want to come. It's a private party for me and two or three ghosts. Say, maybe I should have invited the press. Think of all the publicity."

She flipped through her key ring to find the one for the lobby entrance deadbolt. She prayed Rob didn't notice her hands were trembling.

"Carolyn, you never know what some kook will do tonight." He stepped closer and gripped her upper arms. A burning sensation wrapped around her as if she'd been branded. "Will you listen to me?" he demanded, squeezing her arms.

Their gazes locked. The anger darkening his eyes took her breath away. She separated her lips and tried to draw in a deep breath. Without warning he crushed Carolyn against his chest and kissed her hard, taking full advantage of her open mouth.

She didn't have time to think. She could only feel. Her traitorous body surrendered, and she kissed him back. Her body molded to his, revisiting every hard line and plane she'd loved so well. For a few long seconds, the kiss was ecstasy.

Then she remembered. She remembered he only pretended to care for her when he'd had to.

Carolyn moved her hands to his shoulders and pushed to get free of him. He broke off the kiss, but still clutched her arms.

"Let go of me!" She jerked back completely out of his grasp. "I'm no good-time girl, Robert Ashford. I made a big mistake when I misjudged you so completely. I won't make that mistake again. Oh, but you do your job so well. Your father should be damned proud of you. Even though you didn't find the necklace first, you'll get what you want. The Greystone Inn can only bring your fishing camp next door more business in the future."

"Carolyn, that's not—"

"I don't want to hear it. Just leave! I have to put up with you here when an attorney needs to be present, but otherwise, I don't want to see you and your two faces at Greystone. Get out!" She whirled around and stood with her back to him, her chest heaving.

She'd dropped her keys some time during the kiss. He leaned over to pick them up and held them out at her side. She grabbed them from his hand and looked away.

After a moment of silence, she felt each of his exiting footfalls smash the pieces of her broken heart. She felt the chill in the air that swirled around her and assumed, at first, it was from the open door when he left. When she turned toward the footsteps behind her, she knew differently. Frozen in place, she could only stand and watch.

Lloyd had been crossing the foyer to his den when he heard an auto pull up at the front door.

"I'll get the door, Betty," he volunteered, dismissing Betty with a wave of his hand. He wanted to answer the door in case it was Robert again. He was going to settle this once and for all.

Betty nodded and returned to the kitchen as he swung the door open. "What are you doing here?" he asked gruffly, blocking entrance into the house. "Haven't you done enough?"

Robert took his hat off and held it in both hands. "I've come to see Sara."

Lloyd laughed insanely. "Well, I won't allow it. You may not see Sara." A wild look filled his face. His eyes widened with rage. "You'll never see her again. You murdered Lora as surely as if you'd pushed her down the stairs, and I never want to see or hear you again."

"Please, sir. You can't mean that. I'm sorry for your loss, but I did nothing to cause Lora's accident. Please let me see Sara . . . just for a few minutes."

"You will never see her," Lloyd shouted. "Never! Now get off my property and don't come back again." He slammed the door.

Carolyn winced at the venom in Lloyd's voice. A shiver ran down her back. Tonight she understood Sara's pain over not being able to see Robert again, because it wouldn't be long before Carolyn would never see Rob again. She understood now why she often heard Sara weeping in the night—the same reason she had wept. They had each lost their Robert forever.

Carolyn locked the entrance and ran to her apartment where she rinsed her face with cool water. After forcing some soup down for supper, she remembered she hadn't gone out to be certain the gate on the road was locked. Rob was right about one thing. Halloween was a night on which to be careful. She should be certain it was locked.

Hoping the walk in the cool evening would do her good, she took her flashlight, but left it turned off since the full moon provided enough light to walk safely.

Exiting by the back door, she crossed the blacktopped parking lot to the road. Feeling nervous as the darkness of the woods closed in around her, she was glad her rubber-soled shoes made no sounds. She had enough problems with spirits on her hands without raising any more on Halloween night, she thought uneasily.

When she was far enough around the curve to see the gate, she saw the red pickup parked across the road beyond it. She crept closer to make sure. Yes, it was Rob. The blue light in the cab, probably from the radio that she could hear playing, illuminated his head and shoulders leaning back against the far side window. Though looking like he was asleep at the moment, Greystone's self-appointed guard for the night was on duty.

Carolyn made her way back to her apartment, though tears filling her eyes made seeing difficult. Once safely locked in, she fell on her bed and cried herself to sleep.

The only sounds in Greystone that night were of two weeping women, while out on the road, country music and light snoring floated from the pickup.

"It can't be done, Carolyn. No way." Bill Swenson was pacing the foyer, but Carolyn wouldn't back down.

"It's not even Thanksgiving yet," she told him. "That gives us a whole month. I don't see why we can't open by Christmas."

"I'm trying to tell you why not, but you won't listen."

"Bill, humor me. Get all the foremen together. Talk to them. This place is almost done. Wouldn't all the crews like to be done and go home for Christmas?"

The specialized crews required for a restoration of this scope had not all been available nearby. Suggesting the men would like to be done and home for the holidays was the right button to push for Bill. She knew he was already getting calls from his wife, wondering how long he was going to be able to spend with his family over the holidays.

He nodded slowly. "I'll talk to them," he promised.

"You understand it'll mean committing rooms. Sending out invitations to the grand opening. If we decide it's a go for Christmas, nothing can stand in the way, Bill. Nothing."

"Right, boss."

Carolyn smiled and watched him take the steps three at a time while shouting for one of his men as he went. She went straight to her apartment telephone where she would have privacy and called her mother. She hardly gave Eleanor a chance to get a word in edgewise.

"I'll know for sure this afternoon, Mom, but I think we'll open at Christmastime. I'm saving a room overlooking the lake for you and Dad. Will the period costumes be ready in time?"

"We have all the unsized items that you ordered completed now. We played it safe so we wouldn't disappoint you. If you get us the sizes for the rest ASAP, I know we can do it. There's no need to worry. Say, you're coming home for Thanksgiving, aren't you?"

"I hadn't even thought about it, but yes, I guess I could. I'll have to drive down that morning and leave the next day though. I gave Tulie the whole week off to go home since she won't get away for months after that. We'll be too busy."

"You can take back what we have done by then. Oh, and I'll make sure I have yours ready for a fitting then."

"That'll be great. I can't wait to see them. It's really wonderful of the women in your church sewing group to help."

"Honey, we haven't been this excited over anything in years. It's been just what we needed."

Carolyn heard knocking at her door and ended the call. The knock could only mean it was back-to-work time. Her goal for the next several weeks was to work with Tulie and hire and train the people who would work in the inn after it opened for business. They had to conduct interviews and then spend a good deal of time on the phone checking out previous employers and references.

Along with Tulie, she needed a staff that would be capable of running the inn smoothly—even without her there.

"Carolyn, it doesn't fit." Eleanor appeared aghast at how much Carolyn had changed over the last two months. "I made it exactly like your blue one. That one fit perfectly this summer."

"I know, Mom. I've lost a little weight since then. I'm too busy to bother with much for meals, and I don't see putting the pounds back on in the next few weeks with all I have to get done, so I think you'd better take it in."

Eleanor patiently made some marks with tailor's chalk and helped Carolyn get out of the dress. "Other than being loose, I think it turned out well, don't you?"

"It's beautiful. If the dresses and uniforms from the other seamstresses are as carefully made as this one, they'll all be wonderful."

"We're all so excited being involved in this. It was sweet of you to hire them to work."

"Sweet? No, Mom. Smart. I knew the women in your sewing circle would do a better job than a costume or uniform company could have." Carolyn slid back into her slacks and sweater.

"We had so much fun, too. I took those books you got out from the library to a special meeting, and we came up with the drawings I sent you. When you gave us the go-ahead, we used a Ping-Pong table in one of the members' basements as a cutting table. Then we divided them up so each of us had a couple costumes to take home."

"Wait until the uniform companies get wind of you ladies. You'll be on their payroll for special orders like this one. I would sure recommend you."

"Hey, in there. When is the turkey going to get eaten around here?"

Eleanor opened the bedroom door to her husband. "Just finished, dear." She walked on out toward the kitchen. "Dinner won't be long."

"Carolyn?"

"Come on in, Dad." She rehung the long dress in the closet. "What is it?"

Don walked over to her and took one of her hands in his. "Well, I don't know what to say except that your mother and I are very proud of you. You have taken on so much though, honey, that we worry about you." He didn't let Carolyn speak when she tried to. "I know. I know. It's all going very well." He patted her hand and squeezed it. "And you've got your mother interested in doing something, and she's having so much fun. Well, if there's anything your old dad can do to help, just holler."

Carolyn put her arms around his neck and hugged him. "Thanks, Dad. It's so great to be able to count on both of you."

He held her close. "We love you, Carolyn, you know."

"I know, Dad. You, Mom, Aunt Louise. The love you've

all given me made me strong enough to do this. It means more to me than I can ever say."

She swiped at the tears that crowded out of her eyes onto her cheeks. "Don't tell anyone," she added with exaggerated effect to tease him, "but I didn't know if I had it in me to do this. It must be the genes."

They both laughed and shared another hug before Eleanor called them to dinner.

"That is so hot!" Tulie loved the idea of the resident ghosts at the Greystone Inn. She reread all the stories about them that Carolyn had cut from the papers, and hooted. "It's a great publicity gimmick. You have got to use it in your brochures and the program for the grand opening. It's exciting."

Carolyn winced. To Tulie, this was all an exciting marketing idea. She never saw the misty visitors, or heard the music, or Sara's sobs and Lora's chilling laughter.

And Carolyn couldn't bring herself to admit to Tulie that she had. Tulie never asked if the visitations had been real, and Carolyn didn't volunteer the information. The less said the better. She didn't want to stir up any threatening specters again.

Except for the weeping at night, it had been peaceful for a long time. No one had gotten hurt in weeks. Carolyn liked it that way. She'd even tried to talk herself into believing the haunting wails were the north winds.

"Hey, there's another truck," Tulie called.

Carolyn clapped her hands and grinned. "That must be the piano for the corner of the dining room."

The process of moving it indoors and setting it up took all their attention.

"It has to come to room temperature and humidity before it can be tuned. The guy who does that will be here in two days," the deliverymen told them. "Should be ready by then. In the meantime, don't let anyone play it." The men covered the piano with a quilted cover made to fit and left.

At the end of the day, Carolyn and Tulie were going over the brochure design that would be coordinated with all the printed materials like room service menus, complimentary stationary for the guests, and everything else that would employ the same design. Their materials were spread out across the long reception desk that had been built in across the back of the foyer, or lobby, as it was now called.

They were so engrossed in what they were doing that Carolyn didn't notice at first that the piano music had begun. When it finally registered, Carolyn's first panicked thoughts were that by playing, someone was harming the newly delivered piano. She ran to the dining room door. She slid to a stop and gripped the doorframe.

Sara sat on the bench, her slender fingers flying over the keys.

Carolyn heard the melody, but it wasn't from the inn's piano. It was from the same faraway piano that Sara had been playing for months.

"Did you forget one?" Tulie called from behind her.

"What?" Carolyn whirled back around to face her across the lobby.

"You left the desk so suddenly I assumed you'd thought of one you forgot in there."

Carolyn looked from Tulie to Sara and back. Carolyn heard the music, but her friend made no mention of it. Carolyn saw Sara sitting on the piano bench, but Tulie walked to her side without noticing her. "When you look at the piano, what do you see?"

"A nice shiny black piano, under the cover I mean. All we need now is Stevie Wonder to entertain at the opening."

Carolyn tried to laugh, but she wanted to cry. She looked back at Sara.

Sara's fingers stilled over the keys while she looked out the window into the dark of the evening. Her eyes were brimming with tears.

"Listen, Tulie, I'm beat," Carolyn said, feeling an overwhelming need to be alone. "Let's stop now and start again in the morning. The guy from the ad agency will be here then anyway. He'll know if we've overlooked something."

"Good. I'm tired too. How about going into town and eating dinner with me? I'm tired of getting dinner for one in my little efficiency kitchen."

"Thanks, but by the time I clean up and go into town to eat and come all the way back out . . ." She shrugged.

Tulie had her coat on when Rob came down the stairs after touring with one of the town inspectors who walked on past them with a nod. "Hey, here's just the man I need," she said enthusiastically to Rob. She wrapped her hands around his elbow. "How about going into town for dinner? Check out the competition we'll have at the restaurants there."

Rob looked to Carolyn and back again. "All right," he answered warily.

"Great. You will build up enthusiasm as the evening progresses?" Tulie laughed when Rob responded with a grin and turned back to Carolyn. "You're sure you're too tired to go?"

Carolyn didn't trust her voice to speak. She nodded and managed a bit of a smile as she went to pick up the pile of their papers.

"Aren't you going too, Carolyn?" Rob asked.

"No, I . . . I'm . . . I told Tulie I couldn't go."

The look that flashed across his face was almost one of

anger, she thought. But then he turned back to Tulie with a smile. "Nothing to keep us here then."

"I'll see you in the morning then, Carolyn. 'Night," Tulie called with a wave.

Carolyn managed to call out, "Good night," as they reached the door.

"I worry about her, Rob," Tulie was saying. "Sometimes she looks so pale. You'd think she really had seen a ghost."

The door closed behind them. Alone in Greystone, Carolyn locked the entrance door before walking to her apartment. She stared out the back window into the darkness. Leaning against it with her head leaning on the cold glass, Rob's words echoed in her mind. He was right. There was nothing to keep him there now. If only . . .

"Robert, you shouldn't be here in the rose garden. Father will be so angry if he sees us together."

"I had to take that chance. I couldn't let you go back to the city without seeing you again. I love you, Sara."

"Oh, Robert, I love you with all my heart. But I won't see you again until next summer. I can only hope that by then Father will be more understanding than he has been since Lora . . . fell."

"I know he will be, sweetling. Someday he'll allow us to marry. Sara, please believe that you needn't be so sad. We must be patient, but above all, you must trust me. Believe me when I say I love you and we will be together one day. Trust me."

Sara tried to smile, but the tears flowing from her eyes made the smile a lie. "I'll love you forever, Robert."

"Forever," he echoed.

He kissed her softly and ran back to the cover of darkness on the path through the woods.

Sara had begun to play again. Feeling miserable and

wanting the company, Carolyn left her apartment door open to hear the piano better while she made a cold sandwich for her supper.

Chapter Eighteen

Rob handed Tulie into her car. He shut the door with more force than he'd intended.

She rolled down the window. "Rob, if you'd rather not go, we can make it another night."

"No, I'm sorry. I'm hungry, and as a matter of fact, I can't think of anyone I'd rather be with tonight. You have a way of cheering me up every time we talk."

"You say the sweetest things," she said with that chuckle of hers he was so used to hearing.

"I'll be right behind you in my truck. That way you can stay in town and go home from the restaurant."

"Gotcha," she said as she inserted her key to start her car.

Rob strode to his truck and climbed in behind the wheel. Damn, he was a slow study. When was he going to learn? Carolyn had no intention of going out with him tonight or ever. Why would she want to waste her time with a guy like him?

Why hadn't he listened to her? She'd told him very clearly that the inn was the all-important dream of her life. She didn't want him. Hell, the great way she was handling things, she hardly needed him as her attorney. He looked out over the water and tried for a moment to relax.

"Never see her again . . ." echoed in Robert's mind.

Lloyd had forbidden him to come to Sara's funeral that winter. But he went anyway. Standing apart from the others where he couldn't be seen, he watched the brief service. After-

wards, when Arthur finally persuaded his brother, Lloyd, to leave the family plot where he'd laid to rest his wife and both daughters, the other mourners all left quickly.

Robert watched as the gravediggers filled in the grave. He heard the dirt hitting the polished wood coffin and shuddered.

"Sara," he whispered, tears welling in his eyes. "Know that I love you, but it wasn't enough. I prayed for God to take me to the other side with you because I cannot bear the thought of going on living without you. I even failed at that."

Their work done, gravediggers gathered their shovels and drove off in their truck. Broken only by Robert's footfalls, silence surrounded him as he walked to the graveside. He fell to his knees and laid the yellow baby roses he'd brought on the fresh mound of dirt. Unable to control his emotions a moment longer he fell prostrate onto them and wept. His tears moistened the soil where the fragrant flowers lay.

Knowing his heart would never mend, Robert eventually dragged himself up to his knees. "I'll be near you always, sweetling. I swear it. I will never leave you. If you need me just call my name." He straightened the skewed stems of the delicate flowers and rose.

"Wait for me, Sara. On the strength of our undying love, I promise you that we will find a way to be together for all eternity. Trust me, Sara. I will love you always, and we will be together some day."

Rob started the truck and pulled out after Tulie's car. Damn. He couldn't remain as optimistic as Robert, who hadn't been able to help Sara. Now Rob couldn't help Carolyn—not if she didn't want him to. There was nothing he could do, no matter how much he yearned to. Maybe he would call the company that had inquired about buying his fishing camp. The fact that Greystone was going to open next door should only enhance the value of his camp.

He loved the camp, the woods, and Lost Lake. Leaving it would tear away a part of him that would always remain here. He sighed heavily. But leaving would be a lot easier than staying close to Carolyn every day for the rest of his life and not being able to hold her. She might stay as close as next door, but she would be so far away from him that he could never touch her again.

And he would never stop wanting to.

"I think I've got everything," Carolyn said as her clipboard and note pads clattered down on the table. Her purse followed. She surveyed the assembly of men and women before her. "People. People, can we begin the meeting please?"

The men had pulled several of the individual dining-room tables together to make one long conference table. A representative from every staff area in the inn, as well as one from each contractor still working there sat around it with her, Tulie, and Rob.

"At this point I feel it's very important that we list everything that has yet to be accomplished. If I leave anything out, for heaven's sake, tell me now. It's supremely important for you to keep in touch daily with your crews. Keep checklists and don't scratch anything off the list until it's done to your approval—and to mine, if that's appropriate. Now let's begin. Bill, my first question is for you, and your answer will set the tone for the remainder of the meeting. Can the renovations to Greystone Inn be done by December twentieth? Can we open on Christmas day?"

Bill sighed and shook his head. "I may be crazy, but yes. We can open on Christmas."

Everyone cheered. With a lot of hard work and cooperation, everything, it turned out, could be done by the twentieth. That left a safety net of four days to try everything out and fix what didn't work.

By the time the meeting broke up, Carolyn felt confident of the completion date, but she was so keyed up that if anyone came up behind her and said, "Boo!" she was certain she would hit the high ceiling in one jump.

The men and women conferred with each other and slowly they made their way out of the room after the meeting. Carolyn stood to stack up her notes.

"You've performed a minor miracle here, you know."

Her clipboard clattered onto the table as she jerked around. Rob was lounging in the archway behind her.

"Thank you for saying so, and thank you too, Rob, for staying for the long haul even though you didn't want to." She held up her hand to stop him when he started to interrupt. "Having you here when I needed my attorney to back me up once in a while was a big boost. You smoothed out a lot of rough spots." She felt as if saying so was a load off her conscience. Despite what she'd feared his motivation had been, he had always been helpful. "I know I couldn't have done it without your support."

Carolyn turned back to her papers to restack them. She didn't want to feel the pain always present when she was with him. He didn't have to know the fool she'd been to fall in love with him. The fool she was now to still love him. When would the pain diminish?

Rob pushed off from the door and walked toward the foyer as if to leave. She heard his footsteps crossing the polished marble floor.

"Oh, Rob?"

He turned back to her, but did not retrace his steps. The house was silent, as anyone that hadn't left had gone upstairs.

"Ah, I want to ask a favor. I feel a bit awkward, and I don't want you to say you'll do it, if you'd rather not. Ah . . . I'd like to enlist your help with part of the program at the grand opening gala."

"Anything."

He'd offered *carte blanche.* Why couldn't he mean it? What about his motives? "Wait until you try on the high, starched collar. You may want to change your mind about volunteering."

She'd begun to explain that she wanted him to appear in the opening-night program when a deliveryman arrived. He and his assistant brought in three tall, flat crates made of plywood.

"Oh, they're here," she said, her eyes wide and her face flushed with sudden excitement. She snapped her fingers. "Lars. I have to find Lars. Sign for the crates, will you, Rob?" She raced up the stairs, leaving Rob to sign the receipts and instruct the men to lean the boxes against the check-in desk. A couple of minutes later, Carolyn and Lars came down the main stairway.

"Tiny's bringing the wire," Lars told her.

"I've got the hooks in the apartment. I'll go get them." She raced past Rob without slowing down. Moments later she returned with a small bag.

"Hey, take it easy. We want you to live to the opening," Lars joked.

"Nice to know someone cares," she responded flippantly. She read the labels on the crates and decided, "This one. Open this one first." She crossed her fingers and laughed nervously.

With a dark expression on his face, Rob remained silent and stood with his hip leaning against the desk. Tiny, who'd arrived with wire, helped Lars open it. Inside the carefully constructed wooden crates were oil portraits, each set in an ornate gold frame. They held the first painting up, resting the bottom on the registration counter.

"It's Aunt Louise. I gave the artist photos that Mom and Dad had. Her picture just had to be here in Greystone. Do you like it, Rob?"

He smiled and nodded as he studied the portrait.

"Lift out this one next, Lars." He put Louise down flat on top of the counter and turned to the next crate.

Carolyn bounced a couple of times up on the balls of her feet, her hands gripping each other at her waist. She was nervous and worried enough to feel the upset in her stomach. How would Rob react when he saw the last one? She couldn't mistake Rob's sharp intake of air when he saw the second painting.

"It's you, Carolyn," Tiny concluded as he and Lars lifted it from the crate.

"No, I never looked that sweet," she said with a laugh. "It's Sara Whitney."

"She's the one the paper said fell in love with the guy she never got to marry," Lars explained.

"That's the one," Carolyn responded, hoping they hadn't noticed the catch in her voice.

She didn't dare look at Rob, but she could feel his eyes on her. She looked at Sara with her pale curls framing her innocent face. The white dress she wore had a ribbon tied at the high waist, the same dress she wore when Carolyn saw her in Greystone. Her ringless fingers fussed with the bow.

Carolyn knew the moment she saw the portrait in her parents' attic that it belonged in the Greystone Inn.

"The last one, please," Carolyn requested. She pressed her damp palms against her hips.

Now while everyone's eyes were on the third crate, Carolyn stepped back a few steps and surreptitiously watched Rob. She wanted to see his face when he viewed the last portrait.

"Hey, Rob, it's you."

"Sorry, wrong again, Tiny," Carolyn said softly. "It's the original Robert Ashford." She looked back at Rob who returned her gaze. "I thought I'd have to have one painted from the photos like Louise's, but I didn't. The portrait actually belongs to your grandfather, Rob. He allowed me to change the frame to match the others."

"I've never seen it before," Rob said, staring at the portrait.

"I have Thomas's written permission to hang it in the inn. The ones of Sara and Robert will be hung from the molding over the main stairs where I found the necklace. Aunt Louise is going over the reception desk. I thought she'd like to be there to see everything that is going on at the inn, don't you?"

"I think she'd like that a lot." He looked back at her and their gazes locked.

"I hope you don't suffer any embarrassment by the likenesses being mistaken for you and me. I don't want people to get the idea we're a couple. That was never my intention."

"I know . . ." He cleared his throat. "I knew all along that it wouldn't be, Carolyn," he answered with no show of emotion. He had his lawyer face on again. "Our lives are very different from theirs, as you once explained to me very thoroughly."

She had to look away. Thoughts of what might have been rampaged through her mind. Damn, it hurt. Being around him, seeing him and not being able to hold him, to feel his arms around her. Staying near him this long had cost her dearly.

Owning an inn had been a dream of hers, but what she wanted more was to love and trust Rob and to be loved by him in return forever. That was her chimera.

Thankfully Lars prevented her from making a fool of herself by crying or doing something equally as stupid, by suggesting that now was as good a time as ever to hang the portraits.

Louise went up first. Carolyn winked at her before she joined the others on the stairs to help with the other two portraits.

"Tiny, Lars tells me I have you to thank for finishing scraping the paint off this molding after I quit when I found the necklace."

"Hell, if I'd known a priceless necklace was hidden up there, I would have done it all," he answered, stringing together more words at one time than she'd ever heard him utter.

When the portraits of Sara and Robert were straight and in just the correct position, they all went up the steps to the balcony to view them.

Carolyn heard the music and immediately looked at Rob. He must have heard it, too. Why else would he look down at the dining room and then quickly at her? The melody was light and lovely. A Strauss waltz, she thought. Sara must be pleased with the portraits.

Rob and Carolyn shared a knowing smile. Carolyn looked away as tears stung her eyes. She should have known that hearing Sara was something that they would always share. Perhaps the only thing.

A sudden chill went down Carolyn's spine when she thought about what would happen when the inn was finished. There would be no reason for Rob to come by. She couldn't bear to think of Rob not being around any more. Until now she hadn't realized that pushing for a Christmas opening meant that Rob would be gone that much sooner.

When that happened, she didn't think she could stay on either.

Her dream of a lifetime was becoming a nightmare.

Great-aunt Louise counted down the days to the opening. Each morning Tulie tucked an index card into the frame of her portrait with the number of days left. Nowadays it was even common to see workmen and staff wishing Louise a good day or saying hello in passing.

Aunt Louise would have loved this, Carolyn thought. Maybe somehow she was enjoying it.

Snow came in spurts of a few inches at a time, but nothing blizzard-like. Carolyn kept her fingers crossed. Heavy snow was not uncommon here, but it generally came in January, February and March.

"Let the guests get here safely and then snow us in," she pleaded with the falling flakes one afternoon. Rob drove up when she was out on the steps assessing the weather.

"Hi." Would her heart never stop beating fast when she saw him? Would her arms never stop aching to hold him again? She already knew she would never—could never—stop loving him.

"Hi, yourself." He stepped on the porch next to her. "Ah, I was hoping you might have time to go over my part in the program. We never got to it the other evening. I don't want to make too complete a fool of myself by getting it wrong."

"I'm sure you'll do just fine."

"Well, with your parents coming tomorrow, I thought

you might not have time after they got here." They stepped into the foyer.

"Sure." Her hands trembled in anticipation of being in his arms again. "The reception and dance will be held in the morning room . . . I mean ballroom. That's handy for us because it has a door to my apartment. We'll enter from there. Refreshments will be served in the dining room, and the bar, of course, will be open, too. Overflow dancers can always use the foyer. Oops, I mean the lobby."

He smiled.

"The music will be audible from speakers throughout the first floor and the balcony."

Carolyn walked to the end of the ballroom by the apartment door and pointed to the low platform where the musicians would play. "The master of ceremonies will be at the microphone up there on the bandstand when we make our entrance from my apartment. No one should see us before that, so you should get costumed in there, too."

Rob nodded.

"The emcee will tell the family story, and then we come in. You first. He'll introduce your character by name so you'll know exactly when to walk out."

Rob walked over beside her and executed a bow from the waist with his back to the bandstand. Carolyn clapped for him. "Good. By then he'll get to my part, and I'll come in."

She walked toward him slowly. "I hold out my gloved hand which you take."

Rob took her hand, without a glove this time, and she felt the shock of his warm touch to her toes. He raised her fingers to his lips while his gaze bore into hers.

Carolyn struggled to slow her breathing. There was nothing she could do about her runaway heartbeat. Could he see the pulse in her neck throbbing? She cleared her throat.

"Then the band will start to play." Her voice sounded softer and more breathless. It hardly sounded like her. "You bow to me and I curtsey, and then we dance the waltz a turn around the floor."

He slid his arm around her and pulled her to him. They didn't need a band. They had Sara. She'd been playing a waltz since they'd entered the ballroom. Without breaking their eye contact, they waltzed a circle in front of the bandstand. They stopped, but neither dropped their arms.

"Ah, here's where the emcee . . . ah . . . invites everyone to join us," she said hesitantly, trying to remember what came next.

"Carolyn. Oh, God, Carolyn." He lowered his head toward hers.

"Carolyn?" Tulie called, coming in the door. "Oops. I've done it now, haven't I?"

Rob and Carolyn backed away from each other quickly, their lips never having touched. "No problem, Tulie. Been a long time since I waltzed, so we were just rehearsing for the program. What is it?" Carolyn pressed her hands against her sides to stop their trembling.

"Housekeeping. Upstairs. Have you got a minute?"

"Be right there." She turned back to Rob as Tulie walked away from the doorway. "Thanks, Rob. I think you'll do just fine. If I don't fall on my face in the long skirt, we'll be a hit."

She turned and ran from the room without looking back. When Carolyn caught up to Tulie on the second floor, Tulie probably thought she was out of breath from having run up the stairs.

Carolyn knew better.

* * * * *

Carolyn's parents arrived and settled into one of the lake-view rooms. Her first guests—a very important milestone, even if they weren't paying ones.

They were enthusiastic about the inn and all that had been done since their visit in September. They fell right into the swing of getting things ready, distributing the Victorian costumes to all the workers from the restaurant and bar.

The women tried on their crisp white blouses with high, ruffled collars and leg-of-mutton sleeves. Over that they wore long black pinafores with ruffles around the bodice square and at the hem. The straps crossed at the back and finished in a pert bow at the waist. Deep pockets on the front were just the right size for their order books. Each woman wore a lace-trimmed mobcap that covered her hair and enhanced the Victorian look.

The busboys donned black trousers and collarless shirts with black-and-white striped suspenders and matching arm garters just above the elbow. The waiters added a button-front vest to complete a more formal look for them.

Hired to carry bags and room-service items, the bellhops dressed in red trousers and old-fashioned, waist-length black jackets sporting gold braid and a long row of shiny brass buttons. They wore gloves and little, round, flat red hats with a chinstrap.

Carolyn surmised they hated the hat, but they were good sports about it. When a waitress told one that he looked cute in the hat, he wore it all the time after that with no complaints.

Everyone was getting into the old-fashioned spirit. To try out the new kitchen and new recipes, the restaurant had been open for lunch at reduced prices for the workmen since the previous week. They thought the food was great, but many wished the skirts on the waitresses were shorter.

The holiday decorations went up that week. Carolyn found it easy to hire extra part-time help from Lakeside in addition to the full-time staff. The inn was a welcome boost to the local economy, as well as a place of interest. Many people jumped at the chance to work there to see the inside of the rooms they would never see as guests, but had heard so much about.

Carolyn brought in two tall pines and decorated them with candles like Christmas trees in days of old. One stood between the front entrance and the door to the bar, and one in the ballroom by the bandstand. Of course, the candles were plastic and the flame was a flickering low-wattage bulb, but they were as close to the real thing as she could find.

Evergreen boughs were woven around the railing over the balcony with large, red velvety bows at the posts. Red and white carnations with a sprig of holly graced each white linen–covered table in the dining room. Gaily decorated wreaths hung on every door visible from the lobby. More candles, battery-operated this time, stood in the center of every windowsill of the whole inn. Carolyn planned to leave them in place after the holidays as a year-round welcome sign. Bowls of fragrant potpourri graced every nightstand. The overall effect was one of warm welcome.

The last night before the first paying guest was to check in, all but the most stubborn of problems had been summarily dealt with. Before she officially opened to the public, Carolyn invited all the Ashford family to be her guests, along with her parents and Tulie, for dinner. Before they dined, she led them all on a tour of the whole building. Thanks to the elevator, a delighted Thomas wandered in and out of many of the rooms.

Carolyn stationed Tulie at the desk in a deep-gold Victorian dress that had the typical tall collar with cream-lace ruffles at her neck and wrists. Her skirt bustled and flowed gently to the top of her toes. She and Carolyn both had raced to town for high lace-up shoes when one of the waitresses said she saw them in a local shoe store. The store's owner was surprised by the women's excitement that the old style was currently available.

After the tour, they were all seated around one long table arranged down the center of the dining room. The waitresses poured champagne for everyone, and then Carolyn stood and tapped her spoon against her water glass. The room fell silent.

"I'd like to present a toast." She raised her glass of champagne. "To my parents for their love, support and my mother's help designing and sewing all our uniforms." Everyone echoed her compliments for the beautiful work on the costumes.

Her father teased, "If I'd known you were going to work me so hard after we got here, we wouldn't have come up so early!" Her mother jabbed him playfully in the ribs and told him to behave.

"To Thomas Ashford for your faith in me and the wealth of information you shared about how the house should look after restoration."

He only smiled and said, "We knew you could do it." The others agreed with, "Here, here."

"To John Ashford for your untiring help and advice about the fine print in all the contracts I had to sign to get the job done right."

John raised his glass and told her, "Louise would have been proud of you."

That was almost Carolyn's undoing, but she took a deep breath and continued.

"To Ruth, John's wife, for your patience on all the occasions when John came home late. And for all the dinners you provided for our regular meetings at your house."

Ruth was flustered at the attention, but smiled warmly, saying simply, "My pleasure."

Carolyn turned to her best friend and assistant manager. "To Amatulla, my thanks for all your help, and no less importantly, for the laughter that has rung within these walls since you arrived. I hope you love working here as much as I love having you here."

Tulie looked embarrassed but happy and said, "Girlfriend, it's our dream come true, and I can't thank you enough for sharing it with me." She paused and her expression changed to faux anger. "But I'll never forgive you for letting folks know my real first name."

Everyone including Tulie laughed.

After another deep breath to fortify herself, Carolyn turned to Rob who'd managed to sit at her side despite her efforts to seat his parents between them as a buffer.

"To you, Rob, for helping me almost daily when problems popped up. I will always be deeply grateful for your presence here as . . . as my attorney and as one who cares for . . . for Greystone. Thank you for the craftsmen, the friends you have found to work here. And thanks for wanting Greystone to come alive again."

He nodded but said nothing. Carolyn bit her lip as tears overflowed her eyes, but she turned back toward the others and raised her glass. "To Aunt Louise for having the faith in me to make her dream and mine come true. Here's to you all and to the Greystone Inn," she barely managed. Her lips quivered and refused to smile.

She signaled the table service to begin and sat down to drink a big swallow of champagne. She tried to concentrate on the dry taste and bubbly tickles on her tongue . . . on anything but the look that Rob had given her.

Could he know that she thanked him for the intimate moments they shared? For the memories she would always cherish of him? She patted her cheeks with her napkin. Individual conversations sprang up all around the table.

Carolyn's hands were shaking as she raised her glass for another sip. She knew that Rob was watching her until Ruth, seated on his other side, said something, and he turned to answer her. Only then could Carolyn breathe.

The rest of the meal passed in a blurred montage of gourmet food, compliments, and good wishes. Carolyn thought the food was good because everyone told her so. She hadn't been able to eat or taste much.

She did note that the grapefruit sorbet served between courses to freshen the palate was too soft. She would have to check the temperature of the freezers and have the small pewter stemmed cups in which it was served chilled before use. And that waitress in sneakers would have to at least get black ones. The pink high tops would never do.

By the time the baked Alaska was consumed and the Ashfords had left, her folks seemed more than ready to retire to their room upstairs.

Carolyn was tired, but she knew she was too keyed up to sleep. She wandered back to the dining room and sat on the piano bench, exactly where Sara must have spent much of her time. She could hear the kitchen help talking and laughing as they finished their work and left for home.

Before Tulie left for the night, she brought Carolyn an open bottle of champagne and a couple of glasses. "I can't stand to see this good stuff going down the drain and the bubbles won't keep. You might as well enjoy a glass."

"Won't you join me?"

"I was going to, but frankly, I'm bushed. Everyone's left so I'm going home to bed while I have the chance. I've got to be bright-eyed and bushy-tailed very early tomorrow."

Laughing, Carolyn thanked her and wished her a good night. Tulie left the ice-filled bucket on the dining table closest to the piano and left.

Carolyn put off going to lock the front door as she did each night until the inn officially opened and a staff was on duty throughout the night. She turned to the keyboard instead.

A lot of years had passed since her weekly piano lessons, and other than "Chopsticks", there wasn't another melody she could play well without music. Her fingers idly pressed random notes.

"I hate to tell you, but Sara's got you beat when it comes to playing the piano," Rob said from the lobby doorway.

Chapter Nineteen

Carolyn gasped in surprise and slapped her hand down on the keys. The resultant discord made her fingers leap up as if they had been burned. She hadn't known he was in the doorway behind her, or even in Greystone, until he spoke. It was the final sign they were moving apart forever, she decided, if she couldn't sense he was near.

"Tulie phoned before she left to say there was a glass in here with my name on it." He smiled and walked in toward the champagne. Sliding the stems between the fingers of one hand, he lifted the two glasses and filled them with the cold liquid. He carried them over to the piano and sat down on the bench beside her.

She took the proffered stemware and watched the bubbles break on the surface. He was so close. She could feel warmth from his thighs. She wanted to run, but she couldn't even move away. Except for dancing for a minute or two in the grand-opening program, this might be the closest they would be ever again. Holding the crystal firmly with both hands, she hoped the trembling in her fingers didn't show.

A tiny gasp escaped her lips when Rob gently lifted her chin and turned her head until she was looking at him instead. "You never gave any of us a chance to make a toast to you tonight, Carolyn. You had the dinner so well orchestrated there wasn't a free moment." He smiled and lowered his hand to his thigh.

Carolyn couldn't look away. She wanted to memorize

everything about his face so she could close her eyes and see him again and again, after he was gone from her life.

"If the inn runs as smoothly as dinner, you'll have no problems at all."

"Then you never noticed the fuchsia shoes on the waitress?" she asked, trying to be light.

"I was enjoying having dinner with you too much to notice anything else."

What could she say? All she could do was try to smile. She felt her lower lip misbehaving again. She drew it between her teeth and bit down on it. She wished she didn't have to breathe because doing so meant she had to inhale his familiar spicy aftershave.

"Thanks," was all she said. She sipped a little of her champagne.

"No, Carolyn, thank you. Louise knew what she was doing when she left Greystone to you. Getting to know your parents here this week, I think they'd agree with me. Louise knew you would find the necklace and create the inn she'd only dreamed of."

He raised his champagne flute. "Here's to you, Carolyn. Best wishes and congratulations on having your chimera become reality—the Greystone Inn. I know it means everything to you."

They each sipped the champagne. Carolyn was glad of the chance to look away from the hold his gaze had on her. She idly fingered more of the piano keys, but didn't press them hard enough for the felt hammers to make audible contact with the strings.

"You can't call it my inn, Rob. My name might be on the deed, but I'm just the caretaker here. This is an historical treasure, a piece of yesterday that I've been lucky enough to preserve so our children . . . so that children of tomorrow can see what it was like to live here before tragedy struck the Whitney family."

Carolyn could have kicked herself for stumbling on the words "our children." She couldn't help but think of the children she'd dreamed of having with Rob before . . .

No. She wouldn't think that way. And before she did something stupid like touch his cheek, she needed to move away from his body that still sparked heat deep within her. She rose from the bench to look out the window. "It's snowing," she whispered in an aspirate voice.

Gently falling flakes sparkled in the outside spotlights. The tears in her eyes made them sparkle and shimmer many times over.

"Well, I'll say good night. You must be tired, and I don't want to make you lose any more sleep."

"Thanks, Rob," she said in a hoarse whisper without turning, "for everything."

"Oh, I almost forgot. Thought you might like to know that I'm going to accept an offer I received to buy the fishing camp."

Carolyn jerked around to face him, her heart racing.

"You'll be having new neighbors. We're getting together in January to sign the papers and close the deal. It will be upgraded significantly, so you should like that. You won't have just a row of fishing shacks for a neighbor. They're putting in a new big lodge on the hill behind the dock." He shook his head. "Wait till you see it. They sent me drawings ages ago, when they tried to talk me into selling. I thought you'd like to see them so I've kept them." He shrugged. "But with all that happened, I never showed them to you. I think you'll like the new look. Well, good night."

Carolyn swallowed her gasp as he walked out. Her hand covered her mouth, and she was unable to draw a breath to speak. She couldn't believe what she'd heard. Were the drawings she'd seen that night on Rob's desk the buyer's? But why the drawing of the necklace and the dollar signs? If she'd been wrong about him . . . But he seemed to want to leave Lost Lake. He had no interest in staying near her. A chill circled her heart.

She saw him stop in the driveway to look back at her in the window. It occurred to her that this was the window where they had seen Sara searching for her long-lost Robert. Did the candle that glowed on the sill give her the same ethereal appearance?

Not wanting Rob to see the tears escaping her eyes, Carolyn stepped out of sight from the window and brushed away the wetness from her cheeks with her cold fingers.

Rob stood in the same spot for a long time before she heard his steps crunch in the snow as he walked in the woods.

When she peered out the window again, Rob was gone.

The snow continued to fall through Christmas morning and sent the staff and management of the Greystone Inn into a panic. The plows cleared it from the drive and parking areas with no trouble, but the worry was that guests would cancel rather than drive over bad roads to reach the grand opening the next night.

That did not turn out to be the case. All the invited guests showed up, and then some. The town mayor and his council and spouses came early for the tour, as did the county board members and their guests. Representatives of the state travel and tourism bureau, on whose recommendations so much of the success of the inn rested, came, and so did one of the governor's assistants. Travel-column reporters showed up. All were interested in the emerald necklace discovered in the old haunted house that was now a luxury inn.

"It would be fun to catch a glimpse of the ghost who haunts the inn because she was forever separated from her beau," many of the guests told her.

Carolyn smiled and greeted them all dressed in a white-wool Victorian suit that had a jacket over a bustled skirt with a high-collared lace blouse beneath it. Her hair was long enough to have it styled with curls twisted like springs falling in a cascade over one shoulder. She was thankful her hands were gloved to absorb the damp evidence of her nervousness.

Some of the more outspoken guests quipped that with her white dress and pale complexion, she could pass as the ghost for the night. She smiled more, grateful for Tulie's hint to put petroleum jelly on her teeth and gums so she could keep right on smiling even when her mouth felt dry. So far so good.

At the preappointed time Carolyn, with her mother to help her dress, and Rob, with Lars to be sure the high collar was on straight, disappeared into Carolyn's apartment to get into their costumes for the program.

In the bedroom Carolyn traded her Victorian suit for a 1920s iridescent taffeta ball gown. The fabric was woven of green threads in one direction and black in the other. The overall effect, chosen to enhance the black emeralds, was a shimmering look of green that turned to black one moment and back to green the next as she moved. The neckline was a deep scoop that allowed a peek at the soft contours of her breasts and the shadow between.

"You look beautiful, Carolyn. I just wish . . ."

"What, Mom? What is it?"

"Well, honey, I just wish you seemed happier about it all."

A knock on the bedroom door saved her from having to respond. Eleanor opened it to admit Simons, the jeweler who had been safeguarding the emeralds. He held up the black velvet case and opened it. The emeralds and gold sparkled.

"Oh, they're magnificent."

Gone were any traces of paint. The stones rested securely in their new settings on the original chain. He'd attached a more modern clasp, one that was more dependable than the open hook that had been there.

Rob stepped into the doorway behind Simons, and she felt his gaze as he looked at her from her head of elegantly set curls to the toes of her high-top shoes peeking out from under the long dress. "You look beautiful, Carolyn."

"Thank you, kind sir," she responded with a smile and a curtsey. *Keep it light, Carolyn,* she told herself. *You're too close to tears to blow it now. Taffeta water-spots, and besides, the show must go on.* She smiled more broadly, but she could feel her lips were quivering.

"Mr. Simons, please allow me," Rob said politely as he took the necklace from its box and placed it on Carolyn's neck. Poor Mr. Simons's face fell as if he'd been looking forward to putting it on her. He was so out-charmed by Rob that he never had a chance to object.

Carolyn ducked her head within the ring of his arms as he stepped behind her with the necklace strung between his hands. She couldn't help the shiver when his warm fingers touched the back of her neck as he fastened the treasure in place.

When it was secured, he slid his hands onto her bare shoulders and leaned over to place a soft kiss under her ear. "So beautiful." He stepped back, and she was left feeling cold and bereft.

The popular deep-voiced radio personality who'd been hired as the master of ceremonies came in the door. "Is the beautiful lady ready? Wow, those are some rocks! And you guys look great. Hey, let's get this show on the road."

His good-natured joking was exactly what Carolyn needed to break the spell Rob always cast over her when he was close. She and Rob wished each other good luck.

Rob put his gloves on, and Eleanor helped Carolyn with hers. "Victorian ladies and gentlemen would never dance without gloves," she offered. "I learned that in those books we used to design the uniforms."

Carolyn managed a shaky smile and pressed her cheek against her mother's with her thanks. Eleanor left with Lars so they could see the program from out front with their spouses. Simons wished them good luck and followed the others out.

The emcee stepped out the door and signaled the small band that had been playing quietly. There was a drum roll, a spotlight came on and he stepped out onto the stage. Everyone in the room quieted down to listen.

"Good evening, ladies and gentlemen, and welcome to the Greystone Inn." He paused for the applause. "We invite you to come with us on a trip back in time."

He continued with the history of Greystone, of the Whitney family, and of what had happened nearly eighty years before. When Carolyn wrote the script, she'd left out all Lora's evil jealousy of her sister Sara. The story sounded as if a soft-spoken Robert was told by Sara's blustering father that he'd only have to wait for him to consider Robert's request to marry the young Sara, but his chance never came.

In leaving out Lora's jealousy, she also omitted that Lora had stolen the emerald necklace in order to cast aspersions on Robert. The Ashfords agreed that Lora must have been climbing down from the chair after hiding it when she fell. Carolyn's version in the program left the disappearance a mystery, and led the audience to think that Lloyd was all bluster—that he would have relented and given his permission for the wedding had not tragedy struck.

Lora's death from an accidental fall was included, her mother's death from influenza the following spring, and then Sara's demise soon after from the same illness. Carolyn didn't mention that she thought Sara had really died of a broken heart.

The announcer brought tears to the eyes of some of the audience by the time he spoke of the loss of the potential happiness for Sara and Robert and the fact that Robert never married.

Finally, he told of the house passing down through the Whitney family. He described Louise's efforts to refurbish the inn before she gave up and willed it to the present owner, who had restored it so beautifully.

"But for tonight," he went on, "we invite you to see the house as it might have appeared around nineteen-twenty, back in happier days when the Whitneys summered here. Think of the soft-spoken and proper suitor, Robert Ashford, as he would have looked coming to the house to court his sweet Sara. Ladies and gentlemen, may I present Mr. Robert Ashford, played by his grand-nephew, Rob Ashford."

He swung his arm toward the door to the apartment and the spotlight followed. There was applause as Rob stepped out the door into the spotlight and walked slowly, as rehearsed, to the bandstand where he bowed very formally to the audience.

"A young man of his day would have spent awkward moments in the parlor, now the front dining room, talking with Sara's father until she appeared."

Rob improvised a little and ran a gloved finger inside his high starched collar as if to nervously relieve the pressure on his neck. After a glance at the announcer he stood erect again. The audience loved it and laughed warmly before turning their attention back to the emcee.

"At last his lady love would arrive. Ladies and gentlemen, permit me to present Sara Whitney, played by Carolyn Sara Whitney Matison, the owner of the Greystone Inn."

Carolyn took a deep breath and stepped out into the bright light. All eyes were on her and the necklace as the emcee described how Carolyn had found it. He didn't mention that the scraping hook had been moved mysteriously to make sure she did, however. "You can view the necklace in a special case in the art museum in Albany where it will be on display beginning next week until the owner decides its destiny," he reported.

While he spoke, Carolyn walked slowly to Rob and put her hand in his. She curtsied to his bow. While the emcee finished, they turned to do the same to the audience.

The music began and Rob and Carolyn waltzed in a small circle around the floor in front of the crowd of onlookers. After telling the audience the time supper would be served later, the emcee concluded his remarks by hoping they enjoyed their visit to the Greystone Inn.

The hum of individual conversations that began when he finished was almost as loud as the music. Still dancing, Rob led Carolyn directly out the doors into the lobby all the way to the tall Christmas tree beside the entrance.

The proper Victorian distance between them disappeared as they left the room when Rob pulled her close so her breasts pressed against his chest, her temple leaning against his cheek. She inhaled the scent she would always know as his and felt lightheaded.

When they stopped beside the door that had once led to Lloyd's den, Rob captured her hands and held them against his chest. She couldn't move an inch away, even if she had wanted to. He stared over her head without moving, and she turned to see what it was he was looking at.

Robert stood in the doorway with his hand still on the brass knob. "No, sir, you misunderstand me."

"What?" Lloyd shouted from inside the room. "What do you mean, my boy?"

"Father, don't listen to him," Lora implored. "Of course, I will marry him. We shall be wed . . ."

Sara's fingers flew to cover her mouth. She couldn't believe what she'd just overheard.

Lora never finished before Robert objected again. "No, sir. It is not for Lora's hand that I ask, sir. It's for Sara that I have spoken."

Robert saw Sara at the drawing-room door and held his hand out to her. "Sara," he called, looking relieved to see her. She ran to him. He took her hand, and they turned to face her father. "It's Sara I love, sir."

Lora screamed her denial. "No, Papa, it's not Sara! It can't be her! She has everything—looks, talent, poise. It isn't fair. I'm the oldest. He came asking for me!"

Lloyd was quite out of his ken dealing with a distraught daughter, but he couldn't allow her to continue her tantrum. He expected the women around him to be seen but not heard. Hadn't he chosen his wife because she was reticent and hardly ever said a thing, leaving him a household of peace and quiet that could be broken by no raised voice save his own? He looked at Lora and he couldn't imagine what had set her off.

"That's quite enough, girls. Go to your rooms," Lloyd ordered firmly. Sending his daughters to their rooms was always his first and best line of defense against any perceived misbehavior.

"Robert, I understand now that it is not Lora for whom you ask, but . . . but Sara can't marry you until . . . until her sister is married. The oldest should leave the family fold first and all that," he blustered.

Sara felt stricken. Robert put his arm around her waist to support her, and she leaned on him heavily.

"You can't mean it, sir," Robert ventured hopefully.

"Quite so. I can and I do. That's all I have to say for now. We'll just have to wait and see when her sister marries." He turned back to his daughters. "Go on. Go, the two of you. Go to your rooms. And Robert, I think it would be best if you stayed to dinner another night. Peace will be restored in my house. Peace and quiet. Yes, that's what I want. Peace and quiet." His pronouncement made, he dismissed them with the upward wave of the back of his hands.

Sara and Robert followed Lora out into the foyer. Sara trudged toward the front door clutching Robert's arm, drawing strength from him. Large tears clouded her vision.

"You've ruined everything for me for the last time, Sara," Lora shouted. Sara and Robert whirled around to face her. "If Robert won't marry me, then I'll make sure he never marries you either. Do you hear me?"

Sara gasped at the insane threat, but Lora didn't stop. Her face was deeply colored with anger, her voice filled with hatred. "I swear you'll never be with Robert. Never! Whatever I must do, I promise I'll keep you two apart, even if it takes my last dying breath to do it."

Carolyn was thankful Rob held her close. "Rob, you see them. I know you do. We'll always share that, at least, even if . . ."

Applause broke out in the ballroom. Carolyn was glad for the distraction and wiped away tears with her gloved fingers.

"Carolyn, I must be quick before the emcee finishes with the other introductions and your admiring public claims you. Robert never had a chance to see Sara again because of Lora, but I won't let her or anyone else stop me before you've heard what I have to say. Then I'll walk out of your life and won't bother you again." Rob glanced furtively behind him at the people leaving the ballroom.

"Please, Rob. I was wrong. I won't try to stop you, but you must know that I'm sorry. I was blaming you for things you never did, and I didn't think I could trust you, but I know now there was no earthly reason not to. You weren't trying to keep me from finding the necklace or trying to find it for yourself. Lora was keeping me away from you." Tears welled in her eyes as she clutched Rob's hands to her heart. "Please forgive me for doubting you."

"Oh, Carolyn, I told you this summer that I wished I'd met you before this all started, before you inherited this house. I never really explained why, but if I had, then when I fell in love with you, I could have asked you to marry me. The necklace, all your money, and this inn—they wouldn't have stood between us."

"What did you say?" She held her breath and waited for his answer.

"I love you, Carolyn Matison. I couldn't leave tonight without you knowing that. You climbed into my truck and into my heart the first day I met you. I haven't been the same since. I love you, and despite all your damned money, I still wish I could ask you to marry me."

"But . . ."

"No, hear me out. I know I can't ask you now because

you don't need me anymore. Creating the Greystone Inn from an abandoned building is all you've dreamed of doing, and now you've succeeded and established the dream career you were seeking. I can't begin to compete with all that you have. But you must believe I never wanted any of your money. God, if I thought for one minute you'd marry me, you could give it all away, for all I care. We could live here at Lost Lake or go anywhere you wanted." His shoulders slumped and a look of sadness dimmed his eyes.

"Rob, you love me?" Carolyn asked, barely able to breathe.

"With all my heart, but I know that you could never be content living with me."

"But you'd stay or move away if I wanted you to? Just to please me?"

"In a minute."

"What about your buyer? I thought you sold the fishing camp to get away from me."

He shook his head. "They're coming up in January to sign the papers. We don't have anything in writing yet. I couldn't make myself sign away being near to you until I had to. For all these months, I've hoped that someday you could love me and be content living here with me as my wife. How I've wanted to say, 'Carolyn, will you marry me?' "

"Oh, Rob. Don't you know I love you? You're more important to me than Greystone ever could be. You've proved over and over that I could trust you, but with Lora stacking the evidence against you so I would focus on it, I couldn't believe in you. I didn't think you could possibly love me."

"Never doubt it. I love you. I'll love you forever. Do I have a ghost of a chance you would marry me?"

"No pun intended?" She smiled. "Oh, yes," she whispered. Her arms slid around his neck, and he held her close as their lips met.

The ever-present guard, McNair, who followed the necklace wherever it went, grinned as he kept the gawkers at a discreet distance. But it didn't take a mental giant to figure out what was happening from the way the two of them were kissing.

Rob took Carolyn's left hand and pulled off her glove. He reached into his breast pocket for a ring that he placed on her third finger. The ornate, delicate gold setting held a large, green emerald surrounded with sparkling diamonds.

"Rob, it's beautiful."

"This was Robert's. He intended it for Sara, but I know he would feel good about my giving it to you. Grandpa gave it to me when Louise died. He said I would want to have it now. I thought it would stay in the bank box forever."

She raised her hand to caress his cheek and kissed him. When the reporters saw the ring on her hand, the flash bulbs lit the lobby. The guard could no longer contain the well-wishers.

Carolyn was stunned by their applause and shouts and felt the heat rising in her cheeks. Rob never let go of her waist as he confirmed their conjectures about what had just taken place between the two of them. He shook hands with the people congratulating them.

The emcee, who had discovered what was going on, went back to the microphone, stopped the music and announced their engagement. "Sara and Robert have found their happiness at last," he told the audience dramatically. Everyone clapped, and the band began again.

Carolyn's gaze traveled to the portrait of Louise over the reception desk. She knew Rob was looking there, too, when he spoke with feeling. "Thank you, Louise, from the bottom of my heart for sending Carolyn to me."

"Rob, do you suppose she wanted to bring us together because she knew we'd fall in love?"

"We'll never know, but she was one smart lady."

A movement on the stairs drew Carolyn's attention. "Oh, no. Rob, look on the steps."

Her fist raised in anger, Lora struggled to rise from where she'd fallen. Her mouth moved, but no threats could be heard.

Carolyn and Rob clung to each other. "She can't hurt anyone ever again, Carolyn," he assured her.

Fighting the strength of Rob's and Carolyn's love for each other, Lora lifted her hands. Her fingers clawed at a red fog that rolled down the steps and threatened to envelop her. It swirled around her, pulling her into a whirlwind that distorted her figure and carried her away.

"Rob, she's gone," Carolyn exclaimed.

"And she'll never come between us again." The music coming from the ballroom changed to a waltz, and Rob pulled her into his arms to dance.

"Or between them," Carolyn said, pointing to the balcony where the tall, handsome man's white tails and the delicate blond woman's white dress glistened as they danced. Sara and Robert—somehow they were together at last. Looking at each other as only a couple in love could, they paused briefly and turned toward Carolyn and Rob. The specters smiled, and then turned to dance once again. They twirled in each other's arms as they moved under the arch and disappeared through the locked glass door into Sara's bedroom.

Carolyn had furnished that room with antiques like a museum showroom, as it might have looked when Sara occupied it. Visitors couldn't enter the room, but they could view it through a glassed-in doorway. Sara's diary sat open on the desk, and a glass replica of the black emerald necklace spilled from a velvet-lined jewel box on the dresser doily. A replica of the white dress Sara wore in the portrait was draped over the corner of the bed.

"I don't know how, but I know they're together at last," Carolyn whispered.

"Together forever, just as he promised her they would be. Just as we will be."

Rob bowed his head and kissed her lips as the music ended and the crowd of reporters pummeled them with more questions.

But Carolyn had seen enough in those moments before Sara and Robert disappeared to know for certain.

Sara's chimera had come true.

Epilogue

Though he'd been watching the scene for two months, Carolyn could still see the joy and wonder on Rob's face as he stood beside the fireplace in their house in the woods and watched her nurse their baby, Lane Louise Ashford. A smile of happiness filled her face to match the radiant one already in place on his. Balancing a long garment bag over his shoulder, he kissed her upturned face.

"We won't be long, Rob. You go ahead and get dressed."

"Are you going to have time to tie the fluffy necktie for me?"

"I guess doing it once a year isn't too much to ask," she answered with a laugh as he headed down the hall to their bedroom. She switched Lane to her other breast for the second half of her supper, and relaxed back into the chair, looking at the dancing flames.

What a difference from the nerves and worry of last year's program, when she'd opened Greystone Inn. But what a wonderfully exciting time that had been.

Rob didn't give her any time then to change her mind about marrying him—as if she would have. They were wed in Greystone on a snowy day in late January. She remembered how handsome he'd looked in his black tuxedo, waiting for her in the lobby as she walked down the grand staircase on her father's arm. She wore a long white silk dress with a train that swept the stairs as she descended.

Rob had wanted her to wear the black emerald necklace—for good luck, as Alice had promised. Carolyn didn't want all the problems that went along with having such a valuable piece of jewelry at the wedding, so they worked out a compromise.

Mr. Simons created a clasp that would allow Carolyn to remove the center large emerald from the chain holding the others whenever she wanted to wear it. He attached it to a sturdy gold chain that hugged her neck. She carried a bouquet of yellow baby roses and lilies of the valley that Rob had flown in for her.

At the doorway she kissed her father on the cheek and slipped her hand into Rob's bent arm. Giving her father time to stand beside his wife, Carolyn and Rob joined their families and friends in the ballroom where the ceremony was held.

Tulie, Carolyn's maid of honor, had decorated the ballroom beautifully. The dinner reception she'd arranged went off without a hitch. Carolyn left for her honeymoon knowing the Greystone Inn was in capable and dependable hands.

Soon after that, Tulie had moved into the manager's apartment and assumed the corresponding duties at the inn right up to the wonderful job she'd done preparing for the second annual holiday gala.

Baby Lane came crying into the world early, on November first, feisty from the start, after giving her mother something to worry about on Halloween other than ghosts. Her first name, never used in the generations before in either family, symbolized the new happy family living at Lost Lake. The middle name was in honor of Aunt Louise who had brought Lane's parents together. Her soft black hair was just the color of her father's, while her blue eyes matched her mother's. And if the greedy hunger with which she was eating at the moment foretold the future, she would be an athletic, energetic, and totally modern woman of the twenty-first century.

Carolyn smiled. She remembered the reality check she'd had a week ago when she'd tried on the green ball gown for tonight's program. It had been too tight. Her mom helped redo the bodice by adding fabric they scavenged from the full skirt.

"It looks *tres chic,* but the amount of your creamy breasts that is revealed is no longer merely a hint," Rob had complained. "When I think about all the other men who will be ogling my wife, I wonder if there isn't some lace or something you could put across the top."

Carolyn smiled as she carried the sleeping baby to her crib. She had put one of the battery-operated candles from the inn on her windowsill to function as a nightlight and reached over to switch it on.

Above it hung the sun teaser from her Miami kitchen window, the replica of the stained-glass window above the entrance to Greystone. She tapped it lightly to make it wobble. The light from the candle sparkled in the glass sun. The frowns following the sun around were only in the glass and not in their lives any longer. She sighed with happy contentment.

Carolyn kissed Lane and slipped from the room. Stopping only to help Rob with his tie, she quickly dressed in her ball gown. She slid her engagement ring on next to the gold band she wore alone most of the time, with a baby to care for.

Rob appeared in the mirror behind her. He kissed her bare shoulder. She saw the blue of his eyes turn molten with desire and felt her arms weaken with longing to hold him.

"You look so beautiful," he whispered. His gaze promised a wonderful night of loving upon their return from the party.

The babysitter arrived. Carolyn and Rob would be close by at Greystone, so the new parents weren't worried—at least not about the baby.

Carolyn was excited and a little apprehensive as they pulled up to the service entrance at the back of the inn. "Do you think we'll see Sara and Robert tonight, Rob?"

"Would you be disappointed if you didn't?"

"No, I don't think so. We haven't seen or heard them all year long. I believe they didn't need to stay after they found their happiness with each other."

Rob circled the car to help his wife out. They ducked into the manager's apartment where Tulie was waiting for them. "Mmm, mmm, you look hot," she said as she helped them off with their coats. "Not half bad for old married folks," she added, succeeding in making everyone laugh and relax a little.

With a different armed guard this time, Simons arrived with the necklace. All the emeralds shone brightly as Rob put it around Carolyn's neck. He kissed her shoulder tenderly, and looking down at her fuller breasts, he whispered into her ear, "You're sure you couldn't come up with a piece of lace to fill in across there?" She laughed. It was just the jest she needed to chase away the jitters.

In the glare of the spotlights, the announcer introduced them once again. This year Rob surprised her by handing her a perfect white rose. She brought it to her nose to enjoy the fragrance, and then held it in her hand on his shoulder while they waltzed around the room.

Carolyn and Rob, happy in each other's arms, never looked away from each other. They didn't need the manifestations of Sara or Robert or even Louise's voice to encourage them. Combating Lora's evil no longer captured their joint attentions, as her evil had been totally banished from Greystone.

"I'll always love you, Carolyn."

"And I'll never stop loving you, Rob."

Their love for each other and for their family would bind them together forever.

About the Author

After earning bachelor's and master's degrees, ***Lois Carroll*** taught at a Midwestern state university. She has been writing since her childhood when she received a daily diary as a gift. Writing in her free time while she taught, she wrote several plays that were produced by a touring puppet company. Seeking a career in writing and editing, she then worked as a copy editor at a publishing company. Now living in central New York, Ms. Carroll writes full-time. She has published a dozen women's fiction E-books on the Web as well as short stories and nonfiction articles in national magazines. Writing under pseudonyms, she has also published mystery and romance in paperback and hardcover. A wife, mother, and grandmother, she loves creating stories with happy endings the best. She loves to hear from her readers. You can e-mail her through her web site at: http://home.twcny.rr.com/topromances/lois_carroll/